Wren couldn't stop himself from smiling.

His wonderful, sweet, sexy master had no intentions other than kindness and compassion. He was sitting here with bags under his eyes from exhaustion, and he was thinking of how to make medical exams better for pregnant slave women!

"I love you, but you fucking kill me sometimes," he muttered, squeezing Jere's hand. "So you're gonna get someone for an energy source and to comfort the ladies?"

"That's the plan as I see it," Jere smiled back at him. "Besides, if I were to hire someone, someone *free*, things between you and I would have to change. And I'm not gonna do that. A slave will be mine to do as I please with, and that means I can order her to live in our happy little fantasy world where I'm just a doctor who's in love with his assistant."

"How risqué," Wren smirked at him. "Don't let that power go to your head now!"

"If I do, will you tie me up and beat it out of me?" Jere teased back.

Wren laughed, resuming eating his dinner. He was still a little uncertain, but if anyone could make this work, Jere could. Besides, it hadn't happened yet. They had a while to talk about this, to come to terms with what exactly it would mean for either of them. "So, where are you getting a slave? Do you want one right out of the training facility, or maybe an older woman who's past her prime?"

Jere shrugged. He picked at his food for a moment before answering. "I had actually glanced through the classified ads."

Nobody in Hojer would even consider purchasing a slave from a classified ad, certainly not for any sort of important position.

Also recommended...

You may also enjoy these other ForbiddenFiction works:

Don't... **by Jack L. Pyke**

"Don't... open me." Three simple words that tease Jack, taking him places from his dark past. For Jack, BDSM is a way to resist his worst impulses. Yet, the stranger calling himself The Unknown seeks to use that to seduce him. As Jack slips further down into the abyss, two men hold the power to save him. Will it be Gray, the Master who knows Jack's every secret? Or Jan, the first man to give Jack a reason to hope? With deadly ghosts coming out to play, Jack may lose everything, even his life. (M/M)

http://forbiddenfiction.com/library/story/JP2-1.000134

Nicholi's Vengeance, by J.A. Jaken

Nicholi's world goes up in flames when soldiers invade his country, leaving chaos in their wake. Captured and enslaved in a foreign land, Nicholi struggles to cope with the nightmare of slavery and adapt to the terrifying and inexplicable world he is thrust into. He draws courage from a steadfast determination to get justice for his murdered family and — he hopes — peace to himself by finding and killing the man responsible for the destruction of his village. Yet, through it all, Nicholi's greatest enemy might not be foreign powers or enemy soldiers, or even in the self-serving machinations of his fellow slaves, but himself. (M/M+)

http://forbiddenfiction.com/library/story/JAJ-1.000011

Inherent Risk

Alicia Cameron

ForbiddenFiction
www.forbiddenfiction.com

an imprint of

Fantastic Fiction Publishing
www.fantasticfictionpublishing.com

INHERENT RISK
A Forbidden Fiction book

Fantastic Fiction Publishing
Hayward, California

© Alicia Cameron, 2013

CREDITS
Editor: Rylan Hunter
Cover Photos: Yeko Photo Studio at Shutterstock, Zigf, B-d-s, and Yuri_arcurs at Dreamstime
Cover Design: Siolnatine
Production Editor: Erika L Firanc
Proofreading: Kailin Morgan, JhP323

SKU: AC2-000096-02 FFP
ISBN: 978-1-62234-121-4

Published in the United States of America

DISCLAIMER

This book is a work of fiction which contains explicit erotic content; it is intended for mature readers. Do not read this if it's not legal for you.

All the characters, locations and events herein are fictional. While elements of existing locations or historical characters or events may be used fictitiously, any resemblance to actual people, places or events is coincidental.

This story is not intended to be used as an instruction manual. It may contain descriptions of erotic acts that are immoral, illegal, or unsafe. Do not take the events in this story as proof of the plausibility or safety of any particular practice.

For my mom, who will never read this anyway;
thanks for making me!

Contents

Chapter 1

Stillness

Jere felt a little thrill go through him as he saw Wren come into the room with a sharp knife in his hand, the knife glistening as much as his eyes did in the dim light.

"You're sure you're okay with this?" Wren asked as he came closer.

"Of course," Jere smirked back at him. "Why wouldn't I be?"

"The last two times we tried it you called it off the second you heard the sound of metal," Wren reminded him, coming up to run his hand along the side of Jere's face. "I just want to make sure."

The warm, familiar hand was comforting, chasing away the hesitation. "Yes, but I keep asking you to try again," Jere replied, leaning into the touch. "I'm ready, this time. I liked that you stopped the first two times I asked."

"It's the same courtesy you've always shown me," Wren reminded him. "It's because of him, isn't it? My old master."

"I've played with plenty of people," Jere evaded, although he knew that Wren would see right through him. "He never did anything that I didn't allow him to do."

Wren raised an eyebrow. "For some reason, I doubt he would have been satisfied with that."

Jere was quiet for a moment. Wren knew exactly what had him on edge, what made him hesitant to relax and play with knives in the same way he liked to play with everything else. Wren was a dangerous enough weapon without any tools, but fear wasn't logical. It was completely irrational, but it was fun and sexy sometimes as well, especially with someone he knew he could trust.

"You're not him," Jere mumbled. "And I'm so happy about that."

Wren leaned over, kissed him deeply. "You're not the only one."

"Go slow?" Jere asked, relaxing as Wren's body pressed against his. He felt Wren nod.

"Do you still want this?" Wren checked, holding up the roll of wide tape that Jere had requested. "I mean, you might want to be able to talk."

"I won't want to tell you to stop," Jere insisted. At Wren's doubtful look, he backtracked a little. "If I do, I'll use the mind-connection. You know I prefer that, anyway!"

"All right," Wren agreed, pulling off a length of tape and holding it ominously between his hands.

Jere grinned at the sight. "Now, be the sexy robber!"

Wren waited for a minute, capturing Jere's attention and his trust, and as Jere watched, he could see Wren carefully making his expression blank. Jere didn't have more than a moment to appreciate the change in his boyfriend before he felt the tape being pressed against his mouth, silencing him.

"Don't move," Wren ordered, so much different from just a minute ago.

Jere tried to smile at the sound of Wren's voice. It was harsh, powerful, demanding. It held an edge of threat, promising pain if it wasn't obeyed. That, and the hint of playfulness that Jere had come to associate with Wren, especially in bed.

A hand came up to grab Jere's chin, forcing his gaze upward. He struggled against it for a second, before Wren's fingers squeezed lower and threatened to cut off his airflow. Jere went slack, staring compliantly into his lover's face.

"Enjoying this?" Wren teased, breaking character for a moment.

"*You know I am,*" Jere replied, avoiding speaking out loud with the tape across his mouth and Wren's hand around his neck. He risked a smile. This was familiar territory.

The grip loosened suddenly, and he felt lost, untethered, preferring the threat and fear to the lack of contact. He drew in a shuddery breath as he wondered if he really had been about to be choked. He wondered even more how much he would have liked it. He had never really had anyone choke him, and if he explored it with anyone, he would like it to be with Wren.

His thoughts of what could have been were cut off by the feeling of cold, sharp metal against his stomach, and he froze in place as he felt it trail up, firmly, only the very tip making contact with his skin as the blade sliced through his t-shirt. He held his breath as it was dragged up toward his throat, pressing a little harder to go through the collar of his shirt, then slicing down across his collarbone. He fought to stay still as the sensitive skin was grazed, and his muscles twitched involuntarily.

Wren stopped, freezing in place, brushing his hand along the path where the knife had worked across Jere's body. "Doing okay?" he asked, the concern clear in his voice.

Jere took a moment to steady himself. They had talked about this, multiple times actually, and they had both agreed that breaking skin wasn't going to be part of the game. He trusted Wren not to slip, but more importantly, he trusted him to respect that request. It took him a minute to remember that, though, and when he had finally convinced himself of it he nodded. *"You can't very well take my shirt off with my hands tied, now can you?"* Jere teased, rewarded by a smile from Wren.

The knife continued to slice through the last few inches of fabric covering his arms, which were bound tightly, stretching him backward across the desk. Jere loved the exposed feeling that he had, loved knowing that Wren was the one causing it. He focused on Wren instead of the discomfort that was starting to build as the knife had more access to his skin.

In one quick motion, the entire shirt was ripped away, leaving Jere slightly chilled and even more exposed. The chill was soon intensified as he felt a hand working the fastening of his pants and jerking them down, making him lose his already precarious balance and pulling uncomfortably on his wrists.

Wren's hand caught him by the groin, pushing him back into position and squeezing painfully. Jere responded to the pain by moaning, eager for more.

"Didn't I tell you not to move?"

Jere whimpered and tried not to squirm, unsure whether he wanted to move closer or farther away. He hadn't been able to physically stop himself from moving when he lost his balance, but now he wasn't sure if he could stop himself from grinding against the warm hand between his legs. It was a mix of sadness and relief when he felt the squeezing grip released.

Wren returned to his skin with the knife, starting at the same point on his stomach, this time working down, pressing close, *too* close to very valuable parts. Jere held his breath, holding still, an uncomfortable feeling spreading just before Wren made the knife veer off to the side, grazing against his leg. It was still cold, so cold and sharp against his skin, and Jere clutched at the ropes that bound him in hopes of staying still, staying calm. He didn't want it to stop, not yet, but even more, he didn't want to ask for it to stop and risk that request being ignored.

A warm hand covered his, squeezing tightly and bringing Jere back to the present.

"*You're doing wonderfully,*" Wren's voice was in Jere's head, comforting and familiar. "*I like seeing this side of you.*"

Jere remembered to breathe, a tense, excited sigh. When Wren touched him, the excitement far outweighed everything else. A few seconds later, the knife had traveled down the inner side of each leg, grazing the sensitive skin there, making quick work of the silky boxers.

All Jere had covering him were ropes on his wrists and pants around his ankles.

He shivered.

"Are you cold?" Wren asked, mocking him, pretending to be cruel. Jere had been asked the same question long ago, but this was so different. The slight smile at the edge of Wren's mouth gave him away.

Jere nodded.

"I'm not." Wren whispered in his ear, making Jere shudder more and long to feel the warm breath all over his body.

His longing was quickly sated as Wren pressed against him,

chasing away the coldness. He was hot, burning up, hard and rough and alive! That warmth, Jere wanted to get close to it, wanted to wrap it around himself —

A slap on his leg brought him back to the present, and he stilled immediately, remembering the game.

"Nice to see you enjoying yourself," Wren teased.

Jere let out a muffled gasp as he felt a hand encircle his cock, squeezing it, caressing it, warming it. He focused all his energy on staying still, even when he felt Wren's hand replaced by a wet, velvety tongue that worked its way up and down, making Jere want to scream with frustration. The very edge of teeth grazed the head, and he pressed himself back against the edge of the desk. *Don't move, don't move, don't move.*

The pressure and sucking increased, Wren's tongue kept working, and Jere found himself lost in the sensation. He moaned through the tape, squeezed the rope until his hands hurt, and finally, felt his control slip away as he thrust into Wren's mouth, seeking something, anything, some sort of release.

Everything stopped, leaving Jere desperate to feel Wren's tongue and teeth and hands on him again.

Jere tensed as he felt the knife against the underside of his cock. He somehow managed to remain hard, despite, or perhaps because of the sharp coldness and the fear that came along with it. He longed to feel Wren's lips around his cock again, but the blade of the knife had his heart racing.

"Go ahead," Wren taunted, his voice dark and dangerous. "Don't you want to move?"

Jere stayed still, the sharp edge against his delicate skin enough to freeze him forever. The pressure increased and he yelped, doubting Wren's promise to avoid cutting him. Through his panic, he realized that he could feel Wren's hand pressing into his skin as well, holding him taut, protecting him. If the knife slipped, Wren would cut himself, not Jere, and that realization was enough to bring Jere back to excitement, his cock growing harder as a result of the security.

Jere was relieved to hear a clatter as the knife fell to the floor. The line between uncomfortable and turned on was thin, but Wren had stopped while still on the "turned on" side. Jere felt strong hands squeezing his ass, and he relaxed as he was lifted onto the surface of the desk, lying on his back. His pants were tugged off of his feet unceremoniously, and he felt his legs being lifted up, resting on Wren's shoulders. Unable to do more than glance down, Jere focused on the ceiling and the hands that were now trailing up his body, tracing the red line that the knife had left up his stomach, and continuing to follow that line up his arms, ghosting over his hands, testing the ropes to make sure they weren't too tight or too loose.

He closed his eyes, almost purring under the soft hands, warming every inch that they touched. He wanted more, wanted to feel Wren go from soft to rough, from gentle to punishing and back again like they had so many times. Jere's breath caught as he felt Wren stop exploring his body, grabbing his hips and holding him tightly in place. He trembled as he felt something pressing against his entrance, giving him a few seconds warning before shoving into him.

Gasping, Jere struggled against the ropes as he felt himself being filled, stretched uncomfortably, thrust into before he was ready. He fought, unable to decide whether he wanted to escape the pain of the thrusting or take it deeper, giving himself over to the need that had his cock aching for stimulation. He didn't still until he felt a slap on his face.

He froze, suddenly reminded of his orders not to move. Regaining his composure, and trying to breathe through the pain, he forced himself to stay still again, thankful that the thrusting had stopped while he did.

Finally, Jere was completely still, relaxing and letting the pain wash over him, lessening with each breath. He felt slow, soft thrusting start up again, and he moaned, accepting the pleasure that was being forced on him. This was better, this was more manageable.

For now, anyway.

The slow thrusts didn't last long, and in what seemed like seconds, Jere felt himself being rammed into, almost painfully, the slap of flesh against flesh as bodies collided. The desk was hard, and every time he was lifted off the surface and dropped back down he was sure there would be another bruise.

He had rarely felt better.

It was too much, too good, and Jere found himself unable to avoid bucking up to meet every thrust, driving Wren's cock deeper inside of him, wrapping his legs around Wren's shoulders. Despite the order not to move, Jere couldn't hold back from seeking more contact, more pleasure, and more stimulation.

Both lost in their own sensations, neither seemed to notice.

A few seconds later, Jere felt a hand around his cock again, applying pressure, squeezing in time with the thrusts. He whimpered and moaned, jutting up and down, and gasped suddenly as he felt the tape ripped from his mouth in one burning motion, distracting him only slightly from the other sensations he was struggling not to give in to.

He licked his lips, wincing at how dry they were. The thrusts were growing harder, and he knew he wouldn't make it much longer. He wanted it to last forever, but the waiting tormented him, increasing his desire.

"Please..." he begged, startled at how desperate he sounded.

Cruel laughter. A few more thrusts. A hand resting on his throat, threatening to push down.

He felt Wren inside of him, so close to coming, and he whispered, "Please," again.

The hand at his throat came up to cradle the side of his face.

"Come for me, Jere."

They lay, spent, on top of the desk.

"Fuck."

"I think you just did that, love," Jere muttered, his body still spasming.

Wren laughed, drawing a leg up along the length of Jere's, making him shudder all the more.

"Ow," Jere winced as he moved. He wasn't sure just *what* hurt, but he was pleasantly sure that it was a little bit of everything. "Did you leave a handprint on my face again?"

"I'm sorry," Wren said, grinning and showing only the tiniest bit of remorse. "I got caught up."

"Mmm, it's not as though I didn't like it..." Jere let his voice trail off into a breathy sigh. He didn't just like it, he loved it, and the fact that Wren was as into it as he was made it all the better. He squirmed uncomfortably on the desk. "Untie me?"

"You'd like that, wouldn't you?" Wren smirked, sitting up even as he teased. He leaned over his master and drew him into a long, deep kiss that had them both panting when they finished.

"I liked the knife," Jere admitted, falling silent for a moment, appreciating the sensations, the kiss, the closeness of his lover. How long had they been doing this? Months? It felt like forever. But always new. Infinite first times of amazing, connected lovemaking. "Thank you."

"Any time," Wren replied, playful again. "I love trying new things with you."

Jere felt Wren's hands working the knots on his wrists, and winced a little at the burn.

Wren made a tsk-tsk sound. "Jere, honestly, you really should have let me use the padded cuffs!"

"It would have been out of character," Jere muttered, still too full of post-orgasm bliss to notice that his skin had been rubbed raw. "What kind of robber breaks into an office with padded cuffs?"

Wren pulled him up to a sitting position and lightly pulled his wrists in front of his eyes, displaying the bright red chafe marks. "The kind of robber that doesn't want to hear his victim whine for the next week about how it's too hot to wear long-sleeve shirts to work every day."

"I don't whine!" Jere protested. His whining tone completely contradicted his protest.

Wren pulled him further up, firmly planting him on his feet. "You get to bed; I'll bring in some of the healing cream and some anti-inflammatories. It's really too bad that healing gifts don't work on yourself!"

Jere stopped him, wrapping his arms around Wren's neck, not caring that his wrists continued to burn as he pressed them together. "I don't mind having your marks on me," he countered.

"It is rather sexy," Wren conceded. "But, seriously, off to bed, or I'll 'accidentally' bump into those marks while we're working together tomorrow!"

"Promise?" Jere teased. It was another part of their game lately, seeing how much they could get away with in public. It made the day go by quite quickly... or quite slowly, depending on what they were waiting for.

Wren shook his head a bit as he grinned, and Jere walked off to their bedroom, feeling the pleasant stings and burns across—and inside—his body. He would sleep exceptionally well tonight.

Wren was not far behind with the promised items, and began tending to him as carefully and lovingly as he could ever have asked for. Jere sighed happily as a cool washcloth traced over the line that the knife blade had left on him—not quite drawing blood, but almost breaking skin, here and there. Exactly what he had requested, no more.

"I liked what you did with the temperature," he managed, feeling rather exhausted. "You've been working with it?"

"Yep." Wren could almost feel his lover smile. "That book your mum sent along was really helpful—about being able to speed up molecules to start the fire, and how stopping one or bringing a temperature *down* was really the same thing, but in reverse."

"Tha's good," Jere mumbled, falling asleep under the careful touch. He really was proud of Wren, but complete words and sentences seemed like so much work at the moment.

"Babe, are you that tired?" Wren asked as he slid close and pulled the covers over both of them. "It's still pretty early."

Jere nodded, leaning back as he felt the familiar, warm arms encircling him, and pressing against the body he had come to know so well. *"I'm exhausted. And not just by what you and I do – the clinic is really taking its toll on me, especially with treating the slave population as well... I just feel so drained."* Mindhealing was a complicated process, but at its essence, it required considerable energy from the person doing the healing—in this case, Jere. Good meals and adequate rest had been enough to take care of his body when he first arrived in Hojer and had a reasonable number of patients to deal with, but now that there was an increase due to treating the slave population as well, he found himself on the brink of exhaustion by the time dinner rolled around most nights.

The idea to treat slaves in the clinic had come from their friend Kieran, suggested to her by the anti-slavery organizations she was a member of. In addition to improving the general health of the slaves in Hojer, the hope was that it would have far-reaching impacts on how slaves were viewed in general; encouraging people to view them as human beings, at least. Once Jere had agreed with her proposition to make slave healthcare a priority, the word had been put out through legitimate and less legitimate channels that he was offering lower cost care than the local veterinary specialist. Word of mouth spread the information quickly, and many slaveowners, equally curious and in need of services, showed up at his door in the past few months. A town council meeting was held, which both Jere and Kieran attended, and Jere explained his platform to the town planners and a variety of interested citizens. Now, in addition to his regular caseload, he was taking care of three or four slaves a day as well, treating everything from "accidental" injuries to routine illnesses and sterilizations.

It was this additional work that had Jere so exhausted. His proposal and stated position was that he used less energy on slaves, cutting corners by means of limiting pain reduction and not healing "unnecessary" features like scarring. In truth, he was treating the slaves exactly as he would treat a free person, if not better. The free citizens of Hojer would easily have accepted substandard work, and some might actually have encouraged it, another reminder to their slaves that they were not entitled to the same basic privileges as free people. Jere's own beliefs and standards demanded that he provide slaves with the same care and quality that would be afforded a free person, despite the energy drain. Solutions to that problem were limited, and each presented its own drawback. Quite simply, he could either heal fewer people or obtain more energy, and there were so few ways to accomplish either without letting on to the public that he had taken on more than he could handle.

Wren rubbed Jere's shoulders, soothing the tense muscles. *"If it's taking this much out of you, you know you could always – "*

"No. I'm not doing it, and that's the end of the story." Jere managed to spit some words out loud, offended at the idea. They had talked about it before, much to Jere's chagrin, and the idea of using Wren as an energy source had presented itself as a horrible, if realistic solution. One that Jere was vehemently opposed to. *"Siphoning energy off of other people is just wrong, and I don't want to do it."*

"Jere..." Wren started, but his voice trailed off, replaced by a soft, breathy kiss along Jere's neck, which he melted into immediately. "Can we at least discuss this tomorrow? Please?"

Jere heard the sadness, the worry, the concern in his lover's voice. He knew they were both exhausted, and he knew damn well that he was taking on too much. If it was only him being pushed past his limits, Jere would happily have continued to drag through each day, half-alive and groggy, but it wasn't just about him. Wren was just as tired sometimes, and when he wasn't, he still deserved more than a half-dead lover who couldn't make it through a conversation without falling asleep. Jere knew that his life hadn't really been just about him since he had moved to Hojer, just over a year ago, and met the wonderful, wonderful person he was curled up next to at the moment. As much as he hated to even consider energy transfers, he knew Wren had a point, and at least deserved the chance to try and convince Jere of the benefits. Jere gave in, nodding and curling into his lover's touch. *"Okay. Let's talk about it tomorrow. But you're mine! I won't suck your energy to power the undeserving bastards of Hojer, is that clear?"*

Jere bit back a yelp as he felt a sharp bite on his collarbone.

"Yes, master," Wren answered, sarcastic and playful through the mind connection. *"By the way, you'll be needing a turtleneck to go with those long sleeves."*

Chapter 2
Pregnant Girls and Ideas

Wren woke the next day feeling quite well-rested and happy to feel his master's arm flopped carelessly across his chest, cuddling him like a teddy bear. He drew his fingers along Jere's arm for a minute, back and forth, until he realized how tired he must still be, not to be moving at all. It frustrated him how exhausted his lover was, how kind, how fucking *stubborn* he was being not to do the energy transfer. It was noble, but he didn't want Jere to be noble, he wanted him to be alive.

Still, he was quiet as he slipped from their bed, picking up a robe from the back of the door and draping it over his shoulders as he went to start something for breakfast. Jere often tried to claim that he was "too busy" for breakfast on workdays, but Wren thought that was a load of rubbish. Besides, he finally had someone he enjoyed cooking for and eating with, and he took full advantage of it.

Things between him and Jere had gone fantastically over the past few months. Flipping an egg with ease, he couldn't help but smile as he thought about the horror they had both gone through when Wren had essentially bared his soul — and his gift — to his master.

Looking back, it was odd, really, how upset he had been. How differently he had expected Jere to react. Six, hell, even three months ago, he assumed he would have been killed. Of course not. It made sense now. It was Jere, for Christ's sakes, who loved him, and cared about him, and never did a wrong thing to anybody. It had been quite an upset for them, and it had taken both of them a while to really come to terms with his firesetting gift, and the fire, and everything that entailed, but they had gotten over it. They had worked through it, the same way that they had worked through the nightmares and the fear and everything else.

Wren thought he had used his last bit of luck when Jere was willing to overlook his latent gift, to help him stay hidden and protected from the types of people who would want to experiment on him and worse. He had been jaw-droppingly shocked when Jere had encouraged him in it, suggesting he practice using it, asking him about it and how it felt and all sorts of things. There had been uncertainty, at first, but in those later weeks after everything had been revealed, Jere never really seemed to be bothered by the danger Wren could pose. He was more excited, encouraging Wren to try new feats and learn more about the firesetting gift that he had suppressed for so long. Wren wondered if it was because Jere's gift could be used to harm as well, as Jere had pointed out on numerous occasions. More often, he thought it was just because that's who Jere was; he trusted Wren without question and wanted nothing more than to see him happy. It felt strange; people from Hojer weren't like that, supportive and helpful and devoted, but it fit with Jere.

Wren was equally as awed and surprised by the continued support of Jere's mum, the only other person who knew of his second gift. The first and only time meeting Janet had been filled with fear and worry on Wren's part, but Wren was glad that they had become close in recent months through the exchange of letters. Sometimes, it seemed like she and Wren wrote each other more than she and Jere did, and she often sent along books and articles on the topic of dual-giftedness. She passed on stories of children developing firesetting gifts, how they learned to explore and control them, and how adults coped with gifts that showed up or were identified later in life. They were subjects that nobody in a slave state would ever discuss, and Janet made them feel as normal and exciting as learning a new language. She and Jere were excited for him, which allowed Wren to finally start to accept that part of him that he had been forced to hide away for so long.

In addition to the practical knowledge, Janet provided endless emotional support during a rather rough patch, as he explored the potentially deadly gift he had been given, and tried to cope with the reality that he was ever-so-slightly different from almost anyone he had ever met before. She joked sometimes that she had "adopted" him, but even before that, he had started to think of her as the mother he had never had, the kind of mother who would never have turned her back on her child for being different. She always addressed the letters to Jere, just in case any prying eyes should look at them, but a little star next to the name indicated she wasn't actually writing to her son. Nobody would question a doctor receiving advice or articles on gifts, especially breaking research in the area of dual-giftedness. In such small towns, people consulted their doctor for everything from medical emergencies to general developmental questions such as how to manage new gifts. Wren had no doubts that Jere would cover for him. To his credit, Jere never so much as peeked, he just handed the letters over with a smile.

Privacy was something Wren would never have dared expect, much less ask for; not until recently. It wasn't a right afforded to children, and as a slave, it was safer to expect that privacy would be actively discouraged at every turn. While Wren knew logically that he was a slave, it didn't feel like it most of the time, and he was aware that he was thinking less and less like one with every passing day. There were times that he was still forced to acknowledge that Jere was, among other things, his master, but it was a point that was never enforced in private, never brought up or used as a bargaining chip. He accepted it, Jere pretended to accept it in public, and they continued to live their lives as undisturbed as possible. Perhaps they did live their life in some sort of fantasy world of denial, but it worked for both of them, and that was all that mattered. Wren liked it that way and Jere agreed.

It wasn't as though they were entirely reclusive; Jere went out with Paltrek every other week or so, and sometimes even met up with other friends of Paltrek's, having a good enough time, or so he told Wren. On a few occasions, Dane had tagged along with his master, and he and Wren were "allowed" to sit and stare awkwardly at one another, trying to make polite conversation and wishing they were elsewhere. To be fair, Dane was pleasant enough, but Wren remained detached from him. Although Wren was reluctant to admit it, he preferred to remain somewhat detached from most people aside from Jere. It was safer and more comfortable that way.

They had taken to visiting the library regularly, both to pick up books, and to get out of the house. The librarian, Imelda, was even more sweet and friendly toward Wren than she had been before, now that she wasn't restrained from chatting with him. They shared book recommendations, awaited new editions of books together, and actually interacted as near-equals. She was a good judge of character, and she took Jere at his word when he brushed off any of her concerns of how she should interact with Wren. As a *dular*, she had first-hand experience with feeling inferior to those with mind-gifts, but she had lived in the culture for long enough to know what was and wasn't appropriate. While she didn't explicitly approve of slavery, she was familiar enough with customs to avoid making Wren feel uncomfortable, something he appreciated greatly.

Her niece, though considerably more energetic and not nearly as likely to respect custom, had become a bigger part of their life as well. With school on hiatus for the summer, Kieran had spent hours at their house, *in* their house, doing things that neither Wren nor Jere wanted to know too much about. She claimed to enjoy the silence and the space that the usually empty house provided while Wren and Jere were busy in the clinic, but Wren was pretty sure that things at home weren't well. She made more than one comment about her empathic gift being troubling due to the way the slaves at her parents' house were treated, and nobody needed any sort of gift to see how upset she was when she would show up unannounced and silent. He and Jere both resigned themselves to serving as her safe, happy place to hide when the school year was out.

Kieran was working, seemingly tirelessly, on campaigns for healthcare and slave rights and freedom and everything else she could get her hands on. Fortunately for all involved, it appeared that the group she was involved with had acquired some better leadership than it had at one point, and was organizing toward slow change as opposed to the violent overthrow they had been planning initially. Certainly, there were still talks of rioting and slave smuggling and blackmail, but these were fading away in favor of more reasonable interventions such as abuse protection and human-grade, humane healthcare. The small steps seemed to be working better, and the people involved seemed to be in significantly less danger.

Through his work with slaves in the clinic, Jere was tied up in Kieran's efforts, and Wren found himself drawn in as well. All day, he assisted with every free and slave patient from the moment they walked in the door, and once they finished work for the day, he tried to help his lover cope with the unpleasant realities that they encountered. So many of the harsh facts about slave treatment had been easy enough to overlook in the past, but now they were becoming more visible. The first time Jere had taken away a young woman's right to have children it had made Jere sick. Wren could only stand back and watch, feeling cold and detached and secretly relieved. He would never know for sure, but he doubted he would ever want to bring a child into this world, into a state where they might be enslaved. As a slave, he assumed that the minor inconvenience would be far less unpleasant than risking pregnancy that could ruin one's value.

When possible, Jere pushed back against the normal inhumane treatment. Those people who brought in a slave who was badly beaten or abused were informed, quite curtly, that their charge for the healing would double on each subsequent visit for that reason. Jere justified it not as a compassionate move, which would have swayed nobody, but as a practical measure, a way of keeping his healing gift open for other emergencies. One woman had called Jere's bluff not once, but twice, and glared at him with venom as he told her that she would need to pay four times the amount she had paid on her initial visit, or he would get the police involved. Money seemed to get through to them much more easily than threats or appeals to compassion ever had, and nobody questioned Jere's motivations.

Then again, some things couldn't quite be considered abuse.

The girl couldn't have been more than sixteen or seventeen, barely out of the training institute, and she was being half-dragged by her master, a middle-aged, impatient-looking man, who kept sighing and looking around as Wren perfunctorily handed him the check-in paperwork and instructed him on what to fill out. They had spent hours on the slave paperwork, as Jere kept trying to make it similar to the regular paperwork, and Wren kept gently reminding him that it wouldn't be acceptable that way. The free people of Hojer would demand clear differences between their medical care and that of slaves.

"Can't we wait somewhere else?" the man grumbled, shoving the clipboard in Wren's direction. "I don't want to be seen here with her."

"Sir, I—" Wren stopped as he noticed the presenting complaint that the man had filled out. Pregnancy scare. So, he had raped her, although he probably saw it as simply "using" her as intended. As a result, he impregnated her, and despite his actions, he didn't want anyone to see the consequences. He had no pity for the man, but the girl looked miserable. He forced a smile onto his face, trying for all those present to look like an innocent, pleasant slave. "If you'd like, sir, you may remain in the waiting room while I take the girl back to see the doctor. She can wait in an exam room. Allow me to assure you, they are all fully lockable and safety checked to ensure your property will remain in good condition until it is returned to you."

The man looked around again and nodded. "Yeah. That's fine." He glanced down at the girl, who was crumpled, more than kneeling, at his feet. "Go with him. Don't give him any trouble, either."

She said nothing, just dragged herself to her feet and walked toward the door where Wren waited. He was glad he wasn't a girl. Of all the things he *did* have to worry about, pregnancy had never been one of them.

He directed her to an empty exam room, one that had been designated for "slave use." Jere had railed at that idea, horrified that his clinic should be so segregated. But the free citizens of Hojer would demand it be that way, just like they would demand that the door lock only from the outside. It had taken both Wren's and Kieran's insistence for Jere to finally acquiesce.

Wren told the slave girl that she could have a seat, and pointed to an exam table, the act of putting his hand out to point making her cringe and flinch away. He sighed. Jere would have difficulty with this one.

Heading back into the clinic, he checked in the next patient before stepping back out to find Jere disposing of some gloves and making his way to the list to check who was next.

17

"Is she in there?" he asked, nodding toward the slave exam room. Jere always refused to call it by any name, simply pointing or nodding or referring to it as "in there."

"Yep. She's scared, Jere, watch out."

"I'm sure it'll be fine... but bring a sedative, if you would, just in case?"

Wren nodded, acquiring the injection and returning to the exam room, where Jere sat on a stool next to the exam table. The slave huddled against the wall sobbing.

"Shh, it's okay. It's okay, I won't hurt you."

Jere was speaking so gently, so patiently. Wren couldn't help but love him for it, but it was frustrating as well. The girl would respond just as well, if not better, to a sharp, firm command, and the whole fucking thing would be over sooner. *And* his boyfriend wouldn't waste as much of his time and energy on her.

Jere reached out, placing a tentative hand on the girl's arm. She didn't resist, but started shaking. "It's okay, I'm just checking..." he muttered. A few seconds later, he shook his head. "I'm sorry, honey, you're pregnant."

She sobbed harder.

"It's okay, I... Wren, did her master want it aborted?"

"Yes, sir." Wren had no say in the matter, but he was in agreement. The girl shouldn't have to deal with that. Pregnancy seemed awful, and most probably even more awful for a slave. Everything was more awful for a slave. Better to have it taken care of than to suffer through a lack of medical care and proper nutrition.

"All right," Jere nodded, continuing to speak over the girl's sobbing. "Okay, it's a very simple procedure. I'm going to need you to lift up the gown you're wearing—just up a little, I know, I know, I'm sorry. I'm just going to lay my hand on your stomach, not anywhere else, okay, I promise, this will only be a minute."

"Please, sir," she whimpered. "Please, don't do this! Please, just kill me!"

"It's okay," Jere's voice was strained. "It has to be done... your master could do it in many worse ways than this. I promise, there will be no pain. You won't feel a thing. Would you prefer to be sedated?"

It wasn't meant to be a threat, but Wren understood why the girl took it as one.

"Please, sir, no, I'll be good, I'm sorry, please don't, he'll hurt me!"

"Okay, okay, don't worry about it. We'll just get it done." Jere glanced at Wren. "Go out and inform her master what's happened, and find out if he wants her sterilized so this doesn't happen again."

"Yes, Doctor." Wren pocketed the sedative injection and headed back into the waiting room, informing the still irritable man of the outcome. He agreed to sterilization. Wren couldn't help feeling relieved.

He checked a few more things and arranged some paperwork, wanting to decrease the amount of time he had to spend watching the scene in the exam room. Jere was good at what he did. He was even good at calming down the hysterical ones, but even after all this time, Wren had to admit that it came a bit too close to home for his tastes. It wasn't long ago that he was where that poor girl was. He'd rather not remind himself of that.

Finally, he slipped back into the exam room, not entirely surprised to find the girl clinging to Jere's arm in silent desperation. He waited, sensing that Jere was completing the procedure, and looked down at his feet until he felt Jere acknowledge him. He nodded, knowing Jere would want to know whether to go ahead with the sterilization or not.

Biting his lip, Jere returned his attention to the girl. "Again, no pain... and you'll never be in this situation again."

The girl only nodded, burying her head against Jere's arm like a pillow.

A few minutes later, the procedure was complete, and Jere stood up, looking pale and drained and disgusted. "My assistant will clean you up and see you out."

Wren tried to touch his hand as he walked by, but Jere jerked away.

"Sorry, Wren, I just... I need a minute."

Wren sighed. His master took this too hard.

He approached the girl slowly, certain that cleanup tools for this particular procedure would be terrifying to her. He met her eyes, which were empty and full of tears.

"I have a speed gift. I'm not interested in anything other than cleaning you up. This will be quick. Please cooperate."

She nodded and closed her eyes. Wren completed the procedure, cleaning out what used to be a baby, as well as a considerable amount of blood and fluids. In less than thirty seconds, his job was done, and he directed the still sobbing girl to the waiting room, where Jere was explaining the follow-up care instructions to her master with a sad look in his eyes. The master looked annoyed that he would have to do anything out of the ordinary.

Wren noticed a new patient had come in, plastered a polite smile on his face, and gathered the requisite paperwork for the intake. He hoped the new person didn't notice, but there was a tiny spatter of blood on the sleeve of his shirt. He wondered if they had any of that stain remover left.

Jere was quiet the rest of the day, not saying much until they were seated at the table for dinner. Wren, to his credit, had managed to put together a delicious meal in spite of the busy schedule at the clinic, and had also managed to change clothes not once, but twice. Jere, as was becoming typical, was still in the clothes he had worn all day, and was guzzling another cup of coffee.

"The number of patients is still rising, isn't it?" Jere asked.

Wren nodded. He had been keeping careful track of the numbers since the new policy had taken effect. "It is, though not as quickly as before."

Jere shook his head. "I'm sorry, love, this isn't fair to you."

Wren smiled. As usual, his lover was thinking of everyone *but* himself. "Jere, it's fine! If anything, it's not fair to *you*! You're practically dead on your feet."

"I know, I know..."

"We need to talk about energy transfer, Jere. You've said yourself, it would ease the burden, and I know I can tolerate it. Why are you so opposed to the most obvious solution?"

"Because, I don't want you to be some sort of fucking... energy source for me!" Jere protested, tripping over his own words. His feeble attempts to defend himself only made Wren more convinced that it needed to happen.

Watching his lover struggle with moral issues was bad enough. Watching him retch after particularly unpleasant procedures and abuse tore him apart. Watching him fade away because he was literally being sucked dry of energy and resources and health? It wasn't fair, and it wasn't right, and it wasn't something that Wren wanted to just sit back and let happen. As much as Jere was the doctor, and as much as he was the master, Wren felt like he had to do his part to contribute, and the one thing he could do to help Jere right now was to provide him with energy—at least a little bit—until they could think of something else. They were partners in this, Wren was sure of it. The hard part was convincing him it was the right thing to do.

Wren said nothing. Silence, more than anything, seemed to force decisions out of the man he loved.

"Besides, I've thought of something else," Jere said, looking cautious.

Wren probed at their connection, and felt the apprehension, the uncertainty. He raised an eyebrow, waiting.

"I want to buy a slave."

Chapter 3

Justification

Wren let his fork drop, pushing himself slightly away from the table. "You what?" He tried desperately to convince himself that he hadn't just heard that. It couldn't be true.

"I wanna buy a slave," Jere mumbled, looking away for a second.

Wren tried to breathe calmly, reminding himself that there must be a reasonable explanation for Jere's sudden interest in owning another slave. "Jere...."

"I know, I know, it's not like me, and it's weird, and it's good with just the two of us here, and I *like it* with just the two of us here..." Jere's face looked so drawn. "But I think it would be for the best."

Wren tried hard to focus on one thought. Focusing like the books Janet sent had taught him to do, to control his gifts, to control his emotions. To focus on calm, on Jere, on what they had. To not think about the uncertainty that a slave could bring, or what Jere might want to do with him, or the other slave, or all the bad things that could happen. More than anything, he tried not to think about why his master, who was usually so opposed to slavery, was viewing this as any kind of solution.

"Wren?"

It was too much. They had come quite far, but the threat of another slave was too much for him to think about. He didn't want to hear it, didn't want to hear the soft, familiar voice explain anything to him —

"Wren, love, please talk to me?" Jere's voice coaxed him back to reality. "You've gone all pale and quiet; please let me know what's

22

going on?"

Wren took another deep breath and opened his eyes, which he hadn't quite realized he had closed. "What will my place be, sir?"

He hadn't meant it to come out so harsh, but there it was. It was a question that a slave needed to ask his master, and he had asked it as such. The hurt on Jere's face indicated that he noticed.

"Wherever you want it to be, love," Jere said quietly, looking defeated. "I'd rather it be right where it has been, but that's up to you. You're my boyfriend, my lover... my slave only in name. That doesn't change. I want to figure this out with you."

Wren nodded. He wasn't sure if he believed it. He wasn't expecting to react this way. He hadn't ever expected to have this sprung on him. He assumed that he and Jere would be the only two living here forever. He had made peace with letting Jere use him for energy, but this was different. He felt blindsided.

"Wren, if I was anywhere else, I'd hire an employee. Someone to help out, to lend an extra hand to me and to you, someone to share the burden."

"So hire someone!" Wren clutched at the slightest chance of changing Jere's mind.

"It would have to be off-record, somehow," Jere shook his head. "I can't let on that the addition of the slave population is in any way jeopardizing my ability to heal the free citizens, and I doubt anyone around here with a mind-gift would do something of the sort anyway. They'd ask why I didn't buy a slave for energy."

"A *dular*?" Wren suggested.

"I just don't think a Hojer citizen would work," Jere admitted. "And I'm not sure how comfortable I am with having a stranger lurking around my clinic anyway. We need help, and I think I'd feel more comfortable knowing that nobody was going home to spread gossip."

"I don't need help, and I could share energy—"

"No," Jere cut him off. "Because I won't let you."

Wren seethed at the statement.

Jere shook his head. Wren was certain Jere was feeling his anger though the mind connection and he didn't care. He wanted Jere to know exactly how angry he was, how offended he was at the dismissal. Jere wasn't the only person affected by this, and Wren burned at the fact that Jere seemed to be the only person making the decision.

"Wren, you are *too* valuable! As a person, and as a professional asset—you take care of so much around here, from the house, to the clinic, to me—you need to be at your best at all times, okay? I can't risk collapsing and having you collapse from the same exhaustion, it's dangerous and it's bad practice! Please, trust me when I say that I push myself too far sometimes, and I need to know that you won't be too sapped of energy to help me get back on my feet."

Wren had to admit that Jere had a very good point. Jere was an excellent doctor, and his decisions about the clinic were without fault, always. From a medical standpoint, having two people sapped of their energy was potentially even worse than having just one. While Wren doubted that Jere would ever take that much from him, he understood the logic, and he nodded reluctantly.

"And I love you." Jere added. "I'd do anything for you. It seems so wrong to use you like that, even if I know I'm upsetting you by being stubborn about this."

Wren held back a smile. Jere was always so sweet and well-intentioned. Wren still couldn't put the abrupt dismissal out of his mind, but he wondered if he would have been as dismissive if Jere had offered to do something similar. He couldn't deny that he was as protective of Jere as Jere was of him. "I guess it could work," he admitted.

"And, also..." Jere shrugged a little bit. "I want to get a girl."

Wren felt his eyebrows rise in shock and surprise at this next piece of unexpected news. "I didn't even think you *liked* girls!"

Jere wrinkled his nose at the thought. "Not for more than friends or employees—Wren, Christ, do you really think I'd buy another human being with *those* intentions?"

It really didn't make sense. Of course, Wren didn't think Jere would buy another human being in the first place, and the sudden change had him feeling unbalanced and confused. Wren shook his head. "Then, why?"

Jere reached his hand across the table, taking Wren's hand, which he did not pull away. "I've been thinking about this for a while now, but it really hit me today... that girl that was in? She was so terrified, Wren, so fucking terrified of me and of you and of what would happen to her—always, back home, in the hospitals, we would have had a female doctor or at least a female nurse with her! I could even train someone to do basic exams, probably not on free women, unless they requested it, but certainly on slaves. I just... I just think they'd be more comfortable."

Wren couldn't stop himself from smiling a bit, this time. It made sense that his wonderful, sweet, sexy master had no intentions other than kindness and compassion. He was sitting here with bags under his eyes from exhaustion, and he was thinking of how to make medical exams better for pregnant slave women!

"I love you, but you fucking kill me sometimes," he muttered, squeezing Jere's hand. "So you're gonna get someone for an energy source and to comfort the ladies?"

"That's the plan as I see it," Jere smiled back at him. "Besides, if I were to hire someone, someone *free*, things between you and I would have to change. And I'm not gonna do that. A slave will be mine to do as I please with, and that means I can order her to live in our happy little fantasy world where I'm just a doctor who's in love with his assistant."

"How risqué," Wren smirked at him. "Don't let that power go to your head now!"

"If I do, will you tie me up and beat it out of me?" Jere teased back.

Wren laughed, resuming eating his dinner. He was still a little uncertain, but if anyone could make this work, Jere could. Besides, it hadn't happened yet. They had a while to talk about this, to come to terms with what exactly it would mean for either of them. "So, where are you getting a slave? Do you want one right out of the training facility, or maybe an older woman who's past her prime?"

Jere shrugged. He picked at his food for a moment before answering. "I had actually glanced through the classified ads."

Nobody in Hojer would even consider purchasing a slave from a classified ad, certainly not for any sort of important position. The classified ads were full of trash and rejects, slaves who were only good for sex or hard labor, and even entertaining the thought would be enough to draw disapproval from anyone who knew anything about what was acceptable here. Wren tried to stop himself from grimacing. "Jere, there's a reason that people sell in the classified ads."

"Right. Because they have something to sell." Jere's tone was dismissive, but Wren could sense something underneath.

"Jere, they're..." Wren struggled to phrase his next words carefully so they wouldn't sound as callous as they did in his head. "They're unwanted goods. Slaves that have failed out, that can't be sold elsewhere, that reputable buyers wouldn't purchase. They're...."

"They're people." Jere's tone had a threatening edge of finality.

"Yes, they are," Wren relented. Technically, it was true, but legally, socially, they were less than animals. "I just think it would be best if you went to a facility, or a dealer. A *reputable* dealer. It's not like you don't have the money."

Jere shrugged. "It isn't about the money. I buy everything through ads and other people and stuff. You know, furniture, textbooks — when I was in University — things like that."

Wren just stared at him. Surely, he wasn't comparing such a major purchase to buying trivialities?

"And it's just, I don't know, I mean, I've been reading through some of the ads..." Jere looked away a moment, hesitating in a rather unusual way. "There's a few that look... interesting."

"Interesting?" Wren couldn't imagine what would be interesting about a slave ad. They were horrible things, advertising horrible slaves.

"I just... I mean, I didn't want to do it without talking to you first, but there's one in particular — she sounds... a bit young, but there's just something about the way it's worded..." Jere peeked up at Wren, who just waited. "I don't know, I just feel like we could give someone a new start, you know? Take a chance."

Wren sighed. Jere *would* want to take a chance. He wouldn't want to play things safe or get someone reliable or follow solid advice from someone who had actually grown up in a slave state. "Why is she being sold?" He couldn't believe he was even going along with this.

"Just, uh, something about her not getting along. Difficulty

26

training. And stuff."

"Are you being purposely vague?" Wren challenged him, growing frustrated. He could tell that was exactly what Jere was doing by the stiff way he held himself, not to mention the nervous feelings that were clearly noticeable through the mind connection. When he got no answer, he continued. "How much is she even being sold for, then?"

"Don't worry about it. I've got plenty to cover it."

Wren felt the irritation rising. "Listen, you asked for my opinion—"

"Six thousand denn."

Wren shook his head. "Baby, I know you want to do a good thing, but that's only a step above what the workhouses would pay!"

Jere looked at him, cocking his head ever so slightly. The adorable puppy look worked even when Wren was getting frustrated.

"The workhouses... it's where slaves are sent to die," Wren tried to break it lightly. He was pretty sure he was failing. "Old, sick, chronically disobedient slaves—they get sent there. They pay next to nothing—but it's still better than actually *getting* nothing. They're chained up, doing extremely menial labor—factory work, farm work... things like that. Jere, it's where they send slaves that are unsellable."

Wren watched his master set his jaw, silent. He realized he had actually made him *more* likely to go through with this ridiculous plan. "You would be better off getting a kid right out of the training facility. She'll be skittish, but you can give her a better life. Jere, buying used is like—"

"They're not furniture, they're people!"

Jere's tone was short, which irritated Wren, as Jere had been the one who had just made the same comparison. Combined with the way Jere had cut him off and dismissed him earlier, Wren was starting to feel upset more by Jere's attitude than by the idea of buying a slave. With the anger came the heat, the threatening burn that seemed to start in his stomach and threaten to spew outward. Wren glared silently, feeling somewhat vindicated when he saw Jere frown.

"Wren, I'm sorry, I didn't mean to cut you off, or to get angry, I just... I can't believe I'm actually doing this at all. Thinking about buying a slave. It's hard, but I guess I should have expected it to be hard. Nothing here is easy. But if I have to do it, I'm doing it this way. I think I can feel better about it. Maybe."

Wren could see, in theory, where his master was coming from. "And it's not that I don't support you, I just... I know how it works here, and I know the challenges that a slave like this could bring, and I want..." Wren wasn't actually sure what he wanted. "I want things to stay peaceful around here."

"I'm sure they will," Jere smiled back at him, ever hopeful.

Wren still wasn't so sure, and he doubted that Jere had any idea as to what kinds of problems he might be bringing into their home.

"I'll just set up a time to meet with a few slaves and masters, see how it goes, okay? There's no need to rush into anything. Who knows — maybe you're right after all. You know how much you love being right."

Chapter 4

Better Plans

Wren smiled in spite of himself. He hoped he wasn't right, but he probably was. Jere would have the girls come, and then he would understand. He figured it wasn't worth arguing about now.

Besides, they had almost finished dinner, and Wren had better plans than arguing.

He got up, stacked their plates, and wrapped his arms around his master's neck as he leaned down to whisper in his ear. "Go get into the shower," he ordered. "I'll meet you there."

Glancing up at him, Jere smiled, nuzzling against him for a moment.

Wren was gone in an instant, grabbing up the plates and carrying them into the kitchen. He washed them quickly, as was his habit, plus he wanted to give Jere time to get started and naked and wet... maybe a little bit soapy....

He decided he was done with the dishes when he caught himself stroking a glass rather vigorously. Rinsing them quickly and setting them to dry, he made his way down the hallway, through the bedroom, and into the attached bathroom. He could make out his lover's outline through the shower door. He dropped his own clothes to the floor and stepped in, taking in the wet, dripping form in front of him.

Jere smiled at him, perfectly content, his eyes almost glowing through the water-darkened hair that covered them.

Wren reached out a hand and pushed the hair out of Jere's face, letting his hand linger across his cheek, pulling him close for a kiss. How long had it been since he had felt those lips on his? Only hours?

It felt like forever. He pushed harder, pressing Jere against the wall of the shower, pinning his head in place, wrapping his free arm around to clutch at Jere's back as he ground against his leg.

Jere complied, gasping a bit as Wren's tongue filled his mouth, invading before he was ready, taking him as swiftly as he took him in other ways. After a few moments, Wren pulled back, grinning with satisfaction.

"You need a haircut," he mumbled absently, his fingers twined in Jere's hair.

"Mmm, you need to be kissed some more," Jere replied, leaning forward to draw him in again.

Wren agreed. Even after so much time together, he had never grown bored with kissing Jere, the warm, soft pressure of their lips together, the familiar taste of Jere's tongue in his mouth. As they kissed, Wren trailed his hands over Jere's body, feeling the familiar angles of his hips, the curves of his ass. He caressed the parts that he knew Jere loved having touched, and in return, Jere did the same, drawing a few lusty gasps from Wren. For so many years, Wren had been scared of touch, finding it hurtful and unpleasant, but when Jere touched him, he switched on the most wonderful feelings, coaxing sounds and responses of out Wren that he would have sworn were impossible. They continued to kiss and touch each other until the water started to cool.

"You didn't even get a chance to get clean, did you?" Wren snickered. "I don't know if I want to take you to bed all dirty!"

"But I want to get dirty *with* you," Jere pretended to whine, ignoring the dropping temperature.

"I've got an idea," Wren said, an evil smirk crossing his face. "Down on your knees!"

Jere dropped instantly, giving Wren a playful smile in return. "I like this idea already!"

Wren wrapped his fingers through Jere's hair, tugging softly, playfully. He knew Jere liked having his hair pulled as much as Wren liked pulling it. "You get to work on that, and I'll wash your hair. It'll be like a race — we can see who finishes first!"

"You'll win!" Jere was only half-protesting, his face already close enough that his words sent warm air across Wren's cock.

"Well, then, that means I get the prize, don't I?" Wren grabbed some shampoo and let it splat on Jere's head. "Now, close your eyes, and get going!"

He could feel Jere grinning even as his mouth closed around his cock. Wren moaned as he felt the pressure increase sharply, felt Jere sucking and swallowing and taking him deep, deep into his throat. Wren gripped him by the back of the head, pulling him closer, absently remembering what he was supposed to do. Almost reluctantly, because the feeling of Jere's mouth on his cock seemed too good to ignore, he began to massage the shampoo into Jere's hair, cleaning it as quickly as he could while still enjoying the blowjob he was receiving.

It was a challenge, but Wren managed to get his lover clean, and himself. After battling with the shampoo, he managed to squirt some liquid soap between them, dragging Jere up to rub it across both their bodies just moments before he came, drawing a few protests from Jere.

He pressed a finger to his lips, silencing him. "Hush," he whispered, turning him about somewhat forcefully, placing them both under the cold stream of water to rinse the rest of the soap away. He could have possibly warmed it, but he didn't try. He was too focused on other things. "I win, so I get to say what happens next!"

Jere whined, teasing still, but stayed quiet as Wren grabbed towels and dried them both off in record time, leaving Jere shivering in the cold. He guided Jere out of the shower, led him to the bed, and guided him down to lie on his back, pinning him with his body. Wren concentrated, very carefully, and felt his own body temperature rise. It was new, but he could manage it safely now. He felt Jere stop shivering below him, and they wrapped around each other, their limbs intertwined. He could feel both their cocks pressed between them, hard, ready, waiting. He shuddered at the thought, eager to feel that closeness and connection with Jere again.

"Warmer now?" he managed to ask, leaning down to bite gently at Jere's neck. He dragged his tongue over the bruises he left last night, feeling a tiny bit guilty. It really was a bit warm to be wearing turtleneck shirts, but he had to admit that he liked seeing the marks on Jere.

31

"God, yes, Wren. So fucking hot." Jere was grinding, thrusting against him, driving them both crazy as he increased the heat with his own friction.

Wren reached down, fisting both their cocks, and leaned to whisper in Jere's ear. "I want you inside of me. Want to squeeze around you, feel you deep, deep inside."

"Please..." Jere moaned, squirming underneath him.

Wren leaned forward, draping his body across Jere's and stretching until he reached the lube they kept next to the bed. He sat back on his heels, kneeling between Jere's legs, and grabbed Jere's cock, slathering it with the clear, slippery stuff, and easing some onto his own cock for good measure. He slid into position, feeling his lover's cock at his entrance.

"Wren, do you want—"

"I want you to fuck me." Wren knew what he was asking. He wasn't on the receiving end of their games anywhere near as often as Jere was, and he did rather prefer to be stretched, prepared, taken slowly. But sometimes, he just wanted Jere to fuck him. Wren was too eager to have Jere inside of him, to impatient to wait while Jere took care of him carefully and gently. Tonight was one of those nights, Wren's desire already stoked by their time together in the shower. "Just let me come down slowly, okay?"

"Of course," Jere smiled back at him, his face contorting with pleasure as Wren eased himself down onto Jere's cock the tiniest bit.

Wren bit down on his lower lip, trying to ignore the burn as he felt himself being filled, moving slowly, reminding himself to relax, reminding himself that he was in control. Even after all this time, it was something he wasn't always up to, no matter how good it felt.

Wren felt a hand on his own cock, stroking it gently, and he looked down into Jere's eyes, so patient, so calm. Jere's other hand came up to brush against his chest, tracing an invisible line from his neck to his stomach. There was never any pressure from Jere, he just let Wren take what he needed, or not. Jere's cock was hard and he was breathing heavily, but he didn't so much as move his hips while he waited for Wren to adjust. Wren eased down, inch by inch, until he felt himself fully seated on Jere's cock. He let out a tiny sound, a mix of pain and pleasure, and he gently began rocking, moving up and down, feeling his muscles tense and relax beyond his control.

Jere simply lay there, panting, one hand still gently working Wren's cock while the other clutched at the sheets. "Damn, Wren, you feel so good..."

"You too," Wren smiled, finally finding a comfortable rhythm. Once he started moving, Jere joined him, slowly sliding up and down. Wren started to feel good, the pleasure finally hitting him and making him seek out more contact, more depth, more every-thing. "You want to switch places?"

"Whatever you want," Jere smiled back at him.

Wren knew that Jere was just as comfortable both ways. Hell, Jere seemed to be comfortable fucking in any position—they had tried a lot of them. No, Wren was the one who still had some res-ervations, who sometimes still got a little hesitant to have his big, powerful, sexy man on top of him. But tonight... tonight he wanted it.

He slid off for a moment, thinking back to an uncomfortable incident a few months back that had reminded both of them that neither were acrobats in bed, and rolled onto his back, next to his eager lover. Jere wasted no time repositioning himself, winding his arms under Wren's legs to give him better access. Jere paused for a moment, nipping gently at the inside of Wren's thigh, grinning up at him from below his still-wet hair.

"I can't wait to be inside of you again," he intoned, pressing ever so slightly.

It was a turn-on to hear. It was also a subtle way of asking per-mission.

"Fuck me, Jere," Wren whispered, seductive and needy all at once. "Take me. Hard. Deep. Please."

Jere smiled. He slid in, deep, but not hard. It was better. Wren thought he wanted it hard, but he was wrong. He realized he was completely crazy to think that he wanted the kind of hard fucking that Jere liked to receive. Wren clutched at Jere's arms, and he real-ized that Jere knew better than he did what he wanted, and that real-ization was wonderful. Wren wanted long, sensual thrusts, wanted to feel every inch of Jere inside of him, pushing almost too deep, just for a minute, before pulling back and doing it all over again.

Jere's hands were light on the tops of his legs, just resting, stroking, feeling. Even something as simple as that turned Wren on, and he struggled to hold back his orgasm, wanting the moment to last longer. Wren lost himself in the sensations for a moment, coming back when he felt himself bucking up, trying to take Jere deeper. He reached his arms up, suddenly feeling ungrounded, and Jere shifted instantly, easing Wren's legs down and reaching up to pull him into an embrace. Wren felt his cock pressing between their stomachs, and he squeezed tighter, harder, and came in a flurry of moans and gasps, clutching Jere's back.

Still riding the waves of orgasm, he pulled Jere's head down, whispering in his ear "I want to feel you come inside of me." The words had no sooner left his mouth than he pressed his face into Jere's neck, kissing, hiding, biting... trying to get as close as he could. The skin was salty, familiar, and at the same time uniquely Jere, and Wren couldn't get enough of him.

Jere kept riding him, slowly, carefully, even as Wren felt his own body calming down. Suddenly, he felt Jere's arms tighten around him, and he forced himself to breathe and relax as he felt a few sharp, hard thrusts, that *almost* hurt, followed by the warmth of his lover coming inside of him.

They stayed like that for a few minutes, both gasping and grinning like idiots, before Jere slid out and dropped down on the bed. Wren rolled over to wrap his arm around him immediately. He knew they should clean up, but all Wren wanted to do was cuddle and relish the closeness.

"You mentioned you had plans tonight," Jere said softly, his hand petting Wren's head absently. "I had no idea they were this spectacular!"

"It's been a while," Wren replied, snuggling in closer. "I can't spend all my time tying you up and ravishing you, now can I?"

Jere laughed. "Well, I sure as hell wouldn't complain either way! I've never had a bad time with you."

"Me neither," Wren smiled. It was so true. Of all the terrible sexual experiences he had suffered through, all the ones with Jere had been wonderful.

He felt the tiredness threatening to take him over, and tried unsuccessfully to stifle a yawn.

Jere, looking just as tired, kissed him gently before getting up, retrieving a towel, and cleaning them both up. He returned to bed, carefully pulled Wren over to the cleaner side, and curled up against him.

Wren looked up, sleepy. "I love you, Jere."

"I love you too."

Wren fell asleep with soft lips pressing against his head, the sound of light, familiar breathing lulling him to sleep.

Chapter 5
A Deal

Jere made appointments to view slaves, setting up the arrangements by telegraph or speed messenger, although he did his best to keep Wren out of the process. His lover wasn't actively opposed to the idea, but Jere could tell that he didn't actually support the plan, and he wanted to be as considerate as possible. He would rather have involved Wren in every step, but Wren's reaction made Jere think it would be better this way. Jere wasn't too surprised, but it did make him sad. He couldn't remember the last time he and Wren hadn't seen completely eye to eye on things.

Regardless, he was going to at least see the slaves. He figured he owed Wren, and himself, that much. The worst thing that might happen would be if he couldn't bring himself to buy a slave at all, leaving them still short-handed. For the most part, they didn't discuss it. Wren wrinkled his brow or frowned at him whenever he mentioned it, but otherwise, it was an active non-issue. Jere decided there was no reason to argue about something that might or might not happen in the future; they would deal with it once it became a reality. He loved Wren more than he had ever thought possible, but he was terrible to live with when he was upset, so Jere hoped to avoid that.

Two appointments had taken place already, and hadn't gone well. The second hadn't gone at all, as a speed messenger had arrived an hour before the appointment to inform him that the slave he was interested in was "no longer available for sale." Jere hoped that this just meant that the master had changed his mind, but Wren cynically suggested that perhaps the slave had died. Jere couldn't even think of an appropriate comeback to such a suggestion. The first slave looked to be about eighty years old and was nearly blind. Jere's stomach churned when her papers listed her to be about forty. The life she lived must have been horrible, but there was nothing Jere could do for her, nothing he could use her for. A small part of him was starting to understand what Wren meant when he said that people sold in the classifieds for a reason. But he refused to give up hope.

He had taken advantage of his half-day off on Sunday. The person selling the girl he had mentioned to Wren had agreed that it would work, though he had tried to pressure Jere to pick an earlier date, or to travel to see his "property." Jere recoiled at the thought of travelling to meet this person. What the hell should he think of him as—master? Owner? Either was equally repulsive. Despite having set up other appointments, the whole thing still made him nauseous, and the idea of travelling to look at a slave was just too real. In all honesty, he wasn't sure if he could go through with this—buying a human being? He had enough hang-ups about owning Wren—a fact that he hated and was adamantly opposed to, but that was different. Circumstances were different; *everything* was different when it came to Wren.

But still... Wren was part of the reason why he was doing this in the first place. Although the young slave had insisted that he was fine, that he wasn't tired, that this additional workload wasn't straining on him, Jere could see right through him. The lies were sweet and well-intentioned, but Wren was nearly as exhausted as he was. They had expanded the clinic beyond their means, and despite the good work they did, it was taking a toll on both of them. He wasn't about to let his boyfriend suffer anymore because he was too hesitant to embrace his place in society as a slaveowner.

Jere heard a knock at the door, and reluctantly called for Wren. He tried to insist that Wren didn't need to be present for this part of the process, but, as usual, Wren's insistence was much stronger. And, according to the sweet, bossy thing, much more socially acceptable.

In that same "acceptable" manner, Wren opened the door, bowing slightly to let in a middle-aged man. Jere wasn't sure what was more irksome—seeing his lover bow down to such a creature, or seeing the way he dragged the girl behind him.

"If I may, sir, this is Dr. Peters, my master," Wren said quietly, head down, the perfect picture of subservience.

Jere tolerated it. He *always* tolerated it, because maintaining the illusion kept Wren safe.

The man grunted, ignoring Wren, and continued to pull the girl behind him with one arm as he walked across the room. His other hand was stuck out toward Jere, who resigned himself to the situation and shook it. In all honesty, he was too busy being appalled by what he was seeing.

"Dr. Peters, nice to meet you," the man spoke cordially. "Jasper Mollen."

Jere was pretty sure that he was going to say something polite in return, he was properly socialized and interacted with others, and had even become accustomed to the ways of things here, and then... "Is that a straightjacket?"

The man let his hand drop, chuckling at Jere's discomfort. "That's exactly what it is, Doctor! Best thing I've found to keep the little bitch still, especially while travelling. That's why I tried to get you to come visit at my place—such a liability to transfer them around the state when they're so volatile!"

Jere wanted to be ill. The girl didn't look volatile, she looked terrified. In addition to the straightjacket, which was strapped too tightly to be comfortable *or* safe, she had a gag in her mouth, and what looked like a collar and leash around her neck. She was attempting to make some sort of noise, but all that came out was a muffled groan.

Even through the straitjacket, Jere could see that she was far too thin. By the look of her sunken cheeks and bony legs, he would guess that she was starving. She was small, both short and thin, and Jere could tell that even if she wasn't starving she would be petite. Her facial features were delicate, like the rest of her, and it made the cuts and bruises on her face stand out that much more. Her skin had an unhealthy pallor, nearly blending in with the fading bruises. Jere her skin was darker than his or Wren's, and would probably be even more so when she was healthier. She was clean, surprisingly; Jere assumed that her master must have at least made her shower before showing her off for sale. Still, her hair indicated months of neglect, the dark brown curls matted badly. Anyone who kept a dog in this condition would have it taken away from them, it was appalling to see a human being like this.

"*Jere. Dear. You really have to say something. You're standing there with your mouth open.*" Wren's voice was soft, but insistent in his head. Jere forced his mind and his mouth to work together to speak.

"Uh... yeah. Slaves." That wasn't exactly any better than the awkward silence had been. "Yeah, that, uh, that would make travel hard."

Wren shook his head slightly, trying to conceal a smile, and stepped off to the side of the room, ever the picture of appropriateness.

"Yeah, well, I figured I'd throw it all in for this trip. She's secured, I've got her papers together, and I already showed her to another couple in Lockmane County this morning."

"Oh." Jere felt stupid, suddenly considering that the whole plan to buy another slave was a bad idea. He wasn't quite sure what he had been expecting, but this wasn't it. He had never wanted to bring this sort of suffering into his house. "They, uh, weren't interested, then?"

Mollen shook his head. "Nope. Not quite what they were looking for. Which makes me wonder — well, you're a doctor... why are you buying second-hand? I thought your type usually went straight for the pretty virgins from the training facilities?"

"I, uh..." Jere forced himself to think, focusing all of his energy on making and saying words. "I've had good luck in the past," he managed. It was a lame attempt.

The man shrugged. "Eh, well, whatever suits you. You got any questions, or do you just want to look her over?"

"Um..." Jere put all his willpower into not looking back to Wren for help. For his part, Jere could feel the bastard trying not to laugh. He had told Jere that he was on his own, and Jere had taken that statement to heart. "I, uh... how long have you had her?"

"Tell the truth, not that long," Mollen admitted. He dug into a bag he was carrying and pulled out a thick stack of papers. "It's all in there, all clear and legal, but she's been bounced around a bit. I got her from a friend of mine as a payment for some work I did for him — even the workhouse buying price was worth what I did for him, so I'm not complaining. But it's more of a fight than it's worth to get her to do much of anything, Doctor, I won't lie to you. She's been mine three, maybe four months?"

Jere nodded. He had noticed the way the girl's eyes had gone wide at the mention of the workhouse.

"She can be used in a lot of ways, but I'll tell you, it's a fight to get her to do it. I have four other slaves now, just for myself, and I spend more time disciplining and watching this one than the other four combined. I just want you to know — no refunds, no returns, sale as is, you know? Hope you have something simple in mind to use her for — are you looking for someone for experimentation or something?"

Experimentation? Jere would have been repulsed if he thought the man was so casually referring to sexual experimentation, but a dark, vile part of his mind reminded him that he was most likely talking about medical experimentation. He slammed the idea out of his head, forcing himself to focus on the current situation. He steadied his voice. "I'll certainly find a use for her, Mr. Mollen."

The man laughed, shoving the girl forward unexpectedly. She stumbled, unable to catch herself, and collapsed at Jere's feet. "Well, tie her tightly and she works for that," he said with a lecherous laugh, indicating that he had done that very thing.

Jere knelt down, gripping the girl lightly by her arms and attempting to pull her to her feet. She screamed through the gag and thrashed away from him.

"Little bitch," Mollen muttered, grabbing her by a handful of matted hair and jerking her to her feet. He was silent a moment, then released his grip. "Go ahead, examine her as you need. I've got a full mind-bind on her, she isn't going anywhere."

Jere nodded. He didn't trust himself to speak at the moment. A "mind-bind," which the man had so casually referred to, was actually a complex and potentially dangerous procedure. Essentially, it allowed someone with certain types of mind gifts to take complete and total control of the body of someone to whom they were connected. It was most useful with small children, to keep them still during medical procedures, or even for parents to protect them from doing things like touching a hot stove or something equally dangerous. While it was easy enough to learn with adequate training, it was always risky, and it was almost always unpleasant for the recipient of such treatment.

He started by carefully looking into her eyes, which were a dull green, no doubt affected by poor health and a lack of nutrition. Her gaze was clear and alert, despite the tears that were welling up. He placed his hand on her throat carefully, feeling miserable when he felt, more than heard, a whimper. "Just checking your pulse," he said softly, feeling the strong heartbeat below his fingers. Her heart was racing.

"Wren, get me my medical bag?" he said absently, stopping himself before saying anything inappropriate, like "please" or "love."

"Yes, master," Wren replied, returning in seconds with the requested item and presenting it quite formally to him.

Jere said nothing, but dug into the bag and pulled out his tools. Familiar, safe, non-human tools. He peeked cursorily into the girl's ears and nose, then glanced at her master. "Could you remove the gag, please?"

Mollen nodded. He glared at the girl as he was untying it. "You start your goddamn screaming and I'll break your jaw again, you got it?"

She whimpered, still unable to move. It must have meant yes, because a moment later, the gag was removed. She coughed, but was otherwise still. With the gag removed, the sunken hollows of her cheeks were more prominent, and a small scab was visible on her lower lip. Jere tried not to think about what had caused it.

"Open your mouth, I just want to look," Jere spoke calmly, holding up a wooden tongue depressor as he did.

She did as asked, barely parting her lips, a slight whine escaping as she did. Jere glanced into her throat, even peeked a bit at her teeth and gums. He had read up on medical inspections for slaves, and was even being pressured to attend a training a few towns away to get certification for official inspections. The absolute barbarism of the whole thing repelled him, but he knew it would make him look like he knew what he was doing. What he didn't know was whether that knowledge would destroy what was left of his self-respect.

Satisfied with this part, he glanced at Mollen again. "May I remove the straightjacket? I'd like to see what condition she's in beneath it."

The man seemed to hesitate for a moment. "Well, Dr. Peters, she's pretty scarred up. And I'll warn you—she's a handful at times—hard to restrain, hard to *keep* restrained."

"Do you not have adequate control of her with the mind-bind?" Jere asked, frustrated. He didn't expect everyone to have such superior mind-control as he did, having a healing gift after all, but slaveowners were unlimited regarding what they were allowed to do to keep their slaves under control. Just this once, he promised himself, he could accept taking advantage of that fact if it meant that this terrible examination would be over sooner.

The man reddened. "Of course. I just wanted to warn you. You know. And, uh, I can only hold her for about ten minutes, then the restraints will need to go back on."

Jere rolled his eyes. "That will be adequate." He unceremoniously loosened the straps, his revulsion increasing as he saw the girl wince when the pressure on her arms was released. She wore nothing underneath it, and Jere was startled to see the damage done to the barely developed chest in front of him.

He took note of the scars across her chest and stomach quickly before walking behind her, wishing he had an exam gown or something to give her.

"How old is she?" he asked. He figured it was the polite way of asking, "Is she a fucking child?"

"Fifteen, according to her papers." So she was a fucking child.

Jere literally bit his tongue to hold back the curses he wanted to let out when he saw the girl's back. The scars were deep. The fresh cuts were deep. They covered every inch that was visible from her neck down to the waistband of the skirt she wore, if it could be called that. A ratty piece of fabric, really. The lack of dirt or dried blood indicated that she had been cleaned up recently, but Jere was concerned by the redness and inflammation that he saw around the edges of the newer cuts, indicating a lack of proper medical treatment. He said nothing. He seethed, and tried his best to contain his anger, to stop it from flowing over and becoming noticeable.

"They started her young, because of her gift. Course, it's more work than it's worth to get her to use the damn gift for anything anymore, that's why she bounces around so much."

Jere put a hand on her shoulder, where the damage wasn't as bad. Her skin was cold and clammy. Held securely by the mind-bind, she didn't move, but trembled and whimpered under the light touch.

"What is her gift?"

"Memory. I know, it seems like a mind gift at first, but they classify it as physical—it's actually an enhanced level of regular senses—particularly hearing and vision. I guess there's a similar mind gift, but she doesn't have it. She has almost no psychic ability."

Jere nodded, thoughtfully. It was true, he could feel almost nothing from the girl. As terrified as she was, he should need to block her out—but he was getting little more than he would have from a *dular*. He thought about probing a bit with his abilities, saying it was a wellness check, but he didn't want to scare her. He didn't want to make her start a fight that she would lose.

"I see you've beaten the hell out of her."

Jere glanced back to see Mollen shrug. "Like I said, she requires considerable discipline."

"She's of no use to me if she's dead."

"You can heal her up, I mean—"

"Healing requires time, energy, and resources," Jere informed him, rather curtly. "In general, someone in my profession is compensated as such."

"Oh..." Mollen seemed to think it over. "You're talking about the price, then?"

Jere wasn't quite sure what he was talking about. He wanted to be talking about basic human dignity. He wanted to be talking about right and wrong. He wanted to be talking about abusing a child, but he couldn't have any of those conversations in a place like this. "Yes, I'm talking about the price. What's the going buying price at the workhouses?"

"Four to five thousand," Mollen answered. "Might be more, because there's a lot of years left on her, might be less because she's difficult. But go ahead, look her over, I'm willing to be a bit flexible. You're probably right, she is rather damaged."

Jere hesitated. There was nothing else to see. He had already seen too much, and he didn't want to see anymore.

Suddenly, Mollen reached over, tugging the remainder of the jacket down around her ankles along with the rag that passed for a skirt.

Jere nearly lost his breakfast at the sight, compounded by the pained whimper from the girl. As he stood there, struck dumb, he heard the girl manage to whisper, "Don't fucking touch me."

Grabbing her by the hair to steady her, her master slammed a hand against her backside, covering the already bruised skin with further pain. He pulled back to do it again when Jere grabbed his arm, sparks of psychic pain shooting out before he could stop himself.

"Hands off the merchandise," he growled.

The larger man looked surprised, but backed down. No amount of physical brawn could outweigh the danger that a healer could possess, and upsetting a potential customer was never a good idea.

Without another word, Jere turned back to the girl, forcing himself to look at her. The lower half of her body was as cut up and scarred as the upper half. He felt sick; he wanted to throw up, he wanted to kill the man standing next to him and steal his energy and use it to repair this poor girl.

"She's no stranger to a man's touch," Mollen tried to joke. Jere noticed that he was still rubbing his arm where he had grabbed it. "She'll fight you, obviously, but she fights everything. You expect it from these types."

"Of course." Jere couldn't say more. He couldn't do anything.

"Hey, are you a certified slave inspector? I'd rather pay you to do a complete exam than the thieves at the workhouse. Those bastards rob you blind – plus, it gives her less of a chance to showcase her nasty fucking attitude."

Jere knew what a "complete" exam included. Gynecological, rectal, blood tests, mental wellness scan; the process was incredibly invasive. Even if he were certified, there wouldn't be enough money in the world to make him do that to this girl, who, even as they spoke, was fighting the mind-bind and starting to win.

"Would you take a check?" Jere asked, his voice quiet. After the banking systems had collapsed during The Fall, all forms of payment faced challenges, but checks in particular were targets for fraud and theft, and were still unpopular. Many local businesses allowed customers to set up a credit system, but very large purchases presented continued difficulties, which was the one place where checks proved valuable. Jere dreaded the thought of making the poor girl wait while he retrieved the funds in cash from the bank.

"A wellness check wouldn't be—oh, oh, you want to buy her?" Mollen appeared shocked. Apparently he had given up on selling her.

"Five thousand denn sound agreeable?" Jere said casually. He had no financial distress, but the idea of giving this man less money pleased him.

"Er, yeah, check's fine..." Mollen seemed hesitant. "I think I was aiming for a little more..."

Jere glared at him. "Yes, I'm sure you were, but you just told me you haven't been able to sell her. She's a considerable hassle to you, and you'd have to consider travelling with her, possibly home again, or at least to the workhouses. I'm not completely sure where those are, but I know there's not one right in Hojer, which, again, would mean some travel. I'll need to expend considerable resources to heal her—which was mentioned nowhere in your ad. No, I think five thousand in your pocket is perfectly adequate."

Mollen scowled a bit, but he nodded. "You're right, you're right. I don't want to put up with her anyway."

"Wren, my checkbook and a pen, please?"

Wren shot him a warning look, but fetched the requested items.

"*You cannot possibly be serious!*" Wren hissed through the mind connection as Jere was filling out one of the checks that he thought he would never use.

"I couldn't live with myself if I sent her off with him. It's wrong and it's terrible and I never should have gotten involved!"

"That's what I told you in the first place—Jere, please, this is ridiculous! This is what I warned you about! Just send her off with him and let it be!"

"Wren, no! Look at her! He's... she'll... I just can't!"

"Jere, she'll be trouble! Don't do this, baby, I know you want to be nice, but we—"

"I'm doing it and that's final."

Jere handed over the check. "I assume you brought the necessary paperwork?"

Mollen nodded. "You'll have to take it by the town registry to get it notarized, but you have two weeks to do that here, I think." He pulled out the transfer of ownership paperwork, signing his name and indicating where Jere was to sign.

"You want the straightjacket, Doctor?"

Jere fought to keep the repulsion off of his face. It was, he realized, supposed to be a friendly offer. "That won't be necessary," he said, forcing himself to speak softly. He stepped around to face the girl again, looking into her eyes and speaking quietly. "If Mr. Mollen releases the mind-bind on you, you are to do as I say. I'll have my slave escort you to your room, and I expect you to go with him. He has a speed gift, and I have a healing gift, so between the two of us, you don't stand a chance of escaping. Is that clear?"

She narrowed her eyes, nodding ever so slightly, the tiny amount that she was able to as her previous master's hold was wearing off.

Jere nodded at the other man. "Let her go."

He shrugged, and Jere felt the residual energy of the mind-bind being released. The girl stumbled a few steps before regaining her balance, freeing herself of the straightjacket. She stood, still, in the middle of the room, breathing heavily and glancing around in terror.

"Wren," Jere said quietly, his boyfriend's irritated face almost scaring him. "Show her to her room—the one next to the office."

"Yes, master." Wren's execution was flawless, and, short of the rage beneath the surface, Jere would have had no idea how upset he was.

"Come on," Wren muttered, barely glancing at the girl. After a second, she followed.

Jere finished up the paperwork quickly, sending Mollen on his way. He didn't really want to process it, but he was, once again, a slaveowner. He just hoped things would go smoothly.

Chapter 6
A Master Again

Jere had barely shut the door behind Mollen when he heard the screaming start.

"Get the fuck away from me, you stupid fucking pervert, I'll rip your fucking eyes out for looking at me!"

Jere hurried toward the commotion.

"Just get in the goddamn room, I don't *want* to look at you, for Christ's sake, just do as you're told!"

"Go to hell, you fucking asshole! You're not my master, I don't fucking have to listen to you!"

Jere rushed over to see Wren more or less barricading the doorway with his body, the furious new slave cursing at him, her tiny fists balled up, tears still falling from her eyes. He put a hand on Wren's shoulder. "I've got it from here, love, thank you."

Wren glared at him before walking away.

Jere took his place in the doorway, suddenly a little intimidated by the tiny ball of rage in front of him. The girl shied away from him, on edge, the combination of green eyes and widely dilated pupils making her look almost feral. Jere leaned against the doorframe, trying to appear casual and non-threatening while still blocking her way out. She took a few steps back, quiet for a moment.

"Your papers say your name is Isis?" he asked, trying to keep his voice low, trying to calm her down.

"I don't have a fucking name. They took it from me with everything else."

Jere didn't rise to the bait. "Is there something else you'd rather be called?"

"Go to hell." Her voice cracked as she said it.

Jere knew she was terrified. "I'll stick with Isis unless you tell me otherwise, then." When she didn't respond, he continued. "My name is Jere Peters—I'm a doctor, gifted with mind-healing. You can address me however you feel comfortable."

"Go to hell, Jere."

He sighed, realizing that it might take a while for her to calm down. "Listen, I bought you to help out in the clinic. Feel free to take a few days to get comfortable."

"Fuck you, I'm not helping you with anything!" she snarled.

"We'll see about that," Jere muttered. He wondered if it would be better if he tried to explain how things were here, figuring it probably couldn't be worse. "Listen, I'm gonna be up front with you— I'm an outlander. I don't enjoy the master-slave thing at all. I needed help, and you were it. I expect you to behave like an employee, and I'll treat you as such. I won't do any of the things your last master did to you—I'm not going to punish you, or hurt you, or beat you or rape you or anything like that. I won't experiment on you. I'll take care of you—you can have a good life here."

Isis laughed, an ugly, sad sound. "You fucking liar."

Jere shook his head. Actually, he *wasn't* lying, not that she'd realize it. He continued, making the effort to keep his voice calm and steady. "Listen, Isis, you have some considerable injuries. I'd like to heal them, maybe do a wellness scan while I'm at it, take care of anything that might be bothering you—"

"Don't you dare fucking touch me, you asshole!" Her words were harsh, but she backed away further, in fear.

Jere didn't move. "I won't hurt you, I promise. I can just put my hands—"

"Stay the fuck away from me!" Isis retreated to the far corner of the room. "Don't fucking touch me, and don't fucking mess with my mind! You can fucking kill me, just stay the fuck out of my head!"

She was yelling, threatening even, but she was still shaking, still crying. Jere stayed in the doorway, letting his head drop for a minute. The girl needed healing, but it wasn't an emergency. If he let her calm down, he assumed things would go much more smoothly later. "Okay. Okay. That's fine. I just thought—"

"Don't fucking touch me," she repeated, arms wrapped around herself. She was rocking back and forth slightly.

"If you're hungry, or if you need *anything*, I'll be in the dining room. Right out this door, to your left. If you try to run, you'll be caught and brought back. Please don't force the issue."

She said nothing, and Jere had nothing else to say, so he got up and walked out. He heard the door slam behind him a few moments later, followed by strained cries. He went to the dining room and dropped into a chair, already exhausted. Jere lifted his head to look up at Wren, who was glaring disapprovingly at him.

He sat back, hoping he looked as pathetic as he felt, and held out a hand to his lover. "Honey, I'm sorry."

Wren shook his head, still looking irritated. He did come and take Jere's hand, sitting next to him. "So much for not rushing into anything."

Jere pulled his hand close, kissing it before speaking. "I couldn't, Wren, I just couldn't leave her with him. She'll come around."

"Yeah, and what will you do until she does, Jere?" Wren didn't look much happier, but he at least looked a little less angry. "Fuck. I thought you were going to buy a slave for help around here, not because of some fucking guilt complex or something!"

Jere said nothing. It wasn't completely true, but it wasn't completely untrue, either. He did feel guilty for having anything to do with slavery, and he would have felt even more so if he had let the girl be taken away, but he really did think that she would come around and help out once she was given the chance. "Wren, I'm sorry, I just... I didn't want to wait and give him a chance to hurt her more."

"This doesn't solve any of the problems we had, and now you have some fucking messed-up kid to deal with."

"I know."

"I thought you were going to think about it a little bit, at least hear me out!" Wren protested, shaking his head. "Not that any of it matters now. You bought her and she's here and it's final, right?"

Jere winced, hearing his own words tossed back at him. Wren was pissed at him about this, and he deserved to be. He looked at his lover, feeling guilty, unable to say anything.

"I'm real glad you asked for my input, then," Wren muttered.

Again, Jere was silent, his own feeling of failure preventing him from saying anything.

"You shouldn't have even bothered telling me you were going to do it," Wren continued, a bitter look on his face. "Obviously it doesn't matter how I feel about it. It's your decision, right? Not mine. It's not as if one slave can buy another."

"Wren, it's not like that!" Jere pleaded. "It *does* matter how you feel, and I *do* want your input, but I couldn't just let her go! I know it was a bad idea, and I know you were right about the classified ads, but look at her! She's hurt, she needs help!"

"She'll run the first chance she gets," Wren pointed out, his tone harsh. "You know that, don't you?"

Jere nodded.

"If she's caught outside the house, it will go hard for her. And for you."

And for you, Jere realized. A runaway slave must reflect terribly on the master, and Jere wasn't sure where that would leave Wren. Wren would never mention something like that, though. He nodded again, suddenly feeling overwhelmed.

"Jere..." Wren prompted. "You made your decision. Now you get to decide what to do next. You can't watch her all the time."

"Go into town. Buy a doorknob with a lock." Jere spit the words out as if they were absolutely vile. They were vile; he should be healing the girl, not locking her up. He regretted having to do it, and he felt terrible for dragging Wren into any part of this.

"I'll nail the windows down before I leave." Wren's tone was business-like, but it had lost the anger it held earlier. He had made his point.

"That's—" Jere stopped himself before trying to convince anyone that such measures weren't necessary. "That's a good idea. Thank you for everything. I don't know what I'm doing."

"You're doing the right thing, Jere." Wren came up behind him, putting his arms around his neck. "I wish you hadn't bought her, but now that she's here, you're doing the right thing."

Jere felt nothing over the overwhelming sense of failure.

Wren went outside. As he suggested, he nailed the bedroom

window shut from the outside. Jere sat in the same spot at the dining room table, tracing the patterns in the wood with his finger, wishing he felt more competent. Wren came back inside a few minutes later, pushing a piece of paper in front of him, a pen into his hand. He signed the pass without comment, without responding to Wren's concerned look. He heard the front door shut, and tried to push the confusion out of his head.

Not long after, he heard the bedroom door open, slowly, tentatively. Jere turned to see a vengeful face staring back at him. He stared back, expecting nothing.

"You're fucking going to lock me in."

He nodded. "I don't trust you to stay put. I'm sorry, but it's necessary to keep you safe."

She said nothing. Just glared, peeking out from the doorway. She had the bedspread wrapped around herself, covering her from head to toe. The beige fabric nearly matched her sallow skin, which Jere guessed would be more olive-toned once her health was restored.

"I'll only lock the door when I'm asleep or working," he explained, trying to be fair. "If I'm around, or if Wren's around, you can feel free to move around the house. The bedrooms at the end of the hall are off-limits — mine and Wren's."

"What is he, your pampered pet or something?" she spat out.

"He's my boyfriend. He also happens to be my slave."

"Ha." She rolled her eyes. "Probably just fucks you so you spoil him and treat him nice."

"It would be a waste of energy," Jere said. He wouldn't fight with the girl. He wouldn't lie to her, either. "I treated him just as kindly before we started fucking."

"So you like to rape boys *and* girls, huh?"

It was a poor challenge. "I don't like to rape anyone. I *don't* rape anyone. And I'm certainly not interested in a prepubescent girl-child."

"I'm not prepubescent and I'm not a fucking child!"

Jere was caught off-guard, and couldn't stop himself from laughing. Of all the things that had been done to her, being called prepubescent upset her? He felt a little guilty as the door slammed. "Isis, I'm sorry, it's just — "

"Go and fuck yourself!" Her voice was only slightly muffled through the door. "Don't fucking talk to me!"

Jere sat there, alternating between wanting to laugh at the absurdity and feeling mean for teasing her. Wren returned shortly, new doorknob in hand. He shook his head as he looked down at Jere. "Was I right?" he challenged.

"Yes. You were right," Jere conceded. "You were right, and I'm an idiot."

Wren finally broke into a smile, speeding over and kissing him hard on the mouth. "And hearing you say that is *almost* worth it."

Jere wanted to stay in that moment forever. Nobody else, just him and Wren. He heard the doorknob rattle instead.

"Sick." Isis's voice cut through the sweetness of the scene like a knife. "Bring back the lock and chains?"

"Just a lock," Jere promised. "And like I said, only when no one is here to keep an eye on you."

"Whatever you need to tell yourself," she muttered.

Wren took a step toward the door, new knob in hand, and Isis responded by screaming and slamming the door, yelling obscenities as she did.

"Jesus Christ," he muttered, glancing in Jere's direction.

Jere got up and knocked on the door. "Isis? Listen, we're just going to replace the doorknob. I'm sorry, I should have warned you."

"Jere, you don't have to apologize to her," Wren muttered. "She's hysterical."

"She's scared," Jere retorted. He turned the knob a bit, peeking in to find Isis huddled in the corner of the room again. "Shit."

"I'll change it," Wren said quietly, taking off to retrieve a screwdriver.

"Isis, no one is going to do anything to you, so you can calm down. Neither one of us is really into girls. Or kids. Or slaves. Among, like, a thousand other reasons."

"Then why the fuck haven't you given me anything to wear!" she snapped, not moving from the corner she was huddled in. "I fucking hate people looking at me. But you probably like it—like seeing me scared, like seeing me all fucking beat up and shit. Gets you off, doesn't it?"

"I... what... no!" Jere finally managed an answer. "No. It doesn't. I just—fuck, Wren, get her some clothes!"

Wren glared at him, pointedly dropped the door handle he had just started working on, and sped off. He returned seconds later with an assortment of Jere's t-shirts and pajama pants, tossing them at the girl, which made her flinch, and Jere frown. Without another word, he began finishing the task he started.

Isis made no move, though Jere was pleased to see a look of surprise on her face. Perhaps she hadn't thought her complaints would be addressed after all.

Wren quickly finished the job, perfunctorily testing the handle to make sure it worked as expected and locked as it was supposed to. Without another word, he walked back out to toward the kitchen.

"I'm making lunch," was his parting statement. Jere could feel the irritation and hurt and a slew of other unpleasant things through the connection. Things he would much rather not feel from his lover.

Jere found himself standing awkwardly in the doorway, looking between the door and the girl in the corner. He sighed. "You can wear whatever you want. Sorry. I didn't think about it. Sorry. Um, if you want something to eat, Wren's a great cook. Come out when you're ready. You need to eat, you're obviously very malnourished, and when we get to healing, it will be easier if you have something in your system."

He turned to leave, and was answered with a muttered, "Fuck you," as he walked through the door. This wasn't going well at all.

Chapter 7

Poison

Wren could neither locate nor quell the source of his nervousness as he started throwing things together for lunch. Before he realized it, he was making soup, chopping up the ingredients with a sense of anger that he tried to ignore. It occurred to him that he was making comfort food, something that took more time to prepare than most other meals. He figured he probably needed some time alone anyway. Jere was getting in over his head quite quickly with this girl, and Wren knew that he would be pulled into the conflict. The inconvenience was bad enough, but Jere's attitude was infuriating. One minute, he was tender and caring toward the girl; the next, he was snapping at Wren and dismissing good advice. The girl had barely been in the house for an hour, and Wren was already fed up with her and Jere's reluctance to step up and do what was necessary. It wasn't that he expected Jere to be cruel with the girl, but he was her master. A voice inside his head reminded Wren that Jere was his master as well. Perhaps a heavier hand would have gotten through to her more quickly, if anything would have. At the rate she was going, she was a candidate for being put down if she ever left the house. Wren wasn't sure whether this was a good or bad thing.

Moreover, he didn't like having a slave in the house. *Another* slave, he reminded himself, quite forcefully, even though the reminder stung. It was something he shouldn't forget, something he shouldn't have *allowed* himself to forget in the past few months. It was easy—too easy—to pretend that he and Jere were something different. They were something different, when they were alone, but any little thing could change their relationship. It was a dangerous game, and he knew he should be wary of playing it. The new slave would change things, but perhaps it would be better. If everyone stayed in their places, it would be safer, easier, less terrible if anything were to happen.

The soup came together too quickly, potatoes and vegetables and bacon and cheese, and he even made some quick rolls to go along with it. He debated making other things, but was actually quite hungry, and besides, he couldn't put off seeing his boyfriend forever. He wondered if that terrible girl would be joining them. He kind of hoped she would, because Jere would be happy if she ate, but on the other hand, he liked having Jere all to himself. Wren carried out two bowls of soup and a basket of rolls, relieved to see that they didn't have company.

He set the food down and began eating without saying a word. He was still angry with Jere, but he didn't know if it was worth it to bring it up. He was even less certain whether he could handle Jere dismissing his anger again.

"Wren?"

Wren tensed. For Jere not to even touch the food before speaking meant he was nervous about something, and anything that could make Jere nervous would undoubtedly trickle down to his slave. Wren glanced up at him, a mouthful of roll serving as a good enough excuse for why he wasn't saying anything.

"Love, I'm sorry I was short with you earlier," Jere said, looking every bit as remorseful as he sounded. "I just... I don't know what to do. I thought I did, but you're obviously upset with me. I had no idea I would come across a slave like this."

"Jere, I told you this is what would happen, and now it's happening. I didn't want to be part of it before, and I don't want to be part of it now," Wren was frustrated. He knew it wasn't Jere's fault, exactly, but he had made the decision, and he had made it knowing full well that Wren did not approve. "I don't mind helping you, but I really don't want to get overly involved in this." In Wren's opinion, it was Jere, the master, who should be the one getting "involved."

"I know, and I'm sorry for putting you into the middle of this." Jere smiled at him, tired and apologetic, but still winning. Winning Wren's heart, all over again. That fucking smile got him every time.

The touching moment was interrupted by the door opening. Isis came out, looking ridiculously small and thin, Jere's clothes hanging off of her.

She glared at Jere. "Your food smells good. Any synth crap hanging around for us non-humans?"

As much as Wren's anger at Jere had been sated, his feelings toward Isis remained unchanged. Wren resisted the urge to smack her. Jere had been nothing but kind to her, and all she seemed to want to do was antagonize.

"None of that here," Jere replied, as if this wasn't out of the ordinary. "There's plenty of regular food here for everyone."

Wren observed Isis taking in the scene, seeing him and Jere seated next to each other, identical bowls of soup, small plates for rolls. The picture of domestic peace and happiness. She didn't say anything, but sat down, tentatively, at the other end of the table. She glared at them both.

"So are you gonna hit me now or later for sitting here?" she asked. Wren could see through her bold façade. He could also hear her stomach growling.

"It's fine." Jere was just as calm. "You're welcome to sit at the table."

Jere stood up, causing the girl to jerk backwards in her chair, increasing the distance as much as possible. Wren thought it was quite an overreaction, but couldn't deny that she looked terrified.

"Relax, I'm getting you something to eat," Jere muttered.

He went into the kitchen, where Wren could hear him pulling down another bowl. The fact that Jere was getting it instead of asking him to do it meant that he was quite aware of how much he was taxing Wren. Wren couldn't resist a smug little smile at the thought.

Jere returned, carrying a bowl of soup, which he placed in front of Isis. She cringed back from him, but he didn't respond. He returned to his seat. "Try to eat. You'll feel better with food in your stomach."

"So, what is this, like, poisoned or something?" Isis asked, not even touching the spoon.

"Why would I poison it?" Jere asked, continuing to eat his. "I want you healthy."

"You probably fucking filled it with sedatives and stuff so you can mess with me later," she accused, her eyes growing hard and tight again.

"He could do that if he wanted to anyway," Wren pointed out, irritated with the bullshit. Jere frowned at him. Every comment that anyone made just increased the level of tension in the room.

"There's nothing in it," Jere insisted. "If you don't believe me, I'll swap bowls with you."

"It's probably something that just affects slaves," Isis countered, although she eyed up the food a bit more closely. Wren guessed that she hadn't been fed in days.

"So, take his," Jere indicated Wren's casually. "You've already pointed out that he's my 'pampered pet,' as you so bluntly put it."

"*What the hell, Jere?*" Wren felt the anger blaze over him, choking out his ability to speak out loud. The anger didn't dissipate as Jere chose not to reply to him at all.

"I've told you how I feel about him, what relationship we have; I would never harm him." Jere kept looking intently at his food, refusing to make eye contact with anyone. "Besides, there is no physical difference between people with mind and physical gifts. As a doctor, I can guarantee, it's not possible."

Wren sat there, barely eating, just fuming. Pet? Jere had referred to him as a pet? He wasn't sure what made him angrier, the term, or the suggestion that he hand over his food to this girl. Feeling childish even as he did it, he pulled his bowl closer to himself. He felt like some sort of prisoner, guarding his food, but he didn't particularly care.

"Fine. *Jere.*" Isis continued to glare as she spoke. "I'll eat if I can have your bowl. But I want to see you eat out of this one. With the poison."

"There's no fucking — okay. Fine. Come over here and swap with me, that way I don't have a chance to do anything to it." Jere pushed his bowl away from himself, spoon and all.

Isis approached, tentatively, as if someone would spring at her. Still cautious, she swapped the bowls out, hurrying back to the opposite end of the table as though it were a race. She watched intently as Jere picked up the spoon and continued eating as though nothing had happened.

"Wren, thank you, this is quite delicious, as usual."

Wren nodded, jarred out of his shock and anger for a moment. This was probably the strangest interaction he had ever witnessed between a slave and her master. Or *his* master. Or his *boyfriend...*

Isis watched silently, until Jere had eaten probably half of the soup in what used to be her bowl. Satisfied, she plunged the spoon into her own, eating ravenously, pulling it closer to herself as she attacked it. Jere continued eating calmly, a blank expression on his face. The three of them sat in silence, only the sound of spoons against bowls interrupting. Wren wondered if perhaps they hadn't all been given some sort of hallucinogen, reassured only by the fact that he had been the one who made the food.

Jere got up after a few moments, refilled his bowl, and came back with a second glass of water. He pointedly took a drink from it before glancing at Isis. "Your highness, I've taste-tested this one as well."

Wren turned away to hide the smile on his face. Jere was really too much sometimes.

Isis wrinkled her nose at the thinly veiled joke, but nodded. "All right."

Jere pushed the glass across the table and pushed the bowl across as well. "Here, I can tell you're hungry."

Isis retrieved them just as quickly as she had before, practically inhaling the soup. "Whatever. You probably just want to fatten me up or something."

Her attempts to insult were pathetic. Wren could have done a thousand times better, even at her age, although he had been far too terrified back then. Even so, the fact that she was still trying was rather impressive. Any other master would have slapped the food from her hands and beaten her for disobedience. Clearly, she didn't care about those consequences anymore.

"You're free to help yourself to anything you'd like to eat or drink," Jere was saying, as though nothing unusual was happening. "Kitchen's through there, there's always at least stuff for sandwiches or something. Wren does most of the cooking, I'm sort of a disaster. Do let him know if there's anything you don't particularly like?"

Isis just glared at him. Wren was starting to think that this was her default state of existence. He had no idea how she held on to so much rage; he felt tired just from being angry with Jere for a few hours.

"Is there anything you'd like to do today?"

Jere was addressing Isis again. Wren tried to push away the irritation. Sunday was usually the day that they spent fucking and cuddling and doing a whole lot of nothing. Sunday was a lovely day.

"What the hell do you mean?" Isis mumbled, still inhaling food as if she were afraid it would be taken away. Wren felt a little guilty at the thought, because he knew from experience exactly how that felt.

"I don't know, you don't seem much for chatting, and that's fine. I mean, that's mostly what we do — um, maybe read, play some card games, something like that?"

"I don't need to be fucking entertained," Isis snapped. "I'm fine if you just leave me alone."

Wren resisted the urge to tell her off, but he wasn't getting involved. This was Jere's problem, not his. Still, there was no need for her to be as rude as she was.

"As you like," Jere shrugged. "Feel free to help yourself to anything in the house, though. You live here, it's for you to use."

Isis said nothing, just finished eating quickly. "I just want to stay in my room. Is that allowable, *master*?"

Jere flinched slightly at the word, but nodded impassively. "Fine by me."

She stood, looking lost, then darted into the bedroom, slamming the door behind her.

Wren felt a little relieved. "What a fucking nightmare," he muttered, glancing at Jere as he said it.

"Give her time," Jere answered. "I doubt she's thinking clearly. With the extent of her injuries, I doubt it's possible for her to be thinking clearly." He stood, cleared the table, and strolled into the living room without a word.

Wren sat alone at the table for a while longer. He still felt off. Finally, he got up, walked to the living room, and settled in next to his master. Thinking back on all the times they had spent there in the past, he wriggled around, placing his head in Jere's lap. Jere's hand came down absently, stroking his hair silently for a few minutes.

"Are you okay?"

Jere's voice was comforting, familiar. Safe. Like nothing had changed.

"Yeah," Wren said, distant. "Just... thinking."

Jere didn't reply, which Wren was mostly happy about. He lay still, silent, as Jere flipped through the pages of a book above his head. He was tired, but not exactly eager to sleep, and the physical closeness with Jere helped to soothe some of the frustration.

The evening passed peacefully, and Jere was teasing him into making dinner before he knew it. Isis refused to come out of her room when it was finished, which was fine by Wren, despite the worried look Jere wore. They ate in peace, no ridiculous talk about poison or extraneous cursing at the table. They finished, the cumulative tiredness of the week hitting them both before the sun was even down.

"Let's go to bed," Wren said lightly, rubbing his hand across Jere's arm. "You look exhausted."

Jere bit his lip, thinking, hesitating.

"You need to lock her in, Jere," Wren prompted, knowing exactly what he was so hesitant about. "You didn't have me buy and install a lock so you could *not* use it."

"It's cruel," Jere protested weakly. "She's hurt; what if she needs something?"

"It's necessary to lock her in, and if she won't let you heal her, she must not be hurt that bad."

Jere got up and walked over to the door to the bedroom, knocking on it lightly. "Isis?"

"Get the fuck away from me, you fucking bastard!"

Jere shook his head, looking to Wren for reassurance. He only shrugged. He had given Jere his opinion on the subject already.

Jere pulled the key from his pocket. "Isis, if you'd like me to heal you tonight, now is the time, otherwise we can talk about it tomorrow. I'm locking the door and going to bed for the night. I'll unlock it again at breakfast time."

"Go to hell!" The shriek could probably be heard from the other end of the house.

"Do you need...?" Jere trailed off, mid-question. He left the room for a moment, returning to stand in front of Isis's room with a plate of food. He opened the door and shoved it through, drawing considerable protests from the girl. "If you really need anything, let me know. I'll come and let you out if you need to use the bathroom or whatever."

"Fuck you!" came the muffled reply through the door.

Jere looked defeated as he turned around. Wren came up to him, putting his arms around him carefully.

"She'll be fine," he whispered. "I'm sure she's slept in far worse conditions than being locked in a nice room before."

Wren had intended for the comment to be comforting, but Jere looked disturbed.

"I don't want to treat her poorly, but I don't see any other choice," Jere confessed. "Am I doing the right thing?"

Wren guided them to the bedroom. "Of course you are, love," he rushed to reassure him. "If anything, you're being a little too nice. She doesn't know what to expect." Personally, he thought Jere was being *much* too nice, but anything else wouldn't be Jere, so he didn't mind. At least, not any more than he minded the whole situation.

They got into bed together, curling next to each other.

"I bought a fucking slave." Jere's voice was incredulous and a little scared in the darkness.

Wren couldn't help but shudder just hearing the statement. "*Another* slave," he corrected, idly.

Jere pulled him close and kissed him lightly. "Wren—"

Wren put a finger over his lips. He knew what Jere was going to say. That Wren wasn't a slave to him, that he didn't think of him that way, all sorts of sweet and genuine but ultimately useless things like that. However, Wren was a slave, and he knew better than to forget it.

"Jere, baby, it might be better, I mean, for the girl..." Wren wasn't completely sure what he was suggesting here. "I just think she might be less confused. You know, if you weren't so...."

"Decent?" Jere suggested, smiling playfully. "Sappy?"

"Nice," Wren finally supplied. "Masters aren't nice. Even the nice ones, they're just less cruel and less mean. But they aren't nice; not to their favorite slaves, and certainly not to disruptive ones."

"Hmm, then I guess you shouldn't be so disruptive," Jere teased, trailing his hands along Wren's back and down his hips.

Wren appreciated the touch, but he didn't accept the distraction. He'd had plenty of experience distracting people with sex to know what it looked like. He captured Jere's hands in his own and held them gently. "You can be firm with her, you know. She won't break. You don't need to spend all your time doting on her and worrying over her."

"Wren, Jesus, she's just a kid, and she's scared and hurt," Jere dismissed him. "I can handle her."

"Babe, you've never really had to deal with a difficult slave before..." Wren continued to press him about the issue. The casual way in which Jere was ignoring the big problem here was starting to concern him, and he was irritated that Jere was dismissing every suggestion that he made.

"No, but I've been dealing with people for many years, love," Jere reminded him. "I've had plenty of difficult patients in the past. She just needs a little patience, that's all. Give her time, and I'm sure she'll calm down and fit right in here."

"Jere, I just... do we really have that much time?" It wasn't what he wanted to say. He wanted to ask how damn much time Jere planned on wasting on this girl, and whether that would leave any time for the two of them, and what Jere meant by fitting in, because the kid obviously didn't fit in here in any way. He wanted to ask if there would be time left for him, but that was stupid and childish, and he knew he shouldn't be so worried about himself and his stupid jealousy. He wanted to ask how Jere was so certain about his slave-owning abilities that he could ignore Wren's suggestions *again*, ignoring the fact that he had been asking for help all day. The more Wren thought about that, the more it bothered him, and he let go of Jere's hands before it became obvious how warm his own were growing.

"Love, don't worry so much," Jere smiled at him, that winning smile that usually made all the bad things go away. "I mean, do new slaveowners here go through training or something?"

Wren tried to smile back. "No, but... but most of them don't try to do it like you do." On one hand, Wren adored Jere's gentle, humanitarian methods, but when it came to this girl, it was unsettling.

"Well, my lack of training has already granted me one perfect assistant and boyfriend whom I love more than anyone else, so I'd say I'm at least lucky," Jere pointed out, smirking as he did.

Wren smiled back, but was struck with a moment of pain as he realized that Jere had actually compared him to that girl, actually compared him to a slave. It was true; he was a slave.

"I'm just teasing!" Jere rushed to correct himself, no doubt feeling the hurt through the mind connection. "Look, you know I don't mean that I like... trained you into this, or, or whatever, right?"

It was a conversation they had had plenty of times before. Wren needed reassurance that Jere wasn't forcing him; Jere needed reassurance that Wren didn't feel forced. The fact that they could have this conversation at all made Wren wonder what had him so worried. It made sense that Jere would be resistant to Wren's suggestions that he be firmer with Isis, Jere was reluctant to be firm or harsh with anyone.

"No, of course not," Wren said, making his voice soft and seductive. He was eager to move on, to avoid talking about the friction that had come between them all day, and the uneasy feelings that he still couldn't quite shake. The conversation was too much, too difficult to keep thinking about. "You're right, you are lucky. And now I want to *get* lucky!"

Without another word, he pounced on Jere, pinning him to the bed and kissing him. Jere had tried to distract him with sex earlier, but Wren's skills in that area far outweighed his. Soon, all thoughts of anything that wasn't fucking were driven far away, and they could both retreat into their fantasy world again. It was so much easier than trying to talk about this.

Chapter 8

Out of Control

It was dark, and Wren knew he wasn't where he was supposed to be. The cellar, Wren slowly recognized. But, no, the cellar had been gone for months! Surely, Master Burghe couldn't have been mad at him for not being someplace that didn't really even exist anymore, could he?

A heartbeat later, he felt the whip cutting into his back, and realized that Master Burghe could certainly be mad about that, because he was master and what he said was right, and so even if the cellar had been cleaned out and turned into storage by Jere —

But if Jere had cleared out the cellar....

The sharp, cutting pain in his back was overshadowed by the terror and loneliness and cold he felt in the training facility's industrial plastic beds, where he was strapped down because he couldn't stop screaming again. He couldn't help that he had been screaming, Burghe had whipped the skin off his back again, and earlier, the trainers had passed him around to be fucked with so many different things, things that were never meant to go inside of a human body, and... *it was so terrible, and it burned, the fire burned, everywhere.*

A trainer's voice thundered next to his head and he waited with helpless dread as he felt the restraints being removed, felt himself being pulled from the bed, waiting for whatever was coming next. It wasn't good and it wouldn't be good and the timeline was all wrong, how had Master Burghe gotten him if he was still in the training facility?

"You're going to your master, boy, back where you belong!" the trainer's voice snarled in his ear as he was yanked up by his hair.

"We've found a real special one for you — a healer who can put out that fire inside of you!"

No! No, they couldn't know about that, nobody could know about that! Nobody but Jere....

He found himself in front of a dark figure, hidden by shadows, and the cuts on his skin seemed to burn in agony. The lights flickered, and Wren wondered if he was really on fire.

"What a perfect little toy," Burghe said, laughing cruelly as he moved toward Wren. He tried to pull away, but found himself paralyzed, unable to move, unable to fight. "I can train you into whatever I want. Slut. Tortured lover. You're mine, Wren."

Wren couldn't say anything, couldn't respond, he just sat there as the air was sucked out of his lungs and out of the room. The man was Burghe, of course it was, but it didn't sound like him, the voice was all wrong, it was younger and softer and so hard to place....

The man in front of him stepped closer, moving almost into the light. He reached out a hand and grabbed Wren roughly by the throat as he stepped into the light.

"You're mine, Wren," Jere repeated, his eyes cold and dark. "I own every part of you."

Wren woke with a gasp, unsurprised to find himself curled tightly into the blankets, pillowcase wet from his own tears. He was panting, trying to make up for the breaths he hadn't been able to take while he was sleeping. Dreaming. Having a terrible, awful nightmare. He could still feel the whip on his back, still feel the hand around his throat, squeezing. He couldn't stop shaking. At least this time, he hadn't flung himself out of bed like he had so many times before.

"Are you okay?" he heard Jere ask, mumbling sleepily.

He couldn't throw the image of Jere/Burghe out of his head. He shuddered. "Yeah," he attempted.

Jere might have been sleepy, but he clearly wasn't fooled. His eyes opened halfway, and he sat up. "Wren, love, is everything okay?"

Compared to the nightmare version, the real Jere looked so innocent and harmless, so concerned as he always was. "Yeah, um, I just... I just had a nightmare. No big deal."

Jere lay back down, but kept watching him. "I'm sorry," he said, sincere as always. "Tell me what you'd like me to do and I'll do it."

Wren sighed, somewhat reassured by the familiar routine, the familiar questions that Jere asked so often. He had gone through a phase where he couldn't stand the feeling of another person near him after nightmares, and another where all he wanted to do was to be held as tightly and as closely as possible by the man who loved him. Tonight... tonight he just wasn't sure.

"I just need a minute," he found himself saying. "Bathroom, or something."

He did just that, getting up and walking to the bathroom, looking at his pale face in the mirror. He ran some water, washed his face, and stared at his reflection for a few more minutes, thinking. He hadn't had a nightmare that bad in months, and certainly not one so damn disturbing. It didn't make sense, really, but then, dreams never did. It bothered him that his unconscious mind had the audacity to put Jere in that role, putting him on the same level with the trainers at the training facility and with Burghe.

"Bad brain," he muttered, shaking his finger at his reflection. It was silly, but it made him smile, and after that, he felt he deserved to smile. He decided it was just the stress getting to him.

He returned to bed, crawling under the covers and wrapping his arms around Jere, pulling him close and pressing his face into the back of Jere's shoulder. Jere responded by taking one of his hands and pulling it up for a kiss.

"Everything okay?" he asked, his breath blowing gently across Wren's hand.

Wren nodded. "Yeah. I just want to go back to sleep."

Jere wriggled closer, pulling Wren's arms around him like a blanket. "I wish I could make them go away," he mumbled.

"Me too," Wren agreed. He fell into a light, restless sleep, too afraid to relax for fear of the dream returning.

Wren woke from his half-sleep to Jere tracing kisses lightly across his face. No more dreams. His lover's lips. He wished this was the way he could always wake up. They lay there together in silence until it was almost past time to get up. Wren would have bet denn on the fact that Jere was as unwilling to face the newest addition to the household as he was.

Nonetheless, the day called, and they both got out of bed like the responsible individuals they pretended to be. Jere knocked on Isis's door when he unlocked it. Wren was unsurprised to see her sitting in the far corner of the room, glaring at them. He wondered if she had even slept. Jere told her that there was breakfast and that she had about thirty minutes to use the shower before being locked in again. She told him to fuck himself and an assortment of other things. Wren went to the kitchen to make something to eat, leaving Jere at the table with a kiss.

The girl was troubling. Hell, the girl was trouble. Never in his life had he heard a slave dare to speak to her master in such a way, nor would he ever have wanted to. Any other master, he knew, would beat her within an inch of her life. He still wasn't sure exactly how Jere planned to handle her, but he assumed that wasn't it. Either way, Wren was sticking to his plan to not get too involved. She was disrupting things enough as it was, and his suggestions to Jere were mostly being ignored, so it would be easier to stop making suggestions. He wasn't about to let this slave come between him and Jere.

Isis did come out to use the bathroom at least, but wouldn't come out for food. Jere shoved a plate of toast and fruit through the door before locking it, ignoring the curses.

The morning went well, things at the clinic going smoothly and calmly. Lunch passed, much as breakfast did, with little interaction between anyone, and a plate of food shoved next to an empty one for Isis. Jere didn't say much, but he did seem pleased that she was eating. He seemed irritated in general, and wouldn't really talk about what was going on, aside from trying to convince Wren that he had it under control. Wren didn't believe it, but he accepted it for the moment, as he found himself still struggling to push aside the dream he had had. The details had thankfully faded, but the feeling of heart-stopping panic seemed just around the corner, threatening to catch him by surprise when he was least expecting it.

The constant screaming was taking its toll on both of them, though Wren guessed it affected Jere for different reasons. Wren couldn't help thinking of his days at the training facility, the screams of fellow teens being tortured, knowing his turn would be next. Jere probably just felt guilty about locking the girl away, as if he really had another choice. Wren couldn't resist squeezing Jere's ass when he brushed by him halfway through the afternoon on his way out of the door at the clinic to check on Isis, the surprised smile almost making up for the unpleasant task of taking care of the girl. They were taking turns, much to Wren's chagrin. He thought she was supposed to be Jere's problem, but it seemed like she was just as much a problem to both of them. Still, Jere wouldn't hesitate to help him with anything, and Wren knew he could go and return more quickly than Jere.

He got to the room, and he realized she was in a violent rage. He didn't even bother trying to open the door, he just heard screaming and smashing and breaking, and he retreated back into the clinic. Stopping by the reception desk briefly, he was approached by a concerned looking older man.

"Is everything all right back there?" the man asked. "Sounds like someone's throwing a fit!"

Wren forced a smile. It wasn't all right, but he couldn't say that. "Everything is just fine, sir, my master is in perfect control of the situation. I apologize if the noise level is disturbing you."

The man frowned at him, and for once Wren didn't feel intimidated. The man had actually looked concerned for the mystery person's welfare, which meant he had no idea that it was a slave. No slave would ever scream like that. It must be a free person, if another free person was concerned about their welfare.

Wren went into the exam room, smiling in the fake polite way that meant something was wrong. "*Jere, I need you. As soon as you can.*" Out loud, he simply said, "Dr. Peters, there's someone with a question for you."

"I'll attend to them as soon as I can," he said, quickly wrapping up the procedure he was working on.

"It's that slave, Jere, she's out of control! I don't even know why, she's just screaming and breaking things! The patients can hear it in the waiting room!"

Jere stayed calm as he instructed his patient to "wait a few minutes" to see how he felt after the healing. It was a sad excuse, but Wren had seen it work plenty of times. The lack of knowledge people had about healing was astonishing at times. Jere went into the house first, Wren following closely behind.

The chaos was obvious from the second they walked into the house. Screams, smashing, and pounding on the walls was all that could be heard. Jere rushed to the door, opening it quickly, heedless of Wren's insistence that he be careful. The last thing Wren wanted was for Jere to get hurt by this wild girl. Not only was his boyfriend at risk, but the girl — no, he wouldn't think of what would happen if the girl hurt her master.

"What in the hell are you doing?" Jere demanded, halting Isis in the middle of her destructive rage.

She glared at him and Wren with hatred before throwing the chair she had already broken into the wall again, screaming incoherently.

"Son of a bitch," Jere muttered, taking a few strides into the bedroom.

At the movement, Isis darted away, huddling in the corner where she had been every other time one of them came near. Jere didn't speak, he just took a few more steps toward her, making her cringe away even further, cursing all the time.

"I'm not going to touch you," Jere growled, then glanced back at Wren. "Get everything out of here — the table, the chair, the fucking bed frame. Leave nothing but the mattress. And get the broken shit, too." He turned back to Isis. "And you. If you move from that spot, I *will* fucking touch you. I'll grab you and hold you down and I don't care how much you scream, is that clear? Just stay there and behave."

A litany of curses escaped from the girl, but she didn't move.

Wren watched the scene, feeling sick and scared. He had never seen Jere this threatening, and he didn't want to see it now. His training and his instincts took over, and he had the room cleared in less than five minutes. He tried to remind himself that Jere was just stressed, just frustrated, that he wasn't going to hurt anyone. He tried to convince himself that Jere wouldn't do that, but he was having a hard time believing it.

As Wren moved, Jere just stood there, his face blank, watching Isis tremble and curse at him. Wren could feel through the mind connection that he was confused and angry. He tried not to think of the danger that a confused and angry master could bring. When the room was emptied out, Jere glanced at the slave—at *both* of his slaves, Wren reminded himself—and looked like he wanted to cry for a moment.

Instead, he looked at Isis, still huddled into the corner. "Get up," he said, emotionlessly.

"Jere..." Wren spoke quietly, wishing he could convey in words how he was feeling. How terrified he was that his lover was going to provoke this girl into a physical fight, or something equally terrible, how there would have to be punishments and consequences and how he just didn't want this to happen, because this wasn't how things were supposed to be. How a slave in Isis's position would be so fucking terrified right now that logic would make about as much sense to her as it would to a banana.

"Gonna hit me now?" Isis challenged, standing up and wrapping her arms tightly around herself. Wren was reminded of how she looked in the straightjacket. "Gonna fucking beat me and show me who's boss then? I'm sure you want to. Fuck it. Go ahead. Beat me. Toss me around like I tossed your shit around!"

"I'm not going to hurt you," Jere ground out. "I'm not going to let you destroy my house, either. If you can't keep yourself from doing any more damage, I can restrain you. I'd rather not, but I can and I will. Is that clear?"

Her eyes widened with fear. "You wouldn't," she muttered, backing against the wall.

"I will."

"There's fucking nothing left in here. So you don't need to fucking restrain me. You won't!"

"Isis, the choice is really up to you at this point. You can be reasonably non-destructive, or I can restrain you." Jere sounded calm, detached... terrifying. "Take your pick—medical restraints, a sedative, or a mind-bind."

"No!" Isis protested, turning away. "Fuck you. No!"

"Well, think about it, because it might happen." Jere spun around, motioning for Wren to follow.

Jere stopped at the doorway to the clinic, pressing his head against the wall, as if that would block out the wailing from the other room. "I fucked that up, didn't I?"

"You did the best you could." Wren's voice was soft, almost tentative, and he prayed Jere didn't hear the unspoken word "master" at the end of it. As much as Jere didn't want to be thought of that way, it was how he had acted, and Wren couldn't help responding to the attitude the way he knew was proper for a slave. He had no right to say whether Jere had fucked it up or not, but it certainly wasn't how he had imagined Jere handling such a situation, and it certainly wasn't how he would have *hoped* the situation would have been handled. Then again, all Wren really hoped was that the situation, and the girl, would stay as far away from him as was possible. He hoped to never see such a display from Jere again.

Jere peeled himself away from the wall. "I don't even know what I got myself into," he muttered, stalking off into the clinic.

Wren was relieved when Jere left. As much as his lover was trying to shield his emotions, Wren didn't need a mind connection to know that Jere was beyond frustrated with Isis, and Wren had felt the consequences of a frustrated master too many times to feel truly comfortable that close to him. He took a deep breath, trying to remind himself that Jere was doing what was necessary. Even though he knew he had work to do in the clinic, he stayed behind, just for a minute, just to compose himself. It wouldn't do for the patients to see him upset and scared. At least, that's what he planned to say if anyone asked him. If Jere asked him.

"Please, sir it was me that—"

A rough slap caught him across the face.

"Slave, you just shut the hell up and keep the hell down, or you'll be getting twice what she does, is that clear!"

Wren fell to the ground with the next blow, but he kept quiet as the two trainers forcibly grabbed his training partner, tied her arms to a ring in the wall, and beat her until she stopped screaming. He struggled not to scream with her, but it became easier. It was easier to ignore her screams than to have screams of his own ripped from his throat.

Wren shook his head, forcing the memory out. That's all it was. A memory. It was stupid to even be thinking of something like that. He forced himself back into the clinic, attacking some paperwork with startling viciousness. Paperwork was his problem. Not memories of slaves being punished, and not the defiant girl on the other side of the wall. That was Jere's problem, and as always, it was better to stay out of it.

Chapter 9
Remembering Place

Isis stayed in her room all that day, as well as the majority of the next. Wren was relieved that there were no more confrontations, no more arguments, no more terrifying moments when he had to watch his lover act like someone he didn't know. He knew it was necessary, and he knew he had pushed all along for Jere to be more firm with the girl, but he hadn't expected Jere to be so good at it, and he hadn't expected the cold threats to restrain her. More than anything, he didn't want to be there to witness any of it happening.

The screaming continued, and there was even some banging on the walls, but not enough that the patients complained, and not enough that Wren felt himself worrying about the crazy girl's fate, or his own. After that one time, Jere didn't have to do any more than raise an eyebrow at Isis and she stopped whatever she was doing, retreating to a corner in her room and limiting herself to cursing and screaming. She didn't respond nearly as well to Wren; while she didn't seem as intimidated by him, she seemed less trusting, screaming from the second he opened her door until he closed it, or refusing to eat the meals that he brought her. Wren used it as an excuse to spend less time attending to her.

Things at the clinic were proving to be more challenging than usual, as if some sort of karmic evil had descended upon them for trying to do something nice. A strange flu was going around, despite the temperate weather, and people were literally lining up to be seen and healed.

"With all the goddamn advances in medicine, you'd think they'd have cured colds and flu by now!" Jere griped, taking a quick break

74

to check with Wren on the status of the waiting patients.

Wren grinned back at him. Jere was adorable when he was frustrated with trivial things. "Come on, there is a plus side to it, though!"

Minor injuries and illnesses came with a significant plus side, especially given their current circumstance. At the suggestion of one of Kieran's contacts in another city, Jere had started a questionable medical process which was known as "gleaning"—basically, siphoning a small amount of energy off of the very patients he was supposed to be healing. He healed their illness, as requested, but left them feeling a bit more fatigued and tired than they had been before. The process, while technically unethical, was often practiced in very small quantities—mainly to restore the healer's energy expenditure in cases of emergency. To take it to the level of "gleaning," one not only replaced and restored the energy they used, but took a little extra as well. Wren had been positively delighted when he heard the idea suggested, his delight only slightly dampened by Jere's morally outraged face.

"I still think it's wrong," Jere said, raising an eyebrow. "On principle, anyway."

Wren placed a kiss on his lips. "Well, I say that if they get to use *your* energy, it's the least they can do to donate a bit!"

"For now, I suppose," Jere conceded.

Despite the "gleaning," Jere still looked exhausted by the end of the day, and he was becoming irritable and short, even with his patients. When Wren poked his head into the empty exam room and teasingly warned Jere that he was going to miss dinner if he didn't hurry up, Jere didn't even look at him before snapping, "Give me a goddamn minute, would you!"

Wren retreated into the house without a word, feeling like absolute shit. He vacillated between scared and angry, uncertain whether he was responding as a slave or as a boyfriend. He and Jere teased regularly, he thought it would be acceptable, even thought it would cheer Jere up. He hadn't predicted the snappy response, and the uncertainty left him wondering what else Jere would do. The table was already set and ready for the two of them, but he went and hid in the kitchen anyway, the familiarity soothing the sting of the words a bit.

It wasn't even a minute later that Jere stood in the doorway, his head down with shame.

"It was completely unacceptable of me to say that to you," Jere spoke quietly. "I don't know what the hell I was thinking and I'm sorry."

Wren felt a wave of relief flood over him. "It's okay," he said quickly, trying not to look as upset or as relieved as he really felt.

Jere took a few steps toward him. "No. It's not. I'm tired and cranky and in a bad mood, but that gives me no right to take it out on you. I'm sorry."

Wren closed the distance between them, happy to feel his lover's arms holding him close. "Thank you for noticing," he amended.

"Thanks for not throwing things at me," Jere teased, "although, I can't say I wouldn't deserve it."

They kissed and cuddled as they walked out to the dining room, shifting their chairs closer than usual so they could play footsie under the table while they ate. Isis didn't join them, but the screams and banging coming from her room indicated that she was awake.

"It's stressful." Jere stated the obvious.

"Yeah," Wren agreed. He could have described it in a variety of other ways, but agreeing was the simplest and the least likely to cause future arguments and hurt feelings. Things felt so out of place as it was, he didn't want to contribute to any more upset or confusion.

"It's been three days. I kind of hoped things would have changed by now," Jere admitted. "Even if they didn't get better — even just different would have helped!"

"Well, babe, have you considered..." Wren let the sentence trail off, playing with his food uncomfortably. He started again. "I mean, you seem to have a sort of plan for what to do with her, but it's not doing all that much. Have you considered doing something different? Maybe, I don't know, talking to someone else, someone who has experience with difficult slaves?" *Or crazy people*, he thought, but didn't say out loud.

Jere wrinkled his nose, looking disgusted. "I know well enough what anyone else would suggest, and I'm not going to do anything like that to the poor girl. I'm doing it my way."

Wren sighed. He should have known that encouraging Jere to consult with another slaveowner would provoke instant rejection; Jere worked so hard to avoid putting himself in that category even if it was true. "I mean, I'm not saying you have to do anything awful to her, but maybe have some more boundaries, some more rules — "

"I've got a good enough idea of what I'm doing," Jere insisted.

Wren seriously doubted his judgment, and it bothered him that Jere was being so stubborn on this when he had said countless times over the past few days that he *didn't* know what he was doing, or that he doubted himself. "Jere, you just... you cater to her! I mean, I'm not saying beat her or starve her or something, but if she's too fucking spiteful and mean to come out at meal time, why are you hand-delivering a plate to her? Make her get it herself!"

"My god, Wren, she's just scared!" Jere protested. "It's bad enough that I've promised not to heal her; I'm not going to help her starve to death. You notice she does eat when I bring her food, and she's stopped insisting that everything is poisoned, that's progress. Eventually she'll feel safe and calm down, and then we can put this all behind us. And for what it's worth, it wouldn't kill you to show a bit of compassion, either."

Wren rolled his eyes. As far as he was concerned, the girl was probably drowning in *undeserved* compassion already. "I just think I might have at least *some* insight into what to do with her, you know, what a slave would be expecting, and maybe you'd want to listen to my ideas and try some of them out."

"She's expecting me to hurt her, and I'm not going to do that," Jere insisted. "It's just a matter of waiting it out."

Wren grew more irritated as Jere ignored him again, insisting he knew about something he didn't. "Jere, she thinks you're tricking her. You make all these promises, and they sound too good to be true. She doesn't believe you! I didn't believe you. For months, I was waiting for it all to come crashing down, and the worst I ever did was look at you strangely! Trust me, that was my life for seven years, I'm pretty familiar with how it works. You need to give her some sort of anchor, something that seems familiar coming from a master, even a lenient one."

"I'm her master and I'm doing it my way." Jere's tone stayed the same, but the look on his face was harsh, resolute, and Wren knew better than to press the issue. Years of experience with people more powerful than himself had taught him exactly when they weren't going to budge, no matter how much one cajoled, or begged, or pleaded. Clearly, Jere was at this point, and his decision was really the only one that mattered in the end. Wren let the bitter taste of that fact serve as a reminder that he needed to remember his place in the relationship and his place in the world. Jere was also *his* master, and that meant that Wren needed to accept Jere's way.

"Fine," Wren mumbled, trying to wash his hands of the whole situation. Jere didn't seem angry at him, so he just had to let it go. Just let it go and pretend it wasn't happening. The more he thought about it, the worse it seemed, but he couldn't let himself get angry either. He had said it was fine, and even though it wasn't, he couldn't afford to create any more conflict. It was bad enough that Jere was actively rejecting his advice; if he ordered Wren to agree with it, Wren wasn't sure what he'd do.

"Besides, I don't want you to have to waste your time worrying about this," Jere reached over to touch his arm. It was supposed to be a conciliatory gesture, but Wren just felt confined and oddly threatened. "I know you've been opposed to the idea and this kid in particular from the start, so I want to respect you on that and not drag you into it. It's my problem, and I can deal with it on my own. You just keep being the wonderful man I love and everything will be fine."

It should have been reassuring, maybe even romantic, but Wren just felt like Jere was trying to pacify him. In a way, that would hurt more than outright dismissal, as if he didn't deserve to have an honest conversation about this. No matter how much Jere might be trying not to drag him into it, it was asinine to think that Wren could just stop worrying about it. He couldn't just stop worrying about another slave screaming in the other room and upsetting the master they shared any more than he could stop worrying about the strange way that Jere was acting.

"All right," Wren mumbled, backing down to Jere's request and focusing on his dinner instead.

They finished the meal on an artificially light note. The familiarity and closeness made conversation easy enough, and Wren wasn't even sure whether Jere noticed his unease or not. It didn't help the feeling, but Wren still resisted bringing it up. Maybe it really would be better to let it go. He didn't want to start another argument that he would lose.

After dinner, they stayed at the table, neither one of them eager to make any moves or lock Isis in for the night or think about anything beyond the dining room table. It was Jere's eyelids and head drooping that finally provoked Wren to prod him into action.

"Babe," he said, giving Jere's shoulder a shake. "Come on. We've gotta go to bed. You're clearly exhausted again." Wren just wanted the day to be over.

Jere opened his eyes, and they were red and bloodshot. "Let me go see Isis for a minute," he insisted, dragging himself to a standing position wearily. He went to the kitchen and brought back the plate of food that Wren had dished up for the girl, despite his own better judgment.

Wren shook his head, following a few steps behind him.

Jere knocked on the girl's door, waiting for a few moments while the screaming and cursing became more violent and more targeted at the two of them before opening it partway. "Isis, do you need anything else before we go to bed for the night?"

"I need you to fucking go to hell and die!" she spat out, looking every bit like a wild animal as she huddled in the corner of the room, curled under the blanket she had clearly pulled off the mattress again.

"Bathroom, drink, more blankets?" Jere suggested, his tone growing irritated. "I brought you food."

"Just stay the hell away from me!" Isis screamed. "Fucking kill me!"

"Isis, I'm just trying to help!" Jere replied, exasperated. "What about your injuries? Are you healing? Do you need *anything*?"

"I need you to fuck off before I kill everyone in their sleep!" Isis's anger escalated, as did her volume. "I'm never fucking coming out of here and you can't make me!"

"Fine. Just fucking stay in there, then!" He locked the door roughly, shoved the key into his pocket, and glanced at Wren. "Come on. We're going to bed."

Chapter 10

Facing Reality

Wren followed him automatically, intimidated by his anger. Jere didn't seem to notice as he stomped down the hall, into their bedroom, and ripped his own clothes off, flopping down onto the bed naked and still angry. Wren couldn't help feeling apprehensive as he shed the clothes he had been wearing all day, replacing them with the pajama pants he wore occasionally. Tentatively, he climbed into bed next to Jere, who slid next to him insistently.

"What, are you cold?" His voice was harsh, accusing. It didn't help that Wren could feel the irritation through the mind connection.

"N-no?" He stumbled over his words. "I just, I mean... I can take them off—"

"No!"

It was too quick, too demanding. Wren felt his body go slack as he waited for something, for Jere to strip him, hurt him, vent his frustrations on him.

A soft hand rested itself on his shoulder, pulling him back to the present.

"I'm sorry, Wren," Jere said bitterly, sounding no less frustrated, but very apologetic. "Please... I'm sorry. I'm just upset. I'm not mad at you."

Wren tried not to, but he felt himself start to tremble. This was stupid. He was fine. Jere wouldn't hurt him.

"Come here," Jere beckoned, his grip tightening somewhat.

Wren turned toward him, but didn't move. He didn't want to move closer. He wanted to move far away, where he was safe, where nobody was touching him. He knew it was irrational, but Jere never acted like this. He felt himself growing tense. "Please..." he heard himself whimper.

Jere pulled his arms back immediately, moving to put space between them. Wren felt the emotional connection from Jere being slammed shut, cutting his emotions off. Wren, still uncertain, left his open.

"Do you want to talk about it?" Jere asked.

What Wren wanted to do was run out of this room and hide in his own. The room Jere gave him. The room he rarely ever slept in. What he wanted was to hide away, like he used to, even though he knew it wouldn't solve anything. What he wanted was to yell "stop!" and have things make sense again. What he wanted was for Jere to take care of him, not in the condescending, masterly way he had been, but for real, like the man he had grown to love. He wanted to talk about everything, but only if Jere would listen to him.

"Wren, love..." Jere sat up, shaking his head. "I'm sorry. I can sleep in one of the other rooms."

Wren suddenly launched himself at him, grabbing him around the waist. "Don't go!" he protested, burying his head in his chest. He already felt like he was losing the gentle man he loved, and right now, the only thing he could think of to prevent that was physical closeness. He couldn't bear the idea of Jere being out of his sight, putting even more distance between them.

Strong, familiar arms wrapped around him, holding him close.

"Okay, okay, I won't," Jere spoke softly, that familiar, soothing tone that he had. Wren clung to it as he clung to him. "It's okay. I just wanted you to feel safe, love. And if I'm the one making you feel differently... I'll get the hell out. You shouldn't have to be nervous just because I'm being an asshole."

That wasn't exactly what was going on—not that Wren could really put a finger on *what* was going on—but it was close enough. He pressed closer to his master and breathed in his scent. "*Just hold me?*" he asked, not wanting to say it out loud.

"Whatever you want," Jere whispered into his ear, kissing his forehead gently and leaning back, holding him close as they fell asleep.

Jere woke up surprisingly well-rested, despite being a little sore from cuddling with Wren all night. He was certain that Wren was comfortable — after all, Jere had been used, quite literally, as a body pillow. It was worth it to see his lover's face smiling up at him this morning.

He didn't know what had caused the emotional surge last night, just that Wren was highly upset, and sort of scared. It worried him, but Wren didn't want to talk about it, and Jere felt he had to respect his decision. Jere was taking charge of enough things already; Wren deserved to at least have authority over his own emotional state. Jere guessed that seeing Isis so beat up and upset had stirred up some bad memories. Certainly, Jere's mood hadn't helped *at all*, but Jere was moody often enough that he knew Wren didn't usually respond so badly.

That still didn't give him any excuse for being moody, or an asshole, or sharp with his lover. He felt certain that Wren trusted him, but denying the years of torment Wren had been through and the scars it left on him would do neither of them any good. It was easy to not think about it, to focus on the present, to focus on how far he had come and how strong he was and how well they got along most days. Compared to Isis, Wren seemed so normal and well-adjusted that it was easy to forget he had been just as abused and terrified at one point, and Jere had to admit that he would rather forget it than face it. None of that changed the fact that Wren still needed some gentle handling, and Jere felt terrible for forgetting it.

He couldn't help but be a little frustrated with Isis, the cause of the moodiness and frustration and generally elevated stress level in the house. She got under his skin, and her intensity brought out the worst in Jere, disrupting everything from his sleep, to his work, to his relationship with Wren. She brought out a side of Wren that Jere had never seen, one that surprised and sometimes worried Jere, especially when Wren hinted that Isis needed less kindness instead of more. Jere knew that this had been Wren's experience, but no matter how disruptive Isis was, he didn't think there was any reason that could ever justify harming her. There wasn't anything that Jere thought justified harming anyone so helpless.

The day was surprisingly uneventful. He unlocked Isis's room immediately after he finished up in the clinic, and found her silent and asleep, curled up in a ball in the corner. A noise woke her immediately, and she responded by yelping and protesting that she hadn't done anything. It was her new stock response; she had mostly ceased screaming at him to get out or accusing him of trying to touch her. Jere calmly informed her that it was dinner time before walking out.

She joined them for dinner, to both Jere's and Wren's surprise, and was silent as they ate. Aside from putting away twice as much food as both of the men combined, she was a non-issue throughout the meal, even allowing them to chat about the clinic and remaining politely silent. The destructiveness of earlier was gone, as was the screaming. She even looked calmer.

When dinner was finished, she carried her plate to the kitchen, a far cry from her actions earlier. Jere was just happy she didn't break it. She came back through the dining room on her way to her bedroom, and Jere gasped when he saw a red spot forming on the back of the shirt she was wearing.

"Isis!" he exclaimed, realizing his voice was sharp a moment too late.

She whirled around, arms flying up to protect herself, pressing her back against the wall. "No, don't! I didn't fucking do anything, goddammit!"

Jere stayed seated. "I didn't say you did—calm down. You're bleeding, for Christ's sake, I was just surprised." He wasn't in the mood for a fight tonight. Not when he was this exhausted and worn out already.

Her eyes widened. "It's fine. I'm not complaining or anything. And I'll, I'll wash the shirt and get the stains out and everything, I promise. It's fine, Jere, sir, really!"

Jere sighed. This was really getting ridiculous. The defiance and destruction were bad enough, but he was watching the girl become more and more ill before his eyes. He was a healer, and this girl was sick and injured in his home. It wasn't right, and was his duty to fix it. "Isis, I'm not worried about the fucking shirt. I'm worried about you! You need to be healed."

"Please! No! I promise, I won't break anything!" She tried pleading, but looked more like she was going to bolt.

Jere forced himself to stay seated. "Isis, I won't do anything without warning you. I mean, I'd like it if you'd let me heal you—"

"No!"

"—but since you're so opposed to that, I can tend to it the traditional way," Jere continued, talking over her protests. "Just clean it up, put some antibiotic cream on it, some bandages—"

"No! Don't touch me!" Isis crept along the wall, looking ready to flee.

Jere wanted to kick himself for pushing her too hard. He wanted to get her to see reason, but that seemed so far from possibility that a part of him simply wanted to sneak a sedative into her meal and heal her while she was sedated. It would be easier than the alternative and less miserable for everyone involved, but he didn't want to force it just yet, not when she showed tentative signs of trusting him. "Isis, I won't touch you tonight, I promise, just calm down—"

"Don't fucking touch me ever!" she shrieked, a second before bolting toward the front door.

Wren beat her to it, blocking her way with his body. She curled her arms around herself in a desperate gesture of protection and tried to barrel her way through him, screaming the whole time. Jere's head pounded from the screams, and he was concerned for Wren's safety now as much as he was for Isis's.

"Isis! That is enough! You're not going anywhere, and nobody is going to hurt you!" Jere stood up to assist. "You're safe here. Go back to your room."

"No, fuck you, fuck you both! Get the fuck away from me! *Don't fucking touch me!* Don't you ever fucking touch me, you fucking bastards, fucking goddamn perverts!" She had retreated away from the front door, moving slowly back toward her room. She twisted around and saw Jere standing close to her, prompting her to shriek more loudly and move toward the door again.

Jere saw Wren grab her, hard, by the arm, his fingers digging into her thin skin. When she yelped and pulled away, he shook her. "Do as you're told, he's your fucking master!"

Before Jere could think or do anything else, he was pushing Wren back just as forcefully. "Don't you fucking touch her!"

The words flew out of his mouth as quickly as he had reacted.

He wanted to take them back as soon as he said them.

He really wanted to take everything back when Wren drew back, dead pale, and stared at him with eyes as wide as the girl. Wren didn't say anything, just stared at him, frozen, trembling. He dropped to his knees.

The intensity of the scene had even silenced Isis, who stood, seemingly confused as to whether to be more terrified of her master or her fellow slave.

Jere forced himself to swallow, then addressed Isis in a shaky voice. "Did he hurt you?"

She shook her head slowly. He was only slightly relieved.

"Go into your room. I'm locking the door. I'll bring you medical supplies tomorrow, and if you can manage to take care of your injuries, that's great. I have no desire to touch you, or go into your mind, or do anything. But if your injuries become more infected, if you become sick, I won't let you die. I *will* heal you, and there's nothing you can do about it. I'm a healer. It's my fucking job. I'd rather not have to force it, but if the other option is letting you die, I won't let that happen." He took a few deep breaths, trying to calm himself, trying to make some sense out of what the hell had just happened, in less than five minutes, to bring things to this point.

Jere looked at her, hard, his jaw set. "And if you *ever* try to take off like that again or destroy things like you did earlier, I will restrain you as we discussed. Is that perfectly clear?"

She nodded, silent for once, then backed into her room.

Jere locked the door quickly, and looked at Wren, still on his knees, waiting.

"We need to talk," he said, sullen. He felt sick as he put out a hand to help his lover up and Wren cringed.

Chapter 11

What Angry Looks Like

Wren felt his stomach churn as he followed his master. They were in the bedroom before Wren even realized where they were going. The realization hurt. He didn't want to be punished in the place where they used to make love. He stood awkwardly by the door and watched as Jere sat on the edge of the bed, put his head in his hands, and then leaned back. He didn't know what to expect.

"What the fuck were you thinking?" Jere's voice was dull.

The words were angry, though. That was enough. "I... I'm sorry, sir." Jere didn't answer. Wren felt his palms begin to sweat. "I just... she was being disobedient."

"Wren, you hurt her!"

Wren trembled. Of course. It made sense that he wouldn't be allowed to hurt the new slave. The pretty new kid, the one who needed Jere to fix her. Jere had been nice to Wren when he needed fixing. This girl didn't belong here, but maybe what Jere wanted was someone else to fix. "I, I'm sorry, sir." He braced himself for whatever might come. Pain? It wasn't like Jere, but he had never heard his master threaten someone with restraints, either. He realized that Isis wasn't the only person in the house who could be restrained, and his blood went cold.

Jere was silent for what seemed like forever. Wren tried counting, but he was too anxious to remember what number he was on. He tried breathing deeply and calmly, but every breath was strained, and it wasn't worth it. He panted, shallowly, instead.

Finally, Jere spoke. "I've never actually been angry with you, have I?"

It sounded like he was calm, but Wren wondered if his master was just contemplating what to do with him. "N-no, sir. I don't think you have."

Jere propped himself up on his elbows for a moment, studying Wren before he sat up. "Come here," he said coolly. "Let me show you what angry looks like with me."

Wren swallowed the fear that had taken up residence in his throat and strode toward his master. He deserved whatever punishment he had earned, he would take it and let it remind him of his proper place.

He was in the process of kneeling between his master's knees when Jere caught his hand, pulling him up again.

"No," Jere whispered, shaking his head.

Wren felt himself being pulled up carefully, up to sit on the bed between Jere's legs, in front of him. Jere's arms came around him lightly, resting around his waist, and a second later, he felt his chin on his shoulder. He didn't know what to say. Surely, this wasn't punishment.

"You're terrified," Jere whispered, holding him close. "I never meant for that to happen."

Wren said nothing. Did he really mean it?

"I never meant to put my hands on you, love." Jere sounded so sincere. "I just reacted. I didn't think, I just saw that you were hurting her, and I reacted. Did I hurt you, or just scare you?"

"You didn't hurt me..." Wren mumbled. Saying that Jere "just" scared him was an understatement, if not a straight-faced lie.

Jere was quiet for a moment, holding him, not moving. It felt good. Safe.

"This must be terribly hard for you," he said quietly, after a moment.

Wren nodded. "I'm trying to stay out of it as much as I can. I know you said that it's not my problem, but I can't just sit back and do nothing, and even if I did, it's still hard."

"Yeah, and you've never seen me react this way, have you?" Jere asked, massaging Wren's arms as he spoke. "Never had to see me with a slave like this."

Wren was silent. A part of him wanted to curse Jere for being so good at guessing what he was feeling, but then, he had always been good at that when he tried hard enough.

"Love, help me understand," Jere pleaded. "I'm hurting you and I don't know how — just tell me what's going on?"

Wren was a bit confused. There were too many things at once, too many emotions, too many thoughts. He believed that Jere was angry at him, he could have sworn that he was furious just a few minutes ago. He couldn't tell now. And he trusted Jere, but he was still scared, and he was worried, but he felt safe; at least, he felt mostly safe. He said the most concrete thing in his mind. "I didn't want you to have to hurt her."

"Isis?" Jere seemed surprised. "Wren, why — "

"Because she's trying to force your hand. She's pushing you as far as you'll let her go, and I don't want you to end up having to actually do it, actually discipline her like...."

"Like a master would a slave?" Jere supplied.

Wren just nodded, tears starting to form in his eyes at the thought. "Because, then... then things would change, and it...." He started to sob, silently, as usual.

Jere's arms were tight around him again. "Wren, really, nothing will change between you and me. I promise. I won't be a different person. I won't be some fucking master to you." He laughed. "Honestly, I don't want to be some fucking master to that girl, although I do want to strangle her. I love you. I care about you. I respect you. That's not going to change. *I* am not going to change."

"But things have changed!" Wren protested. As terrified as he was, he'd rather get it all over with now, tell Jere all the things that might upset him so all the consequences would spill over at the same time. "You've changed already."

Jere was quiet for a moment, his breath even on the back of Wren's neck. "I'm not going to say you're wrong, because I'm probably not the best judge of how I'm acting, but I have to admit that I haven't felt that way. Can you help me understand?"

"You don't listen to me," Wren said immediately, the words coming out as an angry whisper.

"I promise, I'll listen," Jere insisted.

Wren shook his head. "No. Not now — all the other times. About

Isis. I try to help you, to give you advice, and you don't listen to me. You disregard what I say like it doesn't matter, and you do whatever you want without even giving me a reason why. I know I shouldn't be telling you what to do, I mean, I am a slave, but I thought—"

"I thought I was just letting you stay out of it," Jere interrupted. "I thought if I made all the hard decisions, it would make life easier for you."

"Sometimes you ask me the questions and you don't listen to what I have to say!" Wren couldn't hold back the anger. "It's like you just want me to tell you what you want to hear. Is that it? Is that all I'm supposed to do?"

"No. No, Wren, I promise, that's not what I want. This is so wrong. I never wanted you to think that." Jere was quiet again, his chin resting heavy on Wren's shoulder. "Look, sometimes you give me advice, and I just don't want to believe it. I want to hide from it, and I guess that when I did that, it made you feel like I wasn't listening, but believe me, I heard everything you told me. And sometimes, I even thought you might be right, but I don't want to be the one who carries out that advice. I don't want to be the one to scare her, or to put restrictions on her. And I guess it was easier to completely push you aside than to tell you that."

Wren thought about it for a minute or two. It did make sense; Jere was always more likely to avoid conflict than to address it directly, although this time his avoidance had come more in the form of very hurtful redirection. "So you don't think that I'm above my place or anything?" he asked with caution.

"No. Never. I don't think that you're always right, but I'll admit that you're right a hell of a lot more than I am. And as far as I'm concerned, your place is still wherever you want it to be. I can't say I approve of you leaving fingerprints on a scared kid, but that has nothing to do with you or her being a slave."

"I just thought it would be better if I did it than if you did," Wren admitted. "As much as I think you need to sometimes, I don't know if I can handle seeing you hurt her."

"You're acting like I'm going to stumble upon the tactics of being a cruel master and turn into some sort of monster. Just because I choose not to act like that doesn't mean I don't know how, or what it would look like. I'm not going to do that to her, Wren. I didn't do it to you, and I won't do it to her. I wouldn't do it to anyone."

"But things were different. Between us, I mean."

"Of course they were—eventually. But not at first—hell, it was months before I so much as looked at you as anything more than an assistant!"

Wren thought that he had sort of always known this, at least, he thought that he *should* have always known this. But a part of him had figured that Jere had always been at least somewhat attracted to him.

"I mean, I thought you were drop dead gorgeous, but that's pretty hard to miss!"

Wren could hear him smirking.

"I found out pretty quickly that you were very bright, and pleasant, and fun to be around, but I never knew, at first, that anything like what we have now would come of it."

Wren reached up to take Jere's hand in his own, squeezing it as he contemplated what he had just heard. He was thankful that Jere gave him the time to process. He had always assumed that Jere was so kind and patient with him because he was into him, or because Wren was so well-behaved and trained. "I never challenged you," he mused.

Jere squeezed his hand back. "No, no you didn't. But I still would have treated you decently."

Wren had to admit that he believed it. He realized that what he had often mistaken in Jere for infatuation or even naïveté was simply kind, decent interaction. Patience. Compassion. Respect for human life and dignity. All the things he hadn't shown that girl.

"Are you still angry?" he whispered, feeling like a naughty child. "You've been blocking emotions."

"I have," Jere answered. "You were having such a hard time figuring out why I was feeling the way I was—it was easier just to block it up. I was hurting you and I wasn't sure what was going on and I thought it would be better to just deal with it myself and save you the drama. And, yes, actually, I am still a bit angry with you."

Wren felt a bit nervous, but none of the terror and apprehension he had felt earlier. "What would you like to do to resolve that?" he asked, carefully.

"I'm doing exactly that right now, love," Jere kissed his shoulder gently.

"But..." Wren was at a loss. This was how Jere dealt with anger? There was no yelling, no hitting, no anything.

"I'm sitting here *with* you. We're talking about it. We're figuring it out. I know you're safe—what more could I ask for?"

Wren knew that Jere could ask for a lot more, but he trusted that he wouldn't. Jere actually wouldn't want anything else, and now that things were calm, Wren could see that. "It was kind of scary—*is* kind of scary. Having you angry. I never wanted to make you angry."

Jere laughed, which Wren found somewhat hurtful. Wren had just been scared, terrified beyond all reason, and Jere was treating it so lightly.

"It happens, Wren! People get angry with each other all the time. I mean, come on, how many times have you been angry with me? Hell, how many times have I pissed you off just this week?"

He had never thought about it that way. He was a slave. His job was to please his master... but Jere never really did want that. More often than not, it left Wren in the difficult position of still working to please his master, while trying to pretend that he wasn't a slave doing exactly that. It was something that Jere never seemed to grasp.

"It's normal relationship stuff—I know, this isn't exactly a 'normal' relationship—and, well, I guess you've never had one—but I swear, it is. Just because I'm angry at you about one little thing doesn't mean I'm a different person, or that I love you any less, or that I'll do anything unusual."

Wren considered this, wondering if he could trust and believe what Jere said. It was true, even when he was mad at Jere, which happened often enough, he would never do anything to hurt him, not even if he could. Even if he was as angry as Jere had seemed... even then, he would want nothing more than to lie in bed with the man he loved and figure out what was wrong.

"I'm sorry," he mumbled, glad his lover couldn't see his face. "I shouldn't have doubted you."

He felt Jere kissing his head through his hair, making him feel safe and loved and protected.

"Darling, you have every reason to be cautious," Jere reminded him, still holding him close. "This is new for both of us, and I'm sure it's going to be a bit more nerve-wracking for you than it is for me—even if I don't say it out loud, it's not that I'm unaware of it. I know... I know how hard you work sometimes. You have a lot of history trying to bite you in the ass."

"Yeah," Wren agreed. It still didn't make him feel much better. It didn't get rid of this dark, scary part of him that pushed around young girls and ignored the pain of others.

"You just take care of yourself, love," Jere advised gently, nibbling at his neck. "You've told me so much tonight that I had no idea about, and I promise, I'll try to make things better. Just tell me what you need. I'll listen."

"We need to talk more," Wren decided, feeling so much better now that they had done so. "And like I said earlier, I need you to listen. I'll help you with this, the whole mess with Isis, but you have to take my advice. I can't feel like I'm talking to a wall that gets angry at me."

"Apt comparison," Jere laughed. "And you have my word that I will. I can't promise you that I'll always take your advice, but I promise I'll listen, and I'll take your lead, and if I can't do it, I'll try to explain why instead of saying no. You deserve at least that much."

"You're too good to me," he muttered, but he was smiling.

"Ha. I treat all my boyfriends this way," Jere teased, prompting Wren to turn around and kiss him.

"You're a smartass," Wren pointed out, squirming around to pin Jere down to the bed, still kissing him.

They indulged in each other for a few minutes before Wren backed off, sliding down a bit to rest his head on Jere's chest. "Thank you. For being so understanding."

Jere's hand came up, cupping the back of his head, caressing him. "Of course, love."

Chapter 12
Compassionate Care

The next few days passed with little event. Jere couldn't help but feel terrible for upsetting Wren so much, and went out of his way at every opportunity to check in with him, to reassure him, to show him how special he was. More importantly, Jere went out of his way to listen to him, not only to the words he said out loud, but the words he hesitated to say, the way his body spoke for him sometimes, the way his tone could convey more than his words. As much effort as he put into calming and containing Isis, he vowed to try even harder to make things work with Wren. It scared him how far he had pushed his lover away, and he wanted nothing more than to bring them close together again.

Wren stayed jumpy for the next few days, but he was able to open up somewhat, talking with Jere and actually relaxing, especially when they were alone. They both worked to make time to talk with each other, and Jere was careful to avoid just talking about surface-level topics. He made a point to think carefully before responding to Wren, making sure he wasn't snapping or dismissive, and Wren noticed, thanking him with words and with touch. It only made Jere more aware of how disconnected they had become. They tried to go back to the way things used to be as much as possible.

Still, there was a serious barrier to "used to be."

Jere had, as promised, delivered some traditional medical supplies to Isis's room the following day: disinfectants, bandages, clean clothes, and water. He knew it wouldn't be enough. He tried to persuade her to take some antibiotic pills, but found them thrown across the room when he checked in later. He struggled, watching her deteriorate more and more with each passing day.

Her defiance and violence weren't going anywhere either, although she was becoming more and more subdued as her physical state weakened her. Screaming, cursing, and yelling — these were now an everyday part of their lives. He and Wren started spending time outside, enjoying the fading heat of summer and wondering when their house could be reclaimed. She didn't attempt to run again. She rarely left her room, and the destruction had mostly stopped as well. Instead, she just huddled in the corner, or, on rare occasions, on the mattress that had been left in the room.

Jere's concern escalated when she stopped eating. He noticed that she had barely touched lunch, but thought that perhaps her ravenous eating had caught up with her. When dinner approached and he unlocked her door, she simply shook her head when he asked whether she was coming out or not. He brought her a plate, but she shook her head.

"I can't eat," she muttered, leaning heavily against the wall. "Can't throw up again."

"Again?" Jere raised an eyebrow. When had she thrown up?

"All fucking day. It's... I tried to... in a pillowcase." Her voice shook a bit, sounding raspy.

"Isis, you should have said something, you could have had a trash bin or something!" He walked over to the mattress, where he saw the pillowcase had done a poor job of containing its contents.

"Ha," she managed, breathing heavily. "Wouldn't want me to have anything else to throw."

He collected the bedding quickly, surprised when she didn't even move in response to his sudden motions. "I just don't want you to hurt yourself," he tried. "Isis, you're very sick."

"Don't touch me," she pleaded, almost lifeless. "You promised. You said you wouldn't!"

Jere sighed. He had promised not to touch her, but now that seemed like a stupid promise to make. Jere realized that he should have insisted, that he should be insisting right now, but the girl seemed to trust him to keep this promise at least, and he had to weigh the importance of keeping that promise against healing her quickly. The longer he waited to heal her, the more difficult it would be, but any gain in cooperation would be priceless. "You're right. I'll stick by my word. But I did tell you that I wouldn't let you die, remember."

"Then I better go quick," she muttered.

"I'll be back to check on you after dinner," he said, quietly.

He deposited the mess of bedding near the washing machine, then went to the dining room where Wren was waiting for him, a questioning look on his face.

"She's sick," he said, by way of explanation, dropping into a chair.

"So heal her," Wren said softly, looking intently at him. "And make her do her own damn laundry."

Jere laughed, knowing Wren wasn't serious about the last part. "I just can't, Wren. I can't force myself on her like that. It's too much—"

"Jere, for fuck's sake, you're a healer!" Wren reminded him. "It's not like you're doing something terrible to her. You're keeping her alive. She's not making sense anyway—hasn't been, for days, and I'm sure she's full of fever and infection and whatnot. Honestly. Besides, think of where we'd be if you let me die when I asked you to!"

Jere's mind flashed briefly back to those days, barely recognizing the people they had both been. He had been so calm, so practical, ignoring Wren's pleas to die under the assumption that he was too injured to understand what he was requesting. Back then, he knew so little about the lives of slaves that he never would have understood that granting a request for death could be a benevolent action. But Wren had acquiesced much more easily than Isis, then and every other time, until they started falling in love and neither of them wanted Wren to acquiesce. Jere doubted that things would be as easy with Isis, although a part of him longed for that simplicity.

"I won't let her die," Jere mumbled. "She's not at risk of that, yet. I know I should do it anyway, you're right, but I just... every time I think I can do it, I go in there and she begs me not to, she reminds me that I promised her I wouldn't. I don't know if I can go through with it."

"Look, you knew it would come to this, why postpone it?" Wren was calm. He was always calm. Jere envied Wren his pragmatic, level-headed approach, a far cry from the moral debates that Jere was torturing himself with.

"Because I told her I wouldn't," Jere admitted.

"She doesn't believe you anyway," Wren pointed out.

"Exactly." Jere saw the question in Wren's eyes, the frustration as good advice was being ignored again. "Look, I should have healed her in the first place, like you said, but I think she's at least starting to trust me on this, and I'm so far in already, I'd rather wait and keep her trust than get the healing done and over with and have her hate me for it. Do you think there's even remotely a chance?"

Wren smiled back at him. "As much as I want her healed, yes, I admit, your bizarre plan does have some merit. And while I still think she'll be angry at you for doing it at all, perhaps it is worth waiting. You do seem to have a way with her, and you're right, it won't be much more difficult to wait at this point. But make sure you heal her completely! I don't think either of us will want to keep waiting for her to be half-dead again."

Jere allowed himself to smile, feeling relief that Wren supported him in this decision.

After dinner was over, Jere checked back on his patient. He couldn't bring himself to think of Isis as his slave; it was too horrible, too real. She was sick, a patient, like Wren had been. She was covered in sweat, pressing her face against the wall in an attempt to cool herself down.

"Do you want some ice or something?" Jere asked, torn apart by her obvious pain.

"I want to die," she rasped out. "I want them all to leave me alone."

He checked on her every hour, watching as she deteriorated before his eyes. He tried approaching her, but her terror and panic just got worse, so he checked from the doorway instead. Sleep was futile, and he debated with himself whether to go on and do it or not, weighing the options over and over again in his mind. He went to check on her again, his concern mounting as he called her name and got no response.

Turning on the light, he saw her lying on her back, pale, sweating, barely breathing. He rushed over and picked her up, heedless of anything else, and was relieved for a moment when she opened her eyes.

"Don't save me," she whispered, only seconds before she started convulsing.

Jere lifted her quickly and carefully, positioning her on the mattress where she would be less likely to hurt herself or him.

"*I need you!*" he called to Wren, trusting him to take care of things while he plunged himself into the girl's mind, somewhat apprehensive about what he might find.

It was a shock, but for different reasons than he would have expected. There was just... nothing. A blank, void expanse. It seemed dark, but Jere surmised that if he was "seeing" nothing, there must be some sort of light. The dream state was always so confusing. He pushed around, exploring what else might be there, what sort of emotional stimuli or images or... but there was nothing. It was eerily like the dream state of a dead person, which he had been unfortunate enough to encounter twice, when his patients' injuries had been too much even for his superior healing gift. But this wasn't the same. He couldn't sense dead people in their own minds, couldn't sense anything, but he could sense Isis, although only very weakly.

It was this presence that he focused on, and felt himself moving toward it, slowly. Not walking, exactly, as there didn't seem to be a floor of any sort to walk on, but moving nonetheless. He closed his eyes, focusing on the psychic sense, and when he opened them, he was quite unsettled by what he saw.

Isis, looking a few years younger than she did for real, was curled up in a pile of tattered rags next to a tiny fire, huddling close to it to stay warm. Around her on all four sides, as well as top and bottom, was a thick metal cage, with almost no space between the bars. Nobody could go in or out. There were cobwebs around the outside. It was a chilling image.

He took a few steps toward her, kneeling down a few feet from the cage. It was so wrong. So wrong that a person should have to build a cage around herself to stay safe from the rest of the world.

"Isis?" he asked softly, relieved when her projection turned to face him.

"You found me," she said, backing into the corner farthest from him.

"I'm sorry..." He didn't even know what to say. She deserved apologies for so many things. "I can't let you die."

"Will it hurt much?" she asked, strangely calm. Her projection seemed so young, so frail.

"Honey, it will hurt more if you resist," Jere said softly, forgetting he was talking to a teenager, and not a little girl, like the projection looked. "Please, don't be scared. All I want to do is help you. You can make it easier on yourself by letting me in."

She glared at him, and the tiny fire in her cage grew larger. "*You* can make it easier on everyone by fucking letting me die!"

Rage. Burning rage. It was all she had left to hold on to.

"I'm sorry." He shook his head, moved toward the projection, and plunged himself through her psychic barriers so he could start healing.

It wasn't easy, although it wasn't as hard as he thought it would be. While she was defending herself with everything she had, she didn't have much in the way of psychic prowess. He shielded her from as much of the pain as he possibly could, clenching his teeth as he absorbed the sensation into himself, instead. She wasn't blocking him so much as battling frantically to escape.

He entered the healing state quickly and began attending to the medical needs. The fever and infection were of utmost importance, and he addressed those at once, assuming that the convulsions she was having were an indication of the severity.

Once this was taken care of, he moved to her actual injuries, starting with her back and legs, where the damage was the worst. He healed them quickly, doubting he would have a second chance, forcing the infection out and the skin to close in its place. He wanted badly to address the scarring, but he knew there wasn't time or energy. Besides, it wasn't really noticeable amongst the mass of old scarring on her body. He wondered how long she had been a slave. The scars were old, some looking to be more than five years old, but they couldn't be; it didn't make sense. They didn't take kids as slaves until they were much older, right? Even if the man who sold her mentioned she had been taken "young."

Once her legs and back were healed to his satisfaction, he moved to her chest and stomach, finding some injuries there, but not nearly as many. He tried not to think about what he was healing, but he knew that there were mostly whip marks and burn marks. Some things looked like pure and simple pressure—a straightjacket tied too tightly, chains and handcuffs cutting into skin. Jere understood why she was so terrified of being restrained. As he continued, he realized her wrist was broken—one of many times, he noticed, and he was amazed that she had never complained about it, never even seemed to favor it. He healed it up, feeling ill. She must have become accustomed to this much pain.

Her previous master had been right—he had most certainly broken her jaw, at least once, along with a series of other bones. Jere realized that most of the abuse hadn't been from her most recent previous master—after all, she had been through a startlingly large number of masters before him. The thought wasn't comforting.

With a sense of trepidation, he examined the rest of her body. He didn't want to, but it was slightly better than examining her in real life, forcing her to accept his touch. It was something he knew he wouldn't be able to bring himself to do. Nonetheless, she seemed to know, to feel it, to grow conscious, and he felt her body struggling to move away from him on the physical plane. He struggled to initiate a mind-bind, reluctant to expend that much energy or to do something so disagreeable. She suddenly went still, and he realized that Wren must have sedated her. He was regretful for a moment, because he didn't want it to come to this, but it was for the best. He continued to heal the tears and rips and infections inside her body, vowing to kill the man who sold her to him if he ever saw him again.

Jere finished and pulled back, unsurprised to find himself crying, or to find Wren wrapping his arms around him, holding him up, all but force-feeding him water and Crucial Care.

He glanced at his watch, needing to know, needing to figure out how much time had passed. Five hours. "I have to get to the clinic," he mumbled. It was an hour past opening time.

"Hush," Wren cradled him in his arms. "You're taking a sick day. I put the Emergencies Only sign out already and I am redirecting people as needed."

"I need to—" he began to protest.

"You need to rest," Wren said firmly, pulling him to his feet and dragging him toward their bedroom. "I sedated the girl, and I've got another injection ready for you if you argue with me."

Jere allowed himself to be guided, helping slightly by staying on his feet, at least. "You wouldn't!" he protested, realizing what Wren had just threatened him with.

"Don't try me," Wren cautioned, but he smiled as he said it, easing Jere into their bed and kissing him. "You said that you would take my lead, and if you recall, I didn't try to stop you from waiting forever to heal the girl. It's your turn. I have everything under control, and I'll wake you up if we need anything. Now, be a good doctor and get some damn rest!"

Jere slept quite well. He woke for a few hours in the afternoon, still feeling a bit groggy, and attended to the few emergency patients Wren had let into the clinic. He ate and promptly went back to sleep. As much as he hated admitting it, it was nice to be taken care of once in a while. The exhaustion wasn't just from healing Isis. Not only was he chronically overworked, but the past week of screaming from Isis and the arguing and tension between himself and Wren had all taken their toll. Wren made sure that he rested and ate well, and Jere followed his orders, as promised. Jere enjoyed the pampering, but it was made even better by the fact that Wren finally looked content again, pleased that Jere had followed his advice without complaint.

Besides, Wren was doing quite well in the clinic on his own, providing medical advice and minor prescriptions and traditional healing methods when necessary. Jere was impressed at the autonomy his once timid slave had acquired, not to mention his almost intimidating proficiency and ease with managing the often panicked patients. By early evening, Jere felt ready to rejoin the world, and he stepped lightly into the clinic, pausing to watch his lover convince a mother and screaming child to leave, assuring her that the little boy would be just fine with a head cold until tomorrow morning.

Wren closed the door to the clinic. "Goddamn whiners," he muttered, jumping as he saw Jere.

Jere grinned at him. "Compassionate care at its best," he teased.

"I didn't realize you were up," Wren smiled back, walking over and kissing him on the cheek before starting to move away.

Jere caught him, pulling him back to kiss him properly. *"What could you possibly be running off to do?"*

Wren broke away slowly. "Clean up. Get ready for tomorrow morning. Start dinner to feed my starving doctor."

"Can I help?" Jere knew it was no use to argue; he'd never convince Wren to take a break when he was this determined.

"Go check on your patient," Wren suggested.

Jere knew it was just a nice way of telling him he'd be in the way if he tried to help. Still, Wren was right, he should see to the girl. "Has she been up and about much?"

"Um... no." Wren bit his lip for a moment, looking away before he finished speaking. "I've kept her sedated all day."

Jere frowned at him. "I guess I can't blame you. But still...."

"Jere, I couldn't," Wren said softly, his eyes begging Jere to condone his decision. "I can't. This is what you do, not me. If she came at me the way I've seen her come at you, I'm sorry, but I wouldn't just tell her to calm down, I'd knock her across the fucking room, and I know you don't want that. I'm willing to help, but handling her when she's upset, that's really more your area. I'm just keeping it at bay until you can deal with her."

Jere nodded. He understood—he had seen Wren interact with others, even in the clinic, and he wasn't exactly the compassionate type there, either. What he lacked in sympathy, he made up for in efficiency, and most patients viewed a reserved slave as more professional anyway. Isis was also excellent at pushing his buttons. "It's fine," he managed a smile. "I mean, I guess it *was* necessary."

Wren smiled at him. "Go check on her. Maybe put on any healing creams or anything you need before she wakes up? She should be out for another hour, at least."

"All right," Jere smiled back at him. He went into the supply room for the ubiquitous healing cream that would speed the rest of the girl's recovery process and headed back into the house, noticing that the door to Isis's room was locked despite the sedation. Wren was always on the careful side, but it still made him uncomfortable to see it.

He opened the door to find her lying there, seeming to sleep peacefully, looking small and vulnerable in his clothes. They had yet to order her anything to wear, because it was hard to guess her size, and she hadn't been exactly helpful in the process. She hadn't complained, either, and Jere didn't mind sacrificing some nightclothes to her.

He went over to the mattress where she slept, sitting on the floor next to it. He reached out and brushed her hair away from her face, lightly pressing his hand to her forehead. Her temperature was normal. He debated doing some sort of wellness scan, checking her injuries from the inside, but it seemed wrong, a betrayal of sorts. He had told her he would only do that to prevent her from dying, and she certainly wasn't at risk of that. He didn't want to admit it, but he was also a little afraid to meet the girl in a more coherent dream state. Nonetheless, he spread the healing cream across her arms and face, attending to the quickly healing skin from the split lip and burn marks from restraints that he had healed.

He hesitated for a moment, then undressed her carefully, revealing the still horrifying pattern of scars and old injuries covering her nearly from head to toe. Despite knowing she would be furious if she woke up, he retrieved a washcloth and water, gently sponging her skin off before applying the cream. The fever and sickness had taken their toll, covered her with sweat. He hoped she wouldn't notice it, or wouldn't be any *more* upset about it than she already was about everything else.

Fortunately, she weighed next to nothing, and he was able to maneuver her body around with ease, cleaning and treating the sensitive skin before dressing her in new, clean clothes. He briefly considered trying to do something with her hair, but he realized he had no idea how to address the mess, and he knew she would be angry enough as it was. He pulled the blanket up around her, wanting to be ill at how innocent and peaceful she looked as she slept. From a professional standpoint, he felt accomplished, proud of the work he had done in bringing the girl back to health, but the injuries that he had become aware of in the process were sickening. It was so much easier to care for patients who went home the next day, who had family or friends to help them recover from the types of damage that physical healing would never address.

Chapter 13

Compliance

Finished doing what he could, Jere went to the kitchen to bother Wren before dinner. Gone were the days when Wren hesitantly asked for his master to clear out; tonight he just tossed the head of one of the fish they were having for dinner at him. Jere tried to dodge it, missed, and ran off to change out of his fish-gut laden work shirt. He spent a few minutes poking at the stain, wondering what kind of fish it was before giving up and dropping it in the clothes hamper. The latest trend in agriculture was "land-fish," a hybrid animal that survived without the need for water. As useful as they might be in landlocked areas, Jere always found them a little dry for his taste, and the concept just struck him as unpleasantly unnatural. He returned to find dinner and Wren at the table, and smiled both at his boyfriend and at the lack of little leg-buds on what he saw were normal fish.

"Spoil all my fun," he teased, taking his seat.

Wren raised an eyebrow at him. "You know I hate people in my kitchen while I cook."

"But I like to watch you," Jere smirked. "You know, when you lean over the stove, I get a wonderful view of your ass!"

They teased and chatted through the rest of dinner. Jere was surprised by how relaxed and revitalized he felt. Sleep, he realized, was a good and necessary thing. They were enjoying dessert, a chocolate cake with rich, chocolate pools gathered on top of and inside of it, when they heard a door open.

Jere turned to see Isis standing there, hesitant, clutching the doorframe and looking like she might bolt at any minute. "Hey," he said, keeping his voice low.

"I asked you not to save me," she mumbled, looking away.

"I know," Jere said. "How are you feeling?"

She was silent for a moment, seeming to think about it. "A lot better. Nothing hurts anymore. You even... you even fixed things you couldn't see."

Jere nodded. "I tried to fix everything I could. I knew you wouldn't want me to do it again."

"I didn't want you to do it in the first place." She might have been trying to sound angry, but all that came across was exhaustion and defeat. "I'm starving, though. Apparently, when you ordered your right-hand-man to sedate me all fucking day, you didn't tell him to feed me."

"Isis, I—"

"He didn't order me to do anything," Wren cut in, shaking his head. "In fact, if I would have asked him, he wouldn't have let me do it. I sedated you because Jere... because *our* master was getting some rest, and I wasn't willing to deal with your bullshit. Don't act like he's the bad guy."

Jere was a bit thrown by Wren's choice of words, but he figured there was a reason behind it. Wren always seemed to have a reason for things like that, even if Jere didn't like the reason. He reminded himself to ask Wren about it later.

Isis nodded, slowly. "That does make more sense." She took a few steps toward the table, eyeing up the cake.

"Would you like a plate and a fork?" Wren asked. Jere tried to bite back a laugh.

Isis nodded. "I haven't had cake in a long time." Her eyes were fixed on it.

"What else would you like?" Wren asked, getting up. "You shouldn't just have cake for dinner, you haven't eaten in days."

"I can eat whatever the fuck I want!" Isis snapped, recoiling away and glaring. When she got no response from Wren or Jere, she calmed a bit. "Um, but yeah, I am hungry. Whatever's fine."

Wren nodded. "I'll heat up what we had for dinner. Give me a few minutes."

Isis nodded, sitting at her usual spot as far from Wren and Jere as possible.

"He just doesn't want you to get sick," Jere spoke quietly.

"I fucking know that," she replied, almost emotionless, despite her choice of words. "As always, he's right."

She was struggling, but she did sound at least a little more rational than she had before. That much pain was bound to bring out the worst in anyone, he figured. "I did wash you off and put some healing cream on you earlier."

"I know." A glare.

"I figured you wouldn't have let me if I would have asked."

"I didn't really have much of a choice, did I?" She kept glaring at him. "You got inside my head, too, you bastard."

Jere nodded. He wasn't sure if she was angry or sad or some bizarre combination. Strangely, she seemed a little disappointed. "I told you I wouldn't let you die." He thought about the cage he had seen her in, in her dream state. So protected, but so unable to reach out or free herself or anything. It seemed miserable.

She said nothing. Wren brought her food, which she devoured, following it with half of the remaining cake. For the most part, Jere and Wren just watched, amazed that someone so small could take in so much food at one time. When she finished, she looked at them, almost defensively.

"I was hungry!" she scowled.

Jere didn't reply. He looked at Wren, instead, noticing that he was nearly asleep at the dinner table. "I think we might be going to bed a bit early tonight," he mentioned, off-handedly.

"If I can't sleep, will you drug me again?" Isis challenged.

"Only if you're hurting yourself," Jere said, not rising to it. "Unless you'd like to be sedated."

She glared at him, but shrugged. "It was nice to be able to sleep," she admitted.

Jere was silent. She was almost, *almost* asking him for something. He kept his voice level. "I'll give you some sleep pills if you'd like—they'll help you sleep, but you won't be completely knocked out. You do need to rest up, finish the healing process."

Isis nodded. "Okay." She looked at him for a moment, then darted into her room.

Jere shook his head. "You should go to bed," he said to Wren, who looked about ready to fall asleep at the table. "Let me clean up and take care of things out here."

"Okay," Wren didn't protest. He leaned forward, kissed Jere ever so gently, and half-stumbled down the hallway.

Jere took a few minutes to clean up, placing the dishes in the sink, covering and refrigerating the leftovers, and wiping off the table. It was not as nice as Wren would have left it, but it would at least be passable for morning. He went through to the clinic, grabbed a sleep pill and a glass of water, and knocked lightly on Isis's door before opening it slightly. He found her sitting in the corner again. He walked over, setting the glass and the pill down near the mattress.

"Why did you save me?" she asked, looking confused. She glanced at the pill.

"Because," Jere said, feeling tired himself. "Because I'm a healer. Because you shouldn't be in pain. Because I didn't buy you to let you die."

"Why *did* you buy me?"

"I need help in the clinic," he answered, quite truthfully. "And I needed someone who wouldn't interfere with the lifestyle that Wren and I have."

"Fucked that up," Isis pointed out.

Jere wondered if she was referring to herself or to him. He figured both were true. He shrugged. "Better than hiring some free person and having them get in our way. There's very few people I let in this house. It wouldn't be safe. For Wren, I mean, for the type of relationship we have."

"Why did you buy *him*?"

"I didn't. I inherited him. And this house and my job."

"Oh. Would you have kept him if he was like me?"

Jere had been wondering this lately. He shrugged again. "Probably. Even if he hated me, I couldn't imagine the thought of selling him. Even when I first met him it wasn't an option."

"Why?" Isis actually risked glancing at him, but hardened her curious look into a glare once she realized he was looking back at her.

"The same reason I can't imagine selling you. Because he is a human being, and he was in pain, and at least I knew that if he was with me he wouldn't be hurt anymore. And then I realized he could be quite helpful. Long before we had any sort of 'relationship,' I was dependent on him just to get through the day. So much of my work here is tied up in him. So much of my life here is tied up in him."

"You can't fucking make me help you," she said, quite determined, as she reached for the sleep pill and downed it with the water. "You can hurt me, but you can't make me do a fucking thing."

"I never said I'd try," Jere said, shaking his head. "And I've said I wouldn't hurt you. Do you need anything else?"

"Before you lock me in for the night?" she snapped. "Fuck you."

"I'll take that as a no," Jere said, stepping out and locking the door behind him. He heard something hit the door, followed by breaking glass. Damn, he really should have taken that. More to clean up tomorrow.

But tonight? He wanted nothing more than to go to bed. He wasn't tired, but Wren was there, and Wren was warm and cuddly and soft. He smiled at the thought, tiptoeing into the bedroom, where Wren had left a light on for him. He stripped and crawled into bed, surprised when he felt Wren move to curl around him.

"Can't sleep?" he asked, running his hand down along Wren's hip, tracing the familiar surface.

"I was sleeping until I heard things breaking," Wren laughed. "She's still a fucking handful."

"Yeah..." Jere shrugged. "I keep thinking she'll come around."

"That's because you're hopeful and optimistic and a little crazy," Wren teased. "You're also the most understanding human being I have ever met."

Jere just smiled. "I couldn't imagine anything else," he admitted. "It's the way I was brought up."

"It would have been nice, I think, to grow up like you did," Wren mused. "I think that's why it's so frustrating to see you killing yourself to make her so happy. Nobody here would do that, Jere. I certainly wouldn't, and I mean, even if she wasn't a slave, a free child wouldn't get to act like that and get away with it."

Jere nodded. It used to seem so horrible, but they had talked about it so many times before, the strict, unforgiving culture, that he just accepted it. "I try to remember it, remember that you're not trying to be cruel to her, but it's hard to reconcile that compliance is valued so much more than compassion. It's so easy to forget that your first instinct when you look at that girl isn't to save her, because mine is, and back home, most people would be in agreement."

"That's about how I feel when I wonder why you aren't bringing her into line," Wren agreed. "It would be bad enough from a free person, but from a slave? It's dangerous. It's uncomfortable to see, unnatural, really, that a slave should act that way, and that her master doesn't respond as expected."

Jere shuddered, the image of land-fish stumbling about on little leg-buds coming into his mind unbidden. Unnatural things had a way of being repellant, no matter how much of an improvement they might be over the normal order. "Is that why you go out of your way to refer to me as master around her? You did it again tonight, and I don't think it was by accident."

"I think it's important that we all stay aware of the facts."

Jere was quiet, resisting the instant desire to contradict him, to say that he was wrong and that they could just avoid it in private. After all, he had promised Wren that he would listen, and this was exactly the kind of topic that he struggled to hear.

"You know, you can ask me why instead of fighting with yourself about it," Wren reminded him playfully. "I promise, I won't bite until we finish talking."

"Fine. Why? Why is it important that we bring up things that we don't want to think about? Why is it important that we keep putting each other in these roles?" Jere frowned, thinking about how little he wanted his own role. "It not like any of us is stupid. We know what we are. Isn't that enough?"

Wren smiled. "I wish it could be, and maybe in your world, it would be, but it isn't enough here. You can't keep flinching every time I, or Isis, call you 'master,' and nobody can afford to forget that we are slaves. If this were a temporary situation, maybe it would work, but I was under the impression that you were sticking around for a while."

"You know I am," Jere agreed instantly. His hopes for leaving Hojer had died long ago.

"Look, even when you thought it might be temporary, I always used to convince you to go along with my advice by telling you that it's the way things are done here," Wren reminded him. "And in the end, this is another one of those situations."

"Yes, and you have always been right," Jere agreed. "Even when I wished you weren't."

It grew quiet, and after a few minutes, Wren leaned over top of Jere, pinning him down lightly, and kissed him, deep, sensually, until they were both moaning.

"Mmm, thought you were tired," Jere teased, not wanting it to stop at all. He wanted nothing more to than to keep touching and kissing Wren all night. "Perhaps you should lie back and let me take care of this?"

"My pleasure," Wren grinned, rolling off and leaning back.

Jere glanced at him, shining under moonlight, his skin still pale, but healthy, soft, wonderful. So much had changed in the last year. No longer was Wren a starving, nervous boy, afraid to so much as be touched. Months of good food had filled him out so that he was healthy and strong, lean from all the running around he did with the help of the speed gift. Jere never forgot how much effort it took for Wren to trust him, even after so much time, and he was grateful that Wren had taken the chance to try so long ago. Jere traced a line of kisses across Wren's chest, down his stomach, playing around his waist for a moment, knowing how much it turned him on, how sensitive the skin there was for no real particular reason. Jere thought he knew all of the sensitive spots on Wren's body, but he was always eager to find more, exploring with his tongue and fingers whenever he got the chance.

After a few moments of teasing, he felt Wren's hands lightly running through his hair, and he smiled, sliding down, letting those familiar hands guide him where they wanted him. Wren was happy to lead, and Jere was just as content to let him. Jere's pleasure came from seeing Wren undone, seeing him forget to be nervous or tentative and just demanding that Jere give him what he wanted. Jere found his lover's cock already hard by the time he got to it, and he wasted no time wrapping his lips around it and swallowing him down.

Wren sighed as Jere pulled him deep into his throat. Jere knew exactly how Wren liked him to move, and he did so eagerly, feeling his own cock grow harder as he took Wren's deeper and fought to swallow around it. He kept up the pressure, dragging his tongue across every inch, and drawing one hand up between Wren's legs as well, trailing a finger up Wren's thigh and making him squirm. He paused for a minute, pulling back and looking into his lover's blue eyes, so full of need. He slipped his finger into his mouth, licking it as he had been working Wren's cock. Jere didn't have to look at Wren to know that he was watching, an eager expression on his face, but he looked anyway, because he loved knowing that he inspired that much need from Wren. He smiled as he leaned back down, positioned his mouth around Wren's cock again, and teased at his entrance with his finger.

Wren tensed a bit, and Jere backed off. It took time, sometimes, not that either of them minded. Jere would be happy to fuck Wren for hours, and on the occasions when they had done exactly that in the past, it had been every bit as rewarding as he had hoped. Now, he pulled his head back so that just the tip of Wren's cock was in his mouth, and he looked up and caught Wren's eyes. Carefully, intentionally, Jere settled his hands around Wren's hips. When Wren smiled and nodded, Jere slid him down, repositioning him, moving him to a better angle. Wren was pliant in his grip. Jere replaced his mouth with his hand, stroking Wren as his breathing sped up. Jere let his tongue wander lower, lapping across Wren's balls, teasing with his hands and his tongue, feeling the way his whole body warmed up. Jere moved slowly down to Wren's ass, his tongue flickering around the tight ring as Wren squirmed and moaned. Jere couldn't stop himself from smiling; he knew Wren loved this, and he loved it too.

He worked Wren with his tongue for a while longer before picking up the pace, jerking Wren's cock faster with his hand, thrusting his tongue in and out just as rapidly. Wren was practically radiating orgasm by the time Jere wet his finger again, this time finding no resistance when he slipped it inside.

Jere's finger found the perfect spot with practiced ease as his mouth descended on Wren's cock again. Wren cried out in pleasure and grabbed Jere's hair tightly, ensuring that he wouldn't go anywhere. Jere wouldn't dream of going anywhere, anyway; he was quite content to stay until he had finished working every last bit of pleasure and happiness out of Wren. He was confident that the moment was coming soon, as he felt the familiar signs of Wren approaching orgasm. Wren's whole body was shaking, rocking in Jere's hands, and he was making sexy gasping noises with every breath. The feeling alone was nearly enough to make Jere come, but he wouldn't, preferring to wait for Wren to orgasm first. It wasn't long before he felt Wren thrust against his finger a few more times, pull his head down forcefully onto his cock, and suddenly Wren was coming, groaning in pleasure.

Jere kept his lips wrapped around Wren, swallowing as he did, the taste of his lover quite welcome and familiar. He kept his hands still, but withdrew his finger gently as he felt Wren relax, the post-orgasm bliss loosening his muscles considerably. He waited for a few minutes, caressing the softening cock with his tongue, and then slid up next to Wren, who pulled him in for another kiss. Jere's cock was rock hard between them, and he reached for it, eager to find his own release while pressed up next to Wren.

"Let me," Wren whispered, half-asleep. "Love touching you."

Jere was happy to oblige. He leaned in for another kiss, at the same time shifting so Wren could reach him more easily. Wren's hand was warm and familiar and firm, and Jere was already worked up from pleasuring Wren. Jere found himself coming in seconds, reaching out to pull Wren closer as he did. A few quick swipes with a pillowcase later they were cleaned up and in each other's arms again, falling asleep.

Chapter 14

Escalation

Wren hoped that the girl would be a bit more cooperative and calm after being healed. Against all odds, he thought that perhaps her violent, rebellious attitude was at least somewhat related to her pain and injuries and fever.

It wasn't.

If anything, the next morning they discovered something far worse than the sick, raving mad child they had dealt with for the past few days.

"Jere, you'd better get in here," Wren yelled upon opening the door.

"What's up?" Jere sounded concerned, but Wren didn't feel the overwhelming flush of shock until his master had turned the corner to see what he saw.

The scene that greeted him was horrifying. Isis was sprawled out on her back in the middle of the room, bleeding from both wrists and shaking. Shards of bloody glass surrounded her.

"Jesus Christ," he muttered, rushing in and dropping to the floor.

Wren cursed under his breath, as he knew the blood would never come out of the pants, not to mention the carpet.

"Supplies, please?" Jere implored, already assessing the damage.

Wren sighed, speeding off to get what Jere would need. He wasn't sure why Jere was so bent on saving the girl. Except he *was* sure, because he knew Jere and he knew this was exactly what Jere would do. Jere was a good person, the type who cared much more about self-destructive girls than bloodstained carpets. As much as he respected Jere for trying, Wren wasn't sure how long he could put up with the stress it was causing them both. He resented Isis for intruding on their lives, and he had to fight with himself not to resent Jere for buying her and keeping her.

He watched, impassive, as Jere took the girl in his hands and healed her again. It was something to watch — no matter how many times he had seen it done, by Jere or by his previous master, the healing process was fascinating, seeing skin knit together on itself, pale faces regain color, gaping wounds stop bleeding. It made his speed gift seem almost insignificant by comparison, although it had been quite useful on many occasions. And the firesetting... well, he still didn't even know what to think about that.

It wasn't long before Jere finished, and he stood up quickly, lifting Isis up and carrying her over to the mattress.

"Could you clean up the glass, love?"

Wren bit back a snide remark, because the last thing he wanted to do right now was clean up glass, but for Jere's sake, he would remain quiet.

The lunch break hadn't gone over much better. After a bit of conning and sweet-talk, Jere got him to check on the girl, and when he came in, he found that she had literally punched and dug through the wall, pulled out a drywall nail, and gouged the skin on her arms with it. She was conscious this time, the nail being more difficult to manage than the glass. She started hurling obscenities at him, and he slammed the door and called for Jere, who showed up looking like a child about to be chastised.

"She's in there cutting herself up again," he said, quietly, hoping to conceal the anger that he had felt since first thing in the morning.

"With what?" Jere frowned at him. "I thought you got all the glass up?"

"I did!" Wren snapped, the accusation pushing him past his limit. "The fucking crazy thing tore the walls apart! Don't act like it's my fault!"

"Sorry," Jere mumbled, opening the door to see what was there.

"No!" Isis screamed, scooting back and banging her head against the wall. "No, don't fucking save me! Let me die, just fucking let me die!"

"Isis..." Jere said quietly. Wren didn't know how he could do it. If it would bring them peace, he would be more than happy to let her kill herself.

"Isis, this needs to stop. I'm not going to sit here and let you kill yourself."

"Then *you* kill me!" she wailed, still banging her head against the wall. "Why don't you? Beat me, hurt me, kill me, but god, stop trying to help me!"

"Isis, you're safe here..." Jere tried, getting nowhere. She banged her head harder against the wall, and his tone hardened. "Isis, for fuck's sake, if you hit your head against that goddamn wall *one* more time I will put you in a mind-bind!"

She stilled, instantly, going white. Wren found himself freezing in place as well, the latent threat of his master's power catching him quite off-guard. He had demanded that Jere be more firm with her repeatedly, and he had imagined feeling vindicated when it happened, but he had never expected his master to become this threatening so quickly or effectively.

"I told you before that you would be restrained if you couldn't stop hurting yourself and I meant it!" Jere snapped, still angry. "So, which is it? Medical restraints, injection, or mind-bind?"

"No," Isis whimpered, curling into a ball in the corner. "No, don't!"

Jere turned, and it was then that Wren noticed the tears in his eyes. "Get the bed restraints from the clinic."

Wren did as he was ordered, trying his best to ignore the screams and pleas from the bedroom. The logical part of his mind realized that Jere sent him for restraints so he wouldn't have to use the mind-bind, because Wren was quicker, maybe even so Wren had a chance to leave the room. But the part of his mind that he tried to keep locked tight against old memories threatened to overtake him, forcing him to remember and relive all the times that he had fetched restraints and chains for his master to use on him. He fought to extinguish the rage that came with the feelings, the sense that nothing was right and he shouldn't have to be a part of this. He wanted to hide, to tell Jere to do it himself, and only the realization that Jere really would do it himself after mind-binding Isis gave him the resolve to pick the restraints out of a drawer.

He returned quickly, and Jere directed him to put the restraints around the mattress, as they would to restrain someone for a medical procedure. Wren could only recall Jere using them in the clinic two or three times in the past year, and the fact that his hands were shaking didn't make it any easier to attach the straps. Once he finished, he stepped back, hoping he wouldn't be needed for anything else. He wasn't sure if he could handle it.

Jere took a step back toward the door, clearing the space between Isis and the mattress. "Isis," his voice was soft and calm again. "We discussed this. I can't have you hurting yourself, and I can't be here to watch you every minute. You won't give me a preference, but I find physical restraints to be the least restrictive, all right? They can be removed at any time, and they have no lasting side effects like chemicals do. You've made it very clear that you don't want me in your head."

She nodded, barely. "Don't fucking touch me," she whimpered, shaking now.

"I'll keep it as minimal as possible," Jere promised. "But you need to cooperate. I need you to lie on the bed, tighten the straps around your legs and one arm. I'll do the last one and check very quickly to make sure they're not too tight."

"No," Isis moaned. "You can't make me!"

Jere was silent a moment. "Yes. I can. But I'd really rather not. Please do as I asked."

"No!" she screamed, but did move toward the mattress. "Please, sir, please don't make me! Please, I won't do it again. You can punish me, I'm sorry, I'll do whatever you like."

Wren could see that it was a lie, but a desperate one. He almost felt bad for her, but a small part of him was feeling justified that some action was finally being taken with her. It was unfortunate that she was being restrained, but Wren was desperate for some sort of order to be reinstated. Everything had been too out of control for too long.

Jere sighed. "I'd like you to do as I asked. I'm not going to hurt you, Isis, I promise. I just need to make sure you're safe."

She sobbed as she did it, but she complied, fastening the straps around her ankles and right wrist, and placing the left one next to the remaining restraint, looking warily at both of them. Jere walked over slowly, pausing next to her.

"I'll be quick about it," he promised. Wren was surprised to see her nod her assent.

In seconds, Jere tightened the strap around her arm, then checked the others for tightness, adjusting both of the restraints on her ankles. "Wren or I will check on you regularly. If you need anything, let us know."

She said nothing, just lay there sobbing.

"I'm going to need to bandage your arms up," he said, suddenly. She nodded, still crying.

"I'm assuming you'd rather have me disinfect and bandage it than do mind healing?"

Again, Isis did nothing but nod and cry.

Wren was off and back quickly with disinfectant and bandages. He might not be able to do anything to stop the girl's behavior, but he could anticipate Jere's needs, and the small act of taking initiative helped him to feel more in control. The grateful smile that Jere mustered helped as well.

Jere knelt next to the bed. Most of the damage was to her right side — presumably, she was left-handed. "I'm sorry. This will sting a bit."

"I don't care," she muttered, defeated.

Jere cleaned her up, drawing pained whimpers, but little else. After he finished and was applying the bandages, he spoke softly. "Isis, this isn't punishment. I want you to know that. I wouldn't do that to you. I just need to make sure you're safe, okay? This is just temporary."

"I fucking hate you," she whimpered. "I fucking hate everything!"

Jere said nothing. He just stood up and walked out of the room without a word. Wren continued to stand there for a moment, absolutely lost and scared, and angry that it had come to this. His master was acting so unusual it was unnerving. His world was coming down around him because of the girl, and Wren barely knew how to process it, much less stop it. He hated feeling so helpless.

He found Jere in the clinic, curled up on one of the exam tables, the grown man looking very much like a child, clutching a pillow to his chest.

"This is wrong," he said tonelessly, hearing Wren come in.

"I know," Wren went to him, comforted him a little. It had almost no effect, but Wren was somewhat relieved by the fact that Jere was bothered by the actions he had been forced to take.

"Her dream state, Wren, it's terrible, she's miserable, even inside her own head, and she's so out of touch with reality. I don't know what to do with it; I've never seen someone so far gone! I feel horrible, like I'm making her that miserable, but I have to help her! All day, I see slaves come in and out of the clinic, and I can't help any of them, ever, but I can help her. I have to!"

Wren didn't necessarily agree with that, but he tried to see it from Jere's perspective, to validate his need to help. "You're showing her more kindness than anyone has in years, baby. Even if she can't accept it."

Finally, Jere sat up, looking at him. "Wren, what do I do? I've never fucked anything up this bad."

"Honestly, sir?" Wren said, startled by the address. He brushed it aside, assuming it was just lingering nerves from the intensity and discomfort brought on by handling the restraints. "She was on her way to the workhouse for a reason. You tried to show her a better life, but she obviously can't handle it. You could always—"

"I would *never* send her there!"

Wren was silent for a moment. It made sense that he wouldn't; Jere was too kind, and it wasn't like he needed the money. As much as Wren resented her presence, he doubted even he could send someone to a place like that. "You could... put her down."

Jere shook his head, eyes closed against the thought. "No. I won't. I mean, I'd do that before I sold her to that workhouse, but I don't want to let that happen. I have to be able to figure something else out."

Wren put his arms around him. "If anyone can, it would be you. And I'll do whatever I can to help you. I promise."

"You shouldn't have to," Jere muttered, leaning into his embrace. "I appreciate it, I just wish... I just wish things were different."

Wren did too. If it had been up to him, the girl would have gotten the beatings she begged for, would have been bound and gagged until she learned to appreciate not being so. When that didn't work, she would have been sold off in a few days, or put down. It might have made him a cold or awful person, but he had himself to take care of, and he worried about Jere as well. It was the fact that it was so important to Jere that kept Wren going, that gave him the strength to fight alongside him. He knew that Jere would do the same, if the situation was reversed.

In addition to providing quiet, calm support for Jere, the best Wren could do was check on Isis, which was starting to be the most dreaded part of each and every day. He thought she would be better once she was restrained, but the second time he went to take his turn to check on her he found her clawing at the palms of her hands, biting the skin on her shoulders, jerking at the wrist restraints until her wrists were purple and starting to chafe, and banging her head against the mattress in a frantic effort to hurt herself. He gave up. He couldn't talk to her. Couldn't bring himself to talk to the kind of person who would willingly bring so much harm and pain to herself. He spent so many years trying to avoid that kind of pain, he hated that she would bring it upon herself willingly. He understood the desire to die; he had shared that same desire for years. But he couldn't deal with the disruption she was causing, and he couldn't deal with the memories that she was dredging up. Wren shook his head, walked out, and got Jere, filling him in briefly.

"Get me a sedative injection," Jere said softly.

Wren returned quickly, handing the needle over to his master without a word. He watched as Jere took it and made his way over to Isis, who screamed and wailed her protests.

"I'm so sorry," he said, kneeling down to be at the level of the mattress she was strapped to. "I think you'd prefer this to the mind-bind."

Isis sounded like a wounded animal, screeching out her pain as Jere took her arm, held it as still as possible, and injected her carefully. In a few minutes, she had stilled, her eyes closing against her will. Still sitting next to her, Jere picked up the edge of the blanket that she had thrown aside and wiped her face clean with it, soothing away the tears as he did.

When the sedation wore off a few hours past dinnertime, and the screaming resumed, Jere was prepared. He pulled another syringe from his pocket, entered the bedroom, and came out only moments later with a drawn look.

"It will last the night," he explained, his eyes looking sad and dead. Wren followed him into their bedroom, putting his arms around him and holding him close as they both fell into a restless sleep.

Chapter 15

Kieran Visits

Wren couldn't throw the chilling feeling that filled his body whenever he thought about the girl in restraints. Or sedated. Or both. He lay cuddled next to Jere all night, barely sleeping, trying to stave off nightmares and memories that he'd rather not be having.

Which had been worse for him, years ago? Being beaten or being restrained, tied up, chained?

It was hard to pick out which was worse. On any given day, he could probably have chosen, picked one or the other. He could have pointed out how one aggravated and exacerbated the other. The memories of both were terrifying and awful. Restraints made him feel helpless, vulnerable, exposed. He couldn't imagine it, now; even though he and Jere liked to play games where Jere got tied up, Wren's body and soul reacted so strongly to the idea that he would never even mention it. Jere, being the attentive man that he was, would never suggest such a thing either, and Jere's attempts to explain why he liked it so much never quite made sense to Wren, although he had to admit he liked tying his boyfriend up whenever he got the chance. He had come to terms with it months ago, and the best he could come up with was that he liked it because Jere did, and he liked it because Jere was safe.

At least when he was being beaten there was a sense of freedom, of movement, a sense that maybe you'd get a chance to move away or escape, even if you knew better than to ever try such a stupid thing. The restraints were just unyielding, merciless. Restraints were a constant reminder of pain, of wrongdoing, of utter helplessness, and the punisher didn't even have to be there to witness it.

He remembered being in them for hours, days even, locked away in the cellar, restrained for no other reason than because Burghe was evil and cruel. He remembered the pain of feeling his joints stretched beyond their proper capacity, the aching of his bones as they pressed into the floor, the cold and unhappiness and the feeling that it would never end. He remembered his sanity slipping, and looking back, he wondered just how similar he may have been to Isis at the time. He had wished he would die, too, although he rarely asked for it, and only tried that once to do it on his own. That had been such a key part of the fire, the hope that he would die and everything would end. Death seemed so simple, so perfect. He was so glad it hadn't ended that way.

Wren's racing thoughts were interrupted by the sun coming up, and a glance at Jere's watch told him it was probably time to get up anyway. He slipped out of bed carefully, trying not to rouse Jere just yet, as he had tossed and turned most of the night.

Their morning routine went as usual, and Wren tried to pretend he didn't know that Jere stopped off to sedate Isis again before she even woke up. He went into the clinic and allowed himself to become blissfully absorbed in his work, the familiar tasks and repetitive actions calming and soothing him in a way that nothing else quite managed to do.

He was filling out some paperwork with just this sort of blissful absorption when he heard two hands slap down on the counter. Reflexively, he ducked, wincing at the display of fear.

"Sorry!" he heard a peppy female voice chime from the other side of the counter. "I forgot, but I'm just so excited to be home!"

Wren shook off the startle and looked up to see Kieran. There were other patients waiting in the office, so he kept his smile small and his voice low. "Hello, Miss Kieran. Very nice to see you."

Kieran scowled playfully at the address. "*Wren!*" she complained. "Don't make me vomit!"

Wren allowed himself to grin back at her. "Are you planning to stay a while, Miss?" He hadn't really expected her to come back so soon; he didn't think that the university had a break at this time of year.

Kieran shook her head. "I'm home for my cousin's wedding,"

she said. "Heading back into the city tomorrow, thankfully, but in order to make it to the ceremony and breakfast in the morning, I had to take a speed train out today, so I figured I may as well take an earlier one and visit you and Jere and see how things are going and get an update on stuff, you know, and, oh, maybe stay the night here, even?"

Wren wanted to laugh and tease her about not standing up to her family, but he was still in front of other people, so he kept a straight face and walked over to the door that would let her through to the clinic. "Perhaps you should speak with my master," he said, a smirk on his face as he let her in.

As the door closed behind her, she stuck her tongue out at him. "Is Jere busy right now?"

Wren nodded, guiding her to the entrance to the house. "The clinic is always busy since we started treating the slave population. Almost more than Jere can handle, really, but he's trying his best."

They walked through to the house, shutting the door behind them and creating a safe space for both of them to talk.

"Is he gleaning?" Kieran asked, seating herself at the table with familiarity.

Wren nodded. "Probably not as much as he should be, but yes, he is doing it, and it's helping a little bit."

Kieran looked at him skeptically. "You're under quite a bit of stress, too, I see."

Wren frowned at her. "Jere and I have both asked you not to use your gift on us."

Kieran laughed. "Wren, for fuck's sake, I don't need any gift to see that you're exhausted! Your eyes are bloodshot, you have bags under them, your shirt is on backwards and it looks like you didn't comb your hair today. Or maybe yesterday, either."

Wren blushed. Was he really that undone? "Sorry," he muttered.

"But now that you mention it..." Kieran got a funny look on her face. "Something is off in this house. Something that's not you or Jere. Maybe not even one of the patients. Is there someone new here?"

Wren was quiet for a moment. Delivering the news to Kieran

had a high likelihood of going very badly, and he was tempted to get Jere and make him tell her, since buying Isis had been his idea in the first place. "Uh... Jere didn't tell you?"

"Tell me?"

"About the other slave he got?" Wren gave in. She would find out soon enough, anyway.

"What!" Kieran gasped, outraged. "You're not serious!"

Wren was silent. He knew she'd feel it out on her own if he didn't tell her.

"Oh my god, Wren, why!" she demanded, eyes wide.

"He rescued a real young kid, couldn't turn her away when he saw how she was being treated." Wren was a little surprised that he was actually defending Jere's decisions, given how many times he had opposed them himself. "We need some help around here, and Jere was also looking for a bit of, well, of an energy source. For when gleaning isn't enough."

Kieran's face showed her distaste at the statement.

"He also wanted a female to help when women are being examined, especially slave women and girls," Wren continued. "Come on, you know Jere, he has all sorts of good, nice reasons for doing everything."

"I guess," Kieran conceded. "It's just, I mean it's wrong, any support of the system...."

"Stop," Wren rolled his eyes. "It isn't like she wasn't a slave already."

Kieran nodded. "So, where is she?"

Wren shrugged. "In her room."

Kieran looked at him for a moment, her eyebrow raised. "Medicated?" she guessed correctly. "Is she ill?"

Wren held his hands up. "Sort of? I don't know. She was awfully beat up when we got her, and wouldn't let Jere heal her for days, and so now she's healed, but she keeps trying to kill herself — cutting her wrists, hurting herself — so I guess you might say she's ill."

"And so Jere's keeping her *sedated*!"

Wren just nodded. In some ways, he felt the same way, outraged that Jere would do such a thing, but the peace and quiet over the past two days had been enough to turn his outrage into tolerance, even relief. "She's up for a while around mealtime, and to shower and stuff."

Kieran stared at him, disbelieving.

"It's just temporary," Wren rushed to explain, even though he didn't really know that for sure. "Just until she calms down, and Jere gets through to her. Kieran, she clawed through the wall and pulled out a nail to stab herself with. She's desperate to die, but Jere's convinced he can save her. And, still, we have the clinic to run. He bought her to make things easier, but things have been twice as hard, here and in the clinic."

Kieran nodded. "Yeah, I guess you should get back to that, right? I'm guessing Jere's probably too busy to come and explain himself until the clinic closes?"

Wren nodded. Judging from the outrage on Kieran's face, it was probably better if she had a few hours to calm down anyway.

"I guess I have some studying to do," Kieran said, still looking dissatisfied. "Let Jere know I'm here?"

Wren nodded, heading back into the clinic. Perhaps it would do Jere good to talk to someone else about Isis, hell, perhaps Isis would benefit from talking to someone other than them. He figured the situation couldn't get much worse.

Jere was torn between feeling pleased and horrified when Wren told him that Kieran was visiting. While he was eager to talk to her, her reaction to his buying a slave was something he figured he could live without. He couldn't stop the wince that came across his face as he asked Wren if Kieran had noticed the new addition to the house. Wren's smirk didn't help him feel much better.

"She's really going to give me shit for this, isn't she?" he mumbled, prompting another laugh from Wren.

When they returned from the clinic, Jere was unsurprised to find the college student curled up on their couch, napping.

"Is she staying here?" Jere asked.

Wren nodded. "Yep. Just tonight, though. The room she was staying in over the summer is all ready to go."

Jere kissed him. "Perfect." He took off to have a shower while Wren made dinner, and was greeted by a half-awake Kieran when he returned to the dining room.

"I see you're acclimating to Hojer and enjoying the luxuries of the slave trade?" she teased.

Jere could tell that she was only half-joking. He sighed. "It had to happen," he dismissed her. "I know Wren told you why. Besides, she can be another warrior for the cause."

Kieran glared at him. "Don't act like this is a joke, Jere, this is serious!"

Wren brought out food, dropping to sit unceremoniously next to Jere while listening to the two free people in the house argue. "You should maybe go and let the topic of discussion come and eat," he said to Jere, quite pointedly.

With a sigh, Jere stood up, moving toward Isis's room.

"What, is she locked in?" Kieran asked, sounding shocked.

"Er... something like that," Jere mumbled. He was a little unsettled when Kieran followed him.

He unlocked the door and tried to slip in without opening it enough for Kieran to see. He had no such luck. Kieran was on his heels, and she gasped when she saw Isis restrained to the mattress.

Jere winced as he felt a light punch on his arm.

"You are not tying her up!" Kieran protested. "Jere, what the hell, how could you!"

Jere unfastened the restraints, freeing the girl who was fortunately still sedated.

"This is just repulsive, I mean, just because she's not acting the way you want her to—"

"She's trying to kill and mutilate herself," Jere said quietly as he stood up, hoping to bring the noise level in the room down a little. "I don't like it either, but it's the only thing I've found that can keep her from hurting herself too badly."

"Well, why do you need to sedate her *and* tie her up *and* lock the door!"

"In case one wears off," Jere answered, though he did have to admit, it seemed a bit foolish now, even to him. "Perhaps I can reconsider that."

Isis, presumably woken by the raised voices, started screaming before she even opened her eyes.

"Dammit," Jere muttered.

"Who the fuck is she? Who the fuck is this bitch! Get her out of here, get her away from me, I don't fucking want her looking at me!" Isis thrashed around on the mattress for a few minutes before seeming to realize that she was no longer restrained, at which point she bolted across the room to the furthest corner from Jere and Kieran.

"Get her out of here! Get all of them out of here! Jere, please, don't let them hurt me, please!"

Frowning, Jere gestured for Kieran to leave. "Sorry," he mumbled, as she rushed out without a word, unusual for the typically verbose girl. He turned to the terrified slave in the corner, encouraged by the fact that she had turned to him for any sort of protection or reassurance. "It's all right, she's leaving."

"What about all the other fucking assholes in here?" she sobbed, looking frantic.

"There's no one else in here," Jere forced his voice to stay calm. "Just you and me. Kieran left, and Wren is still in the kitchen."

"Other people!" Isis protested weakly.

"They're gone, too," Jere gave in, hoping to calm her a bit. "I'm sorry. I shouldn't have let someone else come in here."

Isis said nothing, but continued to shake and whimper.

"Do you want something to eat?" Jere asked. "I can bring it in here if you'd like."

She nodded.

"Promise not to hurt yourself while I'm gone?"

Another nod.

Jere left, retrieved some food for her, and brought it back before anything else, placing the plate, spoon, and plastic cup of water on the floor for her to collect once he left the room. He knew she wouldn't come near him, no matter how much more she seemed to trust him than anyone else.

"Kieran's a friend," he said softly. "She's an anti-slavery activist who's working and going to school in Sonova, where I moved from. I promise, she would never hurt you."

"No," Isis mumbled, rocking back and forth to calm herself

down a bit.

"I know, I'm sorry," Jere said again. "I won't let someone come in here again without your permission. I just didn't think about it."

"Don't let her hurt me," Isis whimpered.

"I won't," Jere promised. "I won't let anyone hurt you. I promise."

Jere waited for a few moments, wishing he knew what else to say or do. He left Isis's room, leaving the door open, and joined Wren and Kieran at the table, still shaken.

"That's why you're sedating her, then," Kieran remarked, more understanding now that she'd seen it herself.

Jere nodded. "I wish I didn't have to. This isn't even the worst of it." He looked closely, realizing that Kieran had tears in her eyes. "You okay?"

She laughed, contrary to her appearance. "The second she regained consciousness she flooded me with emotions. It was all I could do not to huddle in a corner and sob and scream alongside her."

Jere was quiet for a moment. He had never considered just how strongly an empath would feel the emotions of someone like Isis. It was easy to overlook.

"The fucked up thing is, it's almost all regular, plain old emotion," Kieran continued. "No psychic projection at all. Which, I'm glad; she'd kill me if she had that. Jere, you realize, don't you, how terrified she is?"

"I had an idea," Jere nodded. It seemed difficult to miss.

"She's terrified of everything, and angry, and completely and utterly hopeless that anything will ever change," Kieran explained. "It's like she just has this void where any hope or happiness should be, and even something little like an unexpected visitor can suck her down into so much darkness. Be careful with her, Jere, or you'll lose her."

"Lose her, like how?"

"Like she'll go crazy and never come back," Kieran clarified.

The rest of the night passed in relative calm. Kieran was only slightly put off by the emotional overload Isis presented, and a few glasses of wine helped to dim the signal, or so she said. They discussed the current state of the activist group Kieran was involved in, and what sort of work she was doing now, and small but noticeable effects that medical treatment was having across a variety of slave states. One of the first states with medical doctors providing services to slaves had recently passed a law mandating that owners take their slaves to human doctors instead of veterinary practitioners. Slowly, the tides were turning toward seeing slaves as human again. It was a paradigm shift, it was a lot of work, and it was a seemingly endless challenge, but even those small steps were important.

Jere listened with new interest. Kieran's rants always seemed so idealistic, so disconnected from Jere's life in Hojer, but since the conversation he and Wren had the other night about the importance of remembering who was master and who was slave, Jere had been more attentive to politics in general. As Wren had pointed out, he really couldn't just keep trying to ignore the facts, especially not when he had doubled his role of master by buying another slave.

Wren bid them an early goodnight, claiming that he was tired. Jere was pretty sure that he just wanted to give him a chance to talk to Kieran by himself, to seek support and comfort.

"This has to be hard for him," Kieran commented, once they were alone.

Jere nodded. "Gift or just observation?"

Kieran grinned. "Would you kick me out of your house tonight if I said both?"

Jere shook his head. He had assumed as much; despite his and Wren's request that Kieran not use her gift on them, he knew how hard it was to avoid using one's gift.

"It's just a habit. I check pretty much everyone," Kieran admitted. "And I'm getting even better at doing it without detection. But you and Wren both just sort of stick it out there for anyone to see, anyway. Well, you more than Wren."

"Thanks," Jere mumbled. They were silent for a few moments.

"Be careful with him, Jere," Kieran cautioned. "He loves you so fucking much—don't hurt him."

"I wouldn't—"

"Not on purpose, no, but just be careful."

Jere nodded. It was true, what she said, and he wished she could have been here over the past few weeks, could have helped him and

Wren see eye to eye when things were rough. It had been better for a few days now, but he knew that Wren was tense and angry sometimes, and he didn't talk about it. Jere just felt like he was in over his head, lacking the energy to do more than accept Wren's insistence that he was fine.

"Everyone in this house is so uncertain and afraid of what could be — Jere, as much as I hate to say it, you're the master, you've gotta make things clear," Kieran pressured him. "It's not enough to make vague promises. Let them both know what you're thinking and stop keeping so fucking much to yourself! You can't do this on your own, you know, not when there are two other people living here."

Jere mostly agreed. He and Wren had been trying to talk more openly about their problems, and it had helped. Still, he didn't even know how to bring half of his concerns up with either of the other people who lived in the house. "I just keep thinking that Wren shouldn't have to deal with this. It was my idea in the first place; he told me she was a bad idea and I did it anyway, so I should be the one dealing with the consequences."

"Has Wren told you that he doesn't want to help?" Kieran asked, surprised.

"No," Jere admitted. "He more or less told me that I was stupid to try to do it on my own and that he was going to help whether I liked it or not. But I still try not to bother him with it more than I have to, and I still think that he should be able to stay out of it."

"I don't know how you've deluded yourself into thinking that would work, but it's a terrible idea," Kieran pointed out bluntly. "Unless you keep them in separate houses, Wren *has* to be involved, and even then, he has to deal with you, and I don't need any sort of gift to see that you're under a lot of stress and pretty emotional about the whole situation. Wren has to be feeling it too."

Jere nodded. He wished it wasn't true, that Kieran would tell him that Wren was doing fine and seemed completely unconcerned by the situation, but he knew better. "I just wish he didn't feel so pressured."

"And Isis?" Kieran prodded. "How are you feeling about her?"

"Fucking spectacular."

Kieran stared him down, and he was pretty sure she was using her gift on him, but he didn't really care. He wasn't even sure how he felt about Isis.

"Well, of course you're confused!" Kieran confirmed his suspicions about the gift. "You're confused and sad and frustrated and angry. You know, it's okay to be angry at her. She disrupted your life, from the looks of it. I'd be angry, too. But you're also strangely hopeful. You really think you can help her."

Jere nodded. He did, and his biggest fear was that he wouldn't. The alternatives... no, he wouldn't even think of those.

"You're in luck," Kieran grinned. "Because she trusts you. Just a little, but she does. Not just that you'll heal her like a good doctor, or that you'll chase strangers away, but she trusts that you'll take care of her. You're her master, and she accepts it. Build on that. It's your only in."

They talked for a while longer, continuing to discuss how things had been going in the past few weeks. Jere was surprised by how much better he felt after talking with someone outside of the house. As much as he loved Wren, sometimes an outside perspective was more useful, and having a neutral party to bounce ideas off of made him feel considerably better about everything. Kieran bugged him about being more social, and he bugged her about having more fun—after all, it was her first year at University, she shouldn't be spending *all* her time organizing! By the time they went to bed, they were both exhausted, yet slightly revitalized. Jere tried to hold on to the feeling for the future.

Chapter 16
Reactions

The following week passed slowly, painfully. Jere felt sick nearly every day as he continued to shoot chemicals into Isis's veins to sedate her. It got easier for a day or two, out of sheer familiarity, but the fact that he was growing accustomed to it made it all the worse.

Isis, however, did seem to be calming down a bit. The first few days had been rough; she started screaming and injuring herself immediately after waking up, escalating quickly to the point where Jere was forced to sedate her again. After that, it became routine; she would wake up a bit hazy, have something to eat, visit the bathroom and maybe shower, if Jere could convince her or bribe her to do even that most basic grooming. Without encouragement, she preferred lying in bed, heedless of hygiene. Wren had been thoughtful enough to pick up an assortment of brushes and combs and hair products, but they all sat untouched in the bathroom, where they wouldn't be turned into tools for Isis to harm herself with. After completing these limited tasks, she would return to the bed, where she would hold out her arm and glare until she was pricked with the needle. Jere couldn't tell if she wanted it or not. She screamed, cursed at him, and made a general nuisance of herself, but she complied. He thought he might even have seen a smile one day when he told her he wouldn't use the tie-down restraints anymore. He couldn't bring himself to do it, and it was just one more thing that weighed on his conscience.

For the most part, she was incoherent, inconsolable, and destructive. There were, however, a few moments of lucidity interspersed.

Jere went in at night, as was becoming routine, to most probably sedate her, maybe give her a sleep pill if she was feeling cooperative, and lock her in for the night.

She was sitting in her usual corner, banging her head back against the wall.

Jere shook his head. "Knock it off," he ordered, torn between being relieved and feeling like a brute when she froze. He softened his voice. "I don't want you hurting yourself."

"Then why don't you hurt me?" she challenged, wrapping her arms around her knees. "Why don't you hit me, or beat me, or whip me ever? Everyone else does, so obviously it's what needs to be done. I'm a problem, and that's what you do to problems. Why are you waiting?"

Jere grinned at the absurd request. It wasn't a new request, she had asked numerous times before, to the point that Jere was beginning to understand that she believed she really did deserve it. "Like I've said—I don't do things that way."

"Ha. Right. You just lock me up and shoot me up with drugs and turn me into some sort of fucking zombie prisoner. Don't you think they've tried that before? It doesn't work. It doesn't make me better."

"It's just to keep you safe," Jere replied. "You'll be safe here. It will get better."

"Fuck you. No, it won't!" Isis snapped, pointedly turning away from him a bit, although still never taking her eyes off of him. "We'll just play this stupid game until you get too fed up with me, and *then* you'll start hurting me and *then* you'll sell me. I just wish you'd get on with it already."

Jere sat quiet for a moment. Once or twice, he had tried reasoning with her, attempted to convince her that there might be other possibilities than being hurt or sold, but it only made her more agitated. "What's the plan for tonight, then?"

He did rather want to go to bed.

Isis shook her head, shrugged a little, then shook her head again. "I don't fucking know. I'm too tired to try to piss you off tonight. Which is fucking stupid, all I do is sleep."

Jere continued to be surprised by her insightful revelations. For as out of control as she was, she sometimes seemed to know exactly what she was doing. "Sedatives aren't the same as sleeping... plus, you wear yourself out when you're awake."

"Yeah."

Jere waited for a few minutes before pushing a cup of water and a sleep pill over toward her. "It's up to you," he said calmly.

"You drug me all the fucking time now!" Isis snarled resentfully. "Even when I'm not doing anything!"

"I've only ever done it when you're hurting yourself or when you ask me to," Jere reminded her, surprised by the accusation. He thought he had tried so hard to be fair, and in the past few days, she had started to look somewhat content to take the pills he gave her to keep her calm.

"I never ask!" Isis protested. "I know it's going to fucking happen, and that's why I do it! You come in here all goddamn compassionate and shit, and I know you're gonna do it to me before you leave, I just hope that maybe I can make you angry enough to do other things first!"

"Like beat you?" Jere asked, almost rhetorically.

"It'll happen eventually," Isis spat out. "Maybe it'll fix me." With a glare, she grabbed the cup and the pill and threw them across the room. "I'll do the same thing if you put a fucking needle near me!"

Jere leaned back against the wall, dropping to sit. If he waited long enough, he was sure she would blow up and give him a reason to justify injecting her with a sedative. She was right. He did drug her all the time. It was terrible, but it was true. He didn't know how else to handle it.

Isis sat, fuming, tears running down her face which she tried unsuccessfully to wipe away on her shoulder. "Jere?" she said softly, after a minute.

Jere was surprised. She rarely ever used his name without adding a string of curse words to it. "Yeah?"

"Do you think I'll ever...? I mean, would you..." she fumbled, looking down at the floor, at the wall, anywhere but at him. "I fucking hate being locked in here!" she settled, sounding defeated.

"I'm sorry." He meant it.

"I just, I won't go anywhere, I won't do anything, I wasn't really even trying to run that one day, I promise, I just..." she let her voice trail off. "It doesn't fucking matter what happened, does it?"

Jere drummed his fingers against the floor for a second. Did it matter? He was pretty sure that it did. And he doubted she was trying to run. He had scared her. Wren had scared her. And, for as much as she was trying to hurt herself these days, she had been worse then.

"It doesn't matter," Isis mumbled. "Just fucking lock me in. Put the restraints back on too, while you're—"

"Do I have your word that you won't leave this house?" Jere cut her off. "The clinic is off-limits as well."

Isis looked at him warily. "You mean it?"

Jere nodded. He might regret it, but he already regretted locking her up every night, and the fact that she had risked asking him a favor made him wonder if what she needed was a little leniency, a chance to prove herself.

"But why? I mean, I'm still fucking up all the time. You still have to restrain me and drug me and—"

"Do I have your word?" Jere asked again.

Slowly, she nodded.

"All right. It's settled." Jere dug into his pocket and pulled out the keys that locked the door, sliding them across the floor to her.

"You probably have another set somewhere," Isis muttered.

"I don't." Jere waited, not speaking another word for a few moments. He half expected her to throw a fit again, to force him to change his mind, but she didn't. She pulled the keys closer and stared at them, a look of amazement on her face. After a while, she glanced at the door, then back at Jere.

"If you leave here, and you're lucky, Wren or I will catch you and bring you back. If you leave here and you're unlucky, someone from the police force in town will catch you, and I won't be able to protect you. In either case, you won't have this chance again."

Isis fiddled with the keys. "Why are you taking the risk, then? Sounds like an awful lot of work for you, either way."

"Because," Jere shrugged. "I want to help you. To make this easier for you. I'm doing my best to give you everything you ask for."

"Not everything," Isis pointed out quickly.

"I'm not going to hit you!" Jere was just as exasperated by the request as he had been all the other times. He collected himself. "I want to make you comfortable here, as much as possible."

Isis nodded. She retrieved the sleep pill from the floor and swallowed it dry. "Can I have a door that locks on my side so nobody can come in?"

Jere smiled. It was nice to hear reasonable requests, even if it did highlight how paranoid she was. "Not just yet. Maybe after you stop trying to hurt yourself so much, okay? Are you scared about someone coming in?"

"I'm not fucking scared of anything!" she snapped, instantly defensive. Her bravado was withdrawn quickly when Jere didn't respond. "It's just... it's not fair."

"I'll let you know," Jere promised. "I'll get Wren to change it around."

Isis scowled at the mention of Wren's name. "He hates me."

Jere didn't reply. It was pretty true. "You cause a lot of disruption. Wren doesn't like disruption."

Isis yawned, and Jere knew the sleep pill had kicked in. He was glad.

"You really won't lock me in?" she pressed him.

"No," Jere stood and walked toward the door. "Please don't make me regret it."

He went back to the bedroom that he and Wren shared, finding a very angry looking boyfriend sitting on their bed, glaring at him.

"I overheard," Wren said. "I think it's a terrible idea."

Jere couldn't take it. He couldn't take the accusations and defensiveness and attacks from everyone. Even when Kieran had visited, though she had given him some hope at the end, she had attacked him at first. It was too much. "Yeah, well, it's not your fucking decision to make, is it?"

Wren said nothing. Jere's question had been mostly rhetorical, but Wren's pointed silence reminded him painfully how out of line the question had been. He was consumed with guilt as the familiar blue eyes glared at him resentfully, but on the other hand, if Wren wasn't saying anything back, maybe this whole argument would be over.

"It's on me. I'll take care of it," he added, trying to salvage the situation. That was all he wanted, from the start, to take care of everything. He just wished Wren could see it from his perspective instead of taking everything so personally.

Wren shook his head and lay down, facing away from Jere. He was still silent.

Jere cursed, quietly. He stripped his clothes off, turned off the light, and climbed into bed, fully aware that Wren was as far off to his side of the bed as physically possible. Jere wouldn't push him. He lay there quietly, wishing he could sleep. Wishing Wren would talk to him.

"Sometimes, lately, it's like you don't even fucking think before you speak to me."

Jere decided sleep would definitely have been preferable. "I'm sorry."

"Goddammit, Jere, I thought we agreed to be partners on this? You need my fucking help, why can't you just goddamn listen to me for once?"

"I do listen to you. I am listening to you," Jere protested quietly, relieved when he felt Wren turn toward him again. "That doesn't mean that I always have to agree with you, though."

"Right, because it's your fucking decision to make, not mine," Wren snapped.

Jere wondered if Wren had turned toward him just so he could make it clear how angry he was. "I didn't mean it like that," Jere tried to explain. "I meant... you're not the one who goes in there and locks her up every night. You won't be the one who sees the state she's in tomorrow morning. If this was a bad idea, I'll take the blame, I'm doing what I think is right."

"And you never thought of running it past me first?" Wren muttered. "You know I'm not a fan of surprises, and you know that if we wake up and she's gone tomorrow, I'll be right there helping you look for her, regardless of who takes the blame."

Jere considered it, knowing that Wren would be next to him in the search, if it came to that. "I didn't talk to you about it first because I wasn't planning it. I was just talking with her tonight, trying to get her to calm down, and she asked me to leave the door open. I thought it was a good idea."

"Did you even think to ask me what I thought?" Wren asked. "Or did you know I wouldn't approve?"

"I just went ahead and did it because it seemed to make her feel better," Jere admitted, avoiding the question. He hadn't thought to ask Wren, because he had been too busy grabbing at what seemed like the first reasonable request Isis had made in days.

"Do you really think this will help her?" Wren pressed, looking a little less angry.

Jere shrugged. "I don't know. It's too early to tell, really. And what I'm doing now clearly isn't working. Maybe it's time to start trusting her a bit."

"Ha," Wren said, shaking his head.

"Well, what would you suggest?" Jere pleaded. "I don't even know where to begin. All I can do now is keep her alive until something better comes along—if she were a free person back home, I'd take her to a psychiatric hospital!"

"Honestly?" Wren raised an eyebrow. "She's waiting for you to beat her. Hurt her. It's how she organizes her life, by that pain, and if you're not giving it to her, you're lying."

"She won't trust me if I hurt her!"

"She won't trust you if you don't!"

Jere was silent. He didn't know if he could back down on this issue.

"Jere, it's all she knows. She's expecting you to react to her outbursts, and not by giving her a pill and telling her everything will be okay!" Wren pressed. "I mean, a part of me would like to beat her senseless for being so goddamn much trouble, but another part... Jere, you looked through those papers, you *know* how long she's been enslaved."

Jere wished he didn't. At Wren's insistence, he had read over the record a week or so ago, after things started getting out of control. Seven. Seven years old when she was taken. She was only fifteen now, which meant that she had been a slave longer than she hadn't. The record didn't contain any details of her time with any of her masters, but there were plenty, and young girls weren't always safe when they *weren't* slaves.

"It will help her feel normal. It's what she's expecting from you,"

139

Wren finished, looking away.

Jere reached across the distance between them, lightly catching Wren's hand in his own. "Is that... is that how you felt?" They had so rarely talked about those days.

"Honestly, sometimes I still catch myself feeling that way," Wren's voice held a note of regret, sadness. "It's stupid, but it's easier to *know* you're going to be beaten severely than to worry whether you'll be beaten severely. Hope doesn't make things better, Jere, it just hurts more when it inevitably gets crushed."

"I just can't accept that!"

"Well, then, be glad you were never a slave!" Wren snapped back.

"Why can't it be different?" Jere argued. "It's not that I think you're wrong, I just — can't I try this my way?"

Jere sighed when he felt the hand pull out of his grip as his lover moved away again. This wasn't how things were supposed to be. He tried to let the subject drop. "Love, this wasn't what we had planned when we said we'd go to bed early... please, let's not argue?"

"Fine."

Jere was left frustrated and confused again, not knowing whether he should continue to push the topics they had brought up or not. They had talked earlier about spending the night together, quality time, cuddling time. Sexy time. They were both so damn tired lately that this had been getting pushed aside, and Jere hoped that if they could reconnect this way, maybe it would help them reconnect in other areas as well.

Tentatively, Jere slid a few inches closer, reaching out his hand and rubbing it across Wren's back and shoulder, caressing the familiar body that he was so exquisitely familiar with. When Wren didn't move, he hoped it was a good sign, and slid a bit closer, still trailing his hand across his skin.

The feeling of apprehension halted his movement before the words even reached his ears.

"Please stop."

The words were barely whispered, and Jere hated himself for being in any way at fault for their existence. He drew back instantly, throwing his legs over the edge of the bed. "I'll just go," he muttered, feeling defeated. "It's my fault, like everything else."

"You asked for my fucking suggestion, Jere," Wren reminded him, sitting up as well and turning on a light. "You asked for my help, and I tried to give it to you, and all you ever do is argue and ignore me and do whatever you were going to do in the first place. I guess only one of your slaves has to abide by your decisions, and it isn't the girl. So do whatever the hell you want."

Sleeping on the couch would have been easier, but Jere knew it wouldn't solve anything. He turned to Wren, feeling the impact of his statement. "I don't mean to ignore you," he started. "I'm sorry that I did, it's just hard for me to accept a lot of what you're saying. I guess I don't think about what it must be like to be a slave."

"Why should you? You never will be."

Wren looked and sounded angry, but Jere could feel how hurt he was, how much the rejection had hurt him again. "Wren, I'm sorry. I've said before that I'll take your advice and I meant it. What do I do to make this better? Ask, and it's yours."

"I want input on what you do with Isis," Wren said, looking vulnerable, like he was waiting to be rejected. "I'm not going to force you to do anything, but I want you to ask my opinion, and listen to it, and at least consider what I suggest. I want you to stop thinking like a doctor from Sonova and start thinking like a free man who owns slaves in Hojer. I want you to try acting like the master that Isis needs, just to see if it helps, because I think it will, and if it doesn't, then I'll stop pushing so hard."

Jere considered the requests. None of them were over the top, and if it kept Wren from pulling away from him, he was willing to do it no matter how uncomfortable it might make him. "All right. Should I lock her in then, even though I said I wouldn't?"

Wren raised an eyebrow. "Would you, if I asked?"

Jere tried not to shudder. He was so sure that he had made a breakthrough with Isis, that she was starting to trust him, but when it came down to it, he would rather lose her than Wren. "Yes," he said, quietly.

Finally, Wren looked relieved, the tension that had filled his body dissipating for the first time that night. "I won't ask that of you," he said softly, leaning back against the pillows. "All I want right now is for you to come to bed."

Jere did as he was asked, curling up next to Wren, breathing in the scent of him. He wouldn't lose him, not after all they had gone through.

"Thank you," Wren whispered, kissing him. "You have no idea how much this means to me."

Chapter 17
One Option

The next few days passed without major incident. Isis was doing better, relatively, and Jere was pleased to see no indication of running away. The most she did with her newly unlocked door was leave it open, just a few inches, except when she slammed it. It would have pleased him more if Wren hadn't seemed so pissed off about being wrong.

There were still outbursts, constant ones, directed at him, at Wren, at herself, at everything. She was still being sedated more often than not. Jere thought often about Wren's advice to hurt her, like she asked him to, but he immediately discarded the idea every time. He could never do something like that; no matter how good Wren's intentions were in suggesting it, even the thought of it horrified Jere.

Jere still sensed some tension between himself and Wren, but he kept his promise, trying to consult with his lover about Isis, and really considering what to do with her. To his credit, Wren didn't push too hard, seeming to recognize that Jere couldn't turn into a strict master overnight, if ever. He seemed pleased enough that Jere discussed options with him, examining ideas carefully, instead of dismissing them out of hand. Jere would admit that it was difficult, but Wren's advice was starting to have some sway on him. He made small rules, like insisting that she get her own meals and clean up after herself, and he was amazed when she complied with little fuss.

Still, Jere knew that the rest of Isis's behaviors and outbursts were taking a toll on both him and Wren. They shared meals and worked together with practiced efficiency, but neither of them had much energy for anything but talking, and they were little more than bed partners at night. Once or twice, Jere caught Wren looking at him, a puzzled, sad expression on his face, but he had hidden it as soon as it appeared. Jere could feel it in his own exhaustion, in his anxiety at coming back into the house each night, in how snappy and impatient he had grown with everyone. He thought he could deal with it, could handle it on his own and wait out the hard parts, but he didn't realize just how big of an impact it was having on Wren.

Logically, he knew that just *owning* another slave left his lover a bit more anxious, but the exact effects of Isis's loud, angry outbursts, violent reactions, and defiant threats didn't sink in until he and Wren were in the clinic, trying desperately to ignore the pained screaming and wailing from the house. Wren had been holding a vial of medication when a particularly loud thump caused him to jump, dropping it.

With a fearful look in Jere's direction, he backed against the wall, sinking down to the floor. "I, I'm sorry, sir..."

Jere was caught off-guard, and didn't quite respond in the most ideal way. "What's your problem?"

Jere cursed himself when he saw Wren's face, feeling callous for his thoughtless phrasing. It was meant to be a casual question.

Wren continued to sink to the floor, tight and stiff with nerves. "I didn't mean to...."

Jere took a moment to collect himself, drawing in a deep breath. He focused on the connection between him and the man he loved, drawing the feelings of concern and love and care forward, squashing back the irritation and tiredness and confusion. He slowly walked over to where Wren was huddled into a ball on the floor, dropping to his knees next to him and placing a careful hand on his back.

"It's okay," he whispered, rubbing careful circles on his skin. "I'm sorry. I'm sorry you're scared."

Wren didn't respond, just sat there shaking.

Jere leaned in, pressing a kiss to his forehead before ducking down to catch his eyes. "Wren, love, you know I'm not angry with you for dropping something. You know this. You know me better than that."

Wren glanced at him nervously, nodding a little. He moved toward him, and Jere pulled him into his arms, holding him tight, keeping him safe.

"Tell me what's going on?" Jere asked, stroking his hair.

"It's just too much," Wren whispered, hiding his face against Jere's chest. "It's too much—the noise, the screaming, the chaos. I can't fucking sleep at night, I never see you and when I do you're pissed off or sad or irritated. *I* am pissed off and irritated all the time, we're both busier than we ever were before, and it's just, it just reminds me too much of... of everything. Dammit, Jere, this has to stop! I get that you can't help her, I don't think she can be helped, and even if you are trying new things, she's still awful! She has to go!"

Jere tightened his grip, needing the contact as much as Wren did, if not more. "Wren, I'm sorry. I'm so sorry."

"It doesn't make it better!" Wren's words were pained and forced. There was no anger left. "Every time I hear her scream I can't help but remember the training institute. Burghe. Everything. How my life was supposed to be, before you came. How it would be again if you ever... if you...."

"Not gonna happen," Jere promised. "I'm not going anywhere, and neither are you. Wren, I love you more than anything else in this world—nothing will change that."

Wren finally stopped shaking, going still in his arms. "And what about her, then? Where will she go?"

Jere sighed. That was the question that had been weighing on his mind, what exactly to do with Isis. "I'll work on it. I'll take care of this, I promise."

"A lot of good that'll do," Wren muttered, but clung to him anyway. "Please, just think about how I feel?"

Jere kept those words in mind the rest of the day. Wren still looked drawn, but he didn't ask to leave, and Jere needed him, so he didn't offer. When the day was finished and they had eaten dinner as well, accompanied by the presence and defiance of Isis, Wren announced that he was going to have a bath and go to sleep early. Jere didn't overlook the absence of an invitation to join, and he stayed seated at the table for a while after, just thinking, weighing his options.

His reverie was broken by the sound of glass shattering, and he got up with a sigh. He was filled with more trepidation than usual as he walked to the room he had given to Isis, knocking on her door out of courtesy. He was at the end of his rope.

"Go to hell!" she replied.

A few seconds later, Jere heard a muffled yelp and opened the door anyway. He found Isis with her back pressed against the wall, face contorted in pain, blood dripping down her arm again. A quick glance revealed that the window was broken, and while the frame was still nailed in place and much too small to escape through; the glass from it was being used to slice up her wrists again.

"Goddammit, Isis!" he snapped, striding quickly across the room and snatching the glass out of her hand, throwing it aside as she cringed away from him. "This has to stop! Now! All of it! The screaming, the hurting yourself, all of it! It has to fucking stop! I'm tired of sedating you, and I'm tired of healing you, and I'm tired of having you fight me! I've offered you everything, I'll *give* you anything, just fucking cut it out!"

"No you haven't!" she screamed back at him, producing another piece of glass. She struggled against Jere as he tried to take it from her, and they were both on the floor and bleeding by the time he succeeded.

He gripped her wrists to stop her from going for any more glass.

"No! Don't touch me! Don't touch me! You're hurting me! Stop!"

For once, Jere really didn't care if he was scaring her, and he was pretty sure he wasn't really hurting her, either. "What the hell haven't I done for you? What more could you possibly fucking want from me? I've done everything, I feed you, I clothe you, I don't beat you or hurt you or even touch you most of the time, just *what* in the hell more do you want from me! I obviously have no idea what the fuck I'm doing, so name it! I'll do it!"

"I ask for it all the time!" She glared up at him, the dilated pupils almost eclipsing the green. "And you never do it."

"You ask..." Jere let his voice trail off as he realized exactly what she was talking about. "You want me to beat you?"

She nodded.

"You really want that?"

Another nod. A tear fell from her eyes.

Jere let her wrists go and backed away a few steps before standing up. He looked at her, so small and vulnerable, still on the floor. "Get up."

She stood, a bit shaky, and continued to glare at him.

"You want me to hit you?" he asked again. "To beat you."

"I already fucking said I did, didn't I?" she snarled. "Are you deaf or just stupid?"

Jere was silent, weighing his options. He considered his morals, the way he tried to live. He considered the girl's request, delivered as defiantly as possible for someone who trembled and cringed away from him when he so much as looked at her. He considered Wren, and their life, and how hopeless it seemed anymore. It was what Wren had advised, countless times, advice Jere had always rejected for being too cruel, too harsh, too terrible. But Wren's other suggestions had been right, and Jere had no idea what else to do. He had to do something, had to try to do anything he could to take care of this problem. He had promised Wren that much in the clinic earlier. He considered all his options, and realized that there weren't that many. There was really only one.

"Fine." His voice was low, firm, and calm. "Turn and lean against the wall."

Her eyes widened as she heard. She froze, silent, staring at him in shock.

Jere scrutinized her as he unbuckled his belt. Deliberately, he pulled it slowly from the loops, and wrapped the buckle around his fist. He was painfully aware that her eyes had followed his every movement.

He struck her across the legs, barely making contact, certainly not enough to hurt her. She jumped and gasped, staring at him with wide eyes for a moment.

"Turn. Lean against the wall." A part of him couldn't believe he was really doing this, but another part had given up hope that anything would be effective. At least he would be able to prove to Wren that he was following his advice, and if this didn't work... he could admit defeat if this didn't work.

Nodding, without taking her eyes off of him, Isis turned to the wall and braced her hands against it, leaning over as she was ordered to.

Jere felt dizzy and ill.

"You want this?" He struggled not to let his voice crack.

"I don't fucking want anything," she replied, her voice soft. She was looking at the wall, now.

"Isis..." Jere didn't know what else to do. She had asked him to do this, Wren had told him to do it, but he was still the one who could choose to say no, to deny her request and Wren's advice and do what he had always been taught was the right thing. But he had been doing that for weeks, to no avail. "Listen I'm only doing this because you asked me to."

"Yeah, and you should fucking do it already!" The defiant words were overshadowed by the nervousness in her voice. "Maybe you'll fix me. Maybe you'll hurt me enough to make me behave."

Jere was silent for a moment, regretfully considering the scars that he knew already adorned the girl's body. Obviously, those hadn't fixed a damn thing, and he couldn't see how adding more hurt could fix anything either. He considered that maybe it wasn't about the hurt, it was about honoring her requests and playing the role she expected him to. "Isis, this isn't punishment. Is that clear? I am not doing this to punish you."

"My whole life is punishment."

Jere tried not to shudder. "I'm doing this because you asked me to, and *only* because you asked me to. I hate it. I hate that I'm doing this. But I promised you I'd give you what you asked for, and this was it."

"Whatever, just get on with it."

Remarkably, she didn't seem overtly afraid of being beaten. Jere couldn't understand it. Then again, he had never beaten anyone before.

"Here's the deal. Once I start, it's up to me. I decide when I stop, and what I do, and I don't care if you want more or less or different—I get to make the decisions. You get one more chance to call this off — tell me now, is this really what you want?"

Isis was silent for a moment, and Jere felt his hopes rising as he thought she might say no.

"Yes."

One word condemned them both. Jere cursed inwardly, but he couldn't back down now.

He needed to warn Wren. He went for the mind connection. *"I'm about to do something I'll probably hate myself for later. Stay in the bedroom where it's soundproofed better, and close the door if you haven't already. You don't need to hear this; it will only upset you and scare you. No matter what you hear, don't come in this room."*

"Christ, Jere, what's going on?"

"I'm taking your advice and giving Isis what she's been asking for. I'm sorry I didn't tell you sooner, but I know I won't go through with it if I wait. I'm going to be... just remember that you're safe."

Jere knew he would catch hell for it later, but he barricaded his side of the mind connection as tightly as possible without actually severing it. Not only did he know his emotions wouldn't leak through, he knew that Wren wouldn't even be able to contact him that way if he tried.

This resolved, he draw back his arm and brought the belt down upon his slave.

Chapter 18
Mind-Surgery

She was silent, though the impact made her jerk.

He struck her a few more times, watching her body respond to the pain, tensing and jerking each time he hit her. After ten, he noticed she had closed her eyes, and was biting down on her lower lip to keep from crying out. He could imagine the welts he must have been raising on her skin, the bruises that would color later. He swore to himself that he would heal them. Her breathing was ragged.

Jere had no plan, but on a sudden impulse, he reached out and placed his hand on her back, barely touching her.

She screamed and squirmed, but kept position. "No! Don't fucking touch me! Get your goddamn fucking hands off me, I didn't ask for this!"

He brought the belt down twice more, putting pressure on her back with his free hand. "Stop squirming," he ordered, not recognizing his own voice.

"No! Fuck you! Don't you dare! Don't you fucking touch me! This isn't fair! I didn't ask for this, you bastard! Let me go! You're hurting me! Help me! Please stop! Please, no don't do this!"

"I said I get to make the decisions."

The same instinct that had him putting his hand on her had him shoving into her mind the next moment, purposely deflecting the psychic pain away from himself and back to her. He knew it would hurt more than the beating. He could hear her screaming continue.

Once in her mind, he was met with the same dream state that he found the last few times, a girl in a cage. The fire was larger, huge, and the girl was curled around the bars to escape it.

150

"Why are you doing this!" the projection shouted at him.

"Because I have no other options," he answered honestly. "Because there is something... more."

He kept pushing, kept invading, and slowly began to force things out of her memories and into the dream state. Terrible memories, memories of being beaten, held underwater, burned, raped, tortured. A man who would carve his initials into her flesh before raping her, only to have them all painfully healed by a corrupt healer before he sold her. Hunger, loneliness, fear that never ended. A very little girl, Isis at seven or eight, being whipped and locked in a closet as punishment for wetting the bed. The clarity of the memories was so real, so vivid, as to be overwhelming.

"You have no fucking right!" Isis, as a projection, was screaming at him. He could faintly hear her screaming something similar on the physical plane. "Stay out of my head! Those are my memories! Fucking get out!"

Still there was something deeper, something that she was protecting. Jere could feel it, as sure as he would have been able to see someone cradling a broken arm. He pushed harder, despite her protests. Humiliation. Despair. Promises that she would be able to see her parents again, if only she would behave better. Memories formed through the confused and innocent eyes of a small child. A face, a friendly one. Her mother.

He felt her fight back, the first time he had felt any psychic resistance from her. He was so startled that he slipped back from the connection, only to find her jerking away from him, trying to escape his physical grasp. He was on to something, but he needed to get back where he had been.

As she slid down the wall, his forearm caught along the back of her neck, and he used this to his advantage, pinning her by her throat. He resumed the beating, striking her as savagely and as unrelentingly as he could with the belt, not caring whether he got her legs or her lower back in the process. He just needed to distract her energy from her mind. She screamed, drowning out the whistling of the leather and the impact of the thuds against her skin.

He pushed back into her mind, ignoring her screams and begging and protests, pushing back to the memories he had left off on.

Her mother. Her father.

"We'll keep you safe, baby girl. We won't let them take you."

A team of hard-faced men, looking a little regretful as they picked her up and forcefully carried her from the room where her parents stood by, sobbing. A woman with a too-polite smile, "Don't worry. She'll be safe. You can always try for another child."

An elderly man, her first master, looking down at her from a high-backed chair. "You know you're safe here, Isis. Clay, take the girl and give her fifteen lashes for defiance. Feel free to add more if she challenges you."

A pretty young woman, brushing out a 9 year old Isis's hair and catching her eye in the mirror. "You know you're safe here, honey. Just do your work and obey me and your master. We hate having to punish you." The same pretty young woman shaking her head as a beaten and bloodied child was sold on open auction. She had walked in on her husband molesting the child.

Isis, at twelve, clinging to a teenage boy who said resolutely, "Don't worry, I'll keep you safe. I'll hide you from the bounty hunters!"

The teenage boy's face lighting up with glee when he received his reward for capturing a runaway slave.

A thirteen year old girl, in the bed next to Isis, at a training facility. Isis hands her a stolen piece of bread, and the girl asks, "Is it safe?" "It's never safe," Isis mumbles, then grabs the bread back moments before a guard walks in and beats her unconscious for stealing it.

As if Jere wasn't sickened enough by the memories, the next set contained him.

"Isis, that is enough! You're not going anywhere, and nobody is going to hurt you!" Jere stood up, ready to hurt her. "You're safe here."

"Isis, you're safe here..." His tone hardened. "Isis, I will put you in a mind-bind!"

Jere cleaned her wounds after hurting her, tying her down like everyone else did. "I just need to make sure you're safe, okay? This is just temporary."

"It's just to keep you safe. You'll be safe here. It will get better."

Jere felt his resolve start to slip, just a little bit, but he pushed forward. This was it, then. All the times he had promised her safety, all the times he had tried to convince her he wouldn't hurt her, it had only made it worse. She had learned, out of necessity, that safety was a lie. The more anyone said it, the worse it was, and he had said it a *lot*.

He pushed deeper, despite her protests, accessing her thoughts on a neurological level. The areas that were activated by the memories were the most active; even the primitive brain scans of years ago would have been able to detect this. But those with healing gifts could take it a step further, and actually interact with and change people's brains for the better. At one point, it would have been a messy lobotomy; in later years, it would have been complex physical neurosurgery with scalpels and cauterizing guns. With advanced mind-healing, it was as simple as isolating the connections and severing or numbing them. It wasn't a skill that was used often, and it wasn't even a skill that was taught often, but Jere had done it twice in his lifetime, and recognized the necessity of the skill.

He severed the connections between the memories, detaching safety from pain and suffering. He did it carefully, but quickly. Any neurological interference was risky, but then again, the kid was putting herself at risk of dying almost every day. He recognized the evidence of selective mind surgery scars—she had been through similar procedures before, though not nearly as neatly as he had done it. He made a mental note to ask her about it.

He pulled back immediately when he finished, appalled but not surprised to see the dream state that Isis had created crumbling down around both of them, her cage demolished and the fire out and smoky confusion everywhere. He retreated. The projections in the dream state couldn't hurt either of them, but it didn't mean he wanted to see them, either.

The return to reality was jarring and unwelcome. He found himself half-choking the girl, forcing her against the wall with his arm as she gasped for air. He dropped the belt, repulsed, and released his hold on her, his arms coming up to catch her as she fell, sobbing, into his lap. He slid down the wall with his arms around her, both of them landing in a pile on the floor. She clung to him and sobbed like a little child.

"Why?" she pleaded, almost unintelligible over her wailing. "Why the fuck would you do that? Why the fuck would you do that!"

"Isis..." Jere started, unsure of what to say.

"Don't fucking talk to me!" she screamed, but curled up tighter in his arms. "I hate you. I fucking hate you!"

Jere froze for a minute, unsure of what to do. She clawed at his shirt, pulling herself closer, burying her head in his chest. She was shaking. Silently, he reached over and pulled the blanket off of the mattress, wrapping it around both of them. He put his arms around her and rocked her gently, still not saying a word, until he felt her relax a little, her cries slowing down a bit.

Finally, she looked up at him, uncertainty written across her face. He took the corner of the blanket and wiped her tears away, still saying nothing, never loosening the grip he had on her, nor did she loosen the grip she had on his shirt.

"You had no right to take my memories," she said at last, sounding worn out and sad.

"I didn't," Jere responded quietly.

"You're lying!" Isis tried to yell, but it came out sounding defeated. "I've had it done before. *Classified information*, they said I had, so they cut it out of my brain! I can't remember any of it!"

"I didn't take your memories," Jere repeated. "I just removed the connections you had made between them. The memories will be a bit fuzzy for a few days while your brain finishes healing, but they'll come back completely. The connection could even come back, if it gets made again. I didn't *take* any of your memories, I just gave you a chance to see them without so much baggage."

Isis nodded, a few more sobs escaping as she did. "You saw everything. You know how awful I am, you know what I've done!"

"I know what was done *to* you. I'm sorry—"

"Don't." She cut him off, pulling back a bit to glare at him. "Don't apologize for things you never did."

"All right." Jere conceded. "But I'm sorry for the way it happened. I'm sorry that I just hurt you like that."

"I asked you to," Isis said, indifferently. She shook her head, sighing. "Now you know all my secrets."

Jere said nothing. Perhaps the beating and the intrusion meant nothing to her, but it meant a hell of a lot to him. He would remember this guilt until the day he died.

"You know I have a memory gift, right?"

Jere nodded, wondering why she asked.

"I remember all of it. Everything. Every word, every beating, every threat. My life has been nothing but hell and misery and torture since I was seven fucking years old, and I remember every minute of it, except when I've been knocked unconscious. Or the memories they took, but they never took *those* memories. I've had so many people promise me so many fucking things, and it never comes true. Never. And I just... I can't believe anyone."

"I know." He did. He had been witness to the horrors that had put her in this state.

"I just... I just want it all to end."

"I still stand by what I've been saying for weeks —"

"I know, I know, you won't let me kill myself," Isis said, rolling her eyes.

"Right." Jere nodded. She could be so calm and rational when she wanted to be. "That, and... honestly — fuck, I can't promise you'll be safe. I can't promise anyone anything, except what *I* choose to do or not to do. And I *can* promise that I won't do any of those things that have been done to you in the past, and I *can* promise that I will not sell you. Ever. No matter what happens."

Isis was silent for a moment, twisting the end of her hair around her finger. "I shouldn't believe you. I would never have believed you before. But I think I want to."

Jere nodded. Finally, he was making sense to her, and at least some of her actions were making sense to him as well. "All I want you to do is to think of *me* — not anyone else, but think of me and how I've treated you and then tell me if it would be theoretically believable."

Isis was nodding before he even finished speaking. "Of course it is. Of course it fucking is, but it's weird. And it's wrong. And it would mean that you'd be different from literally everyone I've met since I was taken as a slave. How can I even make sense of that?"

"The same way you once made sense of everyone in your life hurting you," Jere suggested. "I'll help you."

"I know. You'd be the first, but I guess you really do want to help me."

They sat there for a few more minutes, together under the blanket. Jere briefly contemplated the bizarre nature of the situation, quickly pushing it out of his head again. He never thought he would be holding the girl while she cried, but he never thought he'd hit her, either. It surprised him how much he was capable of.

"Jere?"

"Yeah?"

"Can I tell you one more thing?"

"Sure."

Isis grinned at him. "You hit fucking hard!"

Jere already feel guilty, so the statement didn't make him feel much worse, but it didn't make him feel any better, either. "Shit, kid, I'm sorry—"

"Don't apologize." Isis raised an eyebrow at him. "You were right. I was asking you to do it. I thought... fuck, I don't know what I thought. I don't think I wanted it to accomplish anything, I was just hoping you would go too far and kill me. And sometimes I like the pain. It makes me feel centered, so I know what to focus on."

"I can heal it," Jere rushed to fix what he thought was a problem. "And your arm, shit, I should heal your arm—it stopped bleeding, which is good, but still—"

"You can heal my arm if you need to, but..." Isis looked down, her face reddening. "Can you leave the rest of it? I like the reminder. I like the pain. It's real, even when I'm not sure what else is."

"But I hurt you!" Jere protested. It was bad enough that he had willingly hit the girl, but when he agreed to do it, he had been planning on healing her afterwards. He didn't know if he could tolerate knowing that she continued to be in pain because of his actions.

"I've had worse," Isis insisted. At Jere's shocked look, she continued. "Look. You didn't make me bleed, or break the skin, even. It hurt like hell and it still hurts and I'll have bruises for a week or so, but I don't care. Jesus, I hurt myself all the time—even when you're not looking, and it's not *just* about trying to die. It calms me down to feel pain, and if you'd really like me to stop causing it myself, then just let those marks stay. Let the bruises come. Please."

Jere shook his head in disbelief, then found himself nodding. "Fine. If you really insist, then fine. But I *am* healing your arm, and if you hurt yourself again I'm healing that, too. No debate."

Isis smiled, holding her arm out to him, now caked in dried blood. "Yes, sir," she said, smirking.

"You don't need to—"

"I *know* that, I'm just doing it to irritate you," Isis said. "Hell, if you had a problem with it, you would have knocked me across the room all the other times I've done it."

Jere couldn't help but smile back at her. "Will you let me in to heal your arm, then?"

She nodded. "It's not like I have much of a choice—as you can see, I don't really have much psychic defense going on."

"I like having your consent," Jere said quietly, earning him another eyeroll. He healed her quickly, smiling when he looked down to see her skin freshly healed and lacking a new scar.

"You're so careful about it," she muttered. "It's not like I'm not covered in old scars anyway."

"Every bit counts," Jere asserted. "If you wanted, I could heal the old ones, but you know how painful it is, and even my healing gift isn't advanced enough to do it painlessly. It would take weeks to fix them all properly."

"I know," Isis shrugged. "Besides. I like them there, sometimes. It reminds me who I am. Who I've been turned into. They're a part of me."

Jere said nothing. Perhaps it was true, but it was a horrible truth. It was a truth that he didn't want to partake in.

"So, what do things look like now?" Isis asked, pulling back a few inches to look him the face.

Jere shrugged. "The same as they did before. We go about our days. If you seriously stop hurting yourself, I won't sedate you again. I'd like you to help out in the clinic."

"Just because I'm a little less crazy doesn't mean I'm going to play slave for you!" Isis snapped, curling her arms around herself.

Jere sighed as he leaned back a bit, away from her. He considered the advice that both Wren and Kieran had given him to be clear about his expectations as a master, and he wondered if Isis's challenges weren't her way of asking him about those same expectations. "First off, you *are* a slave, in case you had forgotten, and I *did* purchase you for a reason. I think it's obvious that I'm not going to be the most demanding master in the world, but I expect you to at least pull your weight around here."

Isis scooted away from him rather pointedly, taking the blanket with her.

"Second, I don't so much expect you to 'play slave' as much as I expect you to 'play assistant.' Or employee, even. You should come by sometime, when Wren and I are working, just see how things are. You can let me know if you have any questions, that sort of thing. I can teach you—"

"I don't wanna learn shit," Isis muttered, scowling. "I just want to be left alone."

Jere stopped himself. *Don't push too hard, don't push too hard.* He took a deep breath. "Sorry. Didn't mean to rush you. Just take it a day at a time. Relax. Read some books, play some solitaire games... I mean, is there anything you'd like me to get you to help pass the time?"

Isis shook her head. "You don't need to get anything for me. But can I have things back? Like... like my bed? Stuff like that? Now that I'm not, you know, breaking them or anything?"

Jere grinned at her. "Certainly. And if you need something to do, I think that carrying it back in here would be a perfect way to spend the day."

She crossed her arms over her chest, looking like any other defiant teen Jere had ever known. "That's not fair! I didn't take them out!"

Jere stood up, laughing for a moment, but quickly stopping when the show of emotion made her cringe away. He held a hand out to help her up. "Well, you were the one who caused them to be taken out, so it really is on you."

"It's still not fair," Isis muttered, though her tone was lighter. "Is there food left? I'm starving."

Jere fought not to start laughing again. Isis was *always* starving. "Sure thing. Come on out and I'll see what I can find."

Chapter 19

Unexpected

Jere made his way into the kitchen, leaving Isis to get cleaned up. He was still a little shocked at what had just transpired. Actually, he was more than a little shocked, and more than a little horrified. After carefully and selectively blocking the majority of most of his all-consuming emotions, he dropped the block on mind connection that he had with Wren, relieved to feel his presence once more.

"Jere? Is everything all right?"

Jere was a little apprehensive *"It, um... everyone's fine, yes."*

"You beat her."

Jere winced. Wren wasn't shocked or horrified, as he was, he simply stated the fact. He hated hearing it put so calmly.

"Would you like a snack?" Jere evaded. *"I know it's the middle of the night, but Isis was hungry, and I could use something. I'm making it."*

"I'll come and talk with you."

Okay, that wasn't quite what he had asked, but Wren was always a bit wary about his cooking. Not that he was cooking, exactly, but he was at least preparing something.

Wren was sitting at the table waiting when he went out. Isis had yet to show up.

"What happened?" Wren asked, a worried look on his face.

"I beat her."

Wren nodded, carefully masking his face.

"What the fuck are you doing up?" Isis chose that exact moment to reappear, blood washed from her skin, face washed, and dressed in clean clothes. Her eyes were still rimmed with red from crying.

"Isis..." Jere warned. He really couldn't handle any more friction between the two of them tonight.

She shrugged, grabbing a sandwich and taking a bite before she even finished plopping down onto a chair. "Sorry," she mumbled around the half-chewed food. "Jus' curious."

"You're awfully chipper," Wren commented, a bit surprised.

"It wasn't like he horsewhipped me or anything," Isis finished stuffing the sandwich into her mouth, swallowing without chewing. "A few good lashes with his belt, which he even offered to heal. Like a gentleman. Fixed my most recent attempt at ending my own life. I think I'm just worn out from the memory surgery thing. Jere, is it normal to feel a bit fuzzy? Like, in general, it's like I have cotton in my head or something."

Jere was still blocking his side of the mind connection, unwilling to let his confused emotions leak over to Wren, but Wren was very pointedly letting his come through, and the outrage and anger that Jere felt was astonishing.

"You did what!"

"She was asking for it!" Jere couldn't stop himself from getting defensive.

"*Nobody* asks for that!"

"She's been asking for weeks, you heard her, and besides, you even agreed it would be a good idea!" For weeks, he and Wren had argued over the fact that Jere refused to take any drastic actions with Isis, and now that he had, Wren was angry instead of pleased.

"Not hitting her, I don't care if you hit her! Jere, you can't just fuck with people's memories! It's wrong."

"Wren—"

"No!" Wren slammed his hand down on the table, causing all three of them to jump. "No! It's not okay! Ever! It's fucking... it's mind-rape, and it's most certainly not what she was asking you to do! It's not what I told you to do!"

Jere felt more defensive. He felt bad enough that he had done everything he did to the girl, and Wren's attack wasn't helping. Of all people, he thought Wren would understand why he had done it; he had been the one demanding that Isis be gotten rid of. "I did what I had to do! I thought you'd be happy that I finally did something!"

Wren stood up, his face a mixture of rage and sadness and hurt and fear. "How could you hesitate to hit her when you would so quickly violate her that way?" He turned away.

Jere jumped up after him, grabbing his shoulder. "Goddammit, I did what was necessary to keep her in line and I *will not* defend myself to you!"

Before he could register what he said or what happened next, he felt the pain explode from the left side of his face, and his vision went black for a few seconds. He reeled backwards, clutching the edge of the table for support. It finally dawned on him what had happened, and he opened his eyes, waiting for the darkness to recede.

"I can't believe you just hit me!"

He heard his voice, sounding more surprised than anything, which matched how he felt. He focused his vision to see Wren on his knees, face pressed to the floor. He looked strangely calm.

"Are you going to punish me?" Wren's voice was unreasonably calm. "I will submit to any correction —"

"No?" Jere cut him off, reaching up to feel the tenderness in his eye. "Fuck, that was... unexpected."

"Everybody's hitting someone! When is it my turn to hit someone?" Isis piped up, sounding entirely unperturbed by the chaos.

"Never." Jere raised a warning eyebrow at her. He turned back to Wren, at a loss for what to say or do. "Get up," he muttered.

Wren stood obediently, but continued to scowl at him. "If you do not wish to punish me, sir, then I would like to be excused."

"What? Yeah, I mean, no, I don't want to — I'm not going to punish you, for fuck's sakes, but Wren, can we —"

Wren had turned and sped off down the hallway.

"Wren, honey, can we talk about this —" The words fell flat in his head and he felt the rough shock of the mind connection being forcibly closed. For the first time in almost a year, he was alone in his head.

"Son of a bitch." He sat down, defeated, and picked idly at a sandwich.

"That'll be a hell of a black eye," Isis observed.

"Thanks for pointing that out. The throbbing pain wasn't indication enough." Jere knew he was being pouty and short with her, but couldn't particularly bring himself to care. "Christ, how the hell do I explain this at work tomorrow?"

"Can't you just heal it?" Isis suggested. "I mean, that is what you do, right?"

Jere shook his head. "Healers can't heal themselves. Only another healer could do that."

"Oh. That's unfortunate."

"Tell me about it," Jere muttered. "Fuck."

"Just say you fell and hit your head on the corner of a table," Isis suggested. "That's what they used to tell me to say when I was little and there was sensitive company. Oh, or say someone else did it. Some spoiled little brat or something. People want to believe lies."

Jere sighed. She was right. There was no way he could let on to anyone that Wren had done this. The implications were terrifying.

"Fuck, even *I* know better than to assault a free person!" Isis said with a grin. "Seems Mister Perfect Slave isn't so perfect after all."

"Don't push it." Jere warned, glaring at her and only feeling a little guilty when she shifted away from him a few inches.

"Sorry." She was silent for a moment. "So, you and Wren, you're like... married? Or something?"

Jere couldn't help but laugh. He was in the middle of a fucking life crisis, and this kid was making small talk? Her first fucking rational conversation in weeks was about his now failing love life. "We're, uh... dating. I guess. Or we were, anyway."

"You live in the same house, share a bedroom, and do disgusting sex things with each other all the time, but with nobody else, and you think you're just dating?"

"Marriage is like... it's just different. We're not married. Hell, I don't even know if he likes me anymore."

Isis laughed, for once sounding uninhibited. "He obviously does, otherwise he wouldn't be so pissed off at you," she pointed out.

"Hell of a way to show it," Jere muttered, his hand moving to his eye again.

"My parents used to argue like you guys do," Isis said, a wistful look on her face. "Um, they never hit each other, and neither of them was a slave, but, you know."

Jere was silent, thinking.

"You should put some ice on that," Isis advised.

"Yes. Yes, I should, which I know, because I'm a doctor."

Isis looked scared again, and suddenly guilty. "This is my fault, isn't it? You and Wren fighting."

Jere shrugged. On the surface, it was true, but he couldn't help but wonder if these same problems wouldn't have come up eventually anyway. "You're making things more difficult, but it's not your fault. It's something Wren and I have to work on. If anything, it's my fault."

"Don't be mad at Wren," Isis pleaded, clearly not believing Jere's insistence that it was his fault. "I know you said you wouldn't punish him, but if you change your mind, punish me instead. If I wasn't here, he never would have hit you, and there wouldn't be any problem. I'd rather you punish me than him."

"There's not going to be any more punishing or hitting," Jere insisted. "Things are out of control enough as it is. Wren and I will work this out."

"Why did you buy me?" Isis asked, almost out of nowhere. But Jere was starting to realize that few things were really out of nowhere with Isis, they just made sense to her in a much different way than they did to anyone else. She had asked the question repeatedly in the past, and Jere realized that it had something to do with a need to be reassured, another way of asking if she would be sold.

Jere was tired and irritated and didn't want to expend the energy to re-explain himself. "I've told you plenty of times. I need help in the clinic."

"But why me? Why not some nice kid from a training facility?" Isis pressed. "What was so fucking attractive about damaged goods that you *had* to have me?"

"The ad didn't make you sound so bad," Jere admitted, honestly. "And when that man came here to show you, and treated you the way he did, I knew that I could never send you home with him and not feel terrible about it. I thought... I thought things could be different for you here."

Isis was quiet for a moment. "I won't ask you to hit me again," she stated. "And I guess I'll never get *you* to fly off the handle and kill me. Maybe I should have tried harder with Wren. But I'm still probably not what you want. Can I just... can I ask you one favor?"

Jere nodded. He didn't even care what it was. He felt so spent already, giving one more favor couldn't possibly drain him any further.

"When you get sick of me, could you promise to just kill me?" She looked up at him from beneath her eyelashes, her dark eyes wary and vulnerable. "Because if this is how it is, if this is how you treat me, and Wren, and how life is here... I couldn't handle going back to the real world. And the cruelest thing you could ever do to me would be getting me used to living here just to sell me off and put me back where I came from. I'd rather die. I can barely handle living now; if I knew it could be good and it wasn't, I couldn't take it."

It was such a weird, sad request. But he knew what she meant, he knew it was true. Condemning her to the sort of life she used to have after treating her kindly would be extraordinarily cruel. "Yes," he said softly. "I'd kill you, painlessly, before I ever sold you off."

"It doesn't even need to be painless," she muttered, looking down at the table. "Thank you."

She walked off, and Jere was left to sit alone with his thoughts. There weren't many, and they weren't good, and he didn't know what to do with them anyway. He went out into the living room and picked up a letter that sat on the table, one his mum had sent him a few days ago. He wished she was here, wished he could talk to her. It didn't matter that he was a grown man or a doctor or a slaveowner or anything else, a part of him wanted nothing more than to have his mum come and fix everything and make it all better. He settled for reading her letter.

Jere,

Honey, I am so sorry to hear that things are rough between you and Wren. Give him a big hug for me, and then give him a big hug from you! You both need to trust each other and help each other out when things get hard like this.

The girl you bought sounds like quite the challenge. Darling, I don't even know what you were thinking — I know you're so kind and compassionate and probably wanted to do something nice, but getting her was sort of asking for trouble. But I know you, and I have faith that you'll be able to help her. You do wonderful things with people, honey, and don't let a few days or even a few weeks get you down. Maybe by the time you get this letter it all will have resolved itself.

I did some research, and there have been documented cases of definitive gifts showing as early as six or seven. Of course, I wouldn't make someone a slave at that age based on something like that, but then I wouldn't make someone a slave at all, ever! The poor girl must have had it so hard. You're doing a good thing, Jere. She'll appreciate it, even if she doesn't show it. Remember, I put up with you as a teenager, certainly you can put up with this kid! You know, you and your sister gave me plenty of grey hairs when you were that age – it's only fair that you get some of it back!

As far as the tension between you and Wren, it sounds like typical relationship issues made worse by the situation. You might not find it as endearing as I do, but struggles like this are part of a long relationship. I know it might not make it any easier, but he does love you, and you love him, and if you both keep that in mind, I'm sure you'll do fine. I never thought I'd see the day, but honestly, you have grown into such a good man, and Wren is certainly bright enough to realize it. Don't neglect the little things – he needs to hear you tell him you love him more now than ever, and you can tell him I said he'd better be saying it back!

You know yourself and your boyfriend better than I do, but I'm certain this is just a passing thing. I've never seen you so completely in love with someone before, and I think it's good for you, even if it is painful at times. Trust yourself and trust your relationship.

I love you!

Mum

P.S. Your sister finally badgered me for your address and won. She said she might show up sometime.

Jere's last letter home had been filled with whining and complaining about how "bad" things were between him and Wren. He would give anything to go back, to have things be that calm, to do it all over again and do it right this time. Reading his mum's words did help him to feel a little better, though. It was nice to have someone to point out the good things about his and Wren's relationship, not to mention boosting him up in that way that only a mother could.

Feeling slightly reassured, he curled up on the couch, falling asleep there for a few hours before work started the next day.

Chapter 20
More Than That

Wren lay in bed, unable to sleep, unable to move, unable to do anything but replay the night's events in his head. He squeezed his hand into a fist, feeling the slight soreness as he did. He could only imagine the mark he had left on his master. The black eye that he knew would be spreading, the same way as the anger and the fear and the darkness had spread through him when he did it. The black eye that would be visible for days, left by a defiant, angry slave.

Strangely, he wasn't nervous about that. If Jere wanted to, he could have him publicly whipped — potentially whipped to death — but Wren trusted his lover enough to know that wouldn't happen. If anything, he had imagined Jere would have hit him back; it was what Wren assumed he would have done if he had been in Jere's place. Jere had just stood there staring back at him with that big, surprised, hurt look on his face. Wren squirmed a bit at the memory, at how caught off-guard Jere had been. He squeezed the fist tighter, this time feeling the familiar warmth of his gift. He had spent so much time in the past worrying about what might happen if his fire-setting gift ever got out of control, but when it came down to it, it wasn't the first thing that he lashed out with.

Not that Wren had really planned it out; it had all happened so fast, he wasn't even sure *what* had happened. He had heard something unthinkable from Jere, something terrible and ugly that he never would have expected from the man he had come to trust so much. Jere had violated that girl's mind, taking advantage of her psychic weakness and lack of defenses to not only pry into her memories, but to change them and alter them. Wren remembered the countless times that his own mind had been similarly invaded; his memories had never been altered that he knew of, but the sensation of another person poking around inside of his head like that was nauseating even so long after. It had never occurred to him that Jere would even consider doing a thing like that, and Wren had felt his opinion of Jere starting to waver from the moment he heard Isis mention it. It left him uncertain, shaken, and helpless.

If Jere could so easily do something like that to Isis, Wren wasn't sure where he would draw the line. He had been trying to understand it, to convince himself that Jere would never do the same to him, but when he confronted his boyfriend about it—his master, he reminded himself harshly—Jere had dismissed him so coldly and been so defensive. In spite of how far they had come together, Wren couldn't help but recognize Jere's tone as that of a master who thought that his slave had overstepped his bounds, and it infuriated him to be placed in that category yet again. Wren knew he had acted on angry impulse, and it wasn't like him, and it wasn't right, it was *never* right to lash out and hurt someone like that, even if he wasn't a slave. And yet, he was still mad at Jere.

Cutting the mind connection had been harsh, and he knew exactly how much it would hurt Jere. Wren felt more guilt about that than anything else, especially because it made it very clear that he wasn't even open to talking about what had happened. But he didn't know what else to say, or to do, and Jere had refused to back down in the moment. Wren needed time, he needed a *lot* of time, and he didn't even know what he needed that time for, just that he needed it and he wanted it and he was going to take it whether anyone else liked it or not. Even though Jere was good at letting him take time, he didn't want it to be a choice, or at least, not a choice that Jere made. Jere was making too many choices lately, and everybody in the house was suffering because of it. Wren wanted to take time on *his* terms.

And so he did, taking his time that night, and the following workday as well. It was strange, hearing Jere get up and go through his usual routine, although Wren noticed that he had slept on the couch the night before. He thought about how he should have been there next to him, sharing a shower, brushing out his hair while Jere brushed his teeth, picking out clothes for both of them because Jere always dawdled or wore things that looked strange together and then insisted it didn't matter because he had the white coat on over the top anyway.

Their life had been so comfortable, and Wren wondered if his or Jere's actions had destroyed that completely.

Wren snuck out for something to eat about an hour before Jere's regular lunchtime, feeling somewhat guilty that he wasn't preparing food for them. A part of him felt vindicated too, but it was weirdly bittersweet. He had hurt his lover physically; what was wrong with him that he wanted Jere to suffer more? He peeked in Isis's door, which was left open, and found her curled up and asleep on her mattress, clearly worn out.

He didn't even know what to think of her. It wasn't that he hated her. He really didn't feel anything but annoyance toward the girl anymore. He wanted her gone, out of their lives, although he figured that the damage that had been done was irreversible now. Perhaps she would make a better assistant for Jere than he would, he mused, not entirely sure where that would leave him. He seriously doubted that Jere would sell him — if only because Jere was so adamantly opposed to slave trade all together. Although, he wasn't quite sure whether his master would let him continue to lounge about and do nothing. It made him a little uncomfortable to realize that if he had been in Jere's place, he would have sold a slave like himself.

That night, he heard a knock at his door. He knew it was Jere, and he said nothing, drawing his knees up to his chest and trying to stay still. Hiding.

"Wren?"

Another knock.

"Wren, love, I'm sorry. I thought I was doing the right thing; I never thought it would upset you this much, but I swear I can explain! Please talk to me? I want to try and make this right."

Wren pulled the covers over his head. He didn't want to hear it. He didn't want to risk hearing Jere say that he didn't have to defend himself, because it was too close to being ordered to obey, and if everything was left murky and confused, Wren could still be angry. If they talked, and Jere really did stick to his convictions, Wren knew that he would have no other choice than to submit. The uncertainty was preferable.

"I see food's gone, so you've been eating. Thank you. Please take care of yourself."

Wren said nothing as his master walked away. Or was Jere his lover, his boyfriend? He still wasn't sure where to draw that line. It was so typical of Jere to appreciate that he was eating, but Wren couldn't bring himself to say anything back, to do anything, to confront him at all. All he wanted was to hide away forever.

The next day went similarly. He waited until Jere was at the clinic before sneaking out of his room, using the bathroom and showering, and heading to the kitchen for food. He spent the majority of the day counting the dust particles that floated past his eyes in the sunlight that streamed in the window. He was bored. He hadn't been bored since he had been Burghe's mindless slave. With Jere, he was always busy, sometimes with work, more often with companionship and conversation. It had been so long since he had been forced to just sit and contemplate life, although it occurred to him that he was the only one forcing himself to do anything. He felt frozen in place.

"Wren? Please, can we try and work this out? Baby, I miss you! Please, just talk to me?" That was the second night. Wren fought back tears as he heard Jere give up and walk away again. He heard him talking with Isis about one thing or another, and it pained him to think of how it should be him out there talking with Jere. He started to wonder if he even deserved it.

The third day, he ran into Isis on his daily trip out of the bedroom, startling her as she was lugging furniture back into her room.

"Fucking Jesus!" she exclaimed, dropping a dresser and nearly toppling over herself. "It's like seeing a ghost, only less friendly!"

Wren brushed past her. "So you're getting furniture back?" he muttered. He couldn't be angry at her, as much as he tried, because she was just... benign. Inconsequential. An inconsequential being who had destroyed his life, and looked ridiculously innocent and helpless lugging around furniture while swimming in Jere's clothes.

"Yeah. Jere said that as long as I wasn't destroying it or hurting myself with it I could have it back," Isis said with a grin. "He's actually... he's been pretty understanding."

Wren nodded. "Of course he has." For a moment, he hated Jere, because he was always understanding, even though understanding wasn't always what he needed to be. Always such a good guy. At least, he was almost always a good guy. Wren didn't know how to reconcile the person he loved and trusted more than anyone else in the world with the person who would violate someone's mind and steal their memories. He didn't know how to reconcile the Jere that he used to know with the Jere he had come to know in the last month or so.

"He misses you, you know," Isis pointed out, struggling with the dresser again.

Wren watched her, impassive. He couldn't allow himself to feel or he'd lose it. He had to struggle to maintain his anger at Jere, and if he allowed himself to think of Jere missing him, he would lose that, and he didn't know what else he had left except fear.

"Mind giving me some fucking help?" she gave in and asked, looking frustrated and exhausted.

Wren said nothing, but grabbed the end of the dresser and helped her to drag it back into her room. She pressured him into helping with the bed frame as well, and the two of them had the room put back together quickly. Wren stood by her doorway for a moment, tired and uncertain as to what to do next. It seemed that even the most basic of human interaction sucked the life out of him. Maybe he just wasn't fit to be around others. Maybe he never had been in the first place.

"You know, he didn't really hurt me."

"It's not about that." Wren wasn't really sure what it was about anymore.

"It was between me and him. My 'master' as you seem to like to point out so much. I kind of figured you'd be happy that he finally let me have it. It's not like I didn't deserve any of what he did."

"It's more than that." Wren turned to walk out.

"Hey, were you gonna make anything to eat? I'm starving, and Jere's terrible at cooking. He tried to cook chicken last night and I'm surprised we didn't die."

"I'm sure you can find something. You eat anything that

moves."

The kid bounced up in front of him, looking bored and energetic and disgustingly content. "It doesn't need to move! Come on. Don't you want to make something? Something with leftovers? Something big enough for two?"

Wren started to walk down the hall. His own appetite had faded.

"Should I tell him you said hello or anything?"

"Don't tell him anything that isn't true." Wren returned to his room and slammed the door. He realized that he should have grabbed a book, maybe something to eat later, but the time had passed, and he kind of liked his dramatic exit. Besides, he could sulk more effectively if he concentrated all his energy on it. Isis was right. He was a ghost.

It was almost comforting when Jere came by that night, although it was also irritating. This was becoming some sort of strange routine, and Wren wished that Jere would just leave him alone to mope. Every time he came by and didn't decide to order Wren out of the room, Wren was reminded again of the uncertainty between them, the empty promises to be equal, the erratic behavior Jere had been showing since he bought Isis.

"Wren? Love, please talk to me?"

Silence.

"Dammit, Wren, we need to talk! This can't go on."

Wren huddled in bed, half-wishing Jere would just storm in and slap him around a bit. He knew how to tolerate an angry master, because at the end of the day, that person would still be the master. An angry boyfriend was something that Wren had no idea what to do with, and worse, he had no idea what to prepare for. He could deal with pain, but the threat of losing what he and Jere had built was too much. The uncertainty was terrible. Ironically, he realized this must have been how Isis felt for so long. He never thought that he would experience the same feelings first-hand.

"I need you, Wren. I need you in the clinic. You have a fucking job, and you need to fucking do it, because I can't do it alone." Jere's voice was demanding, threatening, and Wren was almost relieved to hear his fears confirmed. Then he heard the discouraged sigh, and he recognized that Jere had been bluffing. When he spoke again, his voice had taken on its usual pleading tone. "And dammit, Wren... I just need you. Please, don't do this? You're all I've got. You're all that's worth anything to me. Tell me I didn't throw it away?"

Wren said nothing, this time because he was trying too hard to avoid sobbing audibly. He pressed his face against his pillow, hearing Jere curse as he stomped off. It wasn't fair, none of this was fair, and none of it was how their lives were supposed to be. He couldn't figure out whether Jere needed him as a partner, or as a slave, and he couldn't help but wonder what might happen if he failed to meet either or both of those roles. It seemed so long ago that he had agonized over Jere not needing him at all; the thought that Jere needed him and he might fail was worse. Wren shook with sobs as he wondered if it was possible for him to be needed as both; if it was possible for him to *be* both. At times like this, he didn't think it was. But the cold hard truth was that Wren did have duties as a slave, and he needed Jere as a partner. He had no idea how to do either of those things, and the only person who could have helped him was the one person he was doing his damnedest to avoid. He felt himself sinking deeper into hopeless despair, and he didn't bother trying to stop it at all.

Chapter 21
Coping Skills

Five days.

It had been five days since Jere had laid eyes on his once-boy-friend. Heard him speak. Kissed him. Okay, it had been a hell of a lot longer since he had kissed him. He was utterly miserable.

The one minor point of contact he had with him was last night, when Wren's emotions had plagued everyone in the house, in addition to his screams. He hadn't had nightmares like that in a month. Jere's knocking on the door had brought silence, but little else.

Silence was still a relative term in the house. Isis woke up screaming more often than not, and still had a tendency to burst into crying jags for almost no apparent reason. Jere had taken it upon himself to purchase a set of earplugs, in hopes that he could get *some* sleep at night.

The clinic was a mess, and he had finally caved and taken the rest of the week off as half-days, citing a stomach flu to anyone that asked. For the most part, he sat in the empty clinic anyway, savoring the quiet, missing the past. Missing rational company.

So, when he heard and felt Paltrek approaching his door, he was surprisingly happy to see the man who had turned into somewhat of a close friend. He pulled the door open with a smile.

"Jeremy, word is you're a bit under the weather?" Paltrek said, a smile spreading across his face as he saw his friend looking a bit drawn, but not exactly sick. "Or are you just taking a bit of time out of your busy schedule to play?"

"Hardly," Jere muttered, letting him in and taking his jacket.

"Where's your boy?" Paltrek smirked, noticing the lack of attendance. "I'd think he was the one actually under the weather, but anyone who knows you knows you'd have him healed up and pampered if he got so much as a scratch!"

"My 'boy' is otherwise occupied," Jere replied. Paltrek had been over enough recently that Jere and Wren had dropped their guard a bit around him, and the non-conforming socialite had accepted their relationship somewhat, dismissing it as weird and liberal and "city-like," whatever that implied. For all of Paltrek's flaws, he didn't judge, and once he accepted Jere as his friend, he seemed to accept or at least tolerate the unusual relationship between master and slave.

"Trouble in paradise?" Paltrek smirked, looking a bit surprised when he got a glare in response. "That bad, huh? What did you do? Forget to iron his shirt for him? Leave a dirty dish in the sink?"

"Oh, go to hell," Jere retorted, but couldn't help smiling. Paltrek had long since figured out that Jere doted on his lover, and never missed an opportunity to harass him about it. "And, no, it was... it was something bigger than that."

Paltrek shrugged. "That's why I don't date, Doc. Only one big thing allowed in my relationships, and that's never the problem." He gestured at his groin with both hands.

"And we've crossed into the 'more than I need to know' area," Jere shook his head, leading them into the living room. "So, did you just come here to make sure I wasn't dying and tease me about my love life?"

"Mostly," Paltrek grinned, then reached into the pocket of his pants and pulled out a bottle of undoubtedly overpriced vodka. "That, and I was bored, and I haven't seen you in a while because you've been holing up and being sad or whatever, *and* I picked this up on a business trip and I wanted someone to try it with! It's one of those new vodkas, made with some experimental cross-breed grain. It's supposed to get you twice as drunk, and I think it's supposed to taste like oranges or something. None of that cheap stuff that they make out of whatever they can get their hands on."

Jere grinned. "You know, that sounds lovely. Want a glass?"

"What do I look like, some kind of alcoholic who drinks out of the bottle?" Paltrek was already opening the bottle and drinking out of it. "Yes, I want a glass!"

Jere didn't answer, he just grabbed two and brought them back. They had just tossed back the first proper shot and were sharing their opinions on it when Isis came barreling through, freezing in her tracks as she saw the stranger in her house.

"And just who is this?" Paltrek asked, raising an eyebrow at Jere. "Thought you didn't go for the more delicate sex."

"Who the shiny fuck are you?" Isis spat out, her body tensing as her arms crossed over her chest.

"A guest in your master's house, slave." Paltrek's voice had dropped from casual and playful to serious and threatening. Isis could sense it, and in seconds she flattened her back against the wall, casting a wary eye at Jere.

Jere was a bit startled by the tone as well, but being in no position to be afraid, he simply sighed, tossing back the next drink he had poured himself to boost his courage a bit. "Yes, Paltrek, this is a new slave. Her name is Isis, and I'm not 'going' for her and neither are you. Isis, this is Paltrek Wysocka, and he is a friend and a guest, and I'd appreciate if you'd not be so goddamn rude."

"Well, what the hell is he doing here?" Isis demanded, still backed against the wall.

"Damn, Jeremy," Paltrek shook his head, "she's got quite the attitude."

"Yes. She does." Jere glared at her, a warning look. "Isis, if you can't be polite and socially agreeable, stay in your room!"

"Fuck you, you didn't even tell me you were having company!" Isis snapped.

Paltrek's jaw nearly hit the floor.

"Because I didn't know and it's none of your damn business anyway!" Jere replied. "Paltrek's a friend. He's visiting. Now go!"

"It's not fucking fair. I didn't even mean to do anything!" Isis snapped, looking offended. She took a few steps toward her room, then turned back to look at Paltrek. "Sorry. If I was rude. I just didn't know anyone else was here and we don't get guests much. I'll be nicer next time if *you're* nicer!"

With that, she flounced out of the room, seemingly unaffected. Paltrek, on the other hand, was still staring in her direction in utter shock. Jere wanted to hide under the couch. He chose to hide under another shot of vodka.

"It's smooth," he commented, ignoring the massive disturbance. "I could drink this all night."

"Jeremy, she is *way* out of line!" Paltrek exclaimed. "I mean, even for you—even with your standards, your bizarre leniency. She takes it way too far! It can be dangerous, you know? Slaves can't just run around doing whatever the hell they want and talking back like that."

Jere poured him another drink as well. "She's new. She's adjusting. She doesn't leave the house, and you're only here because I know you won't report me to some authority or something."

"So that's why you've been off-radar for the past few weeks, then? Taking care of her?"

Jere nodded. There was no point in denying it.

"Damn, Jeremy, I know you have a soft spot for the boy, and I don't blame you, he's sweet and obedient and you obviously have some sort of puppy love crush going on, but what the hell is up with her?"

"She's had a rough time," Jere muttered, swirling the clear liquid around in his glass.

"If she were mine, I'd *give* her a rough time," Paltrek shook his head in disbelief. "How long have you had her?"

"A little over a month, now. It's gotten better—no, don't look at me like that, I know what you're thinking, and yes, it *can* be worse. But it's slowly gotten better."

"What did you buy her for?"

"Help around the clinic."

"And?" Paltrek grinned, a bit lecherous. "She's a pretty girl."

"*And* nothing," Jere winced with distaste of the idea. Admittedly, Isis had cleaned up somewhat, detangling her hair into long, dark waves that twisted into ringlets at the ends. He didn't doubt that she'd grow up to be attractive, but first, she'd have to grow up. "Honestly, Paltrek, that's just... wrong. Really. She's a child. And a girl. And a *child*."

"Fine, fine," Paltrek rolled his eyes. "Keep your city-boy panties untwisted. She *is* a bit young looking, even by my standards."

"You have standards?" Jere smirked.

"I like my ladies a bit more developed, if you know what I mean." Paltrek was cupping imaginary breasts, laughing as he inspired another wince from Jere.

"You're just..." Jere shook his head. "So yes, I *just* bought her for help in the clinic."

"Such a valiant, chivalrous man," Paltrek retorted. "I haven't heard any gossip about you expanding your slave count. I'm assuming she's not around the clinic yet?"

Slave count? Jere shuddered at the term. "No, she's not. Why would people gossip about it anyway?"

"Because, you've been here a year and hardly anyone knows you outside of work, and you're an outlander and they all still think you're interesting," Paltrek pointed out. "Nobody believes me when I tell them that you're just a boring workaholic who seems to have committed himself to a domesticated life with his slave."

Jere narrowed his eyes. He knew Paltrek didn't talk about him in so many words, but the idea that his life was being discussed by anyone in this town still irked him. "She hasn't exactly been ready for working yet."

"In a month?" Paltrek shook his head. "That's setting a bad precedent. You'll never get anything out of her that way. I mean, aside from defiance and whatnot."

As if on cue, Jere heard a loud thump from the direction of Isis's room. He squeezed his eyes shut, trying to will it away. Another, louder one came.

"Son of a bitch," he muttered, standing up. "Would you mind, just... just give me a minute?"

"Need some help?" Paltrek offered.

Jere was thankful for the offer, mostly, because it was so friendly and familiar. However, knowing Paltrek and his ways of handling slaves, it was the last thing he would want. "I don't want her hurt. I can manage on my own. Thanks, though."

Paltrek laughed and waved him off, pouring another drink.

Jere went quickly to Isis's room and opened the door, ducking and barely avoiding a dresser drawer that flew toward his head.

Isis froze for a moment, eyes wide at what had almost happened. "I didn't fucking even aim for you, fuck, you always knock! I didn't know!"

Jere ignored what had just almost happened. "What the hell is your problem?"

Isis glared at him, turned to pull another drawer from the dresser, and hurled it across the room, this time in the opposite direction from where Jere was standing. She looked at him after it crashed, defiant despite her trembling.

"I'm not in the mood for this," Jere growled, feeling a bit guilty when his lowered tone made her cringe. "Knock it off or I'll restrain you and *everything* will be taken out of here again. Since Wren's not around to bring me anything, I'll mind-bind you."

She turned away from him, and he could hear her crying. She walked over to the drawer she had just thrown and kicked it, just a little bit, before turning to look at Jere over her shoulder.

He took a few strides toward her.

"Please don't!" she dropped to the floor and skittered backwards, apparently changing her mind. "Please don't, Jere, I'm sorry, I'm sorry I made you mad! I'm sorry!"

Jere knelt as well, hating the feeling of towering over her. She was terrified enough already. "Isis," he spoke softly, trying to keep his voice as calm as possible, even if he was annoyed with her. "We've been over this. If you can't control yourself, we're looking at restraints or mind-bind or injections, and if you're breaking shit, it goes out of your room. Just because I have a guest doesn't mean that's any different."

"I just fucking hate hearing you guys talk about me," Isis squeezed out through her cries. "He's mean. I heard him. He'd hurt me!"

Jere felt himself relax. It was nice to see her have a reason for being so upset for once. "Listen, kid, he'd hurt you if you were his, but you're not, and you won't be, and there's no way I'd let him or anyone else lay a hand on you or convince me to do it either, is that clear? Sometimes, I just need to vent, because my job is stressful and my boyfriend hates me and you're a giant pain in the ass. I'm not asking Paltrek for advice on what to do; I just want him to hear me out. And I suppose he has a right to his opinion as much as anyone does."

Isis nodded, her frantic breathing slowing as Jere continued to speak.

"That being said, if you'd like to help me on my quest to convince him that beating on human beings is barbaric and wrong and counter-productive, you might try being less of a horror when he's here."

Isis managed a small smile. "He scared me," she admitted.

"I'm sorry," Jere conceded. "I'll warn you next time he comes over."

Isis nodded, sitting quietly for a moment. She glanced up at Jere with a sad face. "So... so you're gonna mind-bind me, now?" she cringed as she said it.

"Do you need me to?" Jere asked, surprised.

"Like it's my fucking decision!" Isis snapped. But Jere could see her tremble.

"Isis," he forced himself to keep his tone calm again. "It's not punishment. I know it feels like it is sometimes, but I promise, that's not why I do it. Right now, you look calm and rational and safe. If you can stay that way, I would never dream of putting a mind-bind on you. I just need you to knock off the bullshit. Can you do that?"

She thought about it for a minute, which Jere was both surprised and impressed by.

"I haven't done so well in the past, have I?" she muttered.

"I'm not talking about the past, or even the distant future. I'm talking about right now." Jere looked at her for a moment, catching her eye before asking, "So, can you do it right now?"

She nodded, a bit tentative.

Jere smiled. "Good. Then I'll leave you to clean up this mess. Let me know if anything needs to be replaced, okay?"

Isis nodded. "Why do you put up with me?"

"I'm a bit of a masochist," Jere shrugged, standing up and brushing splintered wood from his pant leg. "And I brought you here. It's my job to make your life tolerable, at least."

Isis stayed on the floor, where Jere figured she would be for at least a little while. He wouldn't really be surprised to find her asleep later; she tended to tire herself out with these little outbursts.

"Thanks," she mumbled, looking at the floor again.

Jere said nothing, but grinned as he walked back out to the living room to find Paltrek peeling the label off the bottle, balling the paper up, and flicking it across the living room.

"Honestly, isn't one child in the house bad enough?" Jere flopped down next to him and resumed the drink that had been so rudely interrupted a few minutes ago.

Paltrek laughed, unconcerned. "You have slaves to clean it up," he reminded him. "Besides, I can't believe you're more irritated with me for tossing some paper around than you were with her destroying that room!"

Jere shrugged. "I guess I just figure she has a reason for what she's doing. It'll pass."

"And Wren?" Paltrek prodded him. "This has an 'inmates taking over the asylum' vibe to it!"

"Yeah, well, it's good that they're not 'inmates' and this isn't a fucking 'asylum,' then!" Jere snapped. He was most bothered by the implication that in either case he would be some sort of jailer. It was a little too close to how he had actually been feeling lately.

"Ah, shit, Jeremy, I'm sorry, I didn't mean to upset you," Paltrek gave him a conciliatory smile. "I mean, neither of them would make it at the estate, but I know you like to do things differently, and I know it works for you."

"Wren is just..." Jere tried to fight back the sadness. "He's not talking to me. Not at all. We had an argument, I guess, and he's been holed up in his room ever since, won't say a goddamn word. I miss him!"

"I'll bet," Paltrek laughed freely, the alcohol doing its work.

"I just... fuck. I don't know what to do!" Jere decided that more vodka was the answer. "What do I do?"

Paltrek laughed. "Kick the door down and smack him until he starts talking to you. Fuck him. Claim him as your own and show him who's boss."

Jere was unperturbed by the comment. It was intended to be flippant. "I didn't ask what *you* would do, I asked what *I* should do!"

"The hell if I know!" Paltrek roared with laughter. "Fuck, Jeremy, the only person I've had more than a two day relationship with in my *life* has been Dane, and we're not exactly dating, so much as enjoying a *normal* master and slave relationship. Buy him flowers or something. Maybe some jewelry."

"Don't be an asshole, he's not some trite housewife," Jere couldn't help laughing despite his irritation. "This is serious!"

"You could always give him head, that always puts me in a good mood," Paltrek suggested.

Jere rolled his eyes. "Funny, but I doubt that would go over so well."

Paltrek tossed down another shot. Jere was pretty sure they were numbering in the double digits by now. "Well, *I* never turn down good head."

"So I hear," Jere replied. Paltrek was as brash about his sex life as he was about everything else.

"Don't worry about it," Paltrek said, a little more serious now. "If the two of you are as madly in love as you seem to be — which is disgusting, by the way — it will blow over eventually and he'll start talking to you again. Do that 'I'm concerned and nice and the best master-boyfriend ever' thing that you do so well, I'm sure he'll come around."

Jere found himself strangely comforted by his friend's words. And then he wondered if he was really just losing his mind if he was comforted by receiving slave-owning and relationship advice simultaneously from Paltrek Wysocka. The vodka kept flowing.

Chapter 22

Regret

The all-too-familiar feeling of a headache pounding its way through his skull was what first woke Jere.

The creepy feeling of eyes on him as he slept jerked him upright.

"What the everloving fuck?" he exclaimed, rubbing his eyes to focus.

"You drool when you pass out drunk," Isis observed.

Jere blinked at her, then wiped his hand off on the couch cushion. Last night... overpriced vodka. Paltrek. Terrible advice. Good advice. More vodka. There may have been tears before midnight. At some point, he must have passed out on the couch.

"What time is it?" he mumbled.

"It's seven-thirty," Isis replied, sounding annoyingly awake. "Your first scheduled patient in the clinic is coming in at nine, and I figured you would want to shower and maybe throw up or eat breakfast."

Jere wondered if he was dreaming. If he was, it was some sort of twisted nightmare. "Since when do you do nice things for... since when do you do nice things?"

"Fuck you."

Despite the message, her tone was still pretty pleasant. Jere shook his head and hid it under a pillow.

"Look, I guess I kinda feel bad about you and Wren fighting, because you're clearly miserable, and so I thought, you know, you don't need to lose your fucking job as well. I think you guys used to be happy, and I don't like that I'm coming between it." Isis forced a glass of water into his hand. "Besides, I've decided I'm a hell of a lot better off with you than I am somewhere else, and if you drown in a pool of your own drool you won't be able to kill me like you promised."

Jere sat up a bit and forced some of the water down his throat. The girl was still completely insane. "You kept me alive so I could possibly kill you one day. Right. Makes perfect sense."

Isis nodded, smiling as if she *had* actually been making sense.

"Fuck. Fine," Jere muttered, sitting up and flopping his legs over the couch. He looked at the girl, sort of blurry, but still clearly awake and peppy. "Can you make toast?"

"You'd trust me to use an appliance?" she smirked.

"Well, since you didn't kill me in my sleep last night, I suppose you can't do too much damage with a toaster."

Jere half-walked, half-stumbled down the hall, leaving Isis to make toast or burn the house down. At the moment, he might feel better if the house were burned down — with him in it. Besides, Wren could put it out with his gift. Even as angry as Wren was, he wouldn't let them all burn to death. For the second time in the week, he regretted not being able to turn his healing gift on himself. As he walked past Wren's room, he regretted fucking things up with him as well. As he heaved into the toilet in the hallway bathroom, unable to make it to his bedroom, he regretted vodka.

He regretted a lot for it being so early in the morning.

A few minutes later, he emerged; dressed, showered, and feeling slightly better. The antacids and painkillers had helped, as well as the water he drank straight from the tap while showering. He found Isis sitting at the table, eating jam with a spoon, while a few pieces of toast remained on a plate. He grabbed one and forced himself to start eating it.

"Want some?" Isis tipped the jar toward him, almost empty.

Jere shook his head. The thought made his stomach turn. "Did you eat any bread, or just jam?" He winced at the thought.

"None of your damn business," Isis muttered, sticking another spoonful into her mouth. When Jere didn't respond, she shrugged. "I had the rest of what was left of the loaf."

Jere nodded. Her moods were just as unstable as ever, and she

remained defensive, upset by the slightest things. She had been no-
ticeably calmer since the surgery, which kept presenting itself in his
mind as "mind-rape," thanks to Wren's accusation. Jere forced himself to remember that it was surgery, and it was necessary, and that
she seemed better as a result. He had never seen her so cooperative,
and while the friendliness today was almost worrying, it seemed to
fit. She had mentioned on more than one occasion that she felt guilty
about the disruption that she had caused between him and Wren,
which surprised Jere. He barely realized that she noticed them at all,
but she continued to prove that she was more attentive than anyone
gave her credit for.

"I'm bored," Isis announced, interrupting Jere's musings. "I'll
help you at the clinic today."

"Be still, my little heart," Jere muttered, still not entirely sure
that he wasn't dreaming.

"Fuck you, then, you can just do it yourself and I'll stay in here!"
Isis snapped, glaring at him again.

Jere dropped into a chair, the typical response from Isis convincing him that he was awake. He realized that his comment had been
flippant, and that he had all but rejected Isis's attempt to help him.
He forced another piece of toast into his mouth. "Hey, Isis, I'm sorry.
I was just surprised. I didn't mean to be rude, but I get it, I was. I'm
not used to you being helpful, but I would love it if you'd come in
with me today."

She nodded, sucking the spoon thoughtfully as she did. "Okay,
then."

Jere said nothing. It was typical of her to get so upset at the per-
ceived slight, only to recover and calm down again almost immediately. It was either that, or she would start screaming and flee from
the room, but at least Jere always knew where he stood with her. Her
outbursts were unpredictable, but she made it clear when she was
unhappy, and she was open to fixing the problems. Jere thought that
it might be better if both he and Wren tried expressing themselves
as clearly instead of hiding and pretending that nothing was wrong.
He finished the toast, and she finished scraping the remainder of the
jam from the jar.

"Get dressed," he suggested, picking up the plate and holding his hand out for the spoon and empty jar.

"In what?" Isis pointed out. "You never bought me any fucking clothes, remember?"

Jere sighed, remembering that little detail. "Yeah, well, we couldn't really get a size for you—the part where you strike out like a wounded animal makes it a bit difficult, you know? I guess you can wear that in—it's not like I'd let you out in front of people or anything."

"I resent that!" Isis scowled at him.

Jere wasn't really sure which part she was referring to, although his best guess was all of it. "If you know what size you wear, I'll work on getting you clothes, otherwise, I guess we can just order some things in each size and let you try them on."

"You care that they fit and stuff?" Isis looked surprised. "I just, I haven't had clothes in a few years. Not like... not like my own, you know?"

Jere nodded. "I want you to be able to look nice. I'm certain that my oversized things aren't the most comfortable."

"I've worn worse..." Isis mumbled, looking away. Before either of them could say anything else, she had bounded up and toward the door of the clinic. "Come on, show me what to do!"

Jere followed. He *did* need the help, even if it came from the source of most of his problems. She wasn't Wren, but she was better than nobody. The clinic was collapsing into mess and chaos. "Do I need to warn you what will happen if you leave the clinic?"

"No!" she pouted. "Don't be so mean!"

He resisted the urge to roll his eyes at the accusation of being "mean" by reminding her to behave. "All right, all right. Come on, then, you can start with some filing. Here, there's this stack of papers, all sorts of different things, just put them into the charts they go in."

"Like... like how?" Isis looked wary.

Jere picked the first one up. "This one, Mirenda Germaine. See, the name is highlighted. Wren has gotten me very trained to highlight the names, because it makes it a lot easier for him. Now, this room is where the charts go, and they have the names on the side, last name first, first name last. Just match them up and put them in the pocket—don't worry about where they go after that, that's Wren's job, and he's likely to kill us both if we mess it up."

"He makes a lot of decisions about this," Isis observed.

"He makes a lot of decisions," Jere agreed. He tried not to think about how much he missed him. "There's also some charts kind of scattered around the office, just pick those up, see if they need anything filed in them, and put them back on the shelf, too."

They went about their day, as though it were normal. Jere, still a bit frazzled, saw patients as usual, and Isis was presumably keeping herself occupied with the charts. Jere wasn't sure why or how it was taking her so long, but he figured that any help was better than no help, and having her occupied set his mind at ease. He checked on her at lunchtime, smiling as she was putting what looked to be the last handful of charts back on the shelf.

"That took forever!" she exclaimed, grinning a bit. "Does it look all right?"

Jere glanced at it, realizing that the charts seemed to be put up in a random order. He hesitated to criticize her when she looked so proud and desperate for praise, but she would find out eventually. "I forgot to mention it, but we do usually keep them in alphabetical order."

Isis said nothing.

"No, no, it's nothing you did wrong!" Jere rushed to correct himself. "I mean, I forgot to tell you, and I'm sure it was in such a mess when you first came in, you couldn't even tell. We just, you know, it's easier that way."

"That's stupid." Isis was glaring down at the floor.

"Hey, come on, once you start helping out a bit more, you'll see—"

"Fuck you, I'm not fucking doing it!" She grabbed the closest chart and hurled it across the room. "This is just stupid!"

Jere sighed. At least had had gotten to enjoy half a day of peace, and it was a lot neater than it had been. He forced his voice to stay low and calm. "Isis, you can't do this here. Go back in the house if you want to throw a fit, and please don't undo all the good work you just did. I do appreciate it, but I can't have patients seeing and hearing you like this."

Scowling, she nodded, stomping out of the clinic and slamming the door behind her. Jere sighed. He knew she was sensitive to criticism, but this was just over the top.

The rest of the day was equally frustrating, the accumulated stress of the past week combining with the residual effects of the hangover to make him an absolute wreck. Dinner wasn't much better, as Isis refused to leave her room, and Jere was tired of eating the same simple foods every night for dinner. When he went to get a spoon, only to find them all dirty, his patience ran out, and he found himself storming to Wren's room and pounding on his door.

"Open the goddamn door, this is getting ridiculous!" He knew it wasn't right, and he knew that he was overreacting to everything, but since he first moved to Hojer, Wren had always been there for him, and he didn't know what to do without him. He pounded harder on the door, hoping that Wren would at least come and tell him to stop.

There was no response.

"Wren, I need you out here. You're the one who holds everything together, and even if you hate me, I can't fucking do this alone. I need your help. Please. The clinic is a mess and the house is a mess and there's no fucking spoons and I need you!"

No response. If anything, it was eerily silent, as if his lover was trying not to make a sound.

"Dammit, Wren, I *will* get a key and open this door!" It was a bold move, and Jere didn't want to make it. He couldn't see any other choice. He knocked again, then went back to the kitchen, where he knew the keys to every lock in the house were, carefully and neatly labeled by Wren months ago.

He selected the one to Wren's room, remembering the discussion they had had when they first found the keys. How he wanted Wren to keep it, because it was to his room. How Wren had laughed and kissed him and told him to keep it with the rest, because the only time they would ever need to use it would be if it got locked on accident. Everything had changed so much since then, it all seemed too fast and too wrong.

He walked back, feeling sick at the thought of entering Wren's room, where he was so obviously not wanted. When he had made the threat, it seemed reasonable, but now that he tried to imagine carrying it out, he felt sick and dirty. He tried the doorknob again, hoping it would be unlocked, and then stood, staring at the key in his hand.

Chapter 23

Explanations

Jere bent down and shoved it under the door before doing anything he would regret.

"It's in your hands now," Jere said, giving up control of the situation. "It was stupid of me to even say, just like it was stupid of me to talk down to you. The more I try, the more I screw up, so I'll just stop trying. I can't stop loving you, but I can stop trying to get you to do something you so obviously don't want to do."

He waited for a few moments, desperately wishing that he would hear something, some response, some protest from Wren. When he continued to hear nothing, he turned to walk away like he had promised.

"Jere."

The word was quiet, but it carried so much longing and regret. Jere turned around, relieved to lay eyes on the man he loved. He felt himself starting to smile, and then Wren was gone, retreating back into his bedroom, but the door was open. Jere followed nervously.

Wren said nothing; he just sat on the bed in silence. Jere was almost glad that he was used to resentful glares. He couldn't feel anything from his lover; Wren had learned to excel at blocking skills, but Jere could see the fear on his face. The way his eyes widened, the tension in his shoulders, the way his arms were braced on the bed, ready at any moment to launch up and off. Jere stepped in front of him, wincing when Wren pulled back, bracing himself for something.

Jere moved on instinct, dropping to his knees and placing his hands to either side of Wren, directing his attention.

"I'm sorry," he started, knowing the words were nowhere near enough. "I know I shouldn't have gotten so defensive, and I know I shouldn't have snapped at you again. You were hurt and confused and all I could think of was how nothing I was doing was good enough. I didn't even try to understand why you were upset."

"Do you know how often I used to worry that you'd invade my mind like that?" Wren asked, his face a careful mask. "I thought I knew you, I thought I could trust that you wouldn't be that sort of person."

Jere thought carefully before responding, not willing to make the same mistake he had before by getting defensive. "I didn't realize that. I promise, I wouldn't do it to you. I wouldn't do it to almost anyone, but I thought it was necessary. Not from any sort of slave-owning perspective, but from a medical perspective. And I know I fucked up by not telling you sooner, or bothering to explain it to you, but I will now. You deserve to understand why I did it."

"Does it matter?" Wren countered. "You're her master. You get to make decisions like that. I should just be thankful it's not me."

Jere didn't respond or argue with the statement. "I still owe *you* an explanation."

Wren was silent.

"Can I tell you a story?" he asked, attempting to look him in the eye, but failing when Wren wouldn't return the eye contact. "Are you listening, or are you too angry and afraid to even hear me?"

"I hear you," Wren muttered.

"When I was on my medical internship year, I spent a month — a short rotation — in a state psychiatric hospital. It was just part of the experience, most of the time I just served as their medical doctor, you know, fixing up people who hurt themselves, checking blood levels, things like that. They do a *lot* of wellness checks in those places. In most private hospitals, psychic surgeries are done by specialists. I'm not a specialist in psychiatric medicine, so I haven't done many. But, in the state hospitals, they can't afford specialists, so their regular doctors do it — we *have* technically had the training."

Wren still said nothing, glaring down at his legs, avoiding Jere's eyes.

"I had a young woman on my caseload, a few years younger

than I was at the time, maybe twenty, twenty-one. Chronically de-
pressed, for as long as she could recall. Thirty-seven known suicide
attempts, non-responsive to medications, no known family. My su-
pervisor suggested a psychic surgery to address some of the asso-
ciations she had made that were making her want to die, and I said
no, absolutely not. I wouldn't hear it. I thought it was terrible, barbaric — nothing better than the lobotomies they used to do hundreds
of years ago. I thought she could surely get better by talking with
her therapist, a wonderful woman with all sorts of emotional gifts.
The therapist suggested I do it too."

Wren had finally looked up, his face drawn and tired. He still
said nothing.

"Do you know where that young woman is now?" Jere asked,
his heart breaking as he looked into the blue eyes that he loved.

"If you're telling me this story, I'm assuming she's a happy,
well-adjusted mother of two with a white picket fence now," Wren
said, spiteful.

"She's dead."

Jere watched as Wren's eyes widened again, this time in surprise.

"She's dead because I refused to make a medically necessary
decision." Jere's voice was harsh, ragged. It hurt to think about. "I
may as well have watched a person bleeding from their neck, and
refused to stitch up the wound. She had a mind gift, you see, she
could enhance the solidity of any matter. Nobody thought much of
it, but she solidified a piece of her hair into a perfectly solid needle.
She used that needle to slice through her arm, layer by layer, until
she had laid open her veins. Since the wound was so precise, and she
knew it would close quickly once she passed out, she solidified her
skin and vein so it couldn't. By the time they found her at the fifteen
minute check, she was too far gone to save. And it was my fault."

Wren took a breath, looking shocked.

"Wren, I may as well have killed that woman myself, and I
couldn't let it happen again. Not because of some misplaced moral
guidelines. I know it's invasive, and I know it's risky, but those are
risks I felt were necessary to take. I didn't do it because she was defiant, or unmanageable, or because she's a slave and I'm her master. I

did it because it was better than watching her die."

"I've never really thought of it that way," Wren said quietly. He seemed less angry.

"No, and I've never thought of how it must feel to worry about it being used for no reason," Jere admitted. "It just isn't done. Not in ethical places, outside of here. I know so much about you, about what you've been put through, and it never even occurred to me that you would have objected to it until you did. I thought I was doing the right thing."

"I probably should have trusted you," Wren mumbled. "I was just so surprised."

"I certainly didn't handle it well," Jere admitted, thinking of his own outrage. "Can I try and explain why I wouldn't justify it to you at the time?"

"Do you have another fitting story?" Wren's tone was teasing, but Jere could tell that he was still angry.

"Not unless you count 'I'm an asshole' as a fitting story," Jere shook his head, relieved when he elicited a slight smile from Wren. "Look, when I did it, I thought that you would approve. I thought I was doing the right thing, I had stumbled on this perfect way to at least try to make things better, and I knew it would have at least some effect. I've been screwing everything else up so badly, the only thing I've got left is my healing gift, it's the only thing I can really trust. And so I did it, and I thought it was so simple, it never occurred to me that even that gets all fucked up in a place like this; that a medical procedure is used to hurt, and when you called me out on it, I just couldn't take it. It seems so stupid, now, because if I had taken a minute to talk to you, it would have made more sense to both of us, but I was too busy trying to salvage my own pride."

"It didn't cross my mind that it was a medical decision," Wren admitted. "I probably wouldn't have questioned you if you did something similar to a free person in the clinic."

Jere nodded. "I know. And I should have realized that it was out of the ordinary for you to get so upset. But even if it had been in the clinic, even if it was an everyday medical procedure that had you concerned, I still should have explained it. You don't have the right to make medical decisions for me, but you do have every right to know what goes on in this house, and know that they aren't going to affect you directly. I fucked that up, and I'm sorry."

"You really thought she would kill herself?" Wren seemed surprised.

"It was the only thing I was sure about," Jere said quietly.

"And there was no other option?" Wren's voice had softened a bit.

"I could have kept her sedated, but that has equally bad effects, if not worse, and it wasn't working, either."

"Did this work?"

Jere shrugged. "I think it helped. She's not a model slave or anything, but she's safer. She's more rational. She even tried to help out for a bit at the clinic today."

"So then, why do I keep hearing her scream, break things?" Wren challenged. "If you like, wiped her memory or whatever, shouldn't she be more compliant?"

Jere shook his head, wishing he had explained things earlier, wishing he could explain it better now. "I did *not* wipe her memory. I destroyed a very specific connection—between being promised that she was safe, and being hurt instead. Her memories of those specific things will be fuzzy, but are probably seeping back in slowly as we speak. She'll recover them all in time, but she might feel differently about them than she used to. In the meantime, she has a chance to build new memories in their place."

"Oh." Wren looked away again. They were silent a moment, before he looked at Jere appraisingly. "Aren't your knees getting sore?"

Jere laughed, not expecting the question. "They hurt like hell."

"Normally, you train for weeks to hold a kneeling position like that," Wren pointed out, smiling a bit.

"I just didn't want to stand over you," Jere confessed. "I know you hate it. It was the best I could do."

"Come sit next to me?" Wren suggested. "I missed you."

Jere hopped up, his knees stinging now that he had relieved the pressure. "Love, I missed you, too. And I felt terrible. I feel terrible. I never meant to hurt you."

"If I recall correctly, it was me who punched you," Wren pointed out. He dropped to rest his head in Jere's lap. "I don't even know *what* I was thinking—maybe I hoped you'd have me killed once and for all."

"Stop!" Jere insisted, his tone light. "I can't handle two suicidal slaves at once. Especially if I'm madly in love with one."

Wren stiffened. "Still?" he asked, his voice barely perceptible.

"Of course," Jere said sincerely, running his hand across his back with care, wanting nothing more than to hold him close and never let him go. "One little argument doesn't change that. Or even a big one."

Wren was quiet, but his hand came up to trace patterns across Jere's leg, almost mimicking the patterns that Jere was tracing along his back.

"Thank you for letting me in here tonight," Jere said quietly. "I felt awful even considering coming in here against your wishes."

"I figured you were entitled to it," Wren shrugged. "But then, when you walked away, I realized that you did at least deserve a chance to tell your side. It didn't seem fair, me being the only one standing in the way."

"I got in the way of things too," Jere pointed out. "Maybe if I would have been civil to begin with, it wouldn't have come to that."

Wren smiled. Jere tried to stop himself from feeling so enamored.

"I've been snappy with you for weeks," Wren pointed out. "I yelled at you, punched you in the face, refused to talk to you, abandoned you at home and at work, and shut down the mind connection in the most hurtful way possible, on purpose. Honestly, I don't think I could fault you if you did take Paltrek's advice and beat the hell out of me."

"You heard that, too?" Jere realized that everyone in the house had been sober and full of memories except him.

"I did," Wren grinned. "You were in fine form."

"I'll bet," Jere smiled down at him. "You know, though, I mean, that I'd never—"

"Yes, dear," Wren teased, putting his arms around him rather awkwardly, given the way they were lying together. "I know very well that you'd never do that. Although, I almost wish you had hit me back. Jere... I'm so sorry!"

Jere pulled him up, holding him close. "It's okay," he said. "I mean, I think I was mostly surprised. Okay, yeah, and it hurt. It is okay, though. I might have had it coming. And in the moment... hell, I couldn't even process it for a while. You do have a pretty good swing."

"Oh, hush," Wren let himself be cuddled. "Put the mind connection back? It's so lonely without you in my head."

"I'd be honored to," Jere initiated it immediately, the old paths and patterns quickly reactivating. Once again, he felt Wren's calm, steady presence, felt the love and concern and compassion that flowed between them. "I missed you so much."

"Let's never do that again," Wren decided, a big smile on his face.

His emotions betrayed the smile, and Jere picked up on the uncertainty and doubt beneath it. He leaned in, kissing Wren lightly, just barely grazing his lips. It was equal parts wanting to kiss him and wanting to explore his reactions through the mind connection before he started blocking again.

"Are you worried about *me*? Or *you*?"

Wren turned away, shy and embarrassed. "I need a few minutes to block, shit!"

Jere shook his head. "You don't have to," he reminded him. "You can feel that way. I was just curious."

Wren stopped his frantic attempt to shield the bad feelings away. "I've had a lot of time to think, lately, and I'm worried that things will change. I don't know what it will be like, and that scares me."

"It might change, love, but it won't be bad. I'll do everything I can to make this work out, to give you what you need. It was my ill-advised decision that changed everything, and we're still dealing with it. I had no idea the impact it would have. How we work, how we interact, those all changed because of it. *This*, this fight or whatever, it's just another example. Nothing's the same, and even if I got rid of Isis tomorrow, it still wouldn't be." Jere couldn't bear the sad look in his lover's eyes. "But here's what will never change: I care about you, more than anything else in the world, even though I fuck it up sometimes. I love you. I need you. And I will never purposely hurt you."

Wren was quiet again. "You said that you got so upset because the only thing you have left is your healing gift, but what about us? Can't you trust me? I want to be there for you as much as you want to be there for me, but it doesn't work when neither of us will work with each other."

"That's true," Jere agreed. So often, he had focused more on the problems they were having instead of the way that they could and did work together. "I forget, sometimes, that I'm not alone in this."

"I think I do too," Wren agreed.

Jere could feel him thinking, feel the mixture of emotions through the connection, and yet Wren didn't seem inclined to speak. He prompted him, ever so slightly. "I've pretty much taken up the whole conversation tonight."

"That's okay," Wren said, holding Jere tightly. "I don't really have much to say right now. I missed you, and I'm glad you told me what you did, but I still need some time to think."

Wren hadn't asked permission in so many words, but Jere could sense the question. He wouldn't demand it; he was making far too many demands of his lover already. Instead, he returned the affection, holding Wren close and giving him the space he needed to figure it out. "Take as long as you need, love. I'll be here when you're ready."

Chapter 24

Cleaning House

Wren was surprised that he was able to sleep that night. He was torn between feeling relieved, scared, and still angry. The apologies and explanations had made things better, but they didn't undo anything, and they didn't make any of the feelings disappear. He didn't know what to do with any of these feelings, and although Jere had promised him that he didn't have to shield them, he did. Maybe not for Jere, but for himself. He wasn't ready to think about them or confront them yet, and most certainly he was not ready to talk about them.

Instead, he had sobbed out his fear and uncertainty and relief while Jere held him, curled up next to him in the small bed that they so rarely used. He said nothing, which Wren was eternally grateful for, and neither of them heard a peep from the disruptive child down the hall. Wren briefly considered that she might be more attentive and considerate than anyone had thought.

The past week had been hell for him, complete and utter hell. He was startled at some point to realize that, while he was logically a bit afraid of being sold or punished in some way, that fear was miniscule compared to his fear of ruining the relationship that he and Jere shared. Love, intimacy, connection—he had never thought that he would have these things, and he realized that he had taken them for granted once he did. It could all be so easily thrown away.

A part of him knew he should invest in maintaining the relationship because it offered him extremely good protection. He hadn't survived as a slave as long as he had without attending to these facets of life. Yet, most of his agonized thoughts didn't come from a slave's perspective, they came from a lover's perspective. He cared about Jere, and he knew that Jere cared about him, and the thought that either of them had ruined that... it terrified him still, as he lay in his lover's arms, watching the sun come up over the trees that skirted the edge of the property, the ones that had been too far away to get caught up in the fire he caused a year ago.

The leaves were turning colors, gold and red and brown. Wren was always amazed to think of the resiliency of nature; pictures of trees from hundreds of years ago showed the same colors, as if all the changes that the world had gone through had no impact on their routine. Some plants had died off, or stopped growing in certain areas, but new ones replaced them, life continued unperturbed by human interference. He couldn't say the same for his own life; the changes he had gone through just in the past year had been massive. Just over a year had passed since Jere had come to Hojer. A year since he killed his first master, and tried to kill himself. A year since he had been rescued and treated kindly and carefully. A year since he first laid eyes on the man he would lay his life down for in a heartbeat.

In some ways, a year was a long time, but sometimes it felt like everything was moving very fast, too fast, really. Their first kiss hadn't even been a year ago, but he felt like Jere had always been a part of him. The week they had spent apart only made that more apparent. When he tried to stop and think about it, he could still barely wrap his mind around the changes that had occurred, making him who he was. A year ago, he would have died at the very thought of disagreeing with his master — now, he had flagrantly disobeyed and disrespected him on numerous occasions, not to mention physically attacking him, and here he was, lying next to him.

They stayed in Wren's room on some sort of tacit agreement, turning it into a transitional place. Going back to their room seemed like too big a jump for both of them. Besides, neither of them minded the small, cozy bed, where they simply held each other and kissed lightly as the day faded into night. Wren had asked that they not talk anymore, not right away. Jere had dumped out his thoughts on everything, but Jere was always better at things like that. He knew how he was feeling and what he wanted, and he was okay asking for it. Wren, on the other hand, needed time to fight with himself and his memories and his expectations. It was too painful to talk right away, and he still needed time to think, now that he knew that Jere was back on his side. It was a lot to process, but Jere had simply nodded, caressing the back of his head like he always did. Wren felt like he slept better that night than he had in weeks.

Morning was upon them too soon, and Wren reluctantly squirmed his way out of Jere's arms. As was typical, Jere mumbled his protests and reached for him, but fell back asleep quickly once Wren was up. Wren grinned, looking down at his sleeping boyfriend, and went to the kitchen, for once to make food instead of squirreling it away back to his room. He was surprised by how low they were on supplies, and he began making a mental list of what he would buy when he went to the store.

Breakfast was ready quickly, and he left the stove on low to keep it warm while he slipped back into the bedroom and placed a kiss full on Jere's lips to wake him up. Jere's eyes flew open, and he smiled, reaching out to pull Wren down on top of him. More than anything, he had missed this, the stolen moments with Jere when they didn't think about work or talk about what needed to be done.

They rolled around together for a while before the smell of breakfast lured them out and into the dining room, where they found Isis setting out plates as though it were an everyday occurrence. Wren wondered if he was dreaming.

"Nice that you started cooking again," Isis grinned at him. "Jere was trying his best to starve me into submission."

Wren rolled his eyes. He wasn't exactly fond of the girl, but he appreciated her efforts, both to help out and to make light of the situation. If anything, she seemed a little calmer than she had been. He considered that Jere might have really done what was necessary.

"Maybe one day, you'll learn how to cook for yourself," he halfsuggested as he brought the food out.

"But what motivation would either of us have when you're so damn good at it?" Jere slid an arm around his waist, nuzzling against his neck.

Wren did his best to set the food down despite the disruption. In truth, he was happy to feel his lover's hand against his skin again.

"Gross," Isis mumbled through a forkful of potatoes that made it into her mouth before anything made it onto her plate.

Wren raised an eyebrow at her before grabbing Jere by the back of the head and kissing him. He knew it was childish, but it was fun, and he had missed having fun. Isis made a face and continued to eat, pointedly pretending they weren't there.

They were quiet for a moment, filling their plates and starting to eat, before Wren decided to inquire about the day. "So, it's a bit... unkempt in here." He was trying to be subtle. "Dirty" was a much more accurate word.

"Yeah." Jere shrugged. "The clinic is, uh..."

"Similar?" Wren assumed, rolling his eyes as Jere nodded.

"Worse," Isis contributed.

"Lovely," Wren shook his head. "Where would you like me to start?"

"Isis, were you planning on helping out today?" Jere asked, hopeful.

Wren fought to keep his face still, fighting the urge to wrinkle his nose in distaste. She'd probably just be in the way.

She shrugged. "I'm not going to fucking file anything, if that's what you're asking."

"That wasn't what I was asking, I was asking if you were planning to help at all."

Wren had no idea how Jere resisted getting angry.

Isis was silent for a few moments. "I guess. I mean, what do you want me to do?"

"Um..." Jere faltered for a moment. *"Wren, could you take charge here? I know that I need you up front at the clinic, people are starting to wonder, and I don't know that I necessarily want to encourage Isis to traipse around the house all day, but otherwise, this is your area of expertise."*

"I'm sure there are a pile of instruments and the like to be washed and sterilized," Wren said. It was one of his least favorite tasks, as the sterilization solution had to be left on for a while, and Wren could work so much more quickly than the chemical could.

Jere smiled, looking hopeful. "Would you?" he looked to Isis.

"You're letting me play with sharp things?"

"Not 'play,' clean!" Wren corrected, unsurprised when she narrowed her eyes at him.

"Is there any reason I should be worried?" Jere asked, his voice calm. Wren could sense the nervousness beneath it.

Another shrug from the girl. "I guess not. I mean, I can always find something to hurt myself with, anyway."

"Right," Jere muttered, then looked to Wren. "You probably need to do your wonderful thing at the front desk. I made a mess of things in there, and if you get a chance, is there something you could do, um..." Jere glanced around helplessly.

"Something about the mess in the house?" Wren supplied, grinning as he made Jere blush. "Yes. You can thank me for having a speed gift later."

Wren started the workday by checking in their first patient, and watching as Jere slipped into mind-healing with him. He smiled, watching the man he loved at work, and then stepped into the prep room. He was surprised to find Isis waiting for him patiently.

"He didn't even yell at you or anything?" Isis said, looking at him warily.

"Who—" Wren stopped himself, realizing what she was talking about. "Jere? No. No, he doesn't. Ever, really. He knows it makes me uncomfortable."

"You hit a free man," she pointed out, a bit in awe. "Your master. You could have been publicly whipped to death for that. Even *I* wouldn't be that bold!"

Wren began pulling down the supplies, eager to escape her gaze. "I wouldn't advise it."

"He thought you hated him."

Wren was only slightly irked at the fact that Jere had talked about him with the girl. He figured Jere needed to talk to someone. He pushed a sponge toward her. "You clean them with this first."

"Did you?" She took the sponge and the first dirty utensil as she looked at him. "Did you hate him, for what he did to me?"

"It was never about you." It was harsh, but true. "It was more than that."

"So you've said," Isis pointed out, grinning at him. "Memory gift, remember? So, do you still hate him, then? Is this some sort of plot so he keeps you in his favor?"

A part of him railed at the very idea of hating Jere; it offended him that Isis would even suggest that he would think such a thing. But he hadn't denied it, either. A part of him could have hated Jere, because if it came down to it, he would rather hate Jere than be afraid of him. He had dealt with so many feelings during those few days, hiding in his room, and he still wasn't sure what they all meant. "I certainly do not hate him. I love him. I never *stopped* loving him. If anything, I was angry, and a little scared, but I love him. And I... I trust him again."

Isis smiled, following Wren's motions as he instructed her. "I'm sorry I fucked things up between the two of you. I thought it would be better if I were just gone, and since he wouldn't let me kill myself, I thought he might go too far and kill me. All I ever do is make everyone around me miserable, and it makes me feel terrible."

Wren shook his head in disbelief, but he chose his words carefully. He had never heard the girl truly apologize before, and he had never stopped to think about why she took the actions she did. "Thank you. It means a lot to me. And I know it would mean a lot to Jere, too."

She nodded. "It's been a long time since I wanted to make anybody happy just because, you know? Like, not because they would beat me or hurt me or anything, but just... because I didn't like seeing them sad. I remember I used to like making people happy."

Wren considered it for a moment, stopping to wonder what Isis might have been like as a very little girl, before she was taken as a slave. It was something that wasn't usually done, thinking about times before someone was taken, but in this house, nothing was done according to custom. It suddenly seemed almost natural to think of his fellow slave as someone who used to be a person, just like Wren used to be a person, instead of a slave. As a slave, Isis was disruptive, annoying, and threatening, but as a free child, she could have been anything. Wren knew that his younger self wasn't even close to the man he had turned out to be, so much had changed since then, including Jere's presence in his life.

Isis interrupted his thoughts. "He really wasn't lying, was he? Jere. When he said I'd be safe here?"

Wren shook his head. "No. He wasn't. He means it—for both

of us."

Wren left the girl to her task, satisfied that she understood. Talking to her was almost unnerving. She was entirely different from the wild beast she had been, but she was certainly still skittish, still guarded. He wondered if he had been that way when Jere first arrived. She was defiant, too, which he certainly wasn't. But then, he had killed his last master, so maybe a little defiance had been hiding inside him after all.

He fell into the routine of attending the front desk easily, smiling at patients as they came in and guiding them through paperwork, cleaning up the front desk and filing area in the short breaks. He was somewhat surprised that everything appeared to have been filed into the appropriate charts, but was at a loss to explain the haphazard order that they had been shelved in. With a sigh, he quickly alphabetized them.

There was a lull, as usual, between the morning rush and the noon rush. People always either wanted to be there first thing, or stopped by before the doors closed for lunch. Inconsiderate, but predictable. Wren seized the opportunity to peek in on Isis, surprisingly engaged and focused on what she was doing, then slipped into the house to address the mess it had become in his brief absence. He seemed to recall sharing the house with a teenager and a grown man, but their ability to pick up after themselves was more comparable to young children.

Light dusting and a sweep of the floors took care of the guest bedrooms, which were never used anyway. Wren grinned to himself, feeling like he was cheating to think that "half" the house was clean already. Jere's office took a minute or two more, as Wren had to retrieve the coffee mugs that Jere had taken as prisoners and dump the trash. On his way between the rooms, he noticed a faint, but unpleasant smell coming from Isis's room. He debated for a moment, not entirely sure he wanted to know *what* it was, but he figured that he should find out.

It took him a few minutes to locate the source of the smell, especially as he was somewhat distracted by the rest of the mess in the room — clothing strewn about, a plate and cup here, something broken there, bloodstains on the floor and wall that would just *not* come up. It was while he was tracking down and attempting to clean the bloodstains that he found the source of the smell.

Beneath the bed, behind a few small dresser drawers that had gone missing, and under a balled up shirt was an assortment of food in varying states of decay, some wrapped in napkins, others still in bowls. The odor was worse, but Wren couldn't help but explore further, gagging as he uncovered something black and green and wiggling. He hoped that whatever it was had just been jarred by his explorations, but considering the state of the mess, he would not have been surprised to see bugs. The thought made him retreat quickly, not at all eager to find out whether his suspicions were correct.

Pressed against the wall at the very back of the pile were a variety of cans and boxes — it explained where all their food supplies had gone, despite nobody cooking. Wren debated cleaning it up, but decided it was most certainly a thing for Jere to see. He could tolerate the girl, and he didn't even mind cleaning up the usual messes that she made, but dealing with things like this was really something Jere would be far better at. Wren didn't understand how someone could live like this, especially when she wasn't being forced to. He had eaten his share of unpalatable items, but never by choice, and never when there were perfectly good things to eat.

He shook his head and cleaned the rest of the room up before strolling into the clinic to check the desk and find their master.

Chapter 25
Reconnecting

Jere caught him in the doorway.

"I need you for something," he said, nonchalantly, although he was grinning a bit.

Wren followed him, and found himself pulled into an empty exam room, the light filtering in from the window making Jere's face glow in front of him.

"Can I kiss you?" Jere whispered, pulling the door shut.

Wren nodded, a thrill of excitement going through him, and Jere pulled him close, wrapping his arms around Wren as their lips met, their bodies folding together like they had so many times before. Wren was still conflicted about his feelings toward Jere; he still hadn't let go of the anger he had clung to for days, and he wondered if he even remembered how to connect with him so intimately. Very quickly, he realized that he had nothing to worry about, because as doubtful as he may have been, his body remembered, fitting against Jere's like it belonged there. Wren felt himself relax in his lover's arms, felt himself melting into the kiss, felt the warm, familiar feeling of love and connection and safety that he always did when he was right where he was supposed to be. He felt Jere stop blocking his emotions, and he was instantly overcome with feelings of relief and gratitude and joy, bursting forth, filling him and exploding across his eyes with bright lights and happy colors.

Their tongues danced with each other, their hands scrabbled across each other's backs to find something to hold, and Wren pushed harder, closer, trying to feel as much of Jere's body as he could. He was desperate to be close to him, as if their skin could erase the distance that had grown between them. He pushed Jere back, hard, aroused when he heard him exhale sharply as his back came in contact with a wall. At first, Wren cursed the wall for being there, for getting in his way, but he started feeling pleased as he realized Jere could go nowhere. For now, Jere was all his, pinned by Wren's body and clearly enjoying it. Still craving more contact, Wren slid his hands under Jere's lab coat, under his shirt, and across his stomach, never breaking contact with his mouth as he did.

Jere squirmed his way out of the coat, freeing his arms up, only to have them pinned above his head. Wren wanted to feel him, to touch him, to re-explore that which had been his and nearly lost. He didn't want any distractions, not even if those distractions came in the form of Jere touching him.

With the grace of practice and ease of a speed gift, he unbuttoned Jere's pants with one hand, pulling them down over his already hard cock, which made Wren's heart race. He captured Jere's cock in his hand and stroked a few times, feeling Jere moan and whimper beneath him. Wren stared into his eyes, loving the way that his boyfriend looked when he was being touched, the look that practically begged Wren to fuck him. Wren kept stroking Jere's cock, but he stuck to slow, short movements that had Jere desperately squirming in an attempt to get more. Jere was really quite beautiful when he struggled like this.

Wren felt himself growing hard as well, just thinking about Jere, touching him, tasting his lips. It had been so long, too long, and Wren could barely contain himself. He felt his temperature rising, and a smile started forming at the edge of his lips.

Before he could stop himself, he had grabbed Jere's shoulder and turned him forcefully around, breaking the kiss. He still held Jere's hands above his head, although he did loosen his grip for a moment, allowing Jere to twist toward the wall. With his free hand, Wren unbuttoned and unzipped his own pants, freeing his cock, and guiding it toward Jere's entrance. He finally paused, realizing how quickly he was moving, and rested his upper body against Jere's back, his lips nibbling on Jere's ear.

"Fuck me," Jere whispered, taut under his touch. He arched his back, sending Wren a clear invitation.

Wren ground against him, biting lightly at his neck. "No lube. You're not prepared." He wanted to be inside of Jere, but he would settle for this, for rubbing against him and thinking about how satisfying it would be to fuck him again.

"Fuck me," Jere repeated, thrusting back against Wren as much as he could. "*I don't care if you hurt me. I want to feel you so bad that it already hurts, just fuck me.*"

Wren didn't feel like arguing. He didn't feel like getting lube. He felt like pounding into Jere until he screamed, and that was exactly what he did. He tightened his grip on Jere's arms with one hand, wrapped the other around to grab Jere's cock, and forced his way into him without hesitating.

They both screamed. The sex was rough, it was hasty, and they both came in under a minute, the burning pain between them enough to make up for the lack of time that they spent doing it. Wren couldn't quite say what was going through his mind, if anything, only that he loved the hot, tight feeling around him. He loved the way he felt Jere shudder as he came, a moment before Wren let go himself, and he loved the way Jere moaned as Wren bit down harder on his shoulder. The pleasure and the pain and the heat between them were the only things that Wren was aware of, and he enjoyed it that way. They stayed like that for a moment, panting and shaking, pressed together against the wall. Neither had the energy or ambition to move elsewhere.

"Fuck," Jere mumbled, his voice cracking. He was gasping for air, his hair damp with sweat, and Wren could feel his legs starting to shake.

Wren let his arms go, carefully, knowing that Jere was all but dangling from his grip. He stayed close, feeling the heat from Jere's body as he supported him, helping him to be steady on his feet. "We just did that, I believe." He slid out, feeling a bit guilty as he heard Jere draw in a pained breath. "Sorry," he whispered, moving away from him a fraction of an inch before he felt Jere's hands on his own, pulling his arms around him, and bringing him closer again.

"Don't apologize," Jere said, still shuddering in the aftereffects of his orgasm. "I feel too good to be apologized to right now."

Wren said nothing, just smiled as he held his lover close for a while longer.

"I can't believe we just had a quickie in the exam room," Jere said, laughing as he recovered and started breathing normally again. "That was unexpected. I really did just lure you in here to kiss you!"

Wren turned him around so they were facing again, kissing him much more gently this time. "Didn't I say I missed you?"

"You did," Jere mumbled, still not moving away. "I missed you, too. Although, Christ, if this is the kind of reward I get from being away from you..."

"Hush!" Wren teased. "Shit, we're gonna have to change. Do you have patients waiting?"

"Nobody that's an emergency," Jere grinned, looking perfectly satisfied.

Wren guided his blissed-out lover to an exam table. "Sit. Stay. I'll bring clothes."

He returned in under a minute, with clean clothes for them both, and they were mostly successful at keeping their hands off each other as they changed.

"By the way," Wren remembered as he helped Jere to button his shirt. "Your new girl has a veritable science project growing under her bed. It's really... it's really fucking weird. You should have a look at it."

Neither of them mentioned it at lunch that day, and Wren subtly found another simple task in the clinic for Isis to work on while he pulled Jere into the house and pointed out the collection of food.

Jere winced at the sight. "Jesus," he muttered. He approached it, seemingly with the same morbid fascination that Wren had, and poked at a few of the dishes. He drew back about as quickly as Wren had, wincing when the smell hit him.

"What do I do with it?" Wren asked, at a loss. "I was going to clean it up, but..."

Jere shook his head. "No, love, I'm glad you showed me. And that you left it. Shit." He stood up, motioning for Wren to follow him out of the room. "Look, you're going to buy supplies today anyway, right?"

Wren nodded, waiting for more. He was interested to see how

Jere planned to handle this ridiculous mess.

"Well, in addition to whatever you were going to buy, can you do me a huge favor?" Jere bit his lower lip, which Wren knew meant he was a bit reluctant to ask.

"Since you asked so nicely." He tried to make light of the situation.

"Pick up as many non-perishable things as you can—they have that whole section for emergency preparation in case of power outages with all the dried meats and vegetables and ready-to-eat meals. And some normal snack foods, too, crackers, cookies, things like that; she does seem to favor sweets. Just anything that could reasonably be kept and eaten without any sort of preparation, okay?" Jere was looking hopeful.

Wren raised an eyebrow. "You're going to stock her little nest?"

Jere shrugged. "I'm going to let her stock it, if she needs to." At Wren's disbelieving look, he continued. "Look, she obviously feels the need to do it, and it's not hurting anybody—it just can't be things like spaghetti and sandwiches."

Wren could see where he was coming from, although he didn't completely agree with it himself. But Jere knew Isis better than he did, and had made much more progress in working with her than he would have thought possible. He wanted Jere to trust him with decisions; this was one that he would trust Jere on. "And this?" He waved a hand at the mess.

"I'll talk to her about it later and have her clean it up," Jere promised. "Don't say anything to her about it, yet."

Wren was at least relieved that he didn't have to deal with the mess himself, and did pick up a wide variety of storable foods while he was shopping that day. Included in his shopping list were also stain removers, paint, and materials to fix at least *some* of the things that had broken. He decided that the quickie that he and Jere had earlier was much more enjoyable than shopping.

By the end of the day, the house had been refilled with supplies, cleaned, and mostly put back in order. Wren had yet to reorder the medical supplies, but a quick glance through the still-haphazard inventory told him there were no dire supply emergencies. He made sure to keep everything stocked at least a month in advance, in case anything should happen. Supply shortages, especially for medical supplies, were a problem in such rural areas, but even large cities had a hard time keeping some stocked items when outbreaks of disease struck. Compounding the problem was the fact that Jere tended toward newer treatments that were rarely used in these parts of the world, and a large majority of their supplies required special ordering anyway.

As much as he hated admitting it, it was rather nice having Isis around the clinic, even though she bristled at being directly ordered to do anything. Slight criticism had her storming away, but Wren couldn't help but notice that even casual praise made her light up and smile. He knew from experience how hard it was to never feel like you were doing things right as a slave, and he guessed that she hadn't done anything worthy of praise in years. While she tended to work slowly, she was careful and surprisingly thorough, and the extra set of hands took quite a bit of pressure off of him and Jere both.

Dinner was similarly peaceful, and Wren found himself appreciating Jere's decision to put off confronting Isis until the work day had passed.

"Isis, we need to have a talk about something," Jere said as Wren cleared away their plates, his voice level and calm.

"I didn't fucking do anything! Don't yell at me!" Isis went from calm to panicked in a matter of seconds, pushing her chair back away from the table and pulling her arms close to protect herself.

Jere was silent for a moment. "I didn't say you did, and I'm not going to yell at you," he said, quieter than usual. "I just need to talk with you about something."

Isis glared back and forth, from Jere to Wren, then back again. Wren felt almost bad for her, watching her breathe heavily and struggle to remain seated.

"I'm really trying to be good," she whimpered.

Jere, to his credit, didn't change his tone a bit. "You're doing just fine. I'm not angry. You're not in trouble. Do you understand that?"

Isis nodded.

"Okay," Jere paused a moment, waiting for some unspoken sign that she was a bit more calm. "Listen, again, nobody is angry at you, but Wren was cleaning today, and he found your stash of food."

Isis said nothing. She went pale, closed her eyes, and started shaking.

"It's okay, you don't have to worry—"

"Please don't starve me!"

Wren had found it hard to feel sympathy for the girl, but her desperate plea pained him in a way he hadn't realized was possible. He knew exactly how it felt.

"He wouldn't do that to you, Isis," he heard himself saying. "I promise. Jere wouldn't do it, and I wouldn't let him."

Her eyes opened and she looked at him and Jere with doubt.

"I have something to show you," Jere said, standing slowly. "Please, come into the kitchen for just a minute? You'll like what you see."

Isis stood, nodding as she followed him. Wren trailed behind them, curious to see what played out. His respect for Jere grew more and more with every minute he saw him with this slave.

Jere opened the pantry, where the supplies were kept. He pointed to the shelf where all the non-perishable things were stored. "Anything you want, help yourself. There are things in cans, things in boxes, things in little individual foil things. You can take as many as you'd like, and you can keep them wherever you want, and if you run out or you want something different, tell me or Wren and we'll get you more. I would *never* try and keep food from you, is that understood?"

Isis nodded, crying now.

"The only rule with this is that you absolutely cannot keep anything in your room that will spoil or go bad," Jere said gently. "That means no spaghetti, no sandwiches, no uncooked eggs. Or cooked eggs, for that matter—no eggs! It smells bad, it attracts bugs, and it's terribly unhealthy for you to eat things like that. Isis, you are welcome to use the kitchen at any time—the fridge, the stove, anything you need, okay? But you can't keep food under your bed. Not food that will go bad."

"I just thought, if you stopped feeding me, that would be better," Isis tried to explain. "I didn't eat it. I didn't want to bother you anymore by being sick again, I just thought that if you locked me in there or forgot or something... I just didn't want to be hungry anymore."

"You won't be," Jere reassured her. "I promise."

Isis balled up her fists and leaned against the wall, dropping to sit on the floor as she sobbed. "I'm sorry. I'm sorry I'm so fucked up! You shouldn't have to put up with this; you should just get rid of me or kill me or something. I'm too fucked up. You're too nice to me, and I'm still doing shit like this, and it's been so long and I'm never going to get better!"

"It's okay," Jere continued, his voice still calm and steady. "You take as much time as you need. You're not hurting anybody."

She finally looked up at Wren. "You must think I'm disgusting. I'm sorry you had to find that and clean it up," she mumbled, clearly mortified that anyone was onto her secret.

"Well..." Wren started, looking to Jere to finish.

"He didn't clean it up," Jere told her, kneeling a few feet away. "I told him not to. I think Wren has enough to deal with without cleaning up rotting food from under a bed, don't you?"

Isis nodded, sniffling a bit.

"Okay," Jere gave her a minute to compose herself. "It's on you to clean it up, throw out anything that has spoiled, and put away the things you shouldn't really eat without cooking them—flour, rice— Isis, you can get sick or hurt your teeth trying to eat those things! I'd feel horrible!"

"I took those things?" Isis shook her head. "I didn't... I didn't realize."

Jere shrugged. "It's okay. You don't have to feel bad about it."

"It won't happen again," Isis said, her voice small and scared. "I really am sorry."

Jere smiled, and Wren chipped in, "Oh, come on, I didn't apologize that much for giving him a black eye! Why don't you go and get it cleaned up so I can take it out with the rest of the trash before I go to bed?"

Isis nodded, fleeing without another word. Wren figured she had been waiting for an escape opportunity. He walked over to Jere, sitting next to him on the floor and putting a hand on his leg.

Chapter 26

Discoveries

"You're good with her," Wren said softly. "I doubt I'd do as well."

"She's coming around..." Jere looked at him doubtfully. "She is coming around, isn't she?"

Wren thought about it. Compared to where she probably should be, not really, but compared to when they found her... "She's made a lot of progress, Jere."

Jere nodded, but Wren could feel the doubt through the mind connection.

"You know, you keep on taking broken slaves and fixing them and we'll have to name your clinic The Home For Recalcitrant and Wayward Slaves," Wren teased, resting his head on his lover's shoulder. It felt so good, so familiar. He had missed touching Jere so much over the past week that it amazed him to think he had gone years without enjoying it.

"Were you so broken when I got here?" Jere smiled back at him. "I seem to recall you being pretty on top of everything."

"I just hid it better," Wren admitted, shrugging. "I had stupidly decided I wanted to live again, after my attempt at ending my life failed so fantastically. And then I found someone worth being on top of..."

Wren let his words trail off, feeling them replaced by a light kiss.

"Wren, she's so fucking young!" Jere muttered, keeping his voice low so it wouldn't carry. "She's just a child!"

"She's a slave, Jere," Wren reminded him. It was strange to think of it that way, because he was a slave as well, but he often felt like he was in such a different category than Isis. "You cease to be a child once you become a slave. You can't be both."

"Wren, she was seven fucking years old!" Jere protested. "Surely she wasn't..."

"Wasn't what?" Wren asked rhetorically. "Beaten? Raped? Terrorized? Baby, you know she was."

"I do. I don't like it, but I do. Wren, fuck, we didn't get to talk about this, but the things I saw when I did the mind-ra—dammit—mind-*surgery* on her... it was so awful! Things you wouldn't do to an adult, much less a little girl! It's sick. Wrong. Awful!"

"That's why they take most kids at thirteen," Wren pointed out. Truthfully, he had never given it much thought. It was just the way things were. Once your physical gift showed and marked you as a slave, your childhood ended. Nobody thought of new slaves as teenagers, not even if their free age-mates were still being treated like children at home. The only difference between a slave at fifteen and a slave at fifty was that slaves were usually used up by fifty.

"Why would they take her so early though!" Jere looked pleadingly at him. "I don't understand!"

It was sad, but Wren laughed at Jere's horror and inexperience with the slave trade. "Jere, a child with a gift like that could be very dangerous—think about all the secrets she could know! All the spying she could be used for."

"Do parents here regularly use their children as spies?" Jere looked skeptical.

"Well, no, but..." Wren paused. He realized he was thinking from the perspective he had been brought up with—that slaves, that people with physical gifts were dangerous, threatening, needing to be controlled. He considered it in light of more abolitionist mindsets, and reminded himself to curse at Kieran next time he saw her for filling his head with propaganda. "But someone wanted to use her that way, and they had every right to do so."

Jere shook his head. "That's fucking cold."

"I know," Wren said quietly. "It is. And it's awful. But that slave has not really been a child in seven or eight years. As long as me, really."

"You know, when I saw the ad, I thought she was fresh from

a training facility," Jere confessed. "I thought she had just run into some hard luck with her first master, maybe a few first masters, maybe just couldn't conform to life as a slave. I thought she was being sold so quickly because she still had some spirit left. I thought it would be great for her here — she wouldn't be so brainwashed yet, wouldn't be so broken. I had no idea that I'd get a child who had been a slave for more years than she had been a child."

Wren put an arm around him, pulling him close. "You are always so optimistic. I doubt she ever saw the inside of a training facility."

Jere shook his head. "She did. It was in her records. For about eight months, when she was thirteen and fourteen. They thought it might straighten her out, but she ended up making things worse for the new slaves, and refused to learn anything. She was deemed unteachable and recommended for use in a brothel or work house. The speed with which she was sold and sold again after that was outrageous."

"How many masters has she had?"

Jere shrugged. "The first kept her for a little over a year. After that, the turnaround was pretty quick — I think it was somewhere in the thirties."

"Damn." Adjusting to a new master was terrible. New rules, new expectations, new punishments — and no idea how to gauge what any of those might be. "Was she always like this, then?"

Another shrug. "The reports are limited, mostly just reasons for sale, but it seems that she was always defiant, but more in a refusing to work sort of way. She realized pretty early on that she would be of no value to anyone if she were dead or disabled, and she held at least some power by refusing to use her gift for her masters."

"Isn't that what got her sold, though?"

"Yeah. I suppose eight-year-olds aren't so good at planning."

Wren shook his head. There was never an age at which one could really say that they felt "prepared" to hand over their life and will to another, to be beaten and raped and neglected and treated worse than some dumb animal. At least most slaves weren't taken until they were teenagers, giving them a chance to have a childhood. "How did she survive this long, though?" he wondered aloud.

"I'm guessing she wasn't always this bad," Jere admitted. "I mean, her last few sales have dropped so significantly in value, have been so quick — I wonder if everyone just thought that since she was young, they could turn her around."

"And in her last few sales, she was set on dying," Wren realized. He knew the feeling quite well. "She had nothing to lose."

"Don't talk about me like I'm not here," Isis said, entering the room again with both arms full of food. Her tone was surprisingly bright.

"Well, to be fair, you *weren't* here, you were in another room," Jere pointed out, looking up at her from his seat on the floor with a grin on his face.

Isis wrinkled her nose as she dumped one armload of food into the trash bin. She didn't say anything more on the subject, but moved to the pantry and began to put the food back in it.

"I thought you said I had taken flour?" she asked, a few items still in her arms. It seemed that she was making somewhat of an effort to return the items to the shelves they had come from. "I didn't find any."

Wren raised an eyebrow. The new bag was sitting in her arms as she spoke, a picture of some sort of tasty baked goods underneath the bold, blue letters reading FLOUR. "And so that bag just jumped into your arms of its own accord?" he teased.

Isis looked down at her items, reddened, and grabbed the bag, shoving it into the pantry without another glance. "Oh, I, uh, I thought it was sugar. Must not have looked at it or something."

Jere was making some light comment about paying attention, but Wren wasn't listening. He thought about the girl's vehement refusal to file anything. The files that were inexplicably put back in random order. The big, block letters on the bag of flour.

"You can't read, can you?" he blurted out, startled by the thought.

She dropped the remaining items to the floor and fled to her room, a string of unintelligible curse words filling the house before the door slammed with enough force to shake the kitchen.

"Shit." Wren leaned against Jere's leg. "Sorry, babe. She was doing pretty well there, too, for a minute."

Jere shook his head. "Don't worry about it. I'll talk to her."

"I didn't mean to call her out on it—I just... I was shocked."

"I am too, actually," Jere agreed. "Although, it explains a lot. But how does she not know how to read? I mean, there are schools here, right? Don't tell me they don't teach kids how to read until after their gift shows or something."

Wren shrugged. "She was taken at seven, Jere," he reminded him. "But that doesn't explain all of it."

Their conversation was interrupted by a loud bang, and Jere got up with a tired look to deal with it. Wren followed silently, feeling rather guilty for his lack of discretion.

Jere knocked at the door habitually before opening it, and Wren gave him credit for not batting an eyelash as Isis smashed a chair into the wall repeatedly, sobbing and cursing intermittently.

"Stop."

Jere didn't even raise his voice, but at the firm tone, Isis let the chair go and collapsed in a heap on the floor.

"Isis, come on, talk to me," Jere muttered, taking a few steps toward her. He stopped before getting too close.

"Fuck you. Fuck both of you. I'm fucking stupid and useless and I can't fucking do anything and all I am is trouble and you should never have fucking bought me in the goddamned first place!"

"Isis, you're not stupid..." Jere started to try to console her.

She interrupted by banging her head against the floor, softly at first, and then with increasing force, obscenities slipping out every time she brought her head back up.

Jere sighed. "Should I have Wren go and get me a sedative, or would you rather I mind-bind you?"

"I don't fucking care!"

Shaking his head, Jere took another step toward her. "Fine, I'll mind-bind you—"

Before he could get close enough to touch her, Isis scrambled away, jumping up onto her bed and pressing herself against the mattress.

"Please, no, please don't, Jere, I'm sorry, I'm so sorry, I'll be good!" Her eyes were wide with panic. "Don't do it, please, just... here, okay, I'm on the bed, and Wren can get the restraints, and you can do that, and I won't fight you, and I won't do anything else and I won't break anything and I'll stop it, I promise!"

Wren was surprised at how quickly she had turned around, how rapidly she had become compliant and desperate to please. He glanced at Jere. "You want me to get the restraints?"

Jere sighed again. He looked at Wren, then back at Isis. "Do I need them?"

Isis shook her head. "Only if it would please you, sir."

Jere laughed, and Wren found himself fighting back the same. The subservient phrase sounded strange from such a rebellious mouth.

"I can do it!" Isis protested. "Like, be a good slave and stuff. You don't have to restrain me. I used to be able to do it all the time, I thought if I was good enough they'd let me go. You don't even have to let me go, just don't hurt me, and I'll be a good slave, I promise!"

Jere stopped laughing, but he still smiled gently as he spoke. "Isis, I don't want you to be a 'good slave,' I just want you to be safe. That hasn't changed."

"I just... every time I think something is going better, I fuck something else up, and then it's bad again, and today has just been — fuck, it's horrible, and you both know how fucked up I am now, and that I'm too stupid to even learn how to read, and..."

"We knew how fucked up you were already, and you're still here," Jere reminded her. "I promise, it's fine. We'll deal with it. And as far as not being able to read — I don't think it's because you're stupid. In fact, I don't think you're stupid at all. I think you were probably snatched up by some slaveowners before you learned a lot of basic things — self-control among them — and never got the opportunity to learn how to read."

"They tried to teach me at school before I was a slave, but they couldn't," Isis mumbled, still looking down. "They said I was like... reading disabled. I couldn't even learn my letters, then. But I always liked numbers and stuff. And drawing. And then when the gift came, I never got to use it for that, because they took me too soon, and so they would take me and have me copy things or reproduce entire letters or books or something, but I never knew what they said. I can't even read my own name unless the letters are made a certain way, and that's just because they had it written on my bed at the training facility I was at. One of the other girls told me it was my name, and she was whipped and then moved to another unit. They were so fucking happy to get me before I knew what I was memorizing for them."

"They purposely didn't educate you, because then you could expose things more easily," Wren was sickened at the realization.

Isis nodded. "I mean, I could still reproduce the papers they had me look at, but I didn't know what they said. I'm fucking stupid."

"I disagree," Jere asserted. "Would you like to learn?"

"How to read?" Isis raised an eyebrow, skeptical.

"Yes."

"You'd teach me how to read?"

"Well, not me," Jere shrugged. "I'm not the best teacher, really, but I know a certain librarian who would probably be up to the challenge."

"She owes you for taking on Kieran as a pet project," Wren teased.

"That, and the addition to the archives I just funded," Jere added. He smiled at Isis. "Besides, it might do you some good to interact with someone other than me and Wren. I'm sure you're getting rather sick of us."

"You're not, like, giving me away, right?" Isis looked nervous again.

"I'm not even letting you out of this house yet," Jere said, equal parts reassuring and frustrated. "Imelda would have to come over here. You're still a bit too volatile to be released on the town of Hojer."

Isis nodded. "I know. And I... I'd like to. I mean, it probably won't work, but I'll try if you want me to."

"I'll let her know when I stop by tomorrow. I'm supposed to pick something up, anyway."

"She's nice, right?" Isis asked, her voice growing tense again. "I mean, you said, you wouldn't let someone hurt me, right? Even if I can't do it? I don't do anything right, what if I'm still bad at it?"

"Imelda's probably the last person in the world who would hurt you," Wren reassured her. "Well, after Jere, anyway. She's a *dular*, too, if that makes you feel any better."

Isis nodded.

"It's okay if you're not good at it," Jere assured her. "I just think you should have a chance to learn."

"Why?" Isis asked. "What do you get out of it?"

"Well, it seems to upset you that you don't know how, and I'd like to at least give you the chance to feel better about yourself," Jere explained. "If something upsets you that much, I'd like to try to help you deal with it."

"Why?" Isis looked confused.

"Because he likes to help people," Wren supplied. "Trust me when I say that Jere of all people doesn't have any other reason for most of the things he does. And now that you're in his life, he'll go out of his way to help you."

Isis didn't say anything, but she looked almost pleased, if not a little confused still. Jere tended to inspire that reaction.

"Are you going to clean this up and go to sleep?" Jere asked. "I'm getting tired, myself."

Isis shrugged. "Probably go to sleep and then I can do this in the morning?"

It was the closest to asking permission Wren had heard from her.

Jere nodded, gracious as ever. "No more hurting yourself. And I want to heal the bruises on your head before you go to sleep."

"It's fine," Isis shook her head. "It doesn't hurt or anything."

"I didn't ask if it hurt," Jere pointed out. "I said I want to heal it. You are not allowed to hurt yourself, and if you do, I'll heal it, end of discussion. I've said I won't let anyone hurt you, and I'm including you in that statement."

Isis nodded. "You can do it now," she mumbled.

Jere went over to her slowly, sitting on the bed next to her. He placed a hand on her forehead, where the bruise was already showing, and Wren could see the healing taking place immediately. As soon as he finished, he stood and moved away before Isis had a chance to even ask him to. Wren was still amazed that the girl had let Jere touch her.

"Goodnight," Jere said softly, earning a slight smile from Isis before she wrapped her blankets around herself.

Jere stepped to the doorway, where Wren still waited, and took his hand. Wren allowed himself to be led away and into the hallway.

"You're so kind," he pointed out, coming up close and relishing in the contact. "You just won't let her self-destruct, will you?"

Jere shook his head. "Not a chance." He pulled Wren in for a kiss, which he was all too happy to return. "Where are we sleeping tonight?" he asked, his voice not nearly as confident as it had been just moments before.

"I'm sleeping with you," Wren declared, intertwining their fingers. "We can sleep in... your bed."

"Our bed?" Jere queried.

"Is it still?" Wren grew a little shy, turning his head into his lover's shoulder. He wasn't really sure.

"I haven't thought of it as anything but in months, love," Jere was leading him down the hallway. "I doubt I ever will."

"So I get my own room and you don't?" Wren asked, only half-teasing.

"I don't want one," Jere shrugged. "I mean, if the past week proves anything, I'm more likely to spend the night passed out drunk on the couch than I am to enjoy sleeping without you. It felt wrong. I should have been the one to go."

"Don't be ridiculous," Wren smiled. "In the future, we'll just make sure that whoever decides to start punching and hiding is the one who has to leave the bedroom."

They reached the bedroom, and Jere collapsed into their bed, pulling Wren down on top of him. "Even better, we could talk about what the fuck happened so we don't end up apart for a week?"

Wren rested on his lover's chest. His master. His best friend. "Please, not tonight?" He couldn't handle it; couldn't handle trying to be serious when his feelings were just now settling down and making sense to him. He couldn't add Jere's thoughts to the mix and hope that either one of them would remain sane. "Today's been crazy enough already."

Jere nodded, holding him close. "Whenever you're ready, love."

Chapter 27
Ready

Isis stayed calm for the next few days, a fact which amazed Wren. He started to see her as potentially contributing to the household, even though she annoyed him on more days than not, and made him feel threatened the rest of the time. She was too unpredictable, and Wren detested unpredictability. But the more she settled in, the more tolerable she was, and she even agreed to pick out clothes. Wren suspected that it was Imelda's influence, when she visited to teach the girl how to read.

"Here, why don't you go ahead and look through these and pick out some clothes?" Jere suggested, handing her a catalogue.

Isis backed away from it, eyeing it suspiciously.

"What on earth could you possibly be afraid of in a catalogue?" Wren commented, exasperated with the girl.

Glaring at both of them, Isis snatched the catalogue up and slammed it in front of her. When she got no reaction from the outburst, she tentatively opened it to the first page. "This is stupid. I don't know what I'm doing."

Jere glanced hopefully toward Wren. "*Please? Help her out?*"

"Isn't it bad enough that I dress you?" Wren teased, not actually too bothered by the request. "Isis, can I help you with something?"

"Don't need your fucking help," Isis muttered, despite the fact that she had just admitted that she didn't know what she was doing. "I don't see what the problem is with what I'm wearing. It's fine. I'm covered. What am I supposed to do, pick out a ball gown? Or maybe a fucking short skirt or something."

Wren rolled his eyes, looking at Jere with a resigned expression.

"I just thought you might appreciate some clothes of your own," Jere explained. "Some things that actually fit you. We've talked about this before. One of these days you're going to trip over those pant-legs and break something."

"Yeah, then you can heal it," Isis mumbled, but a strange look had come onto her face. She toyed with the rolled up sleeves of the sweatshirt she was wearing. "I can get, like, whatever I want? It doesn't have to be, like... you know...." She looked away.

"Nobody here wants you in some sort of skimpy harem out-fit," Wren clarified, remembering his own surprise when Jere let him pick out clothes for the first time. "Choose clothes that you'll be comfortable wearing."

Isis nodded, for once having no smart comeback or disparaging remark. She flipped through a few pages, finding only the men's section and looking increasingly bothered.

"Can I turn it to the right page?" Wren asked. "I have to do it for Jere, too, believe me, I'm an expert on these catalogues by now."

Reluctantly, Isis handed it over, and Wren turned to the wom-en's section. As it was, a child's catalogue probably would have been more appropriate in terms of size, but Wren doubted Isis would ap-preciate cutesy children's prints and styles. Isis took it back silently, clearly trying not to seem too interested. She looked through a few pages, studying them intensely without saying a word. Wren and Jere exchanged glances above her head.

"I guess... I kinda like this," Isis mumbled, pointing to a fluffy turtleneck sweater. "It looks warm."

"Good," Jere encouraged. "What else?"

Isis looked at him warily. "How many am I supposed to pick?"

Jere stifled a laugh. "As many as you want. Ten. Twenty. At least get enough for a week or two; laundry isn't an everyday event around here."

"Oh." Isis looked surprised again. She looked back at the cata-logues, but seemed sort of stuck on what to choose next.

"This looks nice," Wren pointed to a short-sleeved shirt. "I mean, winter has to end sometime, right? You might want some-thing a little —"

The catalogue flew across the room and Isis drew her knees up to her chest, wrapping her arms around them.

Wren sighed. "Okay. Or maybe that wouldn't look nice." He looked to Jere in confusion. *"What the fuck did I do wrong?"*

Jere just shrugged.

"Listen, I'm sorry," Wren tried to make the situation better. "I was only trying to help, and I didn't mean to upset you. But throwing the catalogue across the room isn't getting you anywhere. Tell me what upset you and I'll try to suggest something better, okay? I'm used to picking clothes for Jere; he's not picky. Hell, he'd wear that girlie short-sleeved thing if I ordered it for him."

"I probably would," Jere admitted.

Isis uncurled a little bit, a trace of a smile appearing at the playful teasing. "I don't fucking like people looking at me," she mumbled.

"Okay...?" Wren waited for more.

Isis glared for a moment before continuing. "It's bad enough that I'm all scarred up everywhere, but I don't need to fucking advertise it by showing it off. I want to be covered. Everywhere. All the time. I don't care if it's hot or cold or whatever, I just don't want people to be able to see me."

It made sense why she was so comfortable hiding out in baggy, oversized clothes, and it explained her violent reaction to the short-sleeved shirt.

"Thank you," Wren said softly. "That gives me a much better idea. Now, if I get the catalogue and bring it back here, do you want to keep looking?"

Isis nodded.

"All right." Wren retrieved it, opened it to the page they had been on, and handed it back, pleased when Isis took it without throwing it again. "Toward the back there should be some summer styles; a lot of the looser fitting items have long sleeves and you might even be able to find some with a higher collar that will come up around your neck."

Isis gave the barest hint of a smile as she looked through the catalogue. "How do you know so much about girls' clothes, anyway?"

Wren grinned. "Sometimes when my old master would lock me in the cellar, he'd give me catalogues to use instead of toilet paper. Not that he couldn't afford it, he just seemed to enjoy taking things away from me. You get bored, chained in a cellar for days on end."

Isis nodded, as if she knew exactly what Wren was talking about. The sad thing was, he thought it was very possible that she did.

Wren was glad to see Isis starting to come around, able to complete such seemingly monumental tasks as ordering clothing and not breaking anything. He had to admit that she had a certain sort of sweetness about her when she was happy, and he couldn't bring himself to hate her as much as he once had. If anything, he strove to be at least half as understanding as Jere was. Jere's understanding attitude extended not only to Isis, but to Wren as well, allowing him the space and time he needed to sort out his feelings. He knew he owed some sort of explanation to Jere, even if only to prevent things from getting so out of hand in the future.

Wren often thought about the fight they had had, but he wouldn't say that he felt exactly "ready" to talk about it for another week or so. There was just so much to think about, to process, to figure out how and when and why. The past few months felt as though they had spiraled completely out of control—his, Jere's, or anyone else's. Every day was a challenge just to get by, to keep going, to keep heads above water. The thought that things were a little calmer was almost strange now, as though the chaos had become so normal and commonplace that it was to be expected.

Part of it had been Isis, but Wren wondered if part of it wasn't coming anyway. Isis brought up a lot of things for both him and Jere, but at least on Wren's part, there were a lot of things lurking beneath the surface already, just waited to be activated. Isis had been the catalyst.

So he picked a Saturday night, knowing neither of them had to be at work in the morning, chilled a bottle of wine he had purchased earlier in the day, and he snuck it into their bedroom when Jere wasn't looking.

"*I have a surprise for you*," he teased at dinner, his face impassive and giving no indication of anything happening.

Jere glanced up at him hopefully, raising an eyebrow. "*You're a terrible tease!*" he protested playfully. "*Do I have to do anything to get it? Maybe beg for it? Go down on my knees and convince you I'm deserving?*"

Wren fought to keep the smile off of his face, stabbing at something on his plate and forcing himself to eat it. *"Oh, you'll get to use your lips, tonight..."*

Jere lost the game, barely stifling a laugh.

"You guys are *so* weird," Isis shook her head, continuing to put away food at her usual breakneck speed. "I'm so glad I don't have to hear your perverted conversations."

Neither Wren nor Jere could manage to hold back a laugh at that comment, as it was perfectly accurate. They tried to keep their flirting to a minimum, just to be respectful, but they failed more often than they succeeded. Even on their "successful" nights, where they limited it to the mind connection, they failed pretty solidly. Isis seemed to take it in stride, making faces or snide comments, but generally seeming to ignore it as long as she wasn't being touched. Neither of them would dream of laying a hand on her in that way.

They managed to finish dinner without ravishing each other, which was impressive for both of them. Having another member in the household had put tight limitations on when and where they could have sex. And tonight, Wren had something a little more important that he wanted to take care of.

Jere followed his lead and they entered the bedroom, which Wren had filled not only with the bottle of wine, but also some candles and chocolates. The extravagant treats had cost a small fortune, especially considering that the chocolates had been imported, but it was worth it. Jere's face lit up with surprise and delight when he saw it.

"What's the occasion, love?" he asked, slipping an arm around Wren's waist.

Wren nuzzled against his lover, enjoying the contact. Things hadn't been entirely back to normal yet, but their physical connection was amazing. "I want us to talk tonight, and I figured that since we were going to be talking about unpleasant things, we should do so in the most pleasant atmosphere possible."

"You didn't have to," Jere protested mildly, coming around to face and kiss him.

"I wanted to. And I think I had to. For me," Wren admitted, lingering a moment in Jere's arms before pulling away. "Now, get your ass in bed so we have plenty of time to talk and drink wine and eat chocolates off each other's bodies!"

Jere was in bed instantly, a grin spreading across his face.

Wren poured them each a glass of wine and joined him, snuggling up close and resting his head on Jere's shoulder. He hesitated, caught in the moment, wishing they could stay this way forever with nothing to interfere. Wishing there wasn't this rift between them. Wishing that he didn't feel as if something terrible, like what had happened a few weeks ago, could happen again at any time. Wishing he wasn't so fucked up and scared, and that he could talk to his boyfriend or master or whatever Jere was, and that he didn't have to wonder things like that, and wishing there wasn't some stupid slave reminding him of it every fucking day....

Jere's hand, warm and solid on his cheek, jerked him back to reality. He set his wine glass down before he dropped it.

"Where'd you go, love?" Jere asked.

Wren swallowed. His planning had been fun, and he had this whole idea in his head about how they'd talk and maybe it would be uncomfortable and then they'd laugh it off and go back to the way things were. Now he didn't know where to start.

"You know nothing you can say would make me love you any less," Jere continued to stroke his cheek, very lightly. "Or make me do anything to harm you."

Wren nodded. He knew it. But it still felt wonderful to hear it said again. No matter how much he knew it logically, he could only make himself believe it most of the time. The rest of the time, there was that nagging doubt; that ingrained habit that years of pain had drilled into him.

It was quiet for a moment.

"Shall I start, then?" Jere asked, sipping at his wine and tipping his glass up for Wren to drink from as well.

Wren took the wine, momentarily applauded its quality, and then nodded. He vowed to speak once Jere did.

Jere sat back, allowing their eyes to meet. "I want to start by saying I'm sorry. I fucked things up from the beginning, and I just *kept* fucking them up all along. I never should have gone ahead and decided to buy a slave on my own, because I'm *not* on my own—I'm in this wonderful, beautiful partnership with you, and that means you get to know and contribute to the decisions that affect this household."

"But you did..." Wren protested, letting his voice trail off. Maybe Jere hadn't exactly consulted him, but he had kept him informed.

"Not well enough," Jere admitted. "I tried to tell you what I was going to do, and sometimes I'd do what you told me to do, but I don't think I ever really heard what you were saying. I understood when you'd tell me to do or not do something very specific with Isis, but I don't think I ever really understood how much all of this affected you, and I certainly didn't realize how much it was all hurting you. Even after we started talking more, somehow everything still got looked over."

"I guess I didn't always communicate very clearly," Wren mumbled. The irony of mumbling that statement was not lost on him.

"No, you didn't," Jere said, the potential harshness of his words softened by the way he took Wren's hands in his own, bringing them up to kiss them. "Tell me what happened with that?"

Wren sighed, looking down at their hands, avoiding Jere's eyes. He'd rather not talk about that, but not talking about things was what got them in such a mess to begin with. And it wasn't an order. Not from Jere. "Fear," he said, the first word that popped into his mouth. "Fear of what I didn't know. Fear of change, and losing you, and having things be different. Fear that, every other time, when things were hard, you've been there for me, and you've supported me, and this time you needed me to support you, and what if I failed, and what if things went badly, and you were acting so different!"

Jere sat quietly, stoically, still gently holding his hands.

"I got so fucking jumpy," Wren continued, encouraged by the silence. "The screaming, the yelling, the chaos. It terrified me every time you'd threaten to restrain her, because I know how terrifying it is, how much it can hurt, and I just... I just don't think of you that way, even though I know you had to, and I hated her, I just fucking hated her for bringing that into our life. But then I'd think, well, *you* were the one who brought her here, not her, but I didn't want to be angry at you, because I know how much we were struggling before. But it still hurt to see, and it hurt to have her take you away from me, and I know it's stupid and childish to say I was jealous, but I think that was a part of it, and... god."

He had to stop himself. The words were pouring now like sand out of a sandbag, and if he didn't stop it, he'd empty himself out. He turned away, lying on his side, and tried to fight back tears.

He felt Jere stretch out beside him, one arm going around his waist, seeking his hand. He took it.

"There's nothing wrong with being jealous," Jere whispered, squeezing his hand. "And I think you had every right to be angry at me, even if you won't say it out loud. I should have made more time for you. You should have been able to ask me for more time, to talk to you, to tell you what was going on for me. I was scared too. Scared of fucking everything up. And I thought if I could just handle everything, just fix it all, then that would be better. I thought that if I didn't tell you how worried I was about failing, that I wouldn't worry you, and it would just go away."

"We make the worst team ever," Wren muttered, laughing a bit at the absurdity of it.

"I don't think I realized just how much I needed you until you were gone," Jere admitted. "I got all content and stupid and forgot."

"I didn't know what else to do. I had fucking attacked you, and I knew I should be apologizing or something, but I was still so angry! And nothing could be fixed—I thought you had done something horrible to that girl, and I probably deserved something horrible to be done to me, and still, all I could feel was anger! I couldn't help but think, if you had never bought Isis, we would never have had this problem, and we could have just kept on going like we did."

"At the risk of sounding critical..." Jere hesitated. "Even aside from Isis, it's a problem that you don't talk to me. I need to know when I've done something wrong, or when you're feeling off about something, because then I can work on it."

His master was pleading with him. Begging. Wren would almost rather that Jere was angry. If Jere was yelling, or being critical, or anything else of the sort, at least that would be familiar.

"It's not just you," Jere said softly, stopping for a moment and pressing his lips to the back of Wren's neck. "I need to talk with you, too, more, about what really matters. It can't just be all good things and happiness — we need to talk to each other about the unhappy things, too, the things that scare us. We can't just expect to never have any problems; we need to figure out a way to deal with them."

"What if I can't?" Wren said, his voice barely above a whisper. What if he failed? He couldn't stand the thought of being the one to break what they had again.

"You can."

Jere sounded so goddamned sure. How was that possible? How could he say it like he knew it?

"Do you ever think..." Wren hesitated, unsure of how to phrase the next question. "Do you ever think that we went too fast? Like we'll, I don't know... burn out? Or something?"

"I've thought about it," Jere said quietly. "Because it all seemed to happen so quickly — so perfectly."

Wren held his breath, simultaneously relieved and terrified that Jere had had the same doubts.

"But I think we've always been exactly where we're supposed to be," Jere continued. "Even now. Because, see, I'm planning on years and years and years of being with you, and I'm guessing they won't always be easy, and so now we can say that we've had a hard time and gotten through it and done better."

Wren couldn't hold back the smile on his face. It made sense that this was how Jere could see it. Every setback was a new opportunity for him, not a death sentence. Bad things could be fixed, made better, forgiven. He turned around, so that they were facing each other, and drew Jere close.

"I wish you would have come in and made me listen to you sooner," Wren admitted. "I was too scared and angry to do anything about it."

Jere looked up at him, relaxed against his shoulder. He looked a bit surprised. "Really? Because I felt terrible just doing what I did. Banging on your door every night? Making threats to come in? I still think it was wrong. You deserve your space."

"You deserved me to talk to you!" Wren protested, knowing it was a bit of a losing battle. "Well, I mean, fuck. I guess I should have just talked to you, then."

Jere shrugged, silent, tracing a design on Wren's stomach with his finger.

"You could write me," Jere said, stopping the movement. "If it's too hard to talk, I mean. I could, too."

"Write a letter and deliver it down the hall?" Wren said, laughing a bit. "It sounds ridiculous."

"Look, if either one of us was gone, like, out of town or something, we'd write to each other, right?" Jere pressed.

Wren struggled to come up with an answer. That situation would really never come up but he understood where Jere was coming from. "Yes...."

"And anyone would agree that there was quite a bit of distance between us?" Jere continued.

"Yes," Wren agreed, smiling despite the painful memories.

"So, write me," Jere insisted. "Send up a smoke signal. Train a carrier pigeon to deliver a letter. Do something to let me know what we're going to do to fix things, because it has to be both of us. We can't do it alone, because neither of us is alone. We're terrible at being alone."

"Sometimes, we're terrible at being together," Wren muttered.

"No," Jere insisted. "We're not. Neither of us is. I love you, and I'm willing to fight for you, and last I checked, you feel the same."

"I do," Wren reached down, intertwining their fingers. "I love you more than I've ever loved anyone else. More than I ever thought possible."

"Then we have a damn good start," Jere grinned at him, sitting up a little. "Now, can I kiss you, or what?"

Chapter 28

Edible

Wren felt himself blushing a little. With all the things they had done, kissing should certainly not make him blush, but Jere was so gentlemanly, so adorable.

"Yes," he replied, leaning forward to make Jere's task a little easier.

It was gentle, soft, and passionate; the way Jere almost always kissed him when he initiated it. They liked to play with other things, rough kissing, playful kissing, deep, horny, I'm-fucking-your-mouth-with-my-tongue kissing... but Wren would admit that this was his favorite kind. Slow, careful, undemanding, their lips moved together in a dance they had practiced thousands of times, and eventually their tongues joined the dance, whirling and twisting in and out. At the same time, Jere's hands were touching him lovingly; one caressed Wren's hair slowly, massaging across his scalp without pulling or tugging at him, and the other roamed across his chest. Jere's hand pressed firm against Wren, causing the fabric of his shirt to press into his skin. Wren wanted the material out of the way so he could feel his lover's skin touching his own, like he could feel Jere's tongue against his. Wren often closed his eyes, but he kept them open now, drawing in an excited breath as he met the soft, grey eyes that he knew so well.

"*You are my fucking world,*" Jere spoke through the mind connection.

Wren approved, as it meant more kissing. He wasn't ready for their lips to part.

"*Thank you, for talking with me. I know it wasn't easy, and I'm sorry*

233

that things have been rough. I'll be better, I promise."

Wren heard the words, deeply, feeling both relieved and guilty. *"I'll do my part, too. It's not all on you!"*

"I know," Jere said, finally pulling away, but keeping his hands where they were. "Now, unless you're committed to spending the whole night arguing about who was the bigger asshole, I want you naked and covered in chocolates!"

Wren laughed, shaking his head. It was so typical of Jere, so eager to move on to the next thing. He watched as his lover quickly divested himself of his clothes, tossing them to the floor before hopping onto the bed. Jere came over to Wren and placed his hands on his chest, moving toward the buttons of his shirt.

"May I?" he asked.

Jere *always* asked. Wren loved it so much. Loved that he never forgot, never assumed. He nodded, relaxing as the familiar hands removed his shirt quickly before moving on to his pants. He was naked in seconds, eager to move on to whichever form of touching or sex they both had in mind.

Jere crawled up next to him, whispering in his ear. "Lie back, relax, and spread your arms and legs."

Wren did so, a little hesitantly. He pushed hard to ignore the image of five-point restraints holding him in this position. He knew it was illogical, but old habits died hard, and seeing Jere use them on Isis had left an unpleasant image in his head.

Jere must have noticed, although Wren's blocking skills were excellent and being used to their full extent. Jere ran his hand down Wren's arm, pausing to take his hand when he reached it, and then leaned in and placed an almost chaste kiss on his lips. "I know you're not always comfortable with this much attention," Jere said, looking at him with a serious expression. "And I can see that you don't really like this position, but I want lots of places to cover you in sweet goodness... and then lick it off."

Wren said nothing, but the fact that Jere had noticed made him more comfortable already. He tried to push the other images out of his head.

"So, if you want to do something different, let me know, but what I'd really like is to show you how much you mean to me, how much time I want to put into touching you, and how fucking edible you are," Jere offered, smiling as he said the last part. "But you know I'd never turn down an opportunity to feel your lips on any part of my body, either."

"This is okay," Wren agreed, feeling strangely shy. They had already had every kind of sex imaginable; he was amazed that something so simple and romantic could bring out the blushing.

Jere smiled back at him, an anticipatory look on his face. Wren felt himself relaxing quickly as his lover placed chocolate pieces all over, in every place where Wren was most sensitive. Finally he finished, sitting up and smiling, a very proud look on his face.

"Now you literally look good enough to eat," Jere smirked. "I think I'll start here..."

He leaned down, taking a piece of chocolate from Wren's leg, and eating it quickly.

"Yep, delicious," he announced, leaning in for the next one.

Wren giggled as Jere's lips barely touched the skin on his other leg.

"I think that one was caramel."

The next was a bit higher on Wren's thigh, and he squirmed a bit as he felt teeth grazing the skin underneath, teasing him and making him wish for more.

"It melted," Jere mumbled, still chewing. "Couldn't get a grip on it."

Wren laughed. There was a time when this much attention would have had him squirming away, trying to cover himself. Now, he was simply wondering where Jere's mouth would land next.

A bit higher, where his leg met his torso, Wren felt Jere's tongue teasing around the candy, licking at the edges. He let out a little moan, loving the way it felt. He felt the tongue on his leg stop, and he opened his eyes to see Jere hovering a few inches from his face, chocolate held between his teeth. Wren nodded, and Jere leaned over, passing the chocolate to him with a kiss. The creamy, dark chocolate flavor was delicious, but it was the heightened senses that really got to Wren; he was so turned on that his world seemed to have narrowed to a tiny point, one where all that mattered was Jere and chocolates. Jere watched him as he ate, and Wren was too busy focusing in on Jere's lustful gaze to feel at all self-conscious.

The last two pieces of chocolate on Wren's lower body were eaten the same way, with the addition of Jere carefully licking the melted spots off of him. Wren knew that they would both be a sticky mess by the time they were done, but it was completely worth it. He felt his pulse quicken as Jere moved up, nibbling the chocolates off of his arms, feeding some to Wren, and licking and biting the path where they had melted and dripped a path down Wren's wrists. Wren had never realized just how sensitive the insides of his arms could be, and he struggled to stay still, wanting nothing more than to get as close to Jere as possible and feel him touch every inch of his body. Wren felt himself giving in, moaning with need and clutching at Jere with both hands. As the last chocolate disappeared between them, Wren pulled Jere down for a kiss, tasting the chocolate mixed with everything that reminded him of Jere.

"There's one more..." Jere insisted, pulling away again after only a few moments. Keeping perfect, unrelenting eye contact, he slid down Wren's body, trailing his tongue in a soft line until it reached its goal.

"That's not chocolate..." Wren pointed out, arching his back as the familiar warmth surrounded him. It didn't matter anymore once Jere wrapped his lips around his cock, because from that second on, all Wren wanted was for the blowjob to continue indefinitely.

The things that Jere did with his tongue had always been amazing. Wren had thought at one point that he would grow tired or accustomed to it, but no, it was just as shocking and wonderful every time. "The best head in Sonova," Jere had described it, long ago. Wren thought Sonova was missing out on an awful lot.

Jere kept going, kept working Wren with his mouth until all Wren could do was gasp and reach for him, torn between pulling him down harder and stopping him so that they could do other things. He placed a hand on Jere's shoulder, pushing him back, almost regretting that choice as he felt the fantastic blowjob stop.

"I want you to fuck me," he said, his voice coming out needy and breathy and entirely unusual. "Fuck me and come with me."

Jere grinned up at him, drawing his tongue around the head of Wren's cock slowly, making him squirm some more. "It would be my pleasure, love," he whispered, and Wren could feel the warm air all the way from his cock through the rest of his body.

Jere wasted no time getting down to business, preparing Wren as carefully and thoroughly as possible. Wren, for his part, simply relaxed against the pillows, coaxing his body to relax as well as Jere worked his tongue, his fingers, and copious amounts of lube into him. It wasn't that hard; Wren had gotten so turned on by everything they had already done that he was desperate to feel Jere inside of him. It had been a while, but Jere was skilled at what he was doing, and Wren would bet that Jere knew his body better than he did. Wren allowed himself to focus only on the way that Jere's fingers felt, stretching him carefully and stroking the spots that made him cry out again and again in ecstasy, the way Jere's tongue still flicked over his cock, just enough to keep him excited, but not enough to make him come. After what seemed like an eternity, he felt Jere's fingers gliding in and out of his ass smoothly, creating no other feeling than fervent desire. Wren felt them withdraw one last time, and he didn't have to tell Jere that he was ready. They both knew.

Jere trailed a quick line of kisses from the tip of his cock, up his stomach and chest, and to his lips. "How do you want me?" he asked, nibbling at Wren's lower lip while stroking his cock with his hands.

"Like this," Wren said, eager to feel his boyfriend inside of him.

Jere grabbed more lube, and without looking, Wren knew he was palming his own cock, covering it in lube, getting ready to fuck him. The thought made him shiver in anticipation, grinding against Jere, pushing his hips shamelessly against Jere's hand and seeking out his cock.

"You sure?" Jere said, a bit surprised. The hand that was not lubing his cock up strayed to caress Wren's legs.

Wren pulled back from his horny fantasy enough to really consider it. It was true, his heart did still beat faster when Jere was on top of him like this, and it wasn't all in a good way, but he liked it, too.... Again, he pushed the images of restraints and Jere acting like a tough, domineering master out of his head, focusing instead on the gentle way Jere always held the back of his head while they were kissing, or the patience he took in preparing him, or the way that Jere smiled and kissed him on the lips. He thought of all the other times that Jere had fucked him, no matter where either of them was sitting or standing or lying, and how perfectly wonderful Jere had made him each time.

"I'm sure," he said, finally. "I trust you."

Jere kissed him again, and stayed there, pulling Wren into the moment with his mouth, until Wren finally felt his tense muscles letting go. He felt the tip of Jere's cock at his entrance, and he waited, ready for the thrust, eager to feel Jere inside of him.

As usual, Jere had considerably more patience, waiting until Wren had started to move again, started to breathe again. Until then, Jere kissed him, stroked him with his hands, and waited.

"*I'm ready,*" Wren said, realizing this time that he really meant it.

He could feel Jere smile, ever so slightly, as they continued to kiss and Jere started to slide into him. Wren was surprised, as he often was, even after all this time, that there was no pain, not even the slightest bit of discomfort. Jere's preparation had been perfect.

Slowly, carefully, Jere worked his way in and out, filling him, letting him adjust and accommodate to each thrust. He was finally all the way in, and Wren felt the slightest burn, but it was good, wonderful, sexy. He matched it with heat of his own, reaching out to place his hands on Jere's chest and using his gift just the tiniest bit to create warmth, knowing how much it excited Jere when he did it. As Jere let out a low growl, Wren finally started moving as well, rocking his hips in time with Jere's careful thrusts. It had been far too long since they had done this, and Wren missed the feeling so much. They connected in so many other ways than sex, but Wren sometimes thought that this was the easiest way for him to hear what Jere had to say. Jere's careful lovemaking expressed how valuable and cherished Wren was in ways that words just couldn't express.

They fucked, Wren realized, for quite a while. Jere's patient, non-demanding lovemaking set the pace, and it seemed like time stopped while they thrust and rocked and moaned together. Warm skin and pleasurable touch and the faint, lingering smell of chocolate was all Wren was aware of, and he let it wrap around him, wondering why anyone would ever stop doing something that felt this good. It was Wren who finally caved, feeling his own orgasm almost upon him.

"You almost there?" he mumbled, opening his eyes, which he hadn't realized he had closed. The sight of Jere above him threatened to make him come immediately.

"Mmhmm," Jere moaned, never interrupting his tempo. "Come around me. It'll set me off."

It was the way they usually did it. Jere had impeccable orgasm control.

Wren smiled, reaching up to cup Jere's face in his hand, his other hand creeping down toward his cock. Jere beat him to it, as he always did, so he settled for clutching Jere's ass instead, kneading and squeezing the skin that he was so familiar with. Wren didn't try to rush things, he just relaxed and let the sensations come over him, his orgasm catching him slowly and beautifully, blocking out every other thought that Wren had. He felt his muscles spasm and tighten, filling him with pleasure. As he did, he felt Jere stop thrusting for a moment, staying deep inside of him after a deep thrust as he joined him in reaching their destination. The sense of time stopping didn't go away immediately; it seemed as though that moment lasted forever, sealing them together. Jere collapsed on top of him, which Wren usually didn't prefer, but tonight, all he wanted was to be close. He reached his arms up to pull Jere closer.

They stayed that way for a few minutes before Jere eased himself out, rolled to the side, and flopped down on his back next to Wren, one arm settled rather possessively on Wren's leg. Wren stretched, feeling the relaxed, sated muscles protesting any amount of movement.

"That was wonderful," Wren commented, unable to come up with anything more sophisticated.

"You're wonderful." Clearly, Jere wasn't doing much better in the talking department.

"Thank you..." Wren started, feeling himself being drawn over for a kiss, "for listening to me."

"*Thank you for putting up with me,*" Jere returned. "*I know I haven't been the easiest person to live with, and you're really bearing the brunt of a lot of things, but I promise, things will get better. At least, between us, things will get better. I'll try harder, make sure that I don't ignore you. You deserve this kind of treatment every night, and I'll find a way to give it to you again."*

"*Wouldn't want to miss out on such good sex?*" Wren teased.

"*Wouldn't want to miss out on you.*"

Chapter 29

Guilt

The next few weeks saw a return of some semblance of calm and peacefulness. Jere's hunch was right, Imelda was more than happy to tackle the project of teaching Isis to read. Despite never having children herself, she enjoyed working with young people, and she adopted Isis as quickly as she had adopted Wren years ago, and Jere more recently.

There had been some preparation on all ends, as Jere found it necessary to brief Imelda on Isis's background quite extensively, as well as to prepare Isis for polite interaction. Imelda could be a bit off-putting at first, with her no-nonsense ways, but Isis responded quite well. She seemed to be aware that Jere was trying to help her, and all she asked in return was that he stay in the room with her and Imelda for the first tutoring session. Jere started to realize just how truly afraid she was of new people.

Given her memory gift, she made rapid progress, especially once she relaxed enough to focus on what she was learning. By the second week of instruction, she read simple words with ease, and was beginning to understand the basic way in which sounds and letters interacted. Her childhood difficulty with reading persisted, but her memory gift more than compensated. If Isis had her way, she would have simply had someone read her every word, one by one, as she memorized them. Imelda insisted she learn how to read the proper way, so she could puzzle out new words if needed. The tutoring sessions only had to be stopped once because Isis became too upset, and she solved the crisis that day by locking herself in a bathroom until Imelda left and Jere and Wren coaxed her out.

Although Imelda visited only twice a week, Isis had gone on a sort of permanent hiatus from work. When Jere asked, she simply shrugged or walked away. He didn't push. The fact that he hadn't had to sedate, restrain, or hardly even threaten her was almost worth the lack of help. She kept herself busier now, flipping through books to find words she knew, making lists of words she didn't, and drawing occasionally. Wren had dumped a sketchpad and assortment of papers on her bed after a shopping trip one day. Neither Wren nor Isis mentioned it, to each other or to Jere, but Wren must have picked up on it when Isis was talking about her childhood and learning to read. Jere had to admit, she did seem a lot more peaceful when she was occupied. He was also secretly pleased to notice that Wren had gone out of his way for the girl.

None of that eased up any of the workload at the clinic, and none of it helped to address any of the problems that had prompted Jere to buy Isis in the first place.

Jere was considering these things just minutes before his last scheduled patient came through the door. An older woman, looking quite put-together and equally impatient, strode through the door, leading a young and very sad looking girl behind her.

Wren handed him the paperwork, smiling perfunctorily as he left them.

Jere glanced through the information. "Mrs. Everly, correct?" He tried to smile.

"Ms. is fine, my husband's been in the ground nearly thirty years now," the woman dismissed him. "But yes, that's me, and this is Terramyn."

"Mistress," the little girl whimpered, clutching at her coat and attempting to hide under it.

Ms. Everly sighed. "Terramyn, get up on the table so the doctor can have a look at you."

"I don't want to see a boy doctor!" the child whimpered, clinging more.

Jere winced as he heard the words, especially as he glanced at the reason they had come in. "You want her examined to see if she's been abused?"

"Molested, actually, raped, whatever you'd call it." The older woman shook her head. "And if there's a way to find and charge the person who did it, I'd like that as well. I mean, of course, make sure she's healthy, heal anything that needs it, that *should* go without saying, but I'm likely to kill the person who did this to my gr – my favorite slave's child."

Jere nodded, narrowing his eyes. "Yes, ma'am.... I'm sorry, could we speak in private for a moment?"

The woman nodded, lifted the child up to sit on the exam table, and stepped out into the hallway with Jere.

"She's my granddaughter," she admitted, looking displeased. "My disgusting lout of a son knocked up her mother, who is one of my slaves. Terramyn doesn't know, and you will not tell her. Actually, you will not tell *anyone*, or I'll have you for malpractice."

"Um, certainly, ma'am," Jere said, a bit startled at the threat.

"I stand a fighting chance of keeping her if they think she's just some child I've grown fond of," Ms. Everly admitted. "It's not that unusual. You care for and educate them the same as other children until their gift shows anyway, if they're not put up for adoption like most are. For enough money, there's a chance I might even get to bypass the training facilities and be approved for private training instead. None of that would be possible if they know she's a blood relative. My son doesn't even know, not that he'd care."

"She's still young, ma'am, couldn't she end up with a mind gift?" Jere suggested.

"It's not likely. She's already started to show signs. Unnatural lung capacity. I caught her at the pond with some other children, holding her breath for almost ten minutes! She doesn't mind at all – wants to be like her mother."

"Right," Jere said, even though it didn't make any sense to him at all. The reality of this state still blew his mind on regular occasions.

"It was my son's friend who hurt the child. I'll see that he is destroyed, if it can be proven. Terramyn says she doesn't know who did it, but her mother... her mother had been the victim of this man's attentions plenty of times in the past, against *her* will, unbeknownst to *me*. She thought I didn't care what he did to her, but at least she told me when it happened to her daughter. I was furious when I found out." The woman glanced at the doorway, where the child sat glumly just inside, crying a bit. "She has no idea what I've gone through to keep her safe. Children of slaves are in such a strange category anyway, nobody can agree what to do with them; giving them the life that you would give your own relatives is just unheard of. She just knows that I'm her mother's mistress, and by extension, someone important in her life. But I heard that you treated slaves, and you were an outlander besides, so I figured you would be a bit more sensitive to her situation."

"Definitely," Jere agreed. "I'll handle it with the utmost discretion."

They went back into the exam room, and Jere pulled out a gown, stepping out of the room for a moment so the child could change into it. He wanted, badly, to go and talk to Wren, but he also didn't want to keep the girl waiting any longer. He came back in to find her sobbing in the arms of her grandmother, whom the child would only know as her mistress.

"Hush, child," the woman said, her voice firm, but with the faintest touch of compassion. "Remember what I've taught you about obedience? You must always, always do as I say, immediately, without question, just like your mother does. It's what good girls do. You want to be a good girl, don't you?"

"Yes, mistress," the girl mumbled, still whimpering.

"All right. Now, I'll be right here to hold your hand in case you get scared, but you have to let Dr. Peters do his job, and you can't fight him."

"I just don't want a boy to touch me there again!"

Jere felt sick to his stomach. Sicker than he had in months. This was why he had bought the fucking slave girl, why he had even considered expanding his "slave count," as Paltrek had called it. It was ridiculous that she was sitting around while this little child was so terrified.

"If you'll excuse me for a moment, Ms. Everly," he heard himself saying. "I may have a solution. Please, wait here."

Without a word, he fled the clinic, into the house, and knocked at Isis's door, finding her lying on her bed and reading through a book, making a neat list of words she didn't know next to it.

"I want you to come with me into the clinic for a minute."

"Why?" she raised a critical eyebrow at him.

"Because there's something I want to show you," Jere started out diplomatically. He thought of the little girl's face, so terrified. "Because I never fucking ask you to do anything, and I need you to just come and see this one thing."

Isis rolled her eyes. "Whatever. I'm not doing anything, though."

Jere didn't answer. He led her to the clinic, and into the exam room.

"Isis, this is Terramyn. She's nine years old, and she's the daughter of one of Ms. Everly's slaves. She shows some signs of a physical gift already. She was molested the other night, and Ms. Everly has been kind enough to bring her in to get checked out and try to figure out who did it."

Jere fixed his glare on Isis for another moment before forcing his features into a smile and looking at the young girl. "Terramyn, this is Isis. She is supposed to work with me, but she's not sure if she's ready yet."

The little girl stopped crying for a moment, looking pleadingly at Isis. "Will you be my nurse, miss? I don't want a boy doctor!"

Jere watched Isis as her face went from bored, to appalled, to angry.

Her jaw set, and she turned to him. "A word, please?"

They went not just into the hallway, but into the next exam room, where their voices were less likely to carry.

"Fuck you, Jere!" she snapped, the second the door latched. "How fucking dare you!"

"How fucking dare I?" Jere shook his head. "You've been asking me for months what I bought you for. *This* is what I bought you for. I bought you because nine-year-olds get raped and don't want me to touch them. Adult slave women *also* don't want me to touch them. I bought you because slave men and boys would sometimes prefer someone who looks a little less like the man that torments them every day to take care of them, and women are less threatening. This is why I bought you. But if you're not up to it, or if you're too busy being rebellious and defiant and stubborn, then just walk in there and tell that little girl to go fuck herself."

"I fucking hate you," Isis snarled. "And I'm not doing this for you. I'm doing it for her."

Jere breathed a small sigh of relief. Despite her protests, Isis had agreed to help. "I'll need to set up a mind connection with you. I'll establish it so I can actually feel through your body. I'll stand behind you, with my hand on your shoulder, and I'll guide you through the actions through mindspeak. I won't have to put a hand on the girl."

Isis's glare had turned colder at the mention of the mind connection. "You fucking bastard," she scowled. "You knew I wouldn't be able to say no, not to this! You take it out *immediately* after it's done!"

"Like I'd *want* to stay connected to you," Jere muttered.

Without another word, they went back into the exam room where Ms. Everly was looking confused and irritated, and Terramyn's eyes lit up as she saw Isis.

"Are you gonna be my nurse, Miss Isis?"

Jere watched, amazed, as Isis forced a smile onto her face. She seemed to put aside all of the anger and fear that she usually displayed.

"Yeah, kid, I am," Isis said softly, taking one of her hands. "Dr. Peters isn't even going to touch you. It's just gonna be you and me, okay? Just us girls. Just... people like us."

Jere realized she meant slaves. It was chilling, but the little girl had obviously been taken in by her words. She had calmed considerably, and was gazing at Isis as if she were the only person in the world.

"Just keep your eyes on me," Isis said softly, taking the child's hands in her own. "And like... you know, what I used to do, when something horrible was happening, is I'd think of my favorite place in the world, and pretend I was there."

"What was it?" Terramyn asked, her voice a bit shaky.

Isis shook her head. "It doesn't matter. This is about you. What's your favorite place? Where do you feel safe, like nothing can hurt you, ever?"

"Umm," Terramyn hesitated, looking at the grandmother who owned her. "Sometimes, in the summer, Ms. Everly takes me and

Mommy with her to her cottage in the mountains, and nobody else is there except for us, and there's not as many rules and nobody ever gets in trouble."

Isis smiled, so bright and genuine that Jere was shocked. "Well, then, you think of that place, kid, and you remember everything you can about it, like, what do the walls look like, and are there stuffed animals for you to play with, and just... everything, okay? And nothing will be able to hurt you while you're there. And I'll be right here, the whole time. And Ms. Everly will be right there, too, if you want her to be."

The child nodded, growing silent.

Jere stepped up behind Isis, almost awed by her compassion. "You ready?" he asked quietly, reluctant to interrupt the mood.

She nodded without looking at him.

He placed his hands on her shoulders, allowing his gift to spread out, forming a mind connection between them. As usual, she put up no resistance, having no blocking skills to speak of, and almost as little psychic ability to begin with. Maintaining the mind connection with her was considerably more work than it was with Wren.

"*Good to go?*" he checked.

"*I still fucking hate you.*"

At least the mind connection worked.

"*Just to warn you, the type of connection I'll need to establish in order to make this work is very similar to a mind-bind. I'm sorry I didn't warn you before, but I promise, that's not what it is. You'll still have free rein of your own body and movements. I'll just be able to feel them on my end, too.*"

"*Asshole.*"

Jere could feel the fear, almost paralyzing, seeping through the connection. Without another word, he initiated the deeper connection, the one that would allow him to use her body as a vessel for his own healing gift. He heard her draw in a ragged breath as the feeling settled over her, but she didn't let anything affect the smile that she was giving the little girl.

The process itself was simple and quick. A "rape kit," they had called it, years ago, which Jere always thought sounded like something that one could buy from an arts and crafts store. Now, it also included full healing of any affected tissue, as well as careful examination of any specimen collected. Submission to the universal registry of DNA would identify the culprit within weeks, placing the matter in legal hands, if that option was chosen. Jere had a hunch that Ms. Everly would prefer to take matters into her own hands.

"It's finished," Jere said quietly, withdrawing from the healing connection with Terramyn as well as Isis. "Ms. Everly, would you like the specimen forwarded to law enforcement, or —"

"No, thank you, Dr. Peters, I would like to take it with me. I have my own connections in that regard," the woman said, her lips set tight. "If you don't mind, though, I'd like a word alone with you. If your girl could take Terramyn to the waiting room for a moment?"

Isis at least had the decency to turn her head toward Jere before glaring at him. Feeling helpless, he shrugged. "Isis, please?" He hoped it didn't sound too much like he was begging.

Without a word to either of the free people in the room, Isis picked the child up off the table and took her by the hand. "Come on, let's go see if there's some toys out there."

It was silent in the room for a moment.

"You don't support slavery."

Jere tried not to squirm. "What are you, an empath? Or a thought-reader?"

"Neither," Ms. Everly shook her head at him. "I have considerable influence over the weather, which is neither here nor there, but what I'm also not is blind or deaf or stupid. I've made a good choice coming here. Terramyn could use support, once she becomes Tera."

"Why don't you just move her out of the state before that day comes?" Jere asked, shaking his head.

"Young man, not all problems can be solved by running away to a free state," the woman replied, frowning at him. "You of all people must know this, or you wouldn't be working in a state where you are uncomfortable. My family has lived here for generations — it's not so easy to just pack up and move. There are emotional ties. Terramyn would never want to leave her mother. My slaves are treated kindly, kept safe. At least, I thought they were. I only wish I had realized... I never thought that a child so young would be taken advantage of!"

"My apologies," Jere said quietly. "I didn't realize."

Ms. Everly waved her hand. "It's of no concern. Dr. Peters, I thank you. For your services and your discretion."

Jere nodded, following her lead toward the door.

"There are other slaveowners whose mindsets are similar to mine," she said, cryptically. "I'll pass the word along that there's a doctor in Hojer they can trust."

"Thank you," Jere said, surprised.

They met Isis and Terramyn in the waiting room, where Ms. Everly motioned to the child.

She took one look at Isis and ran up to her, wrapping her small arms around her waist. "Thank you, Miss Isis," she mumbled, squeezing her tightly before running to take her mistress's hand.

The door had barely closed when Isis whirled on him. "Take the fucking mind connection out, now!"

"Fuck. Sorry," Jere muttered, doing as she asked as quickly as possible. Things had been so tense in that room he had forgotten about it.

The second it was severed, Isis stormed off through the door into the house, Jere following close behind.

"You're a fucking asshole and I fucking hate you!" Isis screamed, bursting into tears and storming into her room, slamming the door.

Wren met him at the doorway, eyes wide with shock. "What the hell happened to her?"

Jere sighed. "I guilted her into helping me in the clinic with a nine-year-old rape victim."

Wren winced. "That was a little low."

Jere shrugged. "It wasn't about getting her to work. It was about the kid."

A rageful scream tore through the house, followed by what Jere guessed to be the sound of a fist going through the wall.

"She did it?" Wren said, a bit surprised.

Jere nodded. "She was fucking spectacular. Every fight, every night that I've spent awake, everything was worth it to see that little girl so comforted."

The stream of curse words was clear, even into the kitchen.

There was a second punching noise.

"She's this mad just from being there?" Wren asked, eyebrows raised.

Jere shook his head. "I did it through her. The extended mind connection, like I had talked with you about. It allowed me to avoid touching the patient, but it feels an awful lot like a mind-bind."

"*Really* low, Jere," Wren amended. "I can't believe she let you do it."

"I'm sure she won't let me forget it," he muttered.

It was after dinner that night when Jere finally summoned up the courage to check on her. The pained sobbing had subsided, and Jere could only tell she was awake by the tell-tale scratching of pencils across paper. He tapped on the door lightly.

"Go and die!" he heard yelled through the door. When nothing worse came, he knocked again.

"What the hell do you want?"

It was as close to a welcome as he was going to get. He opened the door, venturing no further than the doorway. He glanced at the wall, which had two fresh holes in it.

"I'm not apologizing," Isis muttered.

"Show me your arms," Jere said, ignoring the rest. She did as he asked, and he was relieved to see only a few scratches from her assault on the drywall. "Be more careful next time," he cautioned.

She pulled her arms back into her sleeves. "You're a fucking asshole."

"What was I supposed to do?" Jere snapped. "She needed something I could never give her."

"What did you do before you bought me?" Isis protested. "I never asked for this!"

"I would have sedated her. Worked quickly, and hoped it wasn't as terrible. I would have had no other choice but to just let her suffer."

"Couldn't Wren do it?" she muttered. "He's a slave, too."

"He's a man, too." Jere pointed out the obvious. "And besides, he's not really the most compassionate person, in case you haven't noticed. He doesn't get emotionally involved with patients."

"That's true," Isis relented.

There was silence for a moment.

"You're an asshole for making me do that."

"You were so good with her," Jere pointed out. He was amazed by the kindness that Isis had shown. It was something he had never expected from her, but she had done it so naturally.

"You make it awful fucking hard to hate you, you know." Isis said.

"Thanks? I think?"

"You just... like..." Isis shook her head in frustration. "You have the best goddamn reasons for doing everything, and you're perfectly nice, and even when you do something slightly underhanded, like tricking me into helping you heal that girl, it's for the nicest fucking reason ever."

"Sorry?" Jere tried. He wasn't sure what to say. She was angry, but he didn't regret his choice. It had helped the child and he saw a side of Isis that he had only seen glimpses of before.

"I'll help you again, if it comes up." Isis said, resolutely. "I don't want to be your office bitch, and I'm doing other stuff now anyway, but if it comes up, I'll do it."

As usual with Isis, Jere needed a minute to process what she said, to realize that she was really going to be agreeable. Even when she did agree to do something, she seemed to need to be disagreeable about it, but Jere was beginning to suspect that it was little more than an act. The pride and happiness that she displayed after helping with something far outweighed her disagreeableness.

"Um... wow, thank you," he heard himself stammer.

"Whatever," Isis dismissed him. "Go fuck Wren or whatever you do at night. Leave me alone. I'm still not sure if I'm done being pissed at you, even if you are some sort of fucking saint."

Jere had no reply to this. He walked out, puzzling over whether he had won or lost the argument. He realized he didn't quite know what the argument was, so could he really win or lose it? Giving in, he walked to the bedroom, dropping down next to Wren and pulling him in for a hot, deep kiss as he did.

Chapter 30

Forgetting

"Mmm, you're in quite a mood," Wren mumbled, quite happily.

Jere responded by dipping down lower, kissing and biting at his neck.

"Fuck, Jere," Wren gasped, his arms coming up to wrap around his lover. He let out a sigh as he felt Jere's teeth come up to nip lightly at his earlobe. Their sex life had gotten back on track along with everything else, but it had been a while since Jere had approached him quite this desperately.

"I want you to fuck me," Jere whispered, his hands coming up to clutch at Wren's chest as he did. "I want you to fuck me so long and so hard and so rough that I forget all the unpleasant shit that happened tonight. The only thing I want to think about is you, how good you feel inside of me."

"That can be arranged," Wren agreed, grinning. He loved these games. Loved the way that Jere surrendered himself to the feelings. He sat up, eager to get things going, and started to pull his shirt off.

"Let me do it?" Jere asked, quiet.

Wren nodded. It was part of the game, sometimes. Jere serving him. He leaned back against the headboard, a playfully evil glare in his eye as he did. "You first. Strip. Show me how much you want it."

Jere obeyed, biting his lower lip in anticipation as he stripped for Wren's amusement. Jere was always nice to look at, but Wren particularly liked these moments. Jere was so calm, so content, so pleased with his own body. His writhing motions were nothing like the expertly trained erotic dances that a slave would perform, but were so much better, so real and alive and passionate. Jere didn't look at him at first, too busy sliding the clothes off of his body, but as he stripped the last piece away, his eyes came up to meet Wren's, the hunger and passion clearly evident. He licked his lips, purposely slow, and smiled slightly. Wren felt himself growing aroused just watching.

Before too much time could pass, Wren motioned for Jere to come closer. The second he was close enough, Wren grabbed him roughly by his upper arms, jerking him close and devouring his lips for a good long while before pushing him back. Jere moaned in response.

"Undress me," Wren ordered, his voice quiet, yet impossibly loud in the silence. Seconds later, he felt Jere's hands, soft but needy, making quick work of his shirt, then stopping to caress his chest. Wren loved to feel his hands, but he loved the game they played as well.

A sharp slap had Jere drawing his hands back in half-surprise, holding one close to him as if it actually hurt. Wren knew better.

"You didn't finish undressing me," Wren pointed out.

Jere looked pouty for a minute, but Wren could see him trying to conceal a smile. He glanced down at the pants he still wore, and Jere leaned over, untying the drawstring with his teeth, and easing his hands around the waistband until Wren lifted his hips so he could slide them off.

"Better?" Jere asked.

"Much," Wren nodded. Without warning, his hand darted out, grabbing Jere by the hair and pulling him down, kissing him again.

Jere's body went nearly limp under the onslaught, his lips and tongue and pleasurable moans the only things indicative of his eagerness. Wren recognized the mood; Jere wanted nothing more than to be taken, to be positioned and used for Wren's pleasure, however Wren wanted him. The control was intoxicating, and Wren felt his skin starting to flush at the thought.

Wren pulled him away by his hair as well. "Do you want me to hurt you?" he asked, softly. Jere usually liked it rough, but some nights, he liked it a step above. He liked it to hurt, and he liked that it was Wren who hurt him. It had taken Wren quite a while to believe this, and longer to accept it, but once he had, he admitted that he liked it as well. Some nights, he liked it a *lot*.

Jere was silent for a moment, clearly thinking about it. He squirmed a bit, and Wren felt him pulling against the grip he had on his hair. Wren didn't loosen his grip, and he knew Jere was pulling to the point of pain. Finally, he nodded.

"Yes," Jere said, barely above a whisper. "I really do."

Wren nodded, still holding him back by his hair. "Any characters, roles, other things you'd like to try?"

Jere shook his head. "Just you. Just hurt me. And fuck me. And don't hold back."

Wren felt an almost terrifying rush of excitement. Sometimes it was easier to play games—pirate and captive, teacher and student, robber and houseguest—they had been through as many as they could think of—but there was something extra intimate about it being just the two of them. There was no story, no "point" to the game, just one person who liked to be used roughly, and another who was starting to like playing roughly with him. Jere enjoyed being brought to the point of pain and pleasure, and Wren loved the satisfaction that he felt in being the one to bring him there, claiming him as his own.

"All right," Wren smiled. "On the floor and on your knees."

Jere did as he was told, and Wren followed him.

"Face the bed."

Wren walked over to the closet where they kept a variety of toys, pulling the bag out with him. He debated between a variety of options available to him, finally settling on a soft, thick length of rope. Turning back to Jere, he saw him peeking over his shoulder, and Wren descended on him immediately, bringing a looped end of the rope down on his back a few times before speaking.

"Didn't I tell you to face the bed?" he demanded, feeling pleased when he saw faint red marks appear on Jere's back.

"Yes," Jere replied, wriggling around a little.

Wren grinned, glad Jere still had his back to him. He was cute when he squirmed.

"Close your eyes," he ordered, grabbing out a blindfold and securing it tightly around Jere's eyes. "Maybe now you'll be a little less tempted to look around."

"I just wanted to see what you were doing," Jere whined, leaning backward to press against Wren's legs.

Wren swatted him a few more times with the rope, encouraged by the happy sounds Jere was making. "Arms behind your back."

In seconds, he had tied him up, not only binding his hands together, but tying them to his feet as well. Jere was stuck on his knees, his arms pulled back tightly and securely. Wren admired his handiwork as well as the sexy man confined by it.

"Are you comfortable?"

Jere squirmed a bit. "No." His tone was sulky, but the smile on his face gave him away.

"Good." Wren walked around him, seating himself on the edge of the bed. He knew he hadn't tied him enough to hurt, but certainly the position was stressful and uncomfortable. He reached out, running his fingers through Jere's hair for a few moments until he relaxed into the touch, rubbing against Wren's hand. When Jere was no longer expecting it, Wren grabbed him by the back of the neck and pulled him onto his cock, pleased when Jere opened up his mouth immediately and wrapped his lips around the head.

"The faster you get me ready to fuck you, the faster you get a different position," Wren informed him, feeling rather evil. He had no intentions of making this end quickly.

"I could do it better if I could use my hands!" Jere murmured, pulling off Wren's cock to do so.

Wren recognized the tone. Jere really did want to be hurt. Wren grabbed him by the jaw, squeezing hard, until he heard him whimper. "You'll do a good job just like you are," he growled, increasing the pressure for just a few more seconds before letting go.

Without another word, Jere dropped down, taking Wren's cock into his mouth in earnest this time, swallowing him deep and working him with the muscles of his tongue and throat. Wren's hand stayed on the back of his neck, but he just let it rest there, bobbing up and down with the rhythm of Jere's head. They both enjoyed the feeling of Wren holding Jere down, forcing him to stay wrapped around his cock for longer and longer, but tonight, Jere's motions were too good to compare with anything he would ever force him to do.

It wasn't long before Wren felt himself growing fully erect, ready to burst, ready to thrust down his lover's throat and come. But he knew there was much, much more to the plans tonight, and he tightened his grip on Jere's neck once again, pulling him back even as he trailed his tongue from base to tip, desperate for more.

Jere allowed himself to be pulled back, but once Wren's cock left his mouth, he let a mischievous laugh slip out. "Do you wanna untie me now?" he taunted, twisting his head to lick and bite at Wren's leg.

"Do you wanna get slapped again?" Wren replied, not loosening his grip in the slightest.

"Maybe."

Wren felt the thrill and excitement filling him, and he pinned Jere between his knees. With his arms tied behind his back, he was completely immobilized. Wren slapped him across the face, not hard, just enough to make him feel it. Jere sighed happily, and Wren added a matching slap to the other side of his face.

"Like that?" Wren taunted, his face only inches from Jere's. He could feel through the mind connection that Jere was pleased, but he still liked to hear him say it. Not only did it reassure him that he hadn't gone too far, it turned him on to hear Jere admit to enjoying it so much.

"Love taps," Jere retorted, his lips slightly open and smiling. "Barely felt them."

It was part of the game. Wren knew better than to mark his master up. They got carried away sometimes, but Jere couldn't exactly go into work with handprints on his face every day, no matter how much either of them enjoyed it. He took a minute to caress Jere's face, thrilled to feel the heat that his hand had left. He trailed his fingers down across Jere's throat, stopping at his chest, pleased when Jere's only response was to draw in a sharp breath.

"Don't move," Wren ordered, stepping off the bed.

"Like I have a choice," Jere pointed out. He might have sounded put-out, if his breath wasn't so shuddery.

Wren snickered, then came around behind him and grabbed the rope connecting his hands to his feet. He focused carefully, felt the temperature around his hands rising. It was dangerous, but he had been practicing. He smelled smoke, and watched as the fibers of the rope began to turn black and singe where he touched them.

"Jesus Christ, are you lighting me on fire?" Jere exclaimed, part of his fear real this time.

"Be quiet and don't move," Wren repeated, trying not to break his focus. Finally, a few seconds later, a small flame jumped up, burned through the rope, and died at the end of Wren's hand. Jere fell forward into the mattress, suddenly not held up any longer.

"Holy shit," he mumbled.

"On the bed," Wren ordered, almost giddy at his most recent feat with his gift. His practice had paid off. He watched, thrilled, as Jere struggled to get up, flopping down on his stomach, as his hands were still bound behind his back.

Wren reached into the bag of toys and pulled out a small riding crop that they had picked up at a slave supply shop when they decided to play naughty pony games one night. Without a word, he brought it down against the backs of Jere's thighs, smirking as he heard him yelp.

"Hey, what was that for?" Jere whined.

Wren laughed, stretching out across him, pressing his erection to Jere's ass. "Because I felt like it," Wren admitted, biting lightly at his neck. "Too hard?"

Jere shook his head. "Do it again?" He craned his head around until Wren could reach his lips, kissing him gently in contrast to the blows. "Please?"

Wren laughed, reassured that he was on the right track. He leaned back and let another volley of blows rain across Jere's legs and ass, increasing in force as he watched Jere rock against the mattress beneath them. He was pretty sure he had never seen anything so sexy in his life.

"Mark me," Jere begged. "I want to see it tomorrow."

Wren smiled. "Oh, I will," he promised. "But first...."

He made quick work of the ropes that held Jere's arms behind his back, freeing them before flipping him over onto his back. Wren smiled again as he saw Jere bend his knees and spread his legs slightly in anticipation. For good measure, and for the added thrill, he gripped Jere's thighs and pushed them up further, spreading them further apart, and was pleased to see Jere keep them there. Wren reached down very briefly into the bag for some lube, dripping a generous amount onto Jere's ass before assaulting it with his hand, working his fingers forcefully inside as Jere screamed in surprise and pleasurable pain.

"You're tight," he whispered, thrusting three fingers into him and meeting a surprising amount of resistance. "I need to fuck you more often."

Jere said nothing, just moaned and thrust back against him. Wren kept at it for a few moments, his other hand forcefully fisting and squeezing Jere's cock, pressing too hard against the head, keeping the pain just at the edge of the pleasure. When Jere was almost lost to the sensation, he withdrew his fingers and let go of his cock, leaning back to apply more lube to his own cock.

"Hold your legs up," he ordered, thrilled when Jere complied instantly, exposing himself without a thought. "Now, tell me how much you want it."

"Fuck me," Jere moaned.

Wren brought the riding crop down hard across the backs of his legs, still red from earlier, stretched tight by the position Jere was holding himself in.

"Tell me how much you want it."

"Please, please fuck me!"

Again, the riding crop came down, and Jere howled and thrust at the air.

"Tell me."

"Wren, please. Please, I want you!" Another slap. "Fuck me hard!" Another slap. "I want you inside of me!"

With one last, bruising slap of the crop, Wren settled into position and thrust into Jere in one smooth motion, meeting no resistance. Jere cried out in surprise, but his yelps quickly turned to those of pleasure as Wren began fucking him hard and fast, putting his speed gift to good use as he pounded in and out of him at a speed no natural human would ever be able to attain. He felt Jere's grip on his legs slip, and he smiled as he felt them wrap around his back, pulling him in tighter and closer. Jere's arms dropped, and he rocked in time with Wren's thrusts.

Wren felt them both about to come, and on sudden impulse, he picked up the crop and laid two more vicious slaps, one on either side of Jere's chest, forcing his orgasm as the second one landed. Wren's orgasm followed in quick succession, the excitement of the night combining with Jere's muscles tensing and moans of pain and pleasure to bring him to the edge almost immediately. Jere's arms came up around him as they rode the pleasure, and Wren jerked the blindfold away so he could look into his lover's eyes, only slightly surprised to see tears. It had happened a few times before, usually when the sex was particularly intense or when Jere was generally overstressed. Wren had been terrified the first time it happened, but Jere always assured him that it was fine. He leaned in and captured Jere's mouth in a kiss, holding them both together as they shuddered and panted and moaned.

It seemed like ages before he was ready to move off of him, but it could only have been a few minutes. He eased himself out, rolled onto his back, and pulled Jere over so he could rest his head on his chest, which Jere seemed more than happy to do.

Wren kissed the top of his head gently. "Did I really make you cry?" he asked. He felt a bit guilty, but also a bit amused.

"Shut up," Jere mumbled, burying his head against Wren's chest. "You did not!"

Wren tried not to laugh. Jere was terrible at lying.

"I didn't think you were going to take off the blindfold!" he complained, still hiding his face.

"I wanted to see your eyes," Wren informed him, rubbing his back carefully, happy to see that he hadn't left any marks there.

"You're mean!" Jere's fake pout was so over the top that even he was laughing as he spoke. "That crop hurts!"

Wren pulled him up by his hair again, softly, this time, and kissed him.

"You're getting quite comfortable with hurting me," Jere commented, his hand going back to rub against the bruises developing on his legs. He smiled like he was savoring the last bite of chocolate. "I remember a time when you were a bit more timid!"

Wren felt himself blushing. He had grown to love these moments as much as Jere did, and he had gotten creative with his games. "What can I say, I know how much you like it."

"Mmm, because you hate it so much," Jere teased.

"I didn't go too far, did I?" Wren was always concerned about this. It had taken him a while to stop being terrified every time he laid a finger on Jere; on nights like this when he took things further he still felt unsure.

"No," Jere said, quite firmly. "It was quite lovely. Exactly what I asked for. And I'll love seeing those marks you left on me in the morning."

Wren grinned. "You know, if you had handled your frustrations this way a few weeks ago, we would have had a lot better sex and a lot less arguing."

Jere laughed. "You're probably right. Although, I don't think either of us was in a place to do this kind of shit. It would have been a race to see who broke down in tears first. *Real* tears."

"You've got a point." It was true. Wren recalled night after night of not wanting to be touched, of not wanting to have sex, of wanting to be held and cuddled but still being afraid of uncertainty and change and the unknown. "It feels better, now."

"It does," Jere nodded. "A lot of things feel better. We're talking more. Dealing with things."

Wren nodded in agreement. "It's still hard, sometimes, things are different than they used to be, but they're okay, I think. I don't feel that fear that I used to. Having Isis here changed things, but it didn't change who you are. You'll still be here for me. I know we'll make it through... whatever."

"I guess that means you're stuck fucking me for a while, then!"

"Can't think of anything I like more."

Chapter 31

Surprise Visitor

A few more weeks passed, calm and regularity becoming the norm instead of the exception. That is, if one considered screams in the middle of the night, crying fits, and self-inflicted, bloody wounds to be calm. Jere was starting to consider that to be true, which he found a little worrying. Isis was actually doing well, she hadn't hurt herself in over a week, all of her problems were happening less and less, and she was bouncing back quicker than she had before when she became upset. It helped that Jere and Wren had learned to identify things that would set her off, becoming more attentive to her eagerness to avoid criticism and to stay occupied. Even so, she found things to become upset about.

Before work, Jere and Wren were finishing breakfast when they noticed Isis standing in the doorway, looking upset.

"I need things," she muttered.

"What kind of things?" Jere asked, surprised that the girl was even asking. She so rarely asked for anything at all.

"Fuck you!" Isis stormed off, slamming her door.

Jere looked at Wren, hoping he would have some sort of insight. "What kind of things does she need? She has everything, doesn't she? Did we miss something?"

Wren rolled his eyes. "She needs sanity."

Only a few minutes passed before Isis returned, standing in the doorway again. "Jere." A glare asked the question more than the words she spoke.

"Yeah?"

Another glare, and Jere wondered whether she was going to ask him anything or not.

"Girl things," she muttered, crossing her arms over herself protectively. "That's what I fucking need." She stormed off.

Jere sat there confused, his confusion increased by Wren's barely suppressed laughter. "What?" he asked, finally. "I don't get it."

"For fuck's sake, Jere, the girl needs something for bleeding," Wren informed him. "Her cycle?"

"Oh." Jere felt monumentally stupid. "I should have figured that out, being a medical professional. And growing up in a house with my mum and my sister."

"I'm surprised she hasn't asked before, although I guess she could be a late bloomer," Wren mused.

Jere thought back to the first day Isis had spent with them, how she had objected to being called "prepubescent" and stormed off. "Or she was so severely malnourished that those functions shut down."

"That's a hell of a reward for feeding her," Wren commented. "You're right, though, she was starving."

"I wonder how long it's been since her body has been anything close to healthy," Jere wondered out loud. "It's likely that her growth was affected as well."

"Oh, damn, if only she had been fed more, she would have been just as violent and big enough to do something about it," Wren poked fun at the subject. "I can pick some things up when I go to the store."

Compared to when Isis first arrived, Jere felt that he and Wren had adjusted pretty well. The lull in violence and crises was a welcome break from the past few months. In spite of everything, Isis had settled into a nice routine in the clinic, taking over a good portion of the necessary cleaning, not to mention assisting with the patients. She had gotten angry and silent both times Jere had approached her about energy transfer, and he wasn't willing to push the issue just yet. She was helpful enough in other ways, especially her ability to soothe and comfort the most terrified of slaves and occasionally free people. It was strange, almost uncanny, but for just a few moments each day, Jere could see her relaxing, connecting with others, showing such warmth and kindness and compassion. He never thought it possible, at least not from her, and it gave him quite a bit of hope for her future.

She continued to take reading lessons with Imelda, progressing rapidly due to her gift. As they continued to work, Jere began to suspect that she looked forward to Imelda's visits more for socialization than for reading help, but he doubted that could be a bad thing. Watching her open up and begin to trust someone other than him was encouraging, and Imelda seemed pleased to provide the girl with support. Isis even dared to approach her with a sheet of words and letters that she recalled from years past, daring to inquire about their meaning. While Imelda hadn't been overly familiar with the symbols and instructions, Jere recognized them as chemical compounds for illicit drugs, some for new ones that Jere had only read about. When asked, Isis just shrugged, and said that her previous masters had used her to copy all sorts of documents, spying over the shoulders of unsuspecting businesspeople who were completely unaware that the little girl next to them was functioning as a recording device.

Most of the specific memories had been stripped in previous mind-surgeries, some leaving huge gaps that Isis couldn't explain, and hated talking about. Some things had been removed so sloppily that there were days, even weeks of her life that she didn't remember, and these upset her more than anything. For a person with a memory gift, simple forgetting did not happen; blacking out whole days should have been unthinkable.

Jere wondered what kinds of people had owned her in the past, that they would expose her to a world of drug trade and secret information trading, only to rip the memories from her head in such an underhanded way. He asked her on a few occasions what else she remembered from those days, and she had simply answered, "everything." Jere realized that, despite the quantity of information she had, most of the secrets were lost in the noise. If she was specifically asked, she could recall every detail of every day of her life since her gift developed, but the simple act of trying to pick out the important parts was beyond her capabilities. More importantly, she didn't like to think about the past, and Jere quickly stopped upsetting her by asking.

He glanced at the mail, perusing Kieran's most recent letter. She had lightened up considerably on her attempts to indoctrinate him into her world, but she still poked and prodded him here and there. His decision to acquire another slave still annoyed her, at least, that's what he figured the sad faces she drew on the borders of the letter signified. Regardless, she wrote that she was coming back home for a break from courses, and was actually planning to stay with her family this time. Jere figured she'd still be around a lot, which might not actually be so bad, after all. Having Imelda around seemed to have been good for Isis, although he doubted Imelda could actually make anyone too anxious. It was too easy to become socially isolated, and now that everything else was falling into place, it only seemed right that friendships and visiting should resume as well. The season for the Winter Holiday parties had started again, and Jere had even managed to attend a few, confident that Isis would be fine for a few hours while he made appearances. He was almost relieved to have an excuse not to host his own party, because even if Isis had been presentable, Jere would have been too exhausted to plan it, and he suspected that Wren felt the same way.

Things were, *finally,* starting to feel right with Wren again. Nervous energy and uncertainty had buzzed between them for weeks, but they were slowly falling back into familiar patterns, spending time together and working hard to avoid and deal with conflicts before they escalated again. In spite of the challenges they had gone through, they both agreed that they had become better at working together, and Jere at least could appreciate Wren even more than he had before. While neither of them was eager to struggle that much again, there was a sense of accomplishment at having gotten through it. Now that things were calm, they were able to communicate more clearly, tackling problems as a team. It helped that neither of them was as tired, and so they both had that much more energy to devote to one another.

The calm was interrupted one night by a knock on the door. Jere felt around briefly, in search of a psychic presence, and got nearly nothing. He wondered who was showing up at the house at this time with such strong mental shields. The person felt familiar, but he couldn't quite place the identity.

Wren got to the door before he did, and Jere heard him saying "Hello, sir," in his ever-demure tone as he was walking out to join them.

He was startled to see his sister's face peeking out from under a hat, a man's suit hiding her more feminine frame. Like Jere, she had inherited height from their father. "Jen?" he gasped.

"I'm going by Peter, at least while I'm here," Jen smiled at him conspiratorially. After all, 'Jennifer Peters' is on the official 'No Entry' watch list!"

"Mum said you got my address..." Jere managed, still in shock.

"Did Mum also tell you that you have terrible manners?" Jen chided playfully. "But don't worry, I'm fine, the speed train ride went well, thanks for asking, and so nice of you to introduce me to your friend."

Jere was speechless for a second. After not seeing or hearing from her in over a year, his older sister arriving unannounced in Hojer came as quite a shock.

She turned to Wren, stuck her hand out, and smiled. "Hi, I'm Jen. Jere's sister. You must be his boyfriend? Wren, right?"

"Uh..." Wren grew red, taking her hand and shaking it awkwardly. "*Jere! What do I say?*"

"Um, yeah," Jere cut in. "Jen, uh... how much has Mum told you about Wren?"

"Not too much, you know how she is," Jen waved him off. "All about letting you have your privacy or whatever. As if I won't get it out of her eventually. She's told me that you and Wren have hit it off quite well, and that he's adorable, and that you two seem very happy together. I never thought I'd see the day! Nor did I think I'd see the day when my little brother would hit it off with someone from a *slave state!*"

She had taken off her coat and tossed it over the couch. Jere could see that Wren was holding himself back from picking it up and putting it away properly.

"No offense, Wren," Jen amended, a moment late. "Mum said that you wouldn't have any problem with what I do, so I figure, you know, you aren't a fan of slave states either. I don't know *why* you'd both choose to live here, but maybe you have some reason."

"Um..." Wren started again, looking helpless.

"Maybe we should, uh..." Jere fumbled. "Let's sit down, have something to drink or something."

They went into the dining room, and Wren took off to get them refreshments.

"He's cute," Jen grinned. "Where can I find one of those?"

Jere was rescued from answering as Isis came out to see what the commotion was. She dropped into a chair, the one farthest from anyone else, as usual. "Who's this?" she asked suspiciously, eyeing up Jen.

Jere didn't know whether to be happy or horrified that Isis was joining them. "This is my sister, Jen. She's uh... in drag."

Jen rolled her eyes at him. "And who might the kid be?" she asked skeptically. "Babysitting or something?"

"Fuck you, I don't need a babysitter!" Isis snapped.

Jere resisted the urge to bang his head on the table. Wren chose that exact moment to return with snacks and drinks, and Jere muttered, "Her name is Isis, and she's a slave, and Wren's a slave, and you should just kill me now and get it over with."

Silence from Jen was scary. It was the precipitant of getting beat up, or yelled at, or tattled on—any of the normal things that a big sister did to her little brother. It didn't matter that Jere was a grown man, he still felt like he was eight years old and Jen was about to tell Mum that he had done something forbidden.

"You own slaves!" she finally exploded, her face expressing her shock and horror better than her tone, which also expressed it pretty well. "You? Own slaves?"

Jere nodded.

Jen huffed. "So *this* is why Mum was so tight-lipped about her visit!"

Jere nodded again.

Jen turned her glare on Wren and Isis, both of whom flinched back a bit. "I'm sorry," she said, her tone a little softer. "It's nothing personal. It's just, this is my brother, and I thought I knew him better than this. Does he at least treat you decently?"

Wren nodded, ever the picture of perfect politeness. Isis laughed. "Jere's awful at being a master. He doesn't beat us or make us work or anything, he's too nice. He treats us way better than he should."

Jen looked confused. "So... wait, he's a bad master because he treats you well?"

"Well, anyone else from here would say he's a bad master," Isis shrugged. "I like him okay. He's nice to me. Usually. And even when he's mean, he's not like, you know... *mean*."

"For what it's worth, 'mean' includes not letting her kill herself," Wren contributed, clearly uncomfortable. Jere appreciated the defense, though.

"Jen, look, it's not what you think, it's—"

"Jere, just shut up before I make you cry like I did when we were kids," Jen snapped, silencing him at least for a moment. She stared around at the three people sitting at the table, finally settling her gaze on Jere. "You know what, go outside, and let me talk to them *without* you in the room."

Isis stood up, her chair flying back from the table as she did. "No fucking way!" she protested. She looked pleadingly at Jere. "Don't make me, I'm not doing it!"

Jere didn't take his eyes off Jen, who was rather taken aback at the display. "Nobody's making anybody do anything."

"*I can talk to her if you want, babe,*" Wren offered, glancing at him out of the corner of his eye.

"*Talk to her only if you want,*" Jere insisted. "*She has no right to come in here demanding shit and telling anyone in here what to do!*"

"*You are adorably protective,*" Wren replied, smiling a bit. "I'll talk alone with you," he volunteered.

Jen had been watching their interaction, a puzzled look on her face. She looked at Jere. "Shut the mind connection down—"

"No." Wren's voice was firm and calm, even though Jere could feel a little apprehension at speaking so boldly to a free person, even a free person who was his sister and who was from a free state. "Don't push your luck. My connection with Jere doesn't get broken for anything, and it's rude of you to even ask such a thing."

Jen sat back, pouting a bit, but she nodded.

Wren glanced at Jere. "I'll let you know if I need anything," he said out loud. Jere placed a hand on his shoulder as he walked by, retrieving a coat for himself and Isis before heading toward the back door.

He glanced at Isis. "Come on, give these two a minute to chat."

Isis followed silently, still a little on edge. They went outside, where Jere realized Isis had actually never been. A thin layer of snow coated everything in sight, but it wasn't nearly as cold as it usually was at this time of year.

"It's nice out here," she commented, looking around. "Christ, I don't remember the last time I left the house. It was summer, I think, when I first got brought here."

Jere bit his lip. He could tell that she didn't mean for it to be a complaint, but it reminded him just how easy it was to overlook her needs. For so long, it had been so much more important to keep her safe, to keep her contained, he hadn't even thought of something as simple as going outside.

"You know, the last couple years, the only time I was ever allowed outside is when I was being sold. Or shown off in order to be sold. Or lent out."

Jere nodded. "You like going outside?" he asked. It was a stupid question, but he felt he had to say something.

"Sometimes." She shrugged. "Usually. I mean, it's hard, because usually going outside meant going somewhere else, and that part I didn't like, but yeah, in general, I do like going outside, because it's not as closed in and there's things I can look at and sometimes I like to draw things I see outside, like, whatever, nature and shit. Or at least I used to. Actually, I loved going outside, when I was a little kid. I think I'd still like it now. I don't really get to think much about what I like."

Jere nodded again. He was preoccupied, thinking about Wren. Worrying about him irrationally. He fought to keep himself from contacting him through the mind connection, just to make sure he was all right.

"Jere, can I ask you a favor?" Isis said, jarring him out of his thoughts.

"Sure."

"Do you think I could, maybe...." Isis was staring at the ground, making patterns in the snow with her footsteps. "I'd like it, you know, if I could go outside sometimes."

Jere thought about it. There was really nothing keeping her in the house, she wasn't locked in or tied up or anything. Not anymore. She didn't try to run off, and he doubted she would, especially if she wasn't provoked, like she was that one time. He nodded, finally. "All right."

Her eyes widened. "Really?"

Jere couldn't help but smile back at her. "Yeah. In fact, I'm sorry I didn't think of it sooner. I don't want to make you a prisoner or something—if you want to come out and walk around out here on the property, or sit out here, or whatever, you can."

She beamed. "Thank you!"

He walked her around, showing her where their land technically ended, separating them from their neighbors, whose house was much farther off. He asked her not to loiter in front of the house, as patients came and went from the clinic. She looked like she would have no problem with that request, which wasn't surprising. Isis preferred to avoid other people most of the time, especially other free people, especially when Jere wasn't around.

They spent about thirty minutes, walking around, commenting on the setting. Jere appreciated the distraction. He was a bit surprised to realize exactly how possessive and protective he was of Wren.

Finally, he felt the familiar presence in his mind, and Wren's voice was teasing in his head. "*You can come in now, I've tamed your sister.*"

Jere returned quickly, Isis on his heels.

Jen looked a little ashamed, which made Jere wonder what Wren had said to her. When he shot Wren a questioning look, he just shook his head and smiled. "*Tell you later.*"

"I'm sorry I was so quick to jump to conclusions," Jen apologized. "I guess I should have known my little brother better than that. Thank you for letting Wren talk to me."

Jere said nothing, just sat down. Isis took her seat at the far end of the table, eyeing Jen suspiciously.

"I'm sorry that I implied that you had to do something you didn't want to," Jen mumbled her apology to the girl. "I didn't realize how it would sound."

Isis shrugged. "It's fine. Whatever." She was content, dismissive, as she always was as long as she wasn't in some immediate crisis. Jere could see that she still wasn't comfortable with Jen, but it was to be expected. Jen was new, and she was pushy, and Isis didn't do well with either.

"I'm glad you and Wren got a chance to talk," Jere said, diplomatically. "I hope he could answer any questions you had about me."

Jen looked at him a bit distrustfully again. "I still can't believe you own slaves."

Chapter 32
Settled Down

Wren had only been a little nervous to speak with Jen. His time with Jere had taught him a lot about judging people, and, more than anything, he was secure and confident that his master would stop anything bad from happening to him. Besides, knowing Jere and their mum, he doubted that Jen could really be that dangerous. He was right.

She was rather intense, and had obviously spent a lot of time working *around* slave issues, and very little time working *with* slaves. The unspoken commands in her voice, the entitlement, the assumptions.... Wren was right in assuming that she had mostly dealt with slavery as a theoretical and political issue. As they spoke, she revealed that she knew very few slaves or even ex-slaves personally, as most of her work was done outside of slave states. She was passionate about the anti-slavery movement, but she had categorized the slave states and their occupants so broadly that she overlooked the subtle nuances of such cultures. Her cluelessness was almost painful, reminding Wren of how Jere had been when he had first come to Hojer. She was well-intentioned, but good intentions only went so far.

When Jere first left the room, Wren was awkward, nervous for a few seconds. He hated talking about himself, and he felt almost as uncomfortable talking about Jere. No matter what his status was with Jere, such open, honest conversation just wasn't acceptable, but Wren knew that Jen would need it as much as her brother did to understand how things were.

"Isis has been with us a few months," Wren found himself saying, finding it easier to talk about someone other than himself or his master. "She was really bad off when we got her, that's part of why Jere bought her; he wanted to rescue her, I suppose. Jere need-ed someone else around the clinic for help, and he wanted a girl to help with the female patients. She's excellent with patient care; you wouldn't know it by meeting her at first, but she's surprisingly com-passionate, and they don't see her as a threat. She seems to have a knack for calming them down, which takes a lot of the pressure off of Jere."

Jen nodded at him.

"She's still a bit jumpy sometimes, and she doesn't like being or-dered around," Wren added, hoping to explain her behavior. "Jere's gotten her to a much better place. She can interact with people and doesn't try to hurt herself anymore. He's not just a good master; he's a good person in general. I can't even begin to explain how much he's done for Isis, or for me."

"How long has he owned you?" Jen asked, looking disgusted by the fact. "Mum just told me that you were dating—how does it go from him owning you to him dating you?"

"Jere has owned me for about a year and a half," Wren told her. "He inherited me with this place. He didn't choose to buy me; I think if it had been up to Jere, he would never have bought a slave, and he wouldn't have stayed in Hojer very long after finding out it was a slave state. I was just another inheritance, and at first, we just worked together before we started doing anything else. We were attracted to each other, and eventually, well, we started doing other things. And then we fell in love."

"Yes, but... he owns you!"

Wren shrugged. "It's not that big a deal. Not really, not any-more. I can't leave here, and Jere wouldn't leave without me, and he can't free me, so we both stay here."

"Do you just pretend he's not your master?" Jen asked, still looking offended.

"Only sometimes," Wren grinned. "We both know it, and we're both aware of it. We'd be lying and stupid if we weren't. But we don't let it affect too many things. We can't change it, so we deal with it. Jere takes care of things that I can't, like legal things, and I let him. I do most of the things around the house, because I have a speed gift, and it's easier for me, and Jere uses his gift for healing, and it tires him out. We make decisions together, at least, most of the time we make decisions together. And when we don't, we sometimes argue about it, but that's working out okay, too. It's more difficult for me, because I have years of experience being a slave, but I guess I'm learning how to argue. We do the best we can do, both of us."

Jen was quiet, but Wren could tell she was dissatisfied.

"He doesn't torture us, or starve us, or beat us," Wren informed her, knowing she must have been wondering about the darker sides of slavery. He bristled at the idea that someone even *thought* Jere would act like that. "He doesn't even talk down to either of us, although all of us yell more than we probably should. And he doesn't touch me without my consent, and neither one of us lays a hand on Isis. We just... we all do our best. It's not an ideal situation, but I wouldn't trade it. I'm happy with Jere, and I know he'd still support me if we weren't together. You shouldn't judge him before figuring it out."

Jen frowned. "I guess I was a bit hasty," she mumbled. "I just... I've worked against slavery for years now, full-time activism, and then I find out that my brother is a slaveowner and has not one, but *two* human beings that he owns?"

"It's a bit of an adjustment, I'm sure," Wren said, conciliatory. "But it's been an adjustment for Jere, too."

He was quiet for a minute, watching as Jen struggled to process the news. He couldn't help smiling a bit at the resemblance between the siblings—Jen's eyes were a light hazel, unlike Jere's grey, but they were the same shape, and the distressed frown on her face was equally familiar to him.

"Jere is willing to let us have our space, make our own decisions, do what we want. Aside from some of the things he's made Isis do to stay safe, he'd never order us to do anything, not even something as little as talking with you, and he doesn't let anyone else order us around, either."

Jen reddened. "I didn't even realize—"

"It's all right," Wren shook his head. "It's hard for people who have always been free, especially people from non-slave-states, to realize that everyday interactions might come across as orders."

"I really didn't mean it like that!" Jen protested. "I just thought... I thought Jere had to get out!"

"I know," Wren shrugged. "But as much as you were telling him to get out, you were telling me and Isis to stay. You don't know either of us, and you have no idea how we react to new people and being separated from one another. I'm mostly well-adjusted, and I know I can trust Jere to keep me safe. A year ago, I wouldn't have been nearly as comfortable, but I wouldn't have even felt safe mentioning it. Isis has been very traumatized, and barely holds herself together on most days. She doesn't like to be alone with anyone but Jere, really, she only tolerates me sometimes. And that's fine. But she's still uncertain about saying no, so it's up to the people around her to offer her that opportunity."

"I'll apologize to her," Jen mumbled.

"I'd advise that," Wren agreed. He was taken by surprise by his protectiveness toward the girl who had turned his and Jere's life upside down.

They continued to talk about less vital things, how the clinic ran, who Jere spent time with, things like that. Wren could sense that Jen was viewing him as someone to be saved or rescued, but by the time he called Jere back in, he felt more like she saw him as a person. It was too easy, sometimes, for people to get stuck on the painful, victimized part. Sometimes Wren felt that he got stuck there as well, too caught up in the past and in his own pain to be able to move forward with Jere.

When Isis and Jere returned, the four of them sat around, an uneasy truce between them initiated by Jen's apology to Isis. They talked about Jere's success in the clinic, which Jen seemed astonished by, and Jen's activist work, which seemed to be quite fulfilling to her, but not exactly financially solid. Both of them seemed amused that Jere had settled comfortably into middle-class before his older sister. Jen was quite pleased when she found out that Jere was participating in some small activism himself.

"Who are you working with?" she asked. "Surely you wouldn't have been inspired enough to get into this on your own!"

Jere laughed before answering. "Kieran Stellan—she's a freshman at SU, started there in spring of last year, moved there from Hojer."

Jen's eyes widened. "Is she the overexcited little blonde who's hell-bent on saving the world? The empath?"

Wren laughed. It was a perfect description of Kieran.

"Yeah, do you know her?" Jere asked.

"I know *of* her," Jen shook her head. "I've been a little underground lately—the college groups tend to be big on visibility."

"Arrest warrants?" Jere assumed.

Jen shrugged. "Not officially, but plenty of districts want me for 'questioning,' and I'd rather not be questioned. But Kieran... she's making quite a few waves."

"Yeah?" Jere prodded.

"Do you know how rare it is for us to get activists from slave states? I mean, she's spent her whole life here, this is *normal*, and she's coming to Sonova to fight it—it's incredible!"

"I suppose," Jere agreed. "She's gotten me to do a bit of work here. I see slaves at the clinic, so they don't get taken to a vet, and I even network with people sometimes."

"That's wonderful!" Jen smiled. "I can't believe your name hasn't been mentioned."

Jere shrugged. "I did ask Kieran not to mention me."

"Afraid I'd find out you were here and come and beat your ass?" Jen smirked.

Jere said nothing, just grinned. Wren knew that was exactly what he had been worried about. Jere was clearly the non-confrontational one in the family.

"So, who wants to hear fun stories about what Jere was like as a kid?" Jen asked, conspiratorially.

Wren grinned, quite eager to hear such stories. He looked forward to the fact that they would make Jere squirm.

"I do!" Isis piped up, grinning.

"You're evil," Jere muttered, but he was smiling, too. It was unclear who he was referring to.

"Okay, so this one time, we're home alone, right, and I decide it would be fun to scare the hell out of Jere."

"Don't tell this one!" Jere protested. It was a weak protest, made weaker by the fact that he was still smiling.

"So I go into the attic, and I dig out this costume that I used to dress as for Halloween," Jen continues, smiling at Jere's misery. "I don't even think it was that scary —"

"It was fucking terrifying!"

" — but little Jerry had always been scared of it," Jen continued, ignoring Jere's protests. "It was this red, devil-looking mask, with horns and hair and big creepy teeth. We always called it the 'Bart' mask, but I have no idea why. Anyway, I wait until he's taking a shower, and I turn off the power to the bathroom."

"See why I was afraid of her?" Jere tried to defend himself, laughing a bit.

"You started screaming like a girl before I even did anything," Jen reminded him, laughing. She pitched her voice up high and shrill. "Oh, help me, I'm so scared and it's dark and I can't see anything and I might die! I'm telling Mum when she comes home!"

"I did not sound like that!"

"The best part is, I don't say anything, right? I just stay real quiet, hiding outside the bathroom door with the Bart mask on. Eventually, he starts to panic, and he starts screaming my name and asking if I'm all right, and I'm about to die I'm trying so hard not to laugh."

"I was convinced someone had broken in and killed you!" Jere protested. "I even got out of the shower and came to rescue you!"

Isis and Wren were both cracking up at the image, and Jere was starting to laugh as well.

"Yeah, so he gets out of the shower, and I can hear him fumbling around and stuff, and so I open the door and turn on a flashlight and shine it on the Bart mask and start yelling, and he screams some more and I rip off the Bart mask and throw it at him and —"

"Don't tell this part!"

" — and he pees himself!" Jen finished, cackling with the evil pleasure that only older sisters know.

Isis was laughing uncontrollably, Jere was grinning despite his embarrassment, and Wren was doing his best to not join in the laughter. After all, it was so mean....

"Aw, come on, you were just little, it happens," he said, trying to salvage the situation for his lover.

Jen stopped laughing for a moment to add in, "Oh, no he wasn't! That's the best part! He was, like, fourteen!"

The laughs escalated even more.

"Yeah, well, if you had been at college it never would have happened!" Jere tried unsuccessfully to defend himself. "That goddamn mask was creepy."

"Remember Mum's face when she came home?" Jen recalled. "I thought she was going to kick us both out of the house."

"Well, to be fair, she came home to her two teenage children in the dark, one holding a flashlight, the other covered in pee and a bathtowel," Jere reminded her.

"Also, you were punching me," Jen added.

"Your poor mum," Wren laughed.

Jen proceeded to tell a few more such stories, although Jere got in a few good ones as well. It sounded like both of them got their fair share of pranks pulled on one another, and while Jen usually came out on top, being older and wiser, she took her fair share of the blame when the time came. Wren enjoyed seeing Jere interact with his sister, yet another piece of his history and who he was. He felt a pang of guilt and sadness that he would never see his own younger brother again, never play such tricks on him, or share stories, or laugh together as adults. He wondered if he and his brother would ever have interacted like that anyway; their family had been so focused on behaving properly and respecting traditions that little time was left for fun or teasing. While he envied Jere's happy childhood, he felt like he was starting to learn how to have that kind of comfort and playfulness. It felt nice to be learning it now, but it seemed so late, like he had missed out on so much. He pushed it aside. There was nothing he could do about it in any case.

That night, he and Jere ended up going to bed rather late, as everyone had stayed up chatting. Surprisingly, Isis had even stayed out with them, mostly quiet, but seeming to enjoy herself. She seemed enraptured by Jen's stories, whether about Jere's childhood or about her work with the anti-slavery organizations. While Isis had come to enjoy Imelda's visits, Imelda was more than old enough to be her mother, if not her grandmother. Wren wondered how long it had been since Isis had a younger woman to talk to, to be a role model, to just be there for her.

"Your sister has quite the stories," he teased.

Jere made a face at him. "Kiss my ass," he teased, but he was smiling.

Wren wrestled him onto his stomach. "Don't mind if I do!" he retorted, kissing and licking and biting his ass and everything else until Jere moaned. They settled a bit, Jere comfortably in his arms.

"God, it's weird having her here," Jere mumbled.

Wren laughed. "It seems to be going well, now that you're past that initial awkward stage."

Jere nodded. "Yeah, I guess. I mean, I haven't seen her in almost two years, and she sees me here? My life... I barely even recognize it anymore. I'm not the same person as I was back then."

"Is that a good thing or a bad thing?"

Jere shrugged. "Both, maybe? It's a good thing that I have you in my life, I certainly like that. I think, overall, it's a good thing. I'm more confident. I'm successful. But it's weird—I've actually started to accept some things in Hojer, like, I just accept that it's a slave state. It's weird to think that I didn't used to, that it used to be an everyday thing to hate this place and assume everyone in it was evil."

"Jere, it's not as if you like it now!" Wren laughed. "You still say that you hate it probably once a week, and you're trying to change things. But you're working on it from the inside, that's what the whole thing was about with buying Isis, wasn't it? Working from the inside, helping people one at a time. Like the clinic."

"That's true," Jere agreed. "I just hope I never get too complacent."

"Between Kieran and Jen, Isis and her problems, and your unwavering moral compass, I don't think that will ever be a problem," Wren teased. "Besides, even when you're accepting of it, you still don't fucking like it. You do the best you can, and that's good enough. Don't beat yourself up over not being able to save the world!"

Jere smiled back at him, tired and happy. "You're right."

"Now, those are words I love to hear," Wren teased.

Their lovemaking was slow and sensual and Wren couldn't help but think about their first few times together. So uncertain, so hesitant. They had both grown together in this and other regards, and now there was a familiarity and comfort between them in and out of bed that could only be forged through time and experience.

Wren didn't spend much time in general thinking about the state of things, or Hojer, or activism. For years, he had been content to worry about his life and stay alive. Even now that he no longer needed to be concerned about such simple things, he was content to spend his spare time fucking Jere and thinking ahead to all the wonderful years they might have together. He had reached the top, he assumed, as far as happiness and fulfillment went. He had a happy life that he enjoyed, people that loved him, work he enjoyed — he didn't want anything else, because as far as he was concerned, he had everything. More than anything a slave could expect. And he had Jere.

Jen stayed for three days, and Wren was glad to get a chance to know her. It was nice, really, presenting himself and Jere as a couple to someone else, someone who cared more about that kind of thing than anything else. Sure, Kieran saw them both for the people they were, but she was so focused on her own thing and her projects, sometimes it was easy to fade into the background. Paltrek, while tolerant, had nothing much to do with Wren, and Wren was perfectly happy with that. No, he felt the same strange comfort with Jen as he had with Janet, without the threat of having his gift probed out and discovered. Jen's ability to psychically manipulate water wasn't nearly as dangerous. The whole family just seemed warm and nice and friendly. He envied Jere again, just a little bit, for growing up in such an environment. But he couldn't hold it against him, not when they were all so willing to take him in as one of their own. Slaves didn't have families, but he certainly felt like more than a "friend" or "acquaintance" with Jere's relatives.

Even Isis started talking with Jen a little bit, though, in typical Isis fashion, she preferred to have Wren or Jere around when she did. But she expressed more interest in Jen than she ever had in any other person, and practically beamed when Jen commented on one of her drawings.

Wren wondered if she might have a little crush, a theory Jere tried to dismiss out of hand. Wren couldn't help but notice it, though, and

279

for a slave, it didn't matter if you were fifteen and the other person was in their late twenties—someone kind and attractive was rare, and someone kind and attractive and not dangerous was almost unheard of. Wren was certain that Jen would be as horrified at the idea as her brother, and would certainly never act on it. That's what growing up in a normal household did for you, apparently, it made you all kind and opposed to abusing others and taking advantage. It was a novel concept, but Wren was starting to like it.

Jen left on a much happier note than she had arrived, having resolved her anger toward Jere remarkably quickly, and getting to know Wren and Isis a little bit. Wren was glad to see his lover and his sister getting along; Jere needed support from home whether he wanted to admit it or not. The short visit took time and energy out of everyone, but it was in the best way, replacing rest and sleep with interaction and laughter. Jen promised to write, and hugged everyone when she left—even Wren, who had to remind himself not to cringe, and even Isis, who stood there looking awkward and confused but a little bit happy. Wren felt like he had another piece of evidence to add to his crush theory.

Jen asked not to be walked back to the speed train, and as she stood in the doorway, putting off leaving, she smiled at Jere. "I can't believe you're settled down and in love and all this craziness! You're all grown up, little brother! Tell me what it's like, sometime!"

Chapter 33
Being There

Paltrek stopped by for a visit the next day, no doubt to inquire and gossip about the "guest" that Jere had.

"It was my sister," Jere brushed off his inquiries. "Which gossipmonger did you hear this from, anyway?"

"Is your 'sister' always a sexy young man?" Paltrek teased, dropping down on the couch. "Annika saw someone while she was out the other day."

Jere shook his head. "Jen's a bit, um, unconventional."

"Annika's going to be as pissed about that being a girl as she was about you being gay!" Paltrek roared with laughter. "God, she's a terrible judge of everything, isn't she!"

Isis walked by, a glare fixed on her face. Despite Jere warning her that Paltrek was coming over, she clearly wasn't happy about it.

"What are you staring at?" Paltrek asked, laughing a bit.

Isis turned her body so her back was against the wall and she was facing the two free men head on. "Not much," she muttered, but Jere detected the waver in her voice.

"Still a little snot, I see," Paltrek turned back to Jere.

"Paltrek..." Jere started, at the same time as Isis snapped "Still an asshole, I see."

Paltrek cursed, Jere leaned forward in his seat, and Isis moved closer to Jere.

"Isis!" Jere warned.

"You're goddamned lucky you're not mine," Paltrek replied, completely ignoring Jere as well.

"I'd rather die!" Isis spat out.

"Both of you, knock it off!" Jere slammed his drink down, catching everyone's attention. He glared, first at Paltrek, who rolled his eyes, and then at Isis, who cringed away. "Both of you are acting like little kids, for Christ's sake!"

"He started it!" Isis protested, at the same time as Paltrek asserted, "She started it!"

"Point proven." Jere sat back, still ready to jump between them should anything escalate. He was confident that Isis was too scared and Paltrek too proper for such a thing to happen. "Isis, you can be polite or you can go in another room."

"That's not—"

"Paltrek, *you* can be polite, or you can go home," Jere continued, despite the outrage of both of the other people in the room. "From where I'm sitting, you're both being snotty assholes, and I don't have time to put up with it. Try to show a little respect."

Paltrek looked pouty, but he slumped back in his seat and ignored Isis.

Isis looked frozen for a few seconds before looking away. "I didn't want to be out here, anyway," she mumbled, leaving quietly.

"You can't ask people to show respect to a slave, Jeremy," Paltrek muttered.

"I'm not asking you to show her respect, I'm asking you to show *me* respect," Jere clarified, irritated at his friend's persistence. "You were provoking her for no good reason, and you know it bothers me. If I thought you were coming over to harass my slaves, I wouldn't have invited you in."

"I guess you have a point," Paltrek shrugged. "I wasn't doing it to piss you off, but I guess I'd be pissed if you came over and started teasing Dane after I told you not to. A man's got a right to take charge in his own house, right?"

"Something like that," Jere half-agreed. It wasn't exactly how he felt, but he appreciated Paltrek's attempt to understand. "Anyway, how is Annika?"

Paltrek laughed. "A bit better, surprisingly. Since she started dating that guy she met at work, she's been a lot less miserable to live with. Even Arae's starting to look a little bit more lively. Seems the new man isn't that fond of a half-dead slave around, so Annika either leaves her be or leaves her home alone for days on end. It's for the best, really, I don't know how much more the girl could have taken."

Jere nodded. He hadn't seen Arae in months; no one had, but he assumed she was better off left alone than dragged about with Annika.

"Makes my life a hell of a lot better, too!" Paltrek pointed out. "Not having that bitch bothering me and causing trouble makes life go a lot more smoothly. Leaves a lot more time for going out and having fun, if you know what I mean."

Knowing Paltrek, that meant going out and getting laid. Jere couldn't say he objected, although he was quite content to stay home with Wren.

"You should come out sometime!" Paltrek encouraged him. "When was the last time you got out of here? You're in danger of becoming a shut-in!"

"It's been a while," Jere admitted. "I've been busy."

"You've been held prisoner by work and that girl," Paltrek commented.

It was true. "I'll let you know when I get some free time," Jere promised. "It's good of you to stop by, though. It's easier, just to have people over. Less work that way."

"Yeah, yeah," Paltrek shook his head. "Wouldn't want to go out of your way to have a good time. Might give people the idea that you have a life or something!"

They chatted for a little while longer, until Paltrek decided to take his own advice and go out and have fun. Jere looked at the clock, saw it was well past midnight, and went into the bedroom, where Wren was curled up reading and shirtless and looking absolutely edible.

"You didn't have to wait up for me," Jere half-protested, climbing into bed next to him.

"Who said I did?" Wren smirked. "You know, this book is really interesting. I may just spend *all* night reading it."

"Really?" Jere started stripping off his clothes. "You'd really want to do that *all* night?"

"Yep." Wren tried to look serious, but the half-grin on his face and the fact that he couldn't stop peeking over the edge of his book gave him away.

"Even if there was a naked man in bed with you, willing to put his tongue anywhere you wanted?" Jere teased, slipping under the covers and maneuvering himself between Wren's legs, which just happened to be spread wide apart.

"Yep," Wren repeated, stifling a giggle. "This is a really, *really* good book."

Jere leaned over to kiss Wren's stomach, peeking up at him from under the book when he lifted it up. "Even if I untie the drawstring on your pants with my teeth, and beg you to fuck me?"

Wren blushed, but tossed the book aside. "You know my weak spots, don't you?"

Jere grinned up at him, using his teeth to pull at the drawstring, and easing the pants off with his hands. The second Wren was naked, Jere pulled Wren's cock into his mouth, making him gasp.

Jere kept going for a while, until Wren was hard and clutching at his hair, and then he pulled back, kissing a trail up Wren's body until he met his mouth, then kissing him for a few minutes. "Am I as good as your book?" he challenged.

"I think I had a chance to get deeper into the book," Wren replied, looking devious. Jere's felt his eyes light up at the suggestion.

Their playful banter, not to mention touching, was interrupted by a knock at the door. Jere raised an eyebrow at Wren.

"I'll get it," Wren muttered. "God only knows what she wants now."

"Wren..." Jere started, letting his voice trail off as Wren dressed himself rapidly. There was no point in arguing, Wren really would be faster. He watched as his lover opened the door partway.

"What?" Wren demanded.

"I need to see Jere."

"What for?" Wren stood in the doorway, but Jere could see that Isis was visibly upset.

"I just fucking need Jere, okay, it's none of your goddamned business!"

Jere was already up and out of bed, tugging a pair of boxer shorts on and looking around for some pants. *"Love, it's okay, I can see what she wants."*

"If you're knocking at the door at two in the morning I'd say it's my goddamned business," Wren snapped back, clearly irritated. *"She doesn't just get to demand anything she wants at every hour of the night!"*

Jere had managed to find pants, and a shirt as well, which he tugged over his head as he walked over to the door. "Wren—"

"Fuck you both, then!" Isis started to storm off.

"Dammit!" Jere stopped, looking nervously at Wren. "I'm sorry. I know you don't appreciate these interruptions."

"No, I really don't." Wren stalked back to the bed, the slowness of his movements seeming purposeful.

Jere hesitated, frozen in the middle of the room. It was clear that Isis needed him, but it wasn't fair to Wren that he kept getting overlooked. "She'll probably be okay," he managed, mostly trying to convince himself. "If she really needs something, she can come back."

"Just go deal with her." Wren had gotten into bed, and he sat there, a stormy look on his face.

Jere took a few steps closer to the bed. "Really, Wren, I'm sure she just—"

"Go and take care of it, Jere!" Wren snapped, turning away. "Just fucking go."

Jere was left with nothing to do but chase after Isis.

Fortunately, she didn't go far. Jere was a bit surprised to find her sitting at the dining room table, a blanket around her shoulders, eyes clearly red from crying. He sat down next to her, silent for a moment. When she stayed silent as well, he asked softly, "What's going on?"

For a few seconds, she sat there looking down at the table, then began to cry a little. She let the blanket drop from her shoulders and held her arms out, revealing deep gashes on both, slicing across the surface in neat, parallel lines.

"I'm sorry," she whispered.

Jere sighed. "What did you do it with?" It wasn't the first time she had come to him with such marks. He tried to keep sharp things out of her possession as much as possible, just to make it harder for this to happen.

"A scalpel I stole from the clinic," she admitted.

Jere nodded, moving a little closer to her. "Give me your hands," he ordered, his voice still soft.

A sob escaped her lips, and she extended her arms until her hands rested in his. "Please don't hurt me," she whimpered.

"Isis, you know I wouldn't," he reminded her, pained that she even worried about that after all this time. "Just relax, I'll fix it and it will be gone in a minute."

"You should hurt me," she muttered, but Jere could feel her going slack mentally.

"Nobody should hurt you."

The healing was quick, the fresh cuts mending quickly and seamlessly. Jere let her hands go, almost reluctantly. A part of him wanted to keep her still, keep her safe. But the best he could do was to keep fixing her and hope it sunk in eventually.

"Do you want to talk about it?"

She shook her head.

"Listen, kid..." Jere shook his head. "I'm glad that you're coming to me, and I would never dream of turning you away, but I'm scared that one day I won't be around and this will happen and you'll end up dead. We've gotta think of another plan."

"I'm not trying to kill myself, I just want to hurt myself, but sometimes I go too far!" she protested, sobbing again. "Please, Jere, I promise, it's not that, you don't need to... to tie me up or give me medicine or anything again, because then I wouldn't even be able to help out at the clinic, and you said it was only if I was really bad and I'm scared and that would just make it worse, Jere, please —"

"Hey, not happening," Jere cut her off, reassuring her quickly. "I'm not suggesting that. I promise. And it was never because you were 'bad,' anyway, but that's not the point. I just... listen, what if this happens and I'm out, or in surgery with someone, or I have a guest visiting?"

"I could wait," Isis mumbled.

Jere sighed. "That's not what I meant. Look, you did a good job tonight letting me know — those were *very* fresh cuts, which means you did exactly what I asked you to do and told me about them quickly." He watched as Isis nodded. "I don't want you to wait, and I don't want you to feel like you have to wait. But here's the thing, though, this isn't stopping, and it almost seems like it's getting worse, and that scares me, so we need to do something about it."

"L-like what?"

Jere was a bit reluctant to share his plan, because he knew she would hate it. She would hate it, and she would hate him for proposing it in the first place, and she would hate him more for insisting upon it.

"I want to open up a mind connection with you and leave it open."

"No! I don't want you in my head like that!" Isis protested. "I thought you said I was doing good! I promise! I'll tell you every time I do it"

"It's not that you're not doing well right now, but it's not working," Jere tried to explain. "Right now, if you're having a problem, I can't tell if it's something big that needs attention right away, or if it's something that can wait, and it's not fair that I have to drop everything to find out every time. It's not fair to Wren that you automatically get to drag me out of bed without even telling either of us what's wrong. I know it can be hard for you too, and I really think this will make it easier for everyone."

"No! Jere, this isn't—"

"It isn't an option." Jere winced at the harshness of his tone. "Look, first off, I open and close a mind connection with you almost every day now, for work or... or this — and you know it taxes both of us each time we do that. Second, it would allow you constant access to me, no matter where I am, so you could always get to me if you needed anything. Third... I'm not giving you the choice. Actually, no, I take that back, but I'm giving you a terrible, shitty choice — you either agree to the mind connection, or you will need to be supervised by me or Wren at all times."

Isis glared at him, crying and seething. "And you'd drug me up when you couldn't watch me?"

287

Jere shook his head. "No. I promised you I wouldn't do that, and I meant it. I don't care if I don't get to sleep for months, I wouldn't do that to you unless you were really trying to kill yourself like you were before."

"Why are you so fucking nice!" Isis sobbed. "I don't want you in my fucking head. I'll never be alone!"

"Isis," Jere waited until she looked up at him again. "Look, it's not about never leaving you alone. I'll give you your space. If you'd like, I won't even use the mindspeak, ever, unless you do first. It's okay. And I'll teach you some blocking skills if you'd like. But you *have* to have a way to get in contact with me at any time. You're scaring me, and I don't like it."

She nodded, squeezing her eyes shut. "Okay. Okay. Do it."

"I'm gonna move closer and put my hands on your head, okay?" Jere said softly, waiting until she nodded to slide his chair closer. She flinched when he touched her, but she held still. The mind connection was made easily, the pathways and connections already established through their close working relationship. The fact that it was intended to be long-term made it somewhat easier to maintain, but it was still more work than the connection he had with Wren. He slid his chair back, letting her have the space she valued so much. "Test it out."

"*I'm such a fucking mess.*"

"It will get better," Jere said. He believed it. "Can I try?"

She nodded.

"*I see you getting better every day. This will pass.*"

"I fucking hope you're right," Isis mumbled. She stood up, wiped away the tears from her eyes, and turned to leave. She paused, just at the doorway. "Thank you for being there when I need you."

Jere sat at the table for a few moments, waiting for his head to clear. It was almost too much, at times, dealing with this kid, but he did really see her improving. Especially when she was occupied, whether it was with drawing or with work or even when she was talking with him or Wren, for a few moments, she started to seem normal. Sane. Put together.

He finally got up and returned to the bedroom, where Wren was lying in the dark, pretending to be sleeping. Jere could feel through the mind connection that he wasn't.

"Please, don't be mad?" he said softly, undressing and crawling into bed.

"I'm not mad at you — hell, I'm not even mad at her. I'm just fed up with dealing with her problems all the time. I can't get a night alone with you."

Jere felt the same way. "I know how much stress this puts on you. I tried talking to her about it, letting her know that you and I need a little space. She did have a good reason, this time. She wasn't just trying to bother us."

Wren huffed. "She cutting herself up again?"

"It's getting better." It wasn't exactly an answer.

Wren was quiet for a few more minutes. "What changed? In the connection?"

"I have an open connection with Isis now," Jere said softly. "You shouldn't notice it much, she has such little psychic presence."

Wren nodded.

Jere could feel his emotions, the confusion, the budding jealousy. Old fears, made new. "Love, it should make it easier for you and me to get some peace. She can contact me without bothering you. I can monitor her without taking away from the little time you and I get to spend together. Are you okay?"

"Yeah." Wren finally turned toward him. "There's enough of you to go around, right?" he tried to joke, but there was fear in his eyes and his voice was unsteady. He was vulnerable.

Jere put his arms around him. "I will *always* have time for you, love. You're my top priority. Always. No matter what else happens in the moment."

Wren kissed him, passionate and demanding. "Thank you," he whispered, then returned to the kissing. "Sometimes I just need to be reminded."

"Whenever you need," Jere promised. They kissed for a few more minutes, and then Jere grinned. "So, I think we started getting *deep* into something before we were interrupted...."

Wren grinned at him, pinning him down to the mattress. There wouldn't be much sleep tonight.

Chapter 34

Repercussions

The mind connection helped, which Jere was quite grateful for. He hadn't been completely sure that he was making the right decision, but he knew he had to do something. To his surprise, Isis wasn't too bad at learning blocking skills, and the fact that she could control how much of herself was shared and accessible made her much happier with the arrangement. She didn't stop hurting herself, but it happened less and less often, and she got better about asking for help to heal it. She assisted in the clinic with more regularity, and things seemed to settle into a pattern. Isis was scared, and she clung to Jere more often than not, but he'd rather have her clinging to him than fighting him. Her clinging, naturally, was purely emotional; she still grew uncomfortable whenever anyone else was within arm's reach.

Wren just seemed happier that the girl wasn't interrupting them anymore, and his jealousy and worries that Jere would cease having time for him seemed to be mostly unfounded. Jere pushed himself to meet the needs of both of the important people in his life, and on more days than not, he felt pretty successful. After Jen's visit, he felt like he and Wren had a cohesion that they had been missing before, and he reminded himself to send her a letter thanking her for her big-sister advice. Paltrek was right when he said he was becoming a shut-in.

Jere walked into the clinic, finding Wren settling in a new client in his curt, business-like manner. He received very few complaints about his "assistant" — what Wren lacked in bedside manner, he far made up for in efficiency and exacting perfection. Even the most demanding of slaveowners had nothing to fault him on, which was

Alicia Cameron

exactly the way Wren wanted it.

Isis, on the other hand, was kept out of the public eye as much as possible. She was helpful around the clinic in general, and she was especially good at helping with slaves and children, and sometimes free women as well, setting them at ease and providing a friendly face in contrast to Wren's business-like demeanor. She was still nervous around free people, and became easily agitated and scared, especially by those who took liberties with her as a slave that they never would have with a free person. It didn't happen often, but one of the male patients had gotten her alone and tried to touch her, and she darted away, screaming and knocking down a cart full of supplies. Wren had intervened quickly, explaining that their master was violently jealous and summoning Jere immediately through the mind connection. If not for Wren's quick thinking, Isis could have been in danger of punishment, and suspicion would have been cast on Jere for allowing such behavior. Jere was forever grateful that his lover had easily portrayed him as the kind of person who was too greedy and possessive to let another person touch his slaves, and he did his best to live up to that role when talking to the other man. Left to his own devices, Jere had to admit, he still felt lost.

After that incident, Isis made herself scarce. She still put in her fair share of work, a feat that Jere was too happy with to comment on, but she tended to stay behind closed doors. Isis preferred locked doors, as long as the lock was on her side. Many times, she could be found hovering around in Jere's shadow, where he could protect her. It was a job he was accepting gracefully, if not willingly.

But her scarcity made her easy to miss. In fact, it wasn't until a growing sense of anxiety hit him with an almost physical sense that Jere realized he hadn't seen her all day. Thinking back, he realized that wasn't right, he saw her at breakfast, but not after that. There had been a surgery, and then he and Wren were talking about things, patients here and there, nothing he really needed Isis for anyway. Still, he usually saw her around.

And there was the anxiety again, stronger now, filling him with a sense of panic that made his stomach clench and his eyes start to water and his palms start to sweat.

Not his anxiety. Not his panic.

291

Jere took a deep breath, strengthened his own mental blocks a bit more, and felt the feeling dissipate almost immediately. It proved that it wasn't his anxiety, but that wasn't far off.

He rushed out to the front desk and grabbed Wren by the arm, pulling him away from the patient he was checking in, not trusting himself to speak until they were behind the door in an exam room.

"Jere?" Wren looked alarmed.

"Have you seen Isis?" Jere asked, his voice high and alarmed.

Wren pulled his arm away, making Jere realize how tightly had had been gripping it. "No, Jere, what's going on?"

"When was the last time you saw her?" Jere debated using the mind connection, trying to find her that way.

"Um, this morning?" Wren shrugged. "She was quiet today."

"Fuck." He had promised her that he wouldn't initiate it, would let her have her privacy, but was this enough of an emergency? She was just starting to trust him.

"Baby..." Wren put a hand on his shoulder, steadying him. "I'll go look through the house and the clinic. I'm sure she's just off hiding somewhere. Probably thinks she did something wrong again."

Jere shook his head, then nodded. "Go, I mean... but this feels wrong."

Wren kissed him quickly on the cheek, then sped off through the house. Jere knew, logically, that it wasn't a long time, but it seemed like Wren was taking forever. While he waited, he pulled back his blocking a bit, the feeling of panic and anxiety threatening to overtake him again. It definitely felt wrong.

Wren returned, his concerned look now matching Jere's. "You're right. She's not here."

"Shit." Jere dropped the block entirely, steeling himself against the wave of panic as he felt out for his lost slave. He found her, alive, panicked, and terrified. "*Isis?*" he tried the mind connection with her, softly, with no response. "*Goddammit, Isis, if you can hear me, you'd better fucking answer!*"

There was silence, for a moment.

"*Jere?*"

He breathed a sigh of relief. "*Who else would it be? Where are you?*"

"Jere, oh god, fuck, please help me! Jere, I'm sorry. I'm so sorry! I fucked up this time. I fucked up really bad, Jere!"

Jere watched his knuckles go white as they clutched the edge of an exam table. He wished he could squeeze the information out of it. *"Isis. Focus. Where are you?"*

"They're hurting me, Jere!"

"Son of a bitch!" Jere exploded, putting his fist through a cabinet door in an attempt to shield Isis from the rage and frustration inside of him. He saw Wren ducking and covering his head, which made him feel considerably worse. Nonetheless, he motioned to him to come closer. To his credit, Wren did so, stopping an arm's length away.

"What do you want me to do?" Wren asked.

"Just calm me down," Jere forced his voice to stay lowered. "She's somewhere and she's being hurt and I can't get her to talk to me while I'm this upset, and I can't relax with her anxiety bleeding over this much."

Wren nodded, coming close and wrapping his arms around Jere's waist. For a moment, he wanted to fight it, wanted to throw off the feeling of constriction and unwanted touch, to attack anything and everything in sight until he escaped. These weren't his feelings. He felt a soft pair of lips touch his neck, just below his ear, and he was torn between leaning into the embrace and pulling away from it. A hand tightened in his hair and held him there.

"Get your shit together," a soft voice whispered harshly. "*You* bought her. *You* let her get into trouble. *You* need to get her out of it. You can do it."

Jere nodded, feeling a bit chastened, but strangely calmed as well. That was Wren. As much as the connection with Isis was filling him with panic, his connection with Wren was filling him with calm, strength, clarity. It helped that his lover's hands were still on him, anchoring him. He cleared his mind, focused on calm and Wren and the hand wrapped in his hair, and attended to the connection with Isis again.

"Can you tell me who's with you?" he asked, calmly this time.

"Jere, please, I'm sorry! I'm so fucking sorry —"

"It's all right. Isis, listen, drop the shields. I can see through your eyes,

if you'll let me."

"Please, Jere, fucking god — "

"Isis. Listen. Relax. Focus on the shields you put up to keep me out, and concentrate on letting me in. I can help you, but you have to let me. This is all you have to do. You don't have to fight anymore. Just relax and let the shields go."

He heard nothing from the other end, and wondered briefly if he'd pushed her too far. He knew he hadn't when the feelings intensified, his own vision clouded, and he saw glimpses of what she must have been seeing. Uniformed officers. Boots. A cement floor and bars.

"She's at the police station," Jere said out loud, only slightly less nervous than he had been before. *"Isis, what are their names? What are the names of the officers?"*

When she was unable to respond, Jere was forced to wait, trying to keep his focus, looking and listening through her eyes until he overheard one of them say a name. Dorsey. That was it, then. An Officer Dorsey.

"I'm coming, kid, don't worry."

He slammed down shields so he could function, the anxiety stopping immediately, the sensation of Wren still wrapped around him suddenly noticeable. He bent his neck to kiss Wren's hand.

"You okay?" Wren asked, eyebrow raised. "I was getting worried there for a minute."

"I have to go. I have to get Isis," Jere mumbled. "Can you deal with the clinic?"

"How long will you be?"

"I... the rest of the day, probably," Jere shrugged. "Tell you what, I'll come back around closing time for absolute emergencies only. Everyone else can wait until tomorrow."

Wren nodded, kissing his shoulder. "Go. Change your shirt. And don't punch anything."

"Thanks, love," Jere muttered, flying out of the clinic and through to the house in an instant. He focused his thoughts, searching around the available consciousnesses for one that would respond to "Dorsey." He was putting his coat on when he landed on it.

"Is this Officer Dorsey?" He realized his voice was a bit more as-

sertive than it needed to be. If he were speaking out loud, one might have said he was yelling.

"*Indeed. Who might I have the pleasure –* "

"*What the* hell *right do you have to detain my girl without notifying me!*" Jere snarled. He realized that he was becoming more, not less aggressive.

There was silence for a few moments, and Jere stormed down the road, willing himself not to literally run to the station and arrive pissed off *and* out of breath. He fumed as he continued to hear nothing from the officer.

"*Sir, may I have your name?*"

Not the response he was looking for. "*Jeremy Peters.*"

"*The doctor, right?*"

Now was *not* the fucking time for small talk. "*Yes.*"

"*Do you treat crazy, too? The damn girl's not making any sense, we thought she was a runaway for a while, except she keeps screaming to see her master. We didn't know who that was, until now.*"

Jere forced himself to calm down. Perhaps this hadn't been intentional, then. But Isis would have named him, and there was still the slave registry, surely... no, it was better just to think it wasn't intentional.

"*I'm on my way to pick her up now,*" Jere said, picking up the speed a bit. He forced himself to stop before begging the officer not to hurt her.

He tried the mind connection with Isis again, but got nothing. Reluctantly, he shielded hard against it. He would be at the station soon anyway.

It didn't feel soon enough, and he would be lying if he told anyone that he wasn't panting just a little by the time he got there. Still, he took a deep breath and reminded himself not to make the problem worse before he climbed the stairs to enter the building.

"Dr. Peters?" A uniformed man stood in front of him, name badge identifying him as the officer Jere had been speaking with.

"Yes," Jere tried not to scowl.

"Officer Kellan Dorsey," the man nodded, ushering him inside. "How'd you get my name?"

"Mind connection with my slave," Jere mumbled, pushing his

way past the officer for a moment until he realized he didn't know where he was going anyway. "Where is she?"

The officer shook his head, walking to a heavy door with an equally heavyset slave standing guard. Once the officer nodded, the slave stood aside and let them pass. Jere bit back a string of curse words when he saw Isis on the floor, hands cuffed, covered in blood and bruises.

"Is this yours?" a woman's voice asked, too thick and cultured, like spoiled milk. A blonde in a business suit stood tapping one impractically high heel, glancing from Jere to Isis and back again.

Jere wanted to ask who the fuck this woman was and what the fuck she thought she was doing, after punching her in the face, but he settled with nodding. "Yes."

"*Jere! I'm sorry, I fucked up Jere, I'm so sorry!*" Isis was crawling toward him, mumbling "I'm sorry" out loud as she did, the metal handcuffs clanging on the floor.

"Allow me to introduce myself," the woman said, grabbing a still-struggling Isis by the hair and jerking her back. "My name is Nicolette Arnsdale, and I'm the head of Slave Control, Regulation, and Enforcement for the state of Hojer."

"Ms. Arnsdale, if you would, please take your hands off my property."

Isis sobbed, her pleas mixing together with wails and whimpers.

"Mr. Peters, how will we know that she won't attack someone again?"

Jere wanted to punch her in her lipstick-encrusted mouth. "How do you know *I* won't?"

At the surprised and startled looks, Jere rushed to cover with something more socially appropriate. "Ms. Arnsdale, let her come to me. I can personally vouch for her control, now that I'm in the room with her."

With a roll of her eyes, the woman let Isis go, dropping her to her face, as her hands were still cuffed behind her back. Not a second passed before Isis crawled over to Jere anyway, and he struggled to stop from scooping her up in his arms and running away with her. He stood there, plotting violence and revenge and anything else he could think of while the girl he had grown rather fond of crawled on bloodied knees to his feet, kneeling and leaning against his legs when she got to him.

It was too much. Jere knelt down, helping her to stand. He glared at the police officer. "Undo the cuffs. If she falls and is damaged, I'll sue for mishandling her."

Dorsey shook his head, but did as Jere requested. Isis dropped back to the floor, wrapping her arms around Jere's legs this time. He forced himself to focus. *"Are you okay?"* He had to ask, and he couldn't ask out loud, and surely she wouldn't blame him for using the mind connection.

He felt her nodding against his leg, still sobbing. So she was terrified and brutalized, but otherwise okay. As if there was an otherwise.

"What the hell happened, and why wasn't I notified!" Jere tried to keep his tone civil, if his words weren't. He doubted he was successful.

"Your girl was out without a pass, Dr. Peters," Arnsdale informed him, looking smug. "Officer Dorsey and his partner tried to apprehend her, but when he did, the girl attacked him! So, after they subdued her, he brought her back here, and I was called in to help assess the situation and repercussions."

"And why wasn't I notified?"

"Dr. Peters, that girl of yours is ridiculously out of control!" Arnsdale sneered. "Wouldn't even tell us your name!"

"It's not true, Jere, I tried, I fucking tried so fucking hard!"

"Well, she did keep begging for her master," Dorsey admitted. "Just... couldn't get a name out of her."

"Jere, they're lying! Please, fuck, you've gotta believe me, Jere, I'm sorry!"

"Isis, hush. It's okay. It'll be okay."

Isis wrapped around his legs, clinging more tightly, until Jere was about to be thrown off balance. He knelt down to pet her head, very gently, and noticed the blood all over her.

"She was beaten." It wasn't a question.

"She resisted." Arnsdale's voice was a challenge. One Jere couldn't afford to rise to.

"What is there, a... a fine, or something?" Jere tried to be nonchalant, tried to bury his anger with an air of being bored and overworked. "Let me take care of it and get home. I have a clinic to run."

"Sir, you realize she assaulted a free man," Arnsdale pointed out. "The law demands a public whipping for such offenses."

Jere felt his heart drop. He looked at the officer. "I apologize, sir... I didn't even ask, are you all right? It's not every day Hojer's finest get attacked by teenaged girls."

Dorsey shrugged. "A bit of a bruise, on my cheek is all. But she did attack me. Law's law."

"You do respect the laws here, don't you, Dr. Peters?" Arnsdale asked, still challenging. "If I recall, you're the outlander who's treating slaves in the Hojer clinic. Quite a difference from a fancy hospital in the city, now isn't it? But surely, even in the city they had laws against violence."

"Yes," Jere managed, shocked and horrified that this woman knew anything about him. Jere nodded. "So what, then, we... find a whipping post, get this taken care of? Is there a person who does this?"

Arnsdale laughed. "Dr. Peters, we aren't living in ancient, uncivilized times, you know." At Jere's doubtful look, she continued. "There's a procedure for this. It has to be announced, formally, and appropriate witnesses gathered. Now, I'm required by law to tell you that you can leave the girl with us until the punishment, which will occur in seven to ten business days, at your convenience, or you can take her out on bail, which we would not suggest—"

"I'm taking her now."

"—as you would be liable for her should she not show up," Arnsdale pursed her lips at him. "Of course, that is your decision, but keep in mind, Dr. Peters, that your ability to own slaves *could* be revoked should a slave on bail escape your possession."

"She won't," Jere growled.

"On the day of the punishment, there will be a fee assessed on you for use of county and state resources, and you'll have the option to have one of our trained professionals provide the whipping, or you may carry it out yourself according to our standards, if you'd prefer."

"I... uh..." Jere wasn't really sure what to do with this. It was too fast. He had to find a way to stop it.

"Don't worry, Dr. Peters, you'll be receiving an informational booklet by mail in the next day or so," Arnsdale smiled at him with no actual kindness. "But while you're here, shall we set the date?"

Jere felt himself spinning out of control. The second Tuesday of Fuck You seemed like an inappropriate answer at the moment, no matter how much he wanted to say it. "Next Sunday," he mumbled, not wanting to believe it himself. "That way I don't have to take as much time off my schedule to deal with this mess. Christ. You can't even subdue a teenage girl around here without getting hurt?"

Dorsey scowled at him, and Arnsdale's too-big smile faltered for a moment.

"Well, Dr. Peters, next Sunday is fine. Make sure you complete the necessary paperwork."

Jere turned, knelt down, and pulled Isis to her feet as gently as he could.

"I'm so sorry, I fucked up bad, I'm sorry," she whimpered, turning into liquid at Jere's touch.

"Get up," he ordered aloud. "*Isis, come on, I promise you'll be okay, but you have to get up and come with me now, all right? You can't resist and you can't complain and... you know what, just don't even talk until we get back to the house. Don't worry about being sorry, just worry about getting home. I'll take care of everything from here.*"

Chapter 35

Good Enough

Wren was furious.

The kid had been doing better, yes, but that wasn't really the point. The point was that his master was out, wasting time, because she had disappeared somewhere. The point was that he had to give other free people the bad news that their doctor was unavailable for an undisclosed "personal reason" — as if they had a right to know everything about Jere's business anyway.

The point was that Wren was a little worried about the girl, and it pissed him off that he cared.

So he processed people, postponed the few that could wait, offered ice water and comfortable seating to those who couldn't, and tried not to worry too much. He felt some of Jere's emotions bleeding through the connection, which was never a good sign, because for Jere to be that out of control, Wren knew he must be extremely stressed. He was a bit puzzled by the amount of anger he was feeling through the connection, and wondered briefly whether it was directed at Isis or not. He realized it wouldn't be. This was the kind of righteous anger that Jere reserved solely for people trying to hurt people he cared about.

A lull in the storm of emotions clued Wren into the fact that Jere was on his way home. He put up a sign indicating that someone would be attending the desk again soon, slipping away before the waiting emergency patients could ask annoying questions. He stepped through to the house and made tea, giving himself something to do other than worry until he heard footsteps at the door.

Wren sped over to open it, despite Jere's frequent insistence that he shouldn't bother, and shuddered at what he saw.

"What in the hell?" Wren gasped at the beaten mess in front of him.

Isis made no move to reply, simply started sobbing harder.

"Get inside." Jere's voice was quiet and strained, and Wren noticed how tightly he was gripping the girl's arm.

Wren took a step back, his mouth still slack with shock, unsure of what to do.

The second Jere closed the door, Isis dropped to the floor, wrapping her arms around Jere's legs and sobbing.

"Please, Jere, I'm so sorry, I'm sorry!"

Jere closed his eyes, sighed, and took off his coat, handing it to a still-shocked Wren.

"I fucked up this time, I know, I know I did, shit, Jere, fuck!"

Jere knelt down beside her, careful of all the bruised and bloodied places, and put his hands on her shoulders. "It's okay. Isis. Everything's going to be fine, don't worry about it."

"I told them!" Isis wailed. "I told them to contact you and they wouldn't, they just kept hurting me!"

"Shh," Jere said softly. "I believe you. I'm sure you did the right thing."

"No I didn't!"

Wren cringed as a fresh round of sobbing started. Fortunately, he had grown a little immune to her outbursts; they happened at the slightest provocation and never resulted in any upsetting consequences. He was more concerned with finding out what had brought her to this point. "What the hell happened?"

"She was out without a pass," Jere shrugged, looking up at Wren helplessly.

Wren raised an eyebrow. This, for being out without a pass? "But—"

Isis was shaking her head furiously. "I assaulted a fucking police officer."

"You did *what*?" Wren gasped. As unthinkable as her actions were, it did explain why and how she had been so badly beaten already.

"I didn't fucking mean to, okay?" Isis snapped, then started sobbing again. "I just fucked up. I never should have... I shouldn't have...."

"It's okay," Jere repeated. "Let's get you healed, and we can talk more about it later. You're safe now."

"No..." she moaned.

"Yes." Jere's tone was firm, but the look on his face was kind, and Wren noticed that his hands stayed gentle on the girl's arms. In spite of the trouble that Isis continued to cause, Jere was compassionate, refusing to so much as lecture her for her mistakes.

"Let's get you in bed and I'll heal you," Jere's tone stayed calm and firm. "You can rest up a bit while I go back to the clinic, and we'll talk over dinner."

Isis stood up and walked with Jere obediently. "You should heal your patients first. They deserve it more. They aren't so fucked up."

"Just do as you're told for once and let me heal you," Jere said, not unkindly, ushering her into her bedroom. He glanced at Wren for the first time, and Wren could see the exhaustion in his face. "Love, could you get me some healing cream, towels to clean her up, and some Crucial Care with half a sleep pill mixed in?"

Wren nodded, rushing off to fetch the supplies. When he returned, he heard Jere explaining that the sleep pill was just to let her rest. Isis didn't seem to have the energy to fight it today.

He stood by, watching and assisting, while his master calmed and healed the sobbing slave who had become a fixture in their home. She didn't speak anymore, which he was rather happy about, and she even drank down the Crucial Care and sleep pill without complaint, muttering something unintelligible as she fell asleep quickly.

He waited for Jere to walk out of the bedroom. "What the hell happened?"

Jere shook his head. "Like she said. She assaulted a police officer. They took their revenge on her in typical style."

"Shit," Wren muttered, slipping his arm around Jere's waist for support.

"Wren, they want to... they want me to..." Jere was fighting back tears, fighting to make words come out.

Wren knew why. "It's harsh, love, but she'll live." The mandated punishments were terrifying — any slave in their right mind knew better than to break one of the state-enforced slave codes.

"I hate it here, Wren," Jere turned to him, burying his head in his shoulder. "I hate this whole fucking town, this whole fucking *state*, and most of the people in it, and I want to kill them instead of healing them every day like nothing is fucking wrong!"

Wren stayed silent, rubbing his lover's back carefully. "If it would change anything, I'd tell you to do it."

It wouldn't change anything, though, and it most certainly wouldn't get Isis *or* Jere out of trouble. But Wren knew that wasn't what his master needed to hear right now. What he needed was support, and maybe a bit of gentle ass-kicking.

"Come on, let's finish at the clinic so today can be over with," he suggested, half-dragging him along.

They finished the work quickly. Jere was moody and irritable, so they mostly stayed quiet, but the way he pressed up against Wren let him know that he needed comfort and closeness. When the last patient was ushered out and the doors were locked, Wren came up behind him and caught him in his arms, holding him tightly.

"I should go check on Isis..." Jere mumbled.

"You should stay right fucking here," Wren growled in his ear, not loosening his grip in the slightest. "Are you okay?"

"No."

Wren stayed there, kissing at Jere's neck, not exactly sexually, but in a familiar, comfortable way, letting him know that he was there.

"Wren, there has to be a way out of this," Jere whispered, sounding defeated. "I can't let this happen."

"You might not have a choice," Wren said quietly. "But ask around — someone might have some better answers than I do."

"Who would I even ask?" Jere protested, turning to face him.

Wren sighed. Honestly, he doubted that it would matter who he asked, law was law. Jere would be no more able to save Isis from a judicial whipping than he had Wren last year, although the consequences were so much more severe this time. "Kieran. Paltrek. Go to the library and look through the codes, see if Imelda will help you. You're not alone here anymore, baby."

Jere nodded, looking a bit relieved. "You're right. I'm not. I have friends... and I have you."

Wren smiled. He doubted he would be of any help in the situation, but at least he would be able to provide some comfort and support. "Of course you do."

They went inside, and Wren prepared a quick, simple dinner, as he hadn't been sure what time Jere would return earlier. By the time it was finished, the smell filled the house, and the sleep pill Isis had taken had apparently worn off, because she emerged from her bedroom looking scared, disheveled and hungry.

Wren brought out the food quickly, and although he didn't want to admit it, he gave the best looking portion to the girl.

"How are you feeling?" Jere asked, staring down at his plate.

Isis shrugged. "Stupid, mostly."

Wren couldn't hold back any longer. "What the *hell* were you thinking?"

"I fucking wasn't thinking, okay!" Isis snapped, sending a fork hurtling across the room. "I obviously fucking wasn't thinking."

Wren sighed. The girl acted as if getting angry at him would somehow undo the damage she had caused by running off.

"Look, I know I fucked up, and I know I'm going to be punished, so... so that's that!" Isis was still trying for defiant, but her voice was shaking too much for her to pull it off. "Are you happy?"

Wren rolled his eyes. Now she was just being obstinate.

Jere finally rejoined the conversation after being unusually quiet. "Isis, nobody is happy about that. Wren's just a little... concerned."

It wasn't completely accurate, but Wren let it slide. It was nice to see Jere try to defend him.

"I'm doing what I can to help you out. I've just reached out through the mind connection to see who else can help. Kieran is coming over tonight to let me know what the options are as far as she knows, and tomorrow morning I'm going over to the Wysocka estate to speak with Paltrek."

Wren raised an eyebrow. "You're voluntarily setting foot over there?"

Jere shrugged. "He doesn't have time to stop by. He said he'd do some research for me tonight, and I'll go over tomorrow to see what he's got."

"You don't have to do this," Isis mumbled, stabbing her food viciously, but not eating it for once. "Just... just let them whip me. I'm the one who fucked up, don't put yourself out for me. You've done enough."

"It's not up to you," Jere said quietly. "I'll do what I can."

Isis pushed her food around in silence for a few more moments before throwing her spoon across the room to join the fork. Wren glanced at Jere, waiting for his cue on what to do. He wasn't eager to see Isis revert back to the way she had been.

"I'm sorry," she whimpered, backing away from the table. "I'm sorry, I can't eat... I just... I need to go." She fled, still sobbing.

Wren and Jere were equally put off from their dinner, so Wren wrapped everything up and stuffed it in the refrigerator. In all likelihood, he would turn it into some sort of stew or casserole if they didn't end up snacking on the meals in the middle of the night. He and Jere lay on the couch together, trying to pretend that the world didn't exist. It was more easily said than done.

Not long after they had given up on dinner, they heard a knock at the door. Wren got up to get it as Jere commented, "It's Kieran," and, indeed, the girl was standing in the doorway with her too-bright smile on her face.

She wrapped her arms around Wren, and he fought not to stiffen too much in her grip. She was harmless, but unexpected touch still put him on edge.

"Wren, it's so good to see you, it's been so long! I miss you and Jere like crazy, *god* staying with my parents is so horrible! How are you? Are you okay? I heard about Isis—it's awful, isn't it?"

"I'm well, doing fine, and yes, it is awful." Wren all but wrestled her jacket from her, smiling despite the situation. Kieran had grown on him, despite his initial reticence. He was relieved when Jere joined them, though, because he instantly became the target of Kieran's energy and attentions.

"Jere!" Kieran pounced on him like a tiger cub. "Oh my god, it's so awful! So awful! I've done what I could, started some research, reached out to my few contacts... this is just such a terrible thing to have happened. I hate it! It makes me want to go back to school *right now* and contact the organization and get them to organize a protest, or a march, or something!"

Wren wasn't surprised to see Jere hugging the girl like she was an old friend. Since Kieran had first come back from Sonova, Jere had clung to her as much as she had clung to him, the familiar attitude and reminder of his hometown so obviously becoming a part of her life. He felt a pang of regret, knowing that he was part of the reason that Jere was staying here in Hojer.

"Let's sit," Jere suggested, ushering them to the dining room.

Wren was quick to suggest tea, which was quickly dismissed in favor of margaritas. Limes hadn't been available last time Wren went shopping, but he doubted that anyone would mind the substitution of the new, greenish-orange citrus fruit that had been on sale. A pitcher was mixed up and poured into glasses in seconds.

"Where's Isis?" Kieran asked, sipping through the salty rim. "I know she's here. I can feel her."

"She's, uh..." Jere hesitated.

"I'm right here," Isis announced, stepping out of her room. "If you're gonna talk about me, I want to be here, and I want a drink, too!"

"You're too young," Jere dismissed her.

"I was beaten by two grown men today, I can have a goddamned drink!"

Wren grinned at her ridiculous boldness, and for once, he agreed with her. He got her a glass and poured her a drink as well, which she choked on at first as she tried it. Jere looked disapproving, but said nothing.

"Are you doing better since the first time I met you?" Kieran inquired politely.

Isis shrugged. "I guess," she said, evenly. "Jere doesn't have to restrain me and keep me drugged up all the time anymore, now."

Kieran winced, shaking her head. It had been quite a point of contention between her and Jere, one that Wren was secretly surprised they had gotten over so well.

"Don't blame him, it was my fault," Isis said with a shrug. "Jere was just doing what he thought was right. Keeping me alive and all that."

Kieran shrugged. "I guess. You seem calmer now."

Isis shrugged. "I am, when I'm not punching cops in the face or something."

They talked for a few hours, but Kieran didn't have much other than friendly support to offer anyone. As Wren feared, the law was solid, especially on such a controversial topic as this, and there also seemed to be some political ramifications. The current president of Hojer was being criticized for appearing "lax" on his slave code enforcement rates, and the opportunity to whip a teenage girl for breaking one of them was too perfect. At another time, Kieran explained, the courts may have been able to be bought off, to be persuaded and changed, but for now, the president of Hojer had the Slave Control, Regulation and Enforcement agency breathing down his neck.

"I feel like I should move, just to spite them," Jere muttered. "Leave Hojer without a doctor until they find someone else and move to another slave state. They wanted me here so goddamned bad, let them see what it's like to go a few weeks without anyone to treat their little illnesses and injuries. Or their slaves!"

Wren was surprised by the bitterness that Jere was showing. As often as he mentioned hating Hojer, he rarely considered seriously leaving.

"I hate to say it Jere, especially because I had a part in it, but you kind of did draw attention to yourself when you opened up the clinic to slaves," Kieran pointed out. She had prodded at Jere until she had every detail of the story, even the insinuation that he didn't respect the laws in Hojer. "You're changing things here, and in other communities, even small changes like that change the way people think about their slaves. The regulation agencies have difficulty with that. They had to see it as a perfect opportunity to bring you back under control."

Kieran continued to explain the political situation, and Wren let his mind wander. Did it matter, really, who was making the laws, who was enforcing them? In the end, his master, his lover, was going to take Isis and force her to submit to her fate. If he had done the same, he wondered if Jere would take him as well, or if he would die trying to help him avoid it. Wren knew that would never be an issue, because Wren would never be that damn stupid. Yet, as he looked at the girl in front of him, he couldn't help but envy her for her bold stupidity.

Kieran stood to leave, and Wren wondered just how much he had dazed out for.

"Jere, I'm sorry I wasn't able to help more, but you know how it is. This is why it's so frustrating to be in these rural outlands!" Kieran was explaining, as if Jere wasn't from Sonova, himself. "I won't be around too long for this visit, I've got meetings and stuff to go to back on campus, but while I'm here, I'll definitely be in touch!" She tapped at her head, indicating the mind connection.

"And Isis, I'm so sorry you have to go through this. You know you have my support, no matter how much it may or may not mean."

Isis shrugged.

"It's nice to meet you again, now that you're... you know..." Kieran, for once, was stumbling over her words.

"Not psychotic?" Isis supplied. "Yeah. I get it. I'm better now. So much better that I'm getting whipped in a few days. But, uh... yeah, it was nice to chat with you."

Kieran left, and Wren felt the familiar sense of relief. Yes, she had grown on him, but her visits were still rather exhausting. The three margaritas he downed weren't helping much either, and he noticed Isis nearly collapsing on the table. Jere, the only one of them that really *should* have been drinking at all according to the slave codes, had barely finished his first. He was sitting there looking defeated and irritable.

"I think it's bedtime," Wren said softly, standing up and glancing pointedly at the others until they rose to do the same. Isis paused by the doorway for a moment, almost about to say something, then she retreated. Wren chose to consider it a good sign, and put his arm around Jere, leading him to the bedroom and helping him to strip off his clothes.

They lay there in the dark for a while, Wren gently rubbing Jere's arms, pressed close behind him, spooning.

"I'm failing." Jere's voice was small, scared, defeated.

"You're doing the best you can," Wren countered. "That's good enough."

Chapter 36

Support

Jere was up quite early the next morning to visit Paltrek, so he was surprised when he spotted Isis sitting at the table. He made them both coffee before pulling up a chair.

"Can't sleep?"

She shrugged. "The sleep pill yesterday made me restless."

It was a lie and he knew it. "You know, if you would have asked for a pass, I would have given it to you."

Another shrug. "I didn't really think about it."

"Where were you headed, anyway?"

Another shrug. This time, she was silent.

"Was there *any* reason you took off yesterday?"

A few moments passed, Isis resolutely staring down at the table. Finally, she glanced at Jere for a moment before answering. "No."

"None at all?" Jere prompted, raising an eyebrow. "Nothing you wanted, no plans or anything?"

"I'm not lying!" Isis protested immediately, calming when Jere just nodded in response. "It just kind of happened."

Jere waited. There seemed to be more to the story, and he was desperate to understand it.

"Look, I just went outside, okay?" Isis muttered, looking down at the table again. "And I thought, you know, maybe I'd go a little farther. Just, like, down the street, or something though, nothing else! It's something normal people can do, and I knew you wouldn't be that mad, and I didn't think anyone would notice. And then I was going to come back, but someone was coming to the clinic, so I went the other way instead, and I kept thinking I was going to get caught, because when I've run away in the past, I usually get caught really quickly. Not that I was running away or anything, I fucking swear, I wasn't doing that, I wouldn't do that!"

Jere nodded. "I believe you."

"But once I started walking... it just seemed fun, you know? Like I was invincible. Like maybe I wouldn't get caught this time, and I could do something that nobody else would ever know about, it would be just mine. And I just kept on walking, and there started to be a lot more people around, I guess because I had gotten into town, which I didn't know, I've never been out around here before, or I would have gone in a different direction. I know I should have come back then, but I was still feeling pretty invincible, because I hadn't been caught yet, and I just kept going." Isis glanced up for a moment before continuing. "I guess I wasn't invincible, though, because all of a sudden, that guy, that officer that I hit, he was there and he asked if I had a pass, and he told me I had to come with him. I was gonna do it, but I just froze, and I stood there, and then I thought that maybe I could outrun him and come back and you would fix it, but he grabbed me when I started to run, and I panicked, and I just tried to get away. I wasn't trying to hurt him, and I wasn't trying to go anywhere. I promise. I like it here."

Jere sighed. For no reason, and with no intention to go any-where or do anything, the kid took off, hit a police officer, and got apprehended. It would have been better if there were a reason, be-cause then there would be something to fix. "Isis, is everything go-ing okay? I mean, other than this?"

"It's fucking going fine!" Isis snapped, although she was less as-sertive about it than usual. "I should be goddamn worshipping the ground you walk on, and instead, I decide to take a fucking stroll through Hojer for no apparent reason and get myself caught and in trouble. I just felt like doing it, so I did it. *I* am not okay, and that's the only problem."

Jere almost wanted to agree, but no, that wasn't right. She was redeemable. She was smarter than this. He had no idea what to do to try and convince her of it, but *he* knew. Maybe that would be enough. He glanced at his watch, realizing he had to go soon if he wanted to catch Paltrek before he left home. But there was one more thing he needed to do.

"Isis..." This was not going to go over well. "You're not allowed out of this house without me. The clinic is fine, but not outside — not even in the waiting room in the clinic." He waited for the fallout.

Isis was silent for a while. Almost too long. When she finally looked up at Jere, the hurt showed in her eyes. "Is this a punishment, or is this because you don't trust me anymore?"

Jere thought about it for a minute, making sure he was answering honestly. "It's because I don't trust you."

Isis actually winced, looking sad and defeated. "I think I would rather it have been a punishment."

Jere nodded. "Me, too."

They sat in silence for a few more minutes before Jere glanced at his watch again. "I should go," he said, softly.

"Are you mad at me?" Isis asked, abruptly, looking at him from the corner of her eye.

Jere laughed. "A bit, yes." He saw her tense visibly, which surprised him, even after all this time. "Relax, kid, I've been much angrier at you before — you tend to be a pain in my ass, after all."

Isis managed a small smile. "I promise, I'll do better."

"I know," Jere smiled back at her. "You're doing better. Everyone fucks up sometimes. You just tend to do so more often and more severely than most."

She nodded, still smiling. Jere couldn't help but feel awful at the thought of what was going to happen to her. "Is there anything I can do to make this better?"

Isis was silent for a while, then shook her head. "There is no 'better' in a situation like this. Thanks for the offer, though."

Jere felt surprisingly good about leaving Isis behind. He might not trust her to go outside alone for a while, but he did trust her to do as he asked and stay in the house unless he was there. Perhaps he had given her too much freedom all at once. As much as he didn't want to treat her like a slave, she was still so young, and even as teenagers, kids needed boundaries.

His mum was going to squeal with delight when he shared this revelation with her. Ten years earlier, he recalled, he was vehemently protesting that statement in his own teen years.

He was met at the door of the Wysocka estate by a smiling slave woman he vaguely remembered from past visits.

"Are you here to see Master Paltrek, sir?"

Jere nodded, unsure of how to speak or address her or behave properly in the Wysocka estate. He was always so uncomfortable in this house. The woman led him up some stairs, and Paltrek met him up there and brought him into his suite. For a man in his mid-twenties living with his father, Paltrek had a damn nice place to live. Paltrek flopped down on the bed, looking carefree and content, which left Jere to awkwardly deposit himself on the small couch across the room. Dane was on the bed with Paltrek, naked or half-naked under the sheets. Jere found that he was neither shocked nor surprised, and that very fact bothered him.

"Any luck?" he asked, hoping Paltrek and his seemingly endless resources had come up with something.

"Not a damn thing," Paltrek told him, the news making Jere sad and frustrated. "If they were demanding she be put down, you could get the punishment lowered to whipping, and you could maybe have the whipping postponed, but it's a solid law. Really solid. Really backed up by a lot of precedents and paperwork and regulations."

Jere cursed, which didn't fix anything, but did make him feel a little better.

"Jeremy, no offense, but even I couldn't get out of this, and I have a hell of a lot more resources and connections than you do," Paltrek reminded him. "This is serious shit!"

"Obviously." Jere was petulant, and he didn't care if his friend knew it.

"Look, just have them do it and get it done with," Paltrek said, shrugging. "You can heal her after and pretend this never happened. I mean, really, what if she had been a free person and she'd done something like this, she'd be locked up in prison or something anyway."

Jere sort of saw where Paltrek was coming from, but it just wasn't the same. "She's just a fucking kid!" he protested.

"Jeremy, she might be young, but she's not too young to know the difference between right and wrong," Paltrek rolled his eyes.

"She shouldn't have done it."

Jere wanted to say it wasn't her fault, but he couldn't, because it was. "It just shouldn't be so harsh," he muttered. "I just... I wish there was some way to get special treatment." He didn't care that it was wrong, or unfair, he just wanted the girl to be safe.

"Your best bet would be checking with your lawyer," Paltrek advised. "I've done as much as I can from my end, checking with my contacts, but if there's a legal loophole that someone hasn't explored yet, that would be the best bet."

Jere nodded. He hadn't thought of that. "I'll stop by there today, then."

"That's the spirit!" Paltrek smiled at him. "And if there's anything I can do for you, anything at all, just let me know. The girl's a rotten spoiled bitch, but you're a good guy. I wouldn't wish this on anyone. I'll help you out however I can."

"Thanks," Jere said, getting up to leave. It wasn't much, but it was nice to know that he had some support. He sometimes felt like he had so little in Hojer.

He stopped off at his lawyer's office, rolling his eyes at the shiny plaque pronouncing "Demlyn C. Montgomery, Attorney at Law." A smiling slave in the reception area went to fetch her master to tell him he had a client.

"Dr. Peters!" Demlyn Montgomery came out, perfectly put together and too happy to see him. "What can I do for you today?"

"Legal advice," Jere muttered, as if it wasn't obvious. He followed the man into his office, and sat down in a comfortable leather chair. "The new slave I bought was in an altercation with a police officer and they sentenced her to be beaten!"

Montgomery sat before him, smiling, as if he were waiting for more. When Jere said nothing, his smile dropped. "And... you would like what, exactly?"

Jere frowned. "I don't want to do it!"

"Oh, well, I'm sure the court will provide someone to administer the whipping. Maybe they didn't explain that well enough, I mean, it would be common knowledge to anyone who was from here—"

"I don't want it done at all!"

"Oh." The lawyer looked a bit awkward. "Well, that's not really an option."

Jere scowled at him. "She's a medical necessity!" Okay, so it was a bit of an exaggeration, but still.

"Even so," Montgomery shrugged. "That's been tried before. That and similar defenses have worked to get the sentence reduced from execution to whipping, but the whipping sentence doesn't get reduced. Ever."

Jere kept scowling, as if his unhappiness could force reality to change.

Montgomery kept talking, clearly made nervous by Jere's unhappiness. "I mean, I can look through the case records again, if you'd like, just to see, but short of a presidential pardon, I don't see how —"

"A what?"

"A presidential pardon — that is, the president could excuse this; he does have the ultimate authority in slave-related cases."

"Do it." Jere ordered. "Do it now, and get it delivered today, and make sure he gets to it as soon as possible, and let me know immediately what happens."

"Well, that would involve considerable work, and —"

"I don't care what it costs, just do it," Jere instructed. This was the first real sign of hope he had heard. "I'll throw in a considerable bonus if it works."

Necessary papers and contracts were drawn up, and Jere signed them carelessly. What matter was a few thousand denn to keep the girl safe? If it worked. He really had no idea if it would work.

He stopped by the library after visiting the lawyer, and had no luck there, other than a supportive hug from Imelda. Support. It was odd, but he really did have it here.

Dinner that night was a somber affair, with Jere sad that he had no good news to report. He didn't even bother sharing the hope of the presidential pardon, because it didn't make sense to get anyone's hopes up. He wanted nothing more than to cuddle up with Wren and let him kiss the day away, and they went toward their room immediately after dinner with those intentions in mind.

"Jere?" Isis was hesitating in the doorway to her room.

"What's up?" he replied, about ready to go. Wren paused as

well, glancing at the two of them.

Isis looked back and forth, hesitant still.

"*I'll catch up in a minute,*" Jere said to Wren. "*Don't have too much fun without me!*"

Wren left, and Isis took a few more steps out, looking warily at Jere.

He dropped into a chair, resigning himself to wait until she came over to talk. She always did, eventually.

"Um...." She came closer, but still stood, tugging awkwardly at the hem of her shirt. "Can I ask you a favor?"

Jere wondered what the kid could possibly ask for that he hadn't already given her. "Okay."

"Um..." She walked slowly to the table, fiddled with a chair for a moment, then sat down, finally glancing at Jere. "I want you to do it."

"To do what?" Jere was confused.

Another few minutes of silence. "To whip me."

Jere's entire being screamed no. His body recoiled at the thought. He forced himself to take a few breaths before responding. "Why on earth would you want me to do that?"

It was obviously the wrong question to ask.

"Fuck you, then, I'm sorry I even asked, never fucking mind!" In an instant, Isis had crossed her arms over her chest, closing off her facial expression except for anger.

Jere wanted to kick himself. He forced his voice to stay level. "Listen, I didn't say I wouldn't do it, I was just curious as to why!"

Isis's expression softened slightly. "I just... you asked if there was anything that could make it better for me, and that would. Like, I mean, I know you, and I guess I trust you, and I know... it would just be better for me. But, if you don't want to do it, that's fine, you can just have someone from the county do it or whatever. Don't worry about it."

Jere didn't quite understand her reasoning, but he never really understood her reasoning. Clearly, it was important to her, and he doubted that it could be that difficult to do.

"Never mind. Don't bother." Isis stood up, stiff and awkward, knocking the chair over as she did.

"Isis, wait!" Jere said, exasperated, stopping her in her tracks. "I'll do it, okay? I don't know why, but if it will make it better for you, I'll do it."

A big smile spread across her face, and she picked up the chair. "Thanks, Jere. I just... I feel better, knowing it will be you."

Chapter 37

Preparations

Wren was naked and ready, hoping Jere would hurry up with Isis and join him. They had both been so worried lately, it would be nice to have a little down time to relax and work off some frustration. He needed it, but more importantly, Jere needed it, and Jere deserved it, and Wren wanted nothing more than to be there to comfort his boyfriend when he was this upset. Okay, and some sex. He'd definitely be lying if he said he didn't want sex.

He was surprised when Jere came in and sat next to him, not bothering to undress, putting a finger to his lips to silence him. Wren realized he was speaking with someone through the mind connection, which was surprising this late at night. So Wren waited, gently running his hands across his lover's back, feeling the reciprocal caresses against his skin.

After a few minutes, Jere turned to him, sighing. "Love..." he said softly, pressing his cheek to Wren's shoulder.

"Jere?"

He sighed again. This couldn't be good.

"Paltrek is coming over tomorrow night."

"Did he find something out to help?" Wren was amazed. He really didn't think it could be done, even by someone with that many resources.

"No." Jere let himself droop down onto Wren's lap. "He's coming over to teach me as much as he can about using a whip and... and... I don't think I can do this!"

"Baby...." Wren was equally repulsed by the idea. Jere shouldn't have to do this; he shouldn't even be thinking it. "Just have someone from the county do it! They have people that they pay to do things like that—you know we can afford it!"

Jere shook his head, sitting up again. "She asked me to do it."

As usual, Isis asked, and it happened. He doubted she had even given a reason why. He doubted Jere would have pushed her to. "I'm sorry," he said, softly.

"I'd rather take the whipping myself than do it to her," Jere confessed. "I hate this."

"I know," Wren kissed his neck, pulling him close as he did. "You're doing the right thing, though—making sure you know what you're doing and all."

Jere nodded, still tense and tight. "It still doesn't feel right."

It wasn't right, and Wren didn't think it was fair of Isis to ask such a thing, but it would do Jere no good to hear that. He had made up his mind, and Wren would back him up in his decision. They were partners in this, that's what they did.

They couldn't do more than hold each other and kiss and cuddle that night. Jere was too tense and nervous, and Wren didn't want to push him. Jere needed to work out his feelings about what he was being asked to do, and Wren admitted that he wasn't comfortable with the idea either. It was disturbing to think of Jere taking on a role like that, even if it was on a judicial order. Wren took some comfort in the fact that Jere was so horrified; it helped to reinforce just how far his lover was from a cruel slaveowner.

Paltrek came in the next day.

Despite the situation, Paltrek was upbeat and smiling as he strolled in the door, Dane trailing behind him with a whip in his hands. Wren raised an eye at his fellow slave, who merely shrugged in response.

"Thank you so much for coming," Jere greeted him, looking uncomfortable as hell.

"Not a problem," Paltrek grinned. "I brought Dane along, too. Figured you could practice on him."

Wren felt his stomach clench, and by the pale look on Jere's face, he was equally repulsed and horrified by the idea.

"I... um... that's...." Jere struggled to complete words, much less sentences.

Awkward silence filled the room for a moment before Paltrek burst out laughing, clapping a familiar hand on Dane's shoulder. "What did I tell you, boy? Didn't I say he'd flip?"

Dane smiled conspiratorially. "Yes, master."

"Dane knows he only gets punished when he's actually done something wrong," Paltrek said, dismissive in his humor. "Besides, Jeremy, I'm sure I'd never hear the end of it from you."

"I... right. Yeah." Jere looked relieved, but still on edge. "Yeah. You got me."

Wren considered the scene. It seemed that the Wysocka boy wasn't cruel just to his slave — the chance to get one over on someone he considered a friend was taken as well. But, in the end, no harm was done. Not really.

"All right, let's get this thing started," Paltrek took charge. "I did bring Dane over to help us, I need to be able to show you places to avoid hitting, and a real human is always better to use than your imagination. Wouldn't want your precious lover to have to sully himself and take his shirt off in front of me or anything."

Wren felt his face growing red. The fact that Paltrek knew about his and Jere's relationship was bad enough; the teasing made him even more uncomfortable.

"Wren, would you go and get us all some drinks?" Jere suggested, providing him with an excuse to leave. Wren nodded, moving a bit more slowly than necessary.

Isis was lurking in the kitchen, an irritated look on her face. Wren ignored her purposefully, getting drinks together.

"This sucks," she mumbled, clearly seeking his attention.

Wren frowned at her. He still wasn't pleased with her decision, and although he thought the punishment was terrible and excessive, he didn't really feel too bad for her. She was a slave, she knew better. "You're not the only one put out by this, you know."

She said nothing, just glared at him.

"Why in the hell would you ask him to do it?" Wren demanded, suddenly enraged. Jere's restlessness last night had kept both of them awake, and they had both been on edge all day. "Why do you have to drag him into this, too? Make him suffer?"

"You don't understand anything, Wren!" she snapped at him.

"It isn't fucking like that!"

"It's not?" Wren's tone was incredulous. "Because I can't see how you wouldn't think that this would make Jere absolutely miserable."

"I know it's going to make him miserable, but he fucking offered!" Isis retorted. "He said if there was anything he could do to make it better, he'd do it! I just... I know he won't enjoy it! He won't enjoy hurting me, and he won't get off on it, and... and I just can't take someone liking it!"

Wren forced himself to calm down. He hadn't really expected her to have a reason—no, that wasn't true; he had expected her to really want to make Jere unhappy because she was.

"You're scared," he realized.

"No shit."

"I didn't think..." Wren let the sentence trail off. He was so used to resenting the girl, he forgot sometimes that she was so young and scared. He hadn't considered that she could be so scared that Jere's misery seemed trivial by comparison. He certainly hadn't considered that he would be so wrapped up in his and Jere's world that *her* misery seemed trivial by comparison.

"Only part of it's the whipping, you know," she muttered. "The rest, it's like... there's gonna be people looking at me, and what if they tie me up, and I can't resist, and I can't do anything, and I just have to sit there and take it and not fight back, or it could be worse for me, and you, and Jere, and I can't do that to you guys. But I think I can do it better if Jere's doing it, because at least he... I trust him."

Wren was quiet. He had underestimated her. She had thought about him and Jere in this decision, a kindness he hadn't afforded her. "Maybe it won't be as bad as you're thinking," he offered, trying to sound hopeful.

Isis shook her head. "I've had it before."

Wren felt his eyes widen. "You've had this punishment before and you still did this?"

"I guess it didn't work the first time," she muttered. "I was twelve. They broke it into two sessions, because I was so young, and because I passed out so soon. That was worse. They literally had to drag me, kicking and screaming, to the second one, because I knew how terrible it was going to be. I said I'd die before I went through that again. I almost did."

Wren was torn. On one hand, he couldn't believe how *stupid* she had been to do something like this... on the other, he understood how having Jere there with her would make it better. In the same, horrible situation, he couldn't deny that he would request the same terrible favor. In a way, he had, when he had been detained for being out with a pass. Having Jere do it wasn't an option that time, and Wren wouldn't have wanted him to do it anyway, not back then, but he had still begged Jere to come with him, to stay, to watch. He hadn't realized at first how strongly it would affect Jere, but even when he realized it, the support had far outweighed any guilt Wren felt. Even now, knowing how much it tore at Jere's heart, Wren had to admit that he would rather have Jere hurt him than risk someone else enjoying the pain. All the same, he'd rather administer the whipping to Isis than see Jere suffer through it.

"You should join us in the living room," Wren suggested. "They'll probably need you."

He returned as Paltrek was explaining to Jere where he should and shouldn't hit. Jere probably already knew the logistics behind this, being a doctor and all, but he seemed comforted to hear it explained. Wren took a moment to look over at Dane's back, and was somewhat surprised at what he saw there. The scars were neither many nor deep, and those that were deeper appeared to be old. By the looks of it, Dane hadn't felt a whip in months, and from what Wren knew, that was the preferred tool of correction at the Wysocka estate.

"You're gonna want to hit hard, man," Paltrek said, almost apologetic, as he guided Jere through the motions of using the whip. "You've read the bylaws, right, about drawing blood and all that?"

Jere shrugged. Wren knew damn well that he had not read them. When the information packet from the court had been hand-delivered by a messenger slave, Jere took one look at it and sent it hurling across the room.

Paltrek shook his head. "Regulation requires that you draw blood on at least half of the hundred lashes. There will be someone there keeping count, although they probably won't let you know how many you're at."

Jere said nothing, he just went paler.

"Now, if someone who knew what they were doing was doing this, they'd keep the first half lighter, and draw blood on the last half, to minimize pain and unintended damage and skin breaks," Paltrek explained. "Of course, *you* will be doing it, so I'm suggesting the opposite. Go in hard at first, get the blood out of the way, and finish with lighter lashes."

"But you just said—"

"If you don't make the minimum amount of lashes draw blood, you'll be ordered to deliver them as well as possible penalty strokes," Paltrek cut him off. "You don't want to end up giving her ten or twenty extra, do you?"

Jere shook his head, looking terrified. "I'll get them out of the way as soon as possible."

"Christ, Jeremy, do you want me to do this?" Paltrek asked, looking concerned. "I've been handling a whip since I was six years old. I wouldn't mind doing it at all."

It was unfortunate that this was the moment that Isis chose to join them, standing in the doorway of the room, trembling.

"That's exactly what you'd like, isn't it, you sick bastard!" Isis snapped, starting to cry. "You've been wanting to get your hands on me since the first day you saw me!"

"Isis—" Jere started.

"Listen, kid, stop being such a spoiled, dramatic little brat!" Paltrek glared at her. "I would love to get my hands on you, and I don't deny that I think a good whipping would curb your attitude a bit, but even *I* don't agree with this. It's too much and it's too severe, and I'd be trying as hard as your master to evade it if possible. However, Dane would never be so damned *stupid* as to get himself into this."

The room was silent for a minute, even Isis was stunned into silence by Paltrek's rejection of the punishment.

"Now, let's get something straight, I am over here as a favor to your master, because he asked for my help," Paltrek continued, his calm arrogance overfilling the room. "I offered to do it for him because it would be faster and easier for me, and honestly, it would be less painful for you. You're going to cooperate, because none of this will work if you don't, and I didn't come over here to waste my goddamned time."

Isis nodded, still looking at the floor. "I still want Jere to do it," she mumbled.

"I will," Jere said quietly.

Paltrek shook his head, then glanced at Isis. "Come over here and take your shirt off so we can see where we can hit your skinny ass."

Wren winced as he heard the order, because he knew what it would cause.

Isis pressed back against the wall. "No!" she shouted, her ferocity in stark contrast to her trembling. "No, I'm not stripping for you, and you can't make me!"

Paltrek threw up his hands and turned away.

Jere came over slowly, giving the girl a good deal of space. "Isis, it's not like it sounds," he spoke softly. "He just wants to show me where are good places to hit."

"No. I'm not doing it."

"Isis, I'll hurt you more if I don't know what I'm doing. This isn't an option."

"No!"

Jere was silent for a moment. "Put on a sweatshirt and leave it unzipped in the back," he said softly. "You won't have to take it off, and I won't let him touch you. Please, work with me on this?"

She stood there a few moments, clearly considering the options. "All right," she said, finally, and went to do as she was asked.

Jere breathed in relief, and turned back to face Paltrek, who was shaking his head. "Don't say a fucking word," Jere muttered. "It's dealt with."

Isis came out, clutching a sweatshirt to her front while her back remained exposed. Wren shuddered at the scars there, a horrific sight he hadn't seen since she first arrived. For the most part, she preferred to wear long sleeves and high collars that covered the majority of her battered body.

Paltrek took a step toward her and she flinched away, cowering as though he would hit her.

"Jesus," Paltrek muttered. He had been rather shocked at the sight of her as well. "I'm not gonna touch you, I promise. Jeremy would kill me on the spot, and I have better plans than dying for tonight, you got it? I'm going to point out spots on you — hold the shirt back a bit so we can actually see your back, all right? Christ, you'll be stripped naked tomorrow anyway."

"I'm sure you'll be happy to watch that!" Isis snapped, despite her fear.

"I'm not even going to come, I've got better things to do with my time than indulge some sick regulation agency's power trip," Paltrek countered. "Now, move the shirt and hold still!"

Isis nodded, doing as she was ordered to. Wren watched in sick fascination as Paltrek reviewed again the places to hit and not hit, advised on the importance of not wrapping the whip around her small body, and answered the myriad of questions Jere presented.

The entire "training" took about two hours. At the end, Jere was mostly able to strike out accurately with a whip, and practiced hitting various things off of the table, as well as striking the wall, Paltrek's expert eye correcting his stance and posture and movements with grace. Isis was able to tolerate the experience remarkably well, even muttering, "Thank you," to Paltrek at the end, which surprised everyone.

Isis moved to the couch, curling up in a ball on one end. Jere went over and sat at the other end.

"Are you okay?"

"It doesn't matter."

Jere sighed, glancing over the back of the couch to look at Wren, pleading for help with his eyes.

Wren just shrugged. There was nothing he could do. "It will all be over tomorrow."

Isis sniffled a little bit. "Jere, can you give me something to help me sleep? Please? I can't... I can't spend all goddamn night thinking about this."

"Of course." Jere was up in an instant, heading into the clinic.

"He'll have you healed up before you know it," Wren said softly, trying to be comforting.

"I know that already." For once, Isis wasn't angry or defiant, just resigned.

Jere returned, got a glass of water, and handed the glass and a pill to Isis, who swallowed it without comment. "You have to cooperate tomorrow, no matter how hard it is."

"I know."

"Make sure you pick the right clothes, and have something to eat, and remember —"

"I *know*, Jere!" She was starting to get agitated.

"And, tomorrow, you know, it's 'master,' and —"

"Jere! For fuck's sake, please, just stop?" Isis snapped, flinging the glass across the room in frustration.

Wren sped to catch it, more because he didn't want to clean up broken glass than anything else. He didn't comment on it at all, because it wouldn't accomplish anything but upsetting everyone further.

"We've talked about this, like, ten fucking times, I fucking know!" Isis snapped, crossing her arms across her chest. "Please, just stop!" She sat there for a few more minutes, all of them did, and then she got up and walked to her bedroom. "Goodnight. I'm looking forward to this being over."

Wren said nothing, but moved a few minutes later, sitting on the couch next to Jere and wrapping his arms around him. "You'll get through this," he whispered. "She'll be fine, you'll heal her up after, and you can put it behind you."

"Yeah," Jere muttered. "I can always clean up the mess later, but I can't stop it from happening. I just feel useless. I can't protect her — I can't protect either one of you. I should be able to do more than just sit back and let it happen!"

Wren kept his arms around him, pulling him close. Jere said nothing, but Wren could feel through the mind connection that he appreciated it, that the touch and physical closeness helped to ease some of the frustration. He didn't envy Jere's position, and the helpless anger was something Wren had felt often enough to know how unpleasant it was. "She's grateful that you're doing it," he reminded him. "It means a lot to her."

"It's not enough," Jere insisted. "I wish I knew how to fight this."

"Come to bed?" Wren suggested. Sex was probably out of the

question, but cuddling wasn't and closeness wasn't, and the sooner they got to sleep, the sooner the whole thing really could be over.

Jere shook his head. "You go on ahead, love. I have something I need to check up on in one of the journals I left in the clinic."

"Work? At this time of night? Baby..." Wren started. He realized that Jere might just want a bit of time by himself. He leaned over and kissed him on the forehead. "Take your time. I'll be there when you come to bed."

Chapter 38

Pain

All three of them were up early the following day. Jere had tossed and turned his way through half the night, until Wren threatened to give him a sleep pill, too. In the end, Wren had decided on holding him down and fucking him slow and deep and hard, forcing his mind to clear of anything but the moment. Maybe it was wrong to enjoy so much pleasure before doing something so horrible, but for the time they were wrapped up in each other last night, Jere hadn't worried about Isis, or regulating agencies, or anything but being taken and filled by his lover.

Jere really wished he was doing that again now.

Isis, of the three of them, looked the most chipper. As advised, she was eating a light breakfast, and had selected clothing that could be quickly and easily removed—as well as put back on. Her disposition wasn't sunny, by any means, but it rarely was.

Jere glanced at his watch, wishing it said something different.

"All right," he spoke quietly. "We should go."

Isis stood up, nodding. "Don't want to be late, right?"

Jere just smiled at her, trying to hide his sadness that she was going to be put through this. There was more he was hiding as well, but it would do no good to reveal that yet. "I'm stupidly planning a half day at the clinic when I'm finished," Jere shrugged, apologetic. "Besides, there's probably some sort of penalty if we're late."

They didn't speak as they walked through town. As arranged, Wren stayed home. They had barely discussed it, but he didn't want to watch, Jere didn't want him to watch, and Isis didn't want anyone to watch. Jere would contact him mentally to help carry Isis home once they were finished.

They walked side by side. Should anyone ask, he would say it was so he could keep an eye on his slave, but truthfully, it was because he thought that having someone walk behind him was stupid, and he didn't want to do it. At least he had a say in this.

Despite Isis's limited psychic presence, Jere could sense her fear and anxiety as they approached the crowd that had built at the designated punishment spot. A stage with a whipping post, both looking like they had been pulled through some sort of time warp from the eighteenth century, stood at one end of the crowd. Jere realized with a bit of relief that the design would allow Isis to stand with her face away from the crowd, toward the back of the building that had been built right up close to it. She wouldn't have to see the crowd and their reaction. It was a small favor.

"I can't do this," Isis whispered, though she did keep walking.

"You have to," Jere whispered back. "You can't resist."

"Jere, I can't do this!" She was still whispering, but the pitch of her voice had risen in terror. She fell back a half step, her footsteps slowing.

Jere hesitated for a fraction of a second before wrapping his arm around her shoulders. To anyone else, it was looking like he was pulling her close just to hug her, maybe even grope her, which was disgusting, but more acceptable. He knew as well as she did that he could all but drag her from this position if he had to.

"You *can't* resist."

She continued walking, her pace forced to speed up. She surprised him by letting her head drop against his chest. "I don't wanna die," she mumbled.

Jere wanted to scream. After weeks of begging to be hurt and killed, *now* she didn't want to die. "*You won't die. I promise. We'll do this, and it will be over. Mindspeak only from here on out, unless it's to say 'yes, master' or some bullshit, okay?*"

She nodded. They had reached the sentencing committee.

"Dr. Peters," The vile bitch was smiling at him, looking smug. Jere struggled to remember her name, instead of just thinking of her as the enemy. Arnsdale, he recalled. "Right on time."

"Yes." He tried to meet her eyes, tried not to squint as he glared at her. He blocked his own emotions down so hard he felt like he was choking on them.

"I hear you've decided to administer the whipping yourself?" Her voice carried an edge of amusement.

"Yes."

She stared at him, as though expecting more. When she got nothing, she continued, mocking. "I do hope for your sake that you are able to deliver an adequate punishment. I doubt you have much experience with slave matters. You have read the section on penalty lashes, yes?"

If she spoke for one more second, he might strangle her, and that would be bad. "I have patients to attend to," he growled. "If you want to have a chat, I'd suggest the corner bar."

It wiped the smile off her face, at least.

"Prepare her and tie her to the post." Her words were clipped, and Jere didn't bother to respond.

He guided Isis carefully to the spot she was to stand in, feeling his stomach roll as she started to tremble in his arms. He could hear Arnsdale droning on behind him, announcing to the crowd what the punishment was for, and the legalese behind it. He was pretty sure she just liked the sound of her own voice.

"One of our trained experts on pain sensation will be overseeing the whipping today," Arnsdale announced, sounding gleeful. "Dr. Peters, I assume you haven't anesthetized the slave or anything so foolish?"

"Of course not!" Jere snapped. No, he had other plans.

Arnsdale addressed the crowd again. "Any attempt to minimize or eliminate pain, whether physical or psychic, can be easily detected. And really, who would want to make a justified punishment less effective?"

The crowd cheered, and Jere hated every one of them.

Isis attempted to unzip her shirt, but her hands were shaking too badly.

"I've got it," Jere whispered, catching her eye as he did. She didn't fight him. The oversized garment fell away quickly, and a quick pull on the tie of the wraparound skirt she wore removed that as well. He never broke away from her eyes, even as tears started to fall. He placed a steadying hand on her shoulder. "*You'll be all right,*" he promised, guiding her closer to the whipping post.

He pulled rope from his pocket. There was some provided, but he figured it would be rough, and he wanted as little discomfort as possible. There would be enough already.

"*Please don't tie me, Jere,*" she pleaded, although she left her hands where he had placed them, the picture of obedience. "*I won't go anywhere!*"

He set his jaw, forcing his face to stay neutral as he tied a careful knot around one hand. "*It's not that, kid, I'm just guessing that you'll pass out before we're done. If you're tied you can't fall and hurt yourself, and it can get done more quickly.*"

"*I still hate it.*"

"*I'm sorry. For everything.*" He finished tying her hands and looked at her one last time, her face twisted with betrayal and anticipation of pain. He had promised her she would be safe. He had lied... mostly. He paused, brushing her hair back from her forehead, allowing his hand to linger on her skin for a moment. She was cold, shivering in the winter air, but Jere hoped it would help to reduce the pain. She looked back at him, confused and scared of the situation, but unafraid of him. Now that he was beating her, she was unafraid.

He stepped back, picking up the whip he had brought with him, the one Paltrek had been so kind as to lend him, the one he had practiced on and become familiar with. He listened to the last of the officer's words, and debated once more the virtues of turning the whip on her instead.

Jere was given the go-ahead to start, and he took a deep breath, steeling himself. He picked up the whip and gave it a few experimental swings, swishing it through the air, wincing when he saw Isis jump.

"*Don't fucking torture me, Jere!*" Her voice was teasing inside his head, but he knew she was scared.

Without reply, he drew back and struck for real, drawing blood, causing her to gasp in pain and shock. He winced as well.

The next few fell more lightly, which was a relief for both of them, but Jere felt another familiar presence poking at his mind.

"*Gonna have to lay it on a little harder, Jeremy, or we'll be here all fucking day. Don't sentence her to more.*"

Paltrek. He said he wouldn't come, but Jere was actually glad that he had. It was nice to know he had one supporter out there in the audience.

"*Thanks,*" he replied, cracking down the whip more viciously. Red blood rewarded his efforts.

"*I'll keep count so you don't have to,*" Paltrek told him. "*Just focus.*"

Jere was a little relieved. It was hard to focus on too much anyway, although he could tell when he was drawing blood quite well. The next few lashes met the goal of drawing blood as well, he could feel it.

Literally.

"*Jere, something's wrong!*" Isis had noticed. "*What's going on, why can I barely feel it? I know I'm bleeding, but it doesn't hurt that bad! What did you do?*"

"*Don't worry about it,*" he gritted his teeth, forcing the block on his emotions to be stronger. "*I told you, you'll be all right.*"

"*Jere, they'll be able to tell, they have the sensation expert guy whatever!*"

"*Don't worry about it.*" He was distracted, and the next one wrapped around her waist ever so slightly. He fought not to cry out like Isis did.

More lashes fell, and he could hear Isis almost screaming through the mind connection. "*You're doing this, aren't you? You're diverting the pain away, but it's not going away, is it, it's going to you! That's how they can't detect it!*"

"*Isis, don't worry about it.*" More lashes. More pain.

"*Jere, goddammit, stop it! I never wanted this! I never asked you to do this! I can take it!*"

"*It isn't up to you.*" With every cut into her skin, he felt the mirror image on his own back, seeming to rip out from inside, lighting his skin on fire worse than he had ever imagined.

"*I'll tell them, Jere! I'll scream it out and they'll know and they'll make you stop!*"

"*Even if I didn't mind-bind you first, all it would do is make my suf-*"

fering useless. They'd add extra lashes to your sentence. Don't make this harder than it is."

"*Jere, no!*" she was screaming, begging inside his head, similar to the pleading and begging she was doing out loud. Anyone watching would think she was just begging for the whipping to stop.

"*I'm putting a damper on our connection,*" he informed her, doing so before she had another chance to protest. She could get through if she really wanted to, probably, but he couldn't take her pleading. Not when he was in this much pain.

The remainder of the lashes must have passed quickly, but they still seemed to take forever. Every one was agony, as Jere felt the burning and cutting on his own skin, and he was horrified as he watched the girl's back turn into a red, angry mess of blood and tissue. At some point, Paltrek was telling him he could lighten up, and it took a few more lashes before the message even registered. Somewhere in the high eighties, he felt Isis drop out of consciousness, and with relief he stopped shielding her from as much of the pain, knowing she wouldn't feel it anyway.

And then it was over. The whole ordeal had taken maybe fifteen minutes, but Jere was shaking and sweating and about to be sick. He called for Wren, knowing he would sound sick and drained. He wanted nothing more than to lie down and cry.

From somewhere on the sidelines, a slave came with a bucket of water, tossing it over Isis and jerking her back to reality with a gasp and a whimper. She sagged against the post, barely held up by the rope around her wrists. Jere dropped the whip and walked to her without a word. He redirected most of her pain to himself again as he went to untie her.

"Typically, a slave is displayed for up to four hours after a public whipping."

Arnsdale's voice was chiding and condescending. It was spoken to the crowd, but clearly directed at Jere.

He turned around, his gaze cold and flat. "*Typically,*" he snarled, "I am not so terribly inconvenienced in the middle of a workday."

He turned back to Isis, untying her hands and supporting her as she sagged into his arms, looking every bit like the beaten, broken child that she was. He bent awkwardly, trying not to jostle her too much, and picked up her clothes from the ground, tying the skirt lightly around her waist, feeling her pain as it grazed the open welts on her back.

"You know, Dr. Peters, added pain and humiliation are excellent deterrents to your slave and to the slaves of others." Her voice grated and rubbed at him.

He focused on the pain, focused on trying to wrap the sweatshirt around the half-unconscious girl in his arms, focused on pure, unbridled hate.

"I also know that those of us who have a sense of shame and a work ethic have much better things to do than getting off on a teenaged girl being brutalized."

He didn't see her shocked face, and didn't care that a good portion of the audience blushed and turned away, embarrassed to be called out on their behavior. Wren was there, looking nervous, and Jere beckoned him close with all the authority in the world, placing Isis in his arms.

"Get her home. Immediately."

"Yes, master," Wren nodded, looking a bit surprised, whether at the direct order or the scene Jere was causing, but he moved quickly, and Jere knew that Isis was safe for now.

He turned back to the enemy, as he had started to think of her. "I read the bylaws quite extensively, and there is nothing there that prevents me from taking my slave home immediately after the whipping is finished. Give me the paperwork to sign off on for finishing this, and stay the hell away from me. Unlike you, I have work to do."

He signed the papers, almost sad that the woman didn't have anything else to say to him. He was in pain, and he wanted to fight, and he wanted someone who deserved to suffer to vent his anger on. He settled with purposely dropping the papers on the ground before storming off toward home.

Chapter 39
Aftermath

Jere didn't think while walking home. He didn't think, didn't feel, and certainly didn't let his unfelt rage filter through to the two slaves who were linked by mind connection to him. He may have fumed a bit.

He barely remembered to close the door, flying through the house and into the clinic, where he knew Wren and Isis would be waiting for him. He expected it, and he expected the concerned look on Wren's face, but he didn't expect the reaction he got out of Isis, even after all this time.

"How fucking dare you!" she screamed, her voice raw and gravelly. "How fucking dare you, Jere!"

He washed his hands quickly, not sure of what to say.

"I didn't fucking ask you to do this! I never fucking asked for any of this!" She was crying as she said it, and Wren all but held her down on the table. "What is fucking wrong with you!"

Jere finally faced her, and her anger was frightening, despite the state she was in.

"Jere, what the hell happened?" Wren asked, clearly overwhelmed. "She's been on about this since I brought her home!"

"Get your goddamned hands off me!" Isis snapped, shoving him ineffectively. "You were fucking in on this, weren't you!"

Wren readjusted his grip on her. "In on what, Isis? I have no idea what you're talking about!"

"Bull fucking shit, Wren, you know—"

"Isis, leave him out of it, he doesn't know," Jere mumbled. He was exhausted and still in pain. The transfer had taken a lot out of him.

"I don't know what, Jere?" Wren raised an eyebrow at him.

Jere gathered supplies methodically. "I blocked the pain from the whipping."

"Don't fucking lie!" Isis snapped, at the same time as Wren asked, "Isn't that a good thing?"

Jere wished the pounding headache would go away. "They have ways of detecting pain blocking by traditional methods. The only way to accomplish it was to redirect the pain."

"What?" Wren was confused.

"To himself!" Isis yelled. "He fucking took it himself! I barely felt it! Even now, I barely feel it."

"That's because *I* still feel it," Jere mumbled. "Come on, let me heal you."

"Jesus, Jere," Wren gasped. The look on his face revealed his shock and horror, but the budding anger was already leaking through the mind connection.

"Fuck you, no!" Isis protested. "I'm not letting you waste any more of your energy on me. I never fucking asked you to do this in the first place!"

"Listen, it wasn't your decision," Jere tried to keep his voice calm. "What's done is done, but please, let me heal you. I won't stop feeling the pain until the wounds are healed, and you're likely to get really sick if you don't let me heal them anyway. If you want to help me feel better, you have to let me heal you."

Isis glared at him for a moment, but nodded. "I fucking hate you, Jere. I just fucking hate you!"

"I know," he muttered, sitting next to her and starting the healing.

It was strange. He was healing her, but he could feel it in his own body, the only time he had ever felt his own healing gift. He couldn't heal himself, but with the special connection he had used, he had essentially inflicted psychic wounds on himself. By virtue of healing her, he could erase these psychic wounds. The quick reduction of his own agony was enough to keep him working steadily until it was done, no matter how weak he felt.

"You should get some rest," he mumbled to Isis, then glanced at Wren. "Take care of her. Some Crucial Care and healing cream would probably be good."

Wren shook his head. "Dammit, Jere," he muttered, stalking out of the clinic behind Isis with the prescribed items.

Jere curled up on the floor and tried to keep himself from shaking. It was too much, mentally, physically, emotionally, psychically—he was drained. He must have dozed off, because the next thing he felt was Wren's arms around him, lifting him, forcing him to drink. The Crucial Care revived his body, but little else.

"What the hell did you do?" Wren asked, barely holding back anger. His hands and voice were still soft and soothing, but Jere could tell that he was displeased. "How could you do something like this without telling me?"

Jere couldn't answer. He had held it together too long, and he couldn't bring himself to do more than follow Wren's lead back into the house. As he passed the hall clock, he was dimly aware that the clinic was set to open in only three hours. Wren pushed him into bed, crawling in next to him and stripping Jere of his clothes. He stopped when he saw Jere's back.

"You're bruised," he said, disbelieving.

Jere nodded weakly. "One hundred lashes."

"But..." Wren traced his hand lightly over the skin, making Jere wince. "But you didn't...."

"It's the reverse of healing," Jere said with a bitter laugh. "By taking so much of the pain, it changes physical chemistry. It's not hard for the brain to convince the body that it's being hurt—blood vessels and skin cells respond to the idea of whipping almost the same way as they'd respond to the actual whipping."

"But you healed it!"

"I healed the psychic injury," Jere tried to explain. He wasn't sure if he was succeeding, because the concept was a bit fuzzy, even to him. "What I couldn't heal was my body's response to the psychic injury. The bruises are real injuries of mine, and while they don't hurt like the psychic pain from the whipping, it is a bit tender."

"Where the hell did you learn how to do this!" Wren demanded. His words were frustrated, but his hands were gentle as he rubbed carefully across Jere's back and neck.

"Fringe medical journal," Jere shrugged. "Imelda got it for me. I told her I was interested in the article on energy conservation."

"So you found an experimental medical article and used it as a how-to model! That's what you were looking at last night before you came to bed?"

"Did I ever tell you about my uncle?" Jere asked, hoping to salvage the situation.

"I don't give a fuck about your uncle!" Wren countered, rapidly growing angrier. "You could have damaged yourself!"

"When I was four, I had this eye thing—hereditary, leads to blindness," Jere explained, heedless of Wren's response. "There's a great surgery they can do, but it's intensely painful, and the patient can't be sedated or it might not work."

"What does this have to do with anything!"

"My uncle was a healer, too. My dad's brother," Jere explained. "Anyway, when my parents found out I was going to have to have this surgery, they wrote to Uncle Armand and asked him if he'd be able to do this for me... what I did for Isis today. Because I was young, and that much pain at that age... it's traumatizing. An adult can handle it better, can tolerate the pain without as much trauma."

"Jere, that's such a sacrifice! Did you even know what this could have done to you? You're marked up! It's not just the pain, it's actual injury. You could have really been hurt!" Wren was outraged.

Jere shrugged. "My uncle couldn't see for a week after the surgery. Once I was healed, the pain stopped, but his ocular nerve swelled in response to the psychic stimuli and he was temporarily blinded."

"Did your uncle have people who needed him, Jere?" Wren demanded. "Did he know what it would do to him, maybe tell the people around him, maybe warn them? You didn't even have any idea what a whipping like that would do to her, or to you!"

"Wren, I knew it wouldn't kill me," Jere pointed out. "How many times did people point out that it wouldn't kill Isis?"

"It's the other things it could do, Jere!" Wren snapped, his voice rising. "What would have happened if you would have passed out? If they would have found out that you were doing this?"

"I wouldn't have let it get that far," Jere said feebly. "I would have stopped first."

"You never know when to stop!" Wren countered. "You just do

whatever the hell you want, because you feel bad about something, and you don't stop to consider the consequences or how it might affect you or me!"

"Wren—"

"Where the fuck would I be if you got caught doing something like this, Jere?" Wren demanded, his eyes communicating his pain as clearly as the mind connection. "I need you, and I need to be able to trust that you won't spring things like this on me. I thought we had agreed to talk about things like this?"

"I wanted to tell you," Jere confessed. "But I knew you'd try to talk me out of it."

"Of course I'd try to talk you out of it! And if you really wanted to be as equal as you say you do, you'd give me the chance to do that. This wasn't a medical decision, Jere, this was a decision that impacted everyone, and you were the only one who had any warning."

Jere was confused. He had tried so hard to do what he thought was right, and again, it was backfiring. "Wren, I couldn't just let her be hurt like that! It's my responsibility to keep her safe!"

"It's your responsibility to make sure that you can still be master for both of us!" Wren pointed out. "It's awful that she was going to be hurt, but your job isn't to save everyone from being hurt, it's to do your duty and make sure you're doing it in the way that people from Hojer will tolerate."

Jere said nothing. He hated that he hadn't considered most of the points that Wren was making, and he felt terrible for thinking he could handle it without his help.

"I accepted that I was and always will be a slave years ago. When the fuck are you going to accept that you're a master? You own two fucking slaves, Jere! You can't ignore it. You can't keep pretending. Either let it be what it is, or...."

"Or what?"

"Or you could lose us both." Wren's tone was still angry, but his face showed the fear underlying it. "Stop pretending. Stop lying to everyone. Stop lying to me, and to Isis, and to yourself, when you act like we're all just friends sharing a house. You're hurting us, Jere. You're the one with the power to hurt both of us, whether you like it or not, fuck, whether you *try to* or not. Have you accomplished anything by starting a fight with the regulation agency? Were you doing Isis a favor by letting her leave the house? Is this what you want to keep happening?"

"I thought I trusted her," Jere muttered. He didn't reply to the other accusations.

"And even if you didn't, if she asked you, you still would have let her! I'm sorry it's hard for you, but it's hard for everyone. It's why I didn't want you to get another slave in the first place." Wren was quiet for a moment, some of the heat going out of his rant. "When it's just me and you, I know that I can trust myself, and I know that I can trust you. But once someone else gets involved, I have no idea what they'll do, and even though you don't want to enforce any sorts of rules, I know that we will all face the consequences. They won't be from you, but they'll be from someone, and when you don't even keep me aware of what you're doing, it leaves me in an awful shitty position. You can't just keep pretending that nothing else exists, Jere, because it does."

"I didn't realize..." Jere started. It occurred to him that no excuse could justify the anxiety his choices had caused Wren over the past few months, not to mention the threat of danger. He changed course. "I'm sorry. Again, I... I don't know what I'm doing, and you're the one who's getting hurt."

Wren was silent, neither accepting nor rejecting the apology. "So you'll just have bruises, from a whipping you didn't get, until they heal?" He didn't sound pleased about the fact.

Jere nodded. "I feel much better now, if that helps."

"Not really," Wren said quietly. "And, in case you were wondering, you have quite a full schedule this afternoon."

Jere sighed. He was so tired. He couldn't do it. But he had to, for so many reasons.

"Use me," Wren said, quietly. "And it's not an offer, it's an order. Take what you need from me to get through the rest of the day, and then we'll have a little nap, and then you can go back to work, as you *insisted* on not taking the rest of the day off."

Jere was silent. He didn't want to do this. He had *never* wanted to do this. He bought the slave girl so he wouldn't have to do this, and now, because of her, and because of him, he was being forced to do it anyway. "There's got to be something else I can do," he protested.

"I don't really think there is, and even so, I'm not about to go looking it up," Wren said bluntly. "Do it. You made the decision about taking the pain for Isis, I'm making the decision about the energy transfer. Unless you really don't want me to help with decisions."

"I do want your help, I just think we should maybe think about this a little more," Jere tried.

"Or do you just want a chance to go behind my back and do something else?" Wren accused. "You promised, Jere. You promised that we'd talk about important things, make decisions together. It didn't mean anything, did it?"

"It did!"

"How could it have? Just do the energy transfer. Don't waste both our energy arguing any more."

Jere doubted he had any other choice "You'll feel weak and tired after I do it," he mumbled, knowing it wouldn't be enough to convince Wren. "And I still need your help in the clinic tonight."

"Do it, Jere. If you really do value my opinion, do it." Wren's face was resolute. "You know, I used to have to work under a whole hell of a lot worse circumstances, before you arrived. One day feeling overworked and weak won't kill me. And I'll make sure that everyone stays loaded up on Crucial Care and coffee. Let me take care of you."

"I love you so much," Jere whispered, pulling him close. "I'm so sorry that I did this without telling you. I never thought of what impact it would have on you."

"Just keep it in mind in the future," Wren said, his anger finally receding somewhat. "Please don't scare me like this again. I couldn't handle it if anything happened to you."

With great reluctance, Jere linked with Wren's mind. Instead of healing, as he had so many times in the past, he reversed the flow of energy and resources, giving himself power and health and energy, while bleeding it out of his lover. He felt guilty, but knew this would be the only time he would ever do it. He'd club a random passerby and siphon off that energy first. When he was finished, he felt tired, still, but not so drained, and he knew he would be able to tend to his patients later on as a result. He snuggled into Wren's arms and fell asleep.

A few hours later came quickly, and Jere woke with a dull ache in his back and what felt like a miserable hangover. As the events from earlier in the day rushed through his mind, he wished he *was* hung over.

Wren was up and moving around already, although more slowly than usual. He handed Jere a set of clothes to wear for work and looked at him wearily.

"I think I forgot what it felt like to be this tired," he said, shooting an accusatory look at Jere. "Come on, let's go load up on food and Crucial Care."

Isis joined them as they did, looking resentful and glaring at Jere the whole time. He dared to ask how she was feeling, and actually had to duck to avoid the fruit that flew at his head.

"You son of a bitch," she snapped, her jaw set tight. "How could you! I was prepared to take that whipping, and I was fine with it! I never asked you to do this for me!"

Jere had taken her complaints and abuse silently earlier, as he had taken her pain. But the moment was over now, and she was safe, and he was tired and cranky and not looking forward to the rest of the day. "I never asked for you to fucking get in trouble, now did I? I made my goddamn decision, just like you made yours, now let it rest!"

This time it was a glass of water, and Wren didn't even bother trying to catch it. It shattered on the wall behind Jere.

"It isn't fucking fair, Jere! I never asked you to do this and you did it anyway and you didn't even fucking ask me!"

"I didn't ask because it wasn't your decision!" Jere snapped, unable to hold back any longer. Pain and exhaustion and a day of doing things he didn't want to do had destroyed his verbal filter.

"Of course it wasn't!" Isis screamed, tears streaming down her face. "Because I'm just a stupid fucking slave, right? Because anything I think or want or need or am capable of just doesn't even fucking matter to you, because despite all of your stupid bullshit, you're the master, and I'm the slave, and so you get to make all the decisions about me!"

Jere slammed his own glass down. At least he refrained from throwing it. He couldn't take it any more.

"It's because you are a fucking child, Isis. It has nothing to do with you being a slave."

She glared at him, silent.

"You're a child, and I'm a grown man. I don't know about this fucking shithole, and I don't want to, but where I come from, this wouldn't be seen as something unthinkable. In Sonova, at least, we value our children, and we keep them safe, and I can guarantee that almost any grown man in the state would willingly take the place of a child if something like that was going to happen to her. And it's not your decision, because I'm the fucking adult here, not you, whether you damn well like it or not!"

"I'm not a fucking child!" Isis wasn't very convincing as she sobbed and stabbed at her food. "I haven't been allowed to be a child in eight fucking years!"

"I'm not saying that you have to be a helpless little girl, but goddammit, when you *are* helpless, let someone help you!" Jere exclaimed. "Give it a try for once. Let yourself be taken care of. Everyone can use some taking care of."

"I take care of myself!" Isis flung herself away from the table, sobbing, and stormed off to her room.

Wren came up behind Jere, putting his hands lightly on his shoulders and massaging, avoiding the bruises. "Everyone can use taking care of? It sounds like you're starting to see reason after all. Maybe I should have gotten you to do the energy transfer sooner."

Jere smiled a little, the touch and the teasing giving him hope that Wren was starting to forgive him for his earlier decisions. "I should have let you help me," he admitted. "I just thought I was doing the right thing. No one from home would have questioned it."

"It's not something people from here would do, babe," Wren reminded him. "I never would have. And as much as it pissed me off, I'm in awe of you for doing it. You're too selfless for your own damn good, sometimes. You just don't have it in you to hurt anybody, do you?"

Jere looked at him for a moment, wishing he could agree without reservation. Instead, he reached up to take Wren's hand. "Come into the clinic. I have something I need to tell you."

They left the house, and Jere led them to a back room of the clinic, far from any patients, and far from where Isis would hear his plans. "I wasn't going to tell you, but it's not right to keep hiding things from you. I need your help on this, and I'm not going to keep it from you. It puts you at risk, and you deserve to know."

He explained the plan, the dangerous, provocative stunt that he and Kieran had devised through a series of conversations through the mind connection. He explained how it had started out as an idle fantasy, but quickly escalated into something real, and he explained how he had been hesitant to share his plan with Wren because he wasn't sure whether he would be supported. Wren listened, holding back judgment until Jere had finished.

"You're right, I don't really support it," Wren said softly. "But I don't really want to fight it, either. You're sure you want to do this?"

Jere nodded. "But I won't, not if it's too much for you, or if you think it's too dangerous. You know more about what's dangerous than I do, and Kieran even admitted that it was her idea of treating slaves that drew attention to us in the first place. Maybe she's pushing too hard."

Wren thought about it for a few moments before answering. "There is danger, but your plan is solid. I think I want to see how this works out."

Jere smiled, relieved that he wouldn't have to choose between his beliefs and his boyfriend again. "Thank you, love."

"Thank you for telling me," Wren replied, leaning in to kiss him. "It means a lot to know that you won't surprise me with this."

The workday began, and Jere dragged himself through it. Wren's energy had revitalized him physically and psychically, but his soul still felt battered. His body felt ancient as he forced himself to see patient after patient. A sudden commotion in the waiting room had him rushing out, and what he saw brought the first smile to his face that he had had for most of the day.

Chapter 40
Women of Importance

At first, Wren couldn't figure out why his master was smiling. Last he checked, Jere was nearly as exhausted as he was, as patients had slowly depleted his energy reserve all day. He had to have been sore from the whipping that wasn't his — Wren couldn't even begin to wrap his head around the enormity of *that* statement. And now there was a panicking pregnant woman in their waiting room, in addition to a crowd of equally panicked people accompanying her, and Isis hadn't been anything but a bother all day, yet there Jere was, in the doorway, smiling. It occurred to him that this must be the situation that Jere had spoken to him about.

"Go get Isis," Jere ordered, startling Wren out of the daze he had been in. "Tell her she is needed *immediately* and I won't take 'no' for an answer."

Wren continued to stare for a moment. Remembering where he was and that there were people all around, he dipped his head in acknowledgement. "Yes, Doctor," he managed, slipping away.

He knocked on Isis's door before peeking in. "Come on, Jere needs you in the clinic."

She glanced at him, disbelieving. "You've got to be fucking joking."

"No. He needs you immediately, and told me to tell you that he won't take 'no' for an answer," Wren recited, hoping that Jere had given him some magic code phrase to convince the girl. "There's chaos over there and we're both drained."

"Both?" Isis raised an eyebrow. "You mean, he...."

"Yes." Wren wanted to blame her, but couldn't bring himself to

344

do it. Jere was right, she was just a child. An annoying and disruptive one, but he found himself surprisingly accepting of having his energy leeched to save her skinny ass from pain. "Now get moving."

Isis said nothing, just got up and followed him. She was as aware as Wren how opposed Jere was to the idea of using Wren's energy, and that fact seemed to have quieted her rage a little bit. As it was, it was already quieted, compared to earlier. She was always up and down, although she had somewhat leveled out in the past few weeks.

As they made their way back over to the clinic, they found Jere already tackling the situation with practiced ease and finesse. He had directed the majority of the people to wait in the waiting room, where they would be less disruptive. The pregnant woman and a woman who looked the right age to be her mother were back in the examination room with Jere.

"Good," Jere nodded, smiling the second he saw them. So much more comfortable and confident in the clinic, he gave orders that were quick, curt, and professional.

Wren obeyed as usual, and even Isis did as she was told—the confused look on her face the only indication that something was off. But Jere so rarely demanded anything of her. Wren played along, trying to downplay his own anxiety.

There was frenzy and flurry, and screaming and a host of other things as Jere did his doctor thing and made sure the woman was healthy, as was the baby inside of her. It was the screaming that got to Wren the most, because it was something he was so unused to hearing inside the clinic.

"Doctor, can't you do anything to stop the pain?" the woman, who must have been the patient's mother, was demanding anxiously. "She is in *agony!*"

"I'm very sorry, ma'am," Jere apologized.

As Wren watched, he could feel the lack of sincerity in Jere's voice.

Jere turned to the suffering patient. "Ms. Clemente, I am truly sorry, but I can't give you any sort of pill or injection—it would harm the baby."

"You're a mind-healer!" the woman moaned, screaming as some sort of baby-making pain ripped through her body.

"Yes, but there was a very unfortunate incident earlier, which drained me of almost all of my resources," Jere explained, in between screams, his voice detached and clinical. "One of my slaves was subjected to a severe whipping, and I simply could not afford to risk her sustaining permanent injury or death. The policy was very inflexible, so I tried to schedule for a slow day, but things like this just can't be planned."

Isis stood silently, holding a tray of supplies for Jere, her face paling when she realized what Jere was talking about.

"My god, is this the girl?" the mother asked, her eyes widening as she looked at Isis.

As if on cue, Isis shrunk down, managing to look smaller and more vulnerable and entirely helpless.

"I'm afraid so," Jere said, quietly. "She's very young — she could very well have died from such a harsh beating, and I'm in no position to be training a new slave to help with such delicate work as this."

The pregnant woman screamed again, clutching her mother's hand, and Wren was pretty sure he could make out some curses to the state alongside the curses to God and babies and everything else.

"That's like..." the mother started, enraged. "That's like disabling medical equipment! That citizens of Hojer need!"

"Indeed," Jere said quietly. "Isis, go and fetch Ms. Clemente and her mother some cool water. It's the best I can offer at the moment."

Wren felt a chill. Jere had explained the plan, but he had been vague on some of the details. The coincidence that was playing out in front of them was just too perfect, and seeing Jere's plan in action was disturbing. To see Jere so detached was particularly disturbing, no matter how justified his actions were.

Ms. Clemente, in her agony, told Jere where he could shove his glass of water. She screamed and cursed and carried on, and Jere just smiled and patted her leg.

Jere's smile might have been comforting, but Wren could see behind it. "There, there, women have been having children without any sort of painkillers for thousands of years. I am deeply sorry.... I just wouldn't want to expend energy that might be needed to revive you or your child in the event that anything unexpected comes up. I have so few resources left after healing my slave."

The scene continued for another two hours. Ms. Clemente screamed and sobbed, her mother begged Jere to do *something*, and Isis and Wren stood by, waiting for orders. Neither of them spoke, and Wren couldn't even bring himself to look at Isis. He wondered, though, if she had figured out what was going on.

The baby came without event. He was small and squalling, but entirely healthy. In a show of compassion and making good on promises, Jere instantly sated the new mother's pain with mind-healing as soon as the baby was found to be healthy. At that point, her happiness overshadowed any pain she was feeling anyway.

The exciting news was delivered to the party in the waiting room, and once mother and child were cleared to go home, a slave gifted with strength was selected from the crowd to carry the new mother home in her arms.

Wren and Isis were cleaning up the exam room when the new grandmother came back to talk to Jere.

"Seeing my daughter suffer like that was something I never imagined," she confessed, looking as worn out as Wren felt. Her words were stilted and short. "I had never considered the... collateral damage of a punishment like that. It affects the whole community."

Jere nodded. "My slaves are not just pretty things to look at or to dust my furniture. They are every bit as important as my medical tools, if not more. I took it as a personal offense."

"I'll speak with my husband about it when he gets back in town," the woman said, resolutely. "This can't be allowed to happen again."

"I'd appreciate that," Jere said. "Congratulations on your new grandson."

"Thank you." She left without another word.

The three members of the household didn't talk as they cleaned up the clinic. By some unspoken agreement, they didn't joke, or laugh, or argue, they just worked as quickly as their tired bodies could manage. Once they finished, they retired to the house, gathering around the table as was custom. Wren supplied them all with Crucial Care and tea. When he sat down, it seemed like a cue, because Jere finally spoke.

"That was the president's wife and only daughter."

Wren let the significance wash over him again. The one person who could have stood in the way of the punishment, so directly impacted. When Jere had quickly explained it to him earlier, the significance hadn't really sunk in, because he was too busy being appalled that Jere would do such a thing to anyone. It was so cold, so calculating, so unlike Jere.

"Did you know?" Isis asked, her eyes wide in disbelief.

Jere shrugged, evasive. "I had it on good authority that it would be today."

Even if Jere wouldn't admit it to Isis, he had told Wren earlier that he knew the president's daughter would be coming in, all part of his plan. "Is she even one of your patients?" Wren asked, doubtful. He didn't recognize her, and he recognized all the patients who had been in before. There was only that one week when he had been out, and surely an expecting mother would have seen her doctor before delivering.

"No," Jere said, looking down at the table. "She's usually seen by the student health clinic in Sonova."

"That's how Kieran knew to tell you about it," Wren said, realization crossing his face.

Jere nodded.

"You set this up!" Isis finally burst in.

"I took advantage of a convenient situation," Jere's tone was hard and sad.

"What does that even mean?" Wren asked. In the rush, Jere had filled him in only on the barest details. He was still curious to find out exactly how the whole plan had solidified.

Jere shrugged. "Kieran got in touch with me through the mind connection the other day after she couldn't find anything to help. She said that the president's daughter had come home unexpectedly from University in the city and would be delivering a baby on Sunday or Monday."

"Was she even supposed to have the baby this weekend?" Isis asked.

Jere shrugged. "I have no way of knowing that. But she had been receiving medical care in Sonova, so it would be unexpected for her to return home to visit this close to her due date."

Wren actively avoided thinking of the varied ways in which one could ensure another person gave birth on a specified date. Those were crimes he didn't want to be even remotely associated with.

"This wasn't an accident?" Wren asked, hoping Jere would deny it.

"An opportunity presented itself, and I took it." Jere was oddly unaffected. "Kieran and some other people might have helped make the opportunity happen; I asked to be left out of that part."

There was silence for a moment. The agonized screams played back in Wren's head, and he had no idea how the same thing wouldn't be true for Jere and Isis.

Finally, Isis broke the silence.

"Jere, that woman didn't do a thing to you!"

"And you didn't do a thing to the people of Hojer who came to watch you be whipped today," Jere countered, his voice strangely calm. "They proved a point. So did I. After all, it was pointed out to me numerous times that the whipping wouldn't kill you. She might have been in pain, but it didn't kill her either."

"Jere, that's just... wrong!" Isis protested, shaking her head. "She was suffering!"

Jere shrugged. "I think I'm starting to learn that there are bigger things than right and wrong."

"Do you really think this will change anything?" Wren asked, still caught up in disbelief.

Another shrug from Jere. "It might not. But there are now two more people who disagree with that whipping. And at least one more person who is going to try and change things."

"You're not allowed to talk to Kieran anymore," Wren half-teased.

Jere smiled back at him, the first real smile Wren had seen in hours. "Actually, I have a feeling I'll be talking to her a lot more, now."

Chapter 41

Partners

The next few days were calm. They all healed, worked, and got along remarkably well. Jere felt Wren and Isis looking at him sometimes, when they thought he wasn't looking, and he knew they were trying to figure him out, trying to understand his motives, trying to reconcile how the healer and peaceful person in their lives could be so cruel and callous.

He understood how he came off that way. He wanted to strike back, and while there was some human suffering involved, he easily dismissed it as collateral damage. After what had happened to Isis, he saw it as a war, the beginning of a war between himself and the people who kept slavery in place. He could leave, but he couldn't take his lover with him, he couldn't take Isis with him either, and he wouldn't abandon either of them in a place like this. Only three days had passed since the whipping, but Jere felt he had drastically changed. He was in the clinic, tidying up after his afternoon patients while Wren was busy out front, when Isis came to talk to him.

"Hey," she started, looking awkward and embarrassed.

"What's up?" Jere asked. She hadn't spoken more than a few words to him since the president's daughter had been in. When she had, she remained angry or irritated, and he found it best to just leave her be. She helped Wren with what he needed, and that was enough. None of the three of them had any energy to spare at this point.

"I just, um...." She fiddled with a syringe until Jere's raised eyebrow cued her to stop. "I never said thank you."

Jere was confused for a moment. "For?"

"For the whipping," she shrugged. "For saving me from the pain. For healing me. For not, you know, leaving me up there, or making it worse, or anything like that. For taking the pain for me."

Jere was quiet for a moment. She had been so angry, he really wondered if she did hate him for doing it.

"I shouldn't have gotten so upset," she admitted. "I know... I know you better than that. To think that you'd just make the decision because you were the master. I just don't know what to do when people are nice to me. It's not something that happens very fucking often, you know? I'd rather get hurt than let someone else get hurt for me. And usually, that works pretty well. Nobody has volunteered to save me in years."

Jere smiled. "It was the least I could do," he said sincerely. "I'm just glad you're not upset."

"Oh, don't get me wrong, I was pissed," Isis reminded him. "And I still wish you would have told me beforehand—not that I would have let you do it, then, but still. I'm glad you did it. I've never had anyone care about me like that, not since... not since I was taken away from my parents."

He didn't exactly think of himself as a parent to this kid, but he certainly wanted to protect her. He cared about her. She was like the little sister he never had; he couldn't imagine *not* protecting her.

"I'm glad that I'm here with you and Wren," she admitted. "And that you didn't let me die."

"Having you alive is certainly preferable to the alternative," Jere agreed. "I'm sorry it took this long for you to feel comfortable here."

"You can use me for energy," she said softly. "I know that's part of what you bought me for, and I don't mind. I feel like I have too much anyway."

Jere was absolutely shocked. He had given up hope on this, committed to feeling exhausted and gleaning from healthier patients. After the difficulty she had presented, he was happy that she wasn't causing problems, and her limited help at the clinic took some of the strain off of him and Wren. While he had grown very fond and protective of Isis, he had given up on the hope that she would ever serve as an energy source.

"Don't look so surprised," Isis teased. "I mean, I'm always so happy to go along with whatever you have planned!"

He laughed. It was ridiculous. A few months ago, he would never have expected this. Now, she was sitting here joking and laughing and willingly volunteering her energy for him. He forced himself to sound at least a little bit serious. "Thank you," he said. "It means more to me than just not feeling exhausted all the time."

Isis shrugged. "Yeah. I can be nice when I want to. I'm gonna go help Wren out. Don't die of shock or anything while I'm gone."

And she left, bouncing out of the room as though nothing concerned her. Maybe it didn't. She always seemed at peace once she had made up her mind about something. Jere decided to do the same.

After dinner that night, Jere showered, and came out to find Wren and Isis sitting on the couch, chatting like things were normal. It seemed like they were normal. As strange as it was, Jere felt like he had unintentionally carved out a normal life for himself and two slaves. The fact that these two could get along despite all the problems they had faced still amazed him, and it warmed his heart to see how much Wren had taken to the girl lately. As much as Wren might try to be cold and callous and disconnected, he just didn't seem to have it in him anymore.

Jere looked at the empty couch, and decided he didn't want to sit on it. He wanted to sit by Wren. He walked over and dropped to the floor, squeezing in between Wren's legs and resting his back against the couch. He didn't interrupt their conversation, just pressed his head against Wren's legs and listened. They weren't talking about much, something that had come up at the clinic that day. He closed his eyes for a moment, focusing on the peace in the room until he heard his name.

"Jere, you kill me," Isis was laughing, her legs pulled up underneath her on the couch, wearing an oversized sweatshirt that had to be his or Wren's. She looked like a normal teenaged girl.

"What?" he asked, perfectly content.

"You're supposed to be the master and you're on the floor while the two of us are sitting up here," she pointed out the absurdity of it.

"I like it here!" he protested, cuddling up to Wren a bit more.

"Yeah, he's between my legs where he belongs," Wren smirked, his hand coming down to play with Jere's hair.

Isis made a face. "You guys are disgusting," she teased.

"Be nice or I'll start making out with him right here," Wren threatened playfully. "After all, he is so irresistible—"

Isis cut him off by throwing a pillow at him. "Jerk," she muttered, but she was still smiling. She settled back against the arm of the couch. "You're lucky I like you guys!"

Wren laughed. "Yeah, you're not so bad, yourself. I mean, you know. Sometimes."

They sat there quietly for a while longer. Jere loved the feeling of Wren playing with his hair, touching his head and massaging at all the right places.

"What happens now?" Isis asked. "I mean, I've been living here for months, and I still don't really get how you guys work."

"How we work?" Jere asked. "What do you mean?"

"I mean, do we just... do whatever we want?" Isis seemed a little lost. "Like, sit and chat on the couch, or work, or—things are so calm."

"Things were calm like this most of the time before you got here," Wren commented, for once not making it sound like a criticism. "You can join us in the calm," he added.

Jere reached up to grab his boyfriend's hand, squeezing it. He spoke to Isis, though. "This is more like what I first imagined, when I brought you here," he confessed. "I never wanted conflict. I wanted to add someone to our house, to our life. Someone we could trust and work with and get along with."

"*That's an awful lot of 'we' and 'our,' babe,*" Wren spoke through the mind connection, teasing lightly. Jere knew he deserved the teasing; it really had been more of his decisions overshadowing everything else.

"Thanks for letting it be me," Isis blushed. "I have no idea what I did to deserve it."

"It was the screaming," Wren teased. "Jere's a sucker for ear-splitting screams and a lack of sleep. Really, part of your charm!"

Isis rolled her eyes. She glanced down at Jere. "So are we like... activists or something?"

Jere noticed her inclusion of herself in the "we," but didn't comment on it. He shrugged. "I don't know. I don't really know how I'd define it, or if it would even be beneficial for us to be seen that way. A few months ago, I would have said no, but the idea holds more and more appeal each time I think about it. I know I'm going to push for changes, but subtly."

"No offense, but that thing the other day wasn't subtle," Isis pointed out.

"There were worse ways I could have handled it," Jere shrugged. "That was actually one of the more cilivized plans. We can't do anything too drastic; you would both be at risk if we were too visible. But I can't just sit back and do absolutely nothing, either, not after all this. I want to at least try to make things better."

They talked for a few more hours, lofty ideals of humane treatment and progress and changing the world passing between them along with cups of tea. Jere was perfectly content to sit at Wren's feet, and Wren was perfectly content to serve them all tea. Isis seemed to just be taking it all in. The changes in her life over the last few months had to have been overwhelming, but they were slowing. Jere figured that they were at a pace she could handle for once, and she trusted him and Wren enough to enjoy some of them. As it grew late, they parted ways, and Jere allowed Wren to help him to his feet and pull him into the bedroom.

"You have no idea how hot you got me all night," Wren whispered in his ear as they walked down the hallway. "All I wanted to do was take you right then and there!"

"I like this idea," Jere all but melted at his touch. "But the bed is probably a better option."

Wren nipped on his neck as they went through the doorway. "What, do you want it all soft and gentle and comfortable?" he teased.

Jere was craving exactly the opposite. "No. I want something to cushion me so you can fuck me harder without breaking bones."

Wren's smile grew big and predatory. "You are so fucking hot right now."

Jere said nothing, but writhed under the hands that pulled him possessively close. Wren kissed him brutally, insistently, leaving him breathless and wanting more.

"I'll be careful of those delicate bones, but I would really like to fuck you so hard you feel it for the next week," Wren whispered in his ear, his voice nearly bringing Jere to his knees. "Would you like to be fucked like that?"

Jere felt a thrill go through his body. He glanced at Wren's face, excited to see his eyes almost glowing with dark desire. "Yes," he answered, wondering exactly what Wren had planned for him.

"Get your clothes off and get on that bed before I fuck you against the wall," Wren growled, already stripping off his own clothes.

Jere felt himself growing hard at the rough command, and he rushed to do as he was told. He was excited, naked and moving toward the bed when Wren caught him, threw him down, pinning him on his stomach and grabbing him by the hair.

"You're not moving fast enough," Wren decided, using his speed gift together with Jere's willingness to jerk him into the desired position quickly, on his back, his legs spread wide and arms above his head. "Stay," Wren ordered, smacking Jere's thigh to make his point.

Jere didn't say anything, too busy feeling the rush of adrenaline flooding his body as he contemplated what Wren was going to do with him. Wren returned in almost no time with the padded cuffs that Jere had become so fond of. Jere's pulse quickened at the sight of them.

"I am gonna fuck you so hard tonight," Wren whispered, making Jere moan in anticipation. A few seconds later, the cuffs were attached, and Jere tugged at them, testing their tightness.

They were tight. Jere smiled, pulling at the cuffs in anticipation, then gasped, startled and thrilled to feel Wren's mouth wrapping around his cock, swallowing it and pulling off quickly, leaving Jere to struggle and beg for more.

"Rules haven't changed," Wren taunted. "You stay still, I keep going. You move, I stop. Or maybe I'll think of other consequences."

"Please, Wren," was all Jere could manage. Feeling Wren take his cock into his mouth was wonderful, and knew he would enjoy the consequences just as much if he earned them.

Laughing, Wren resumed the task, the vibrations making it that much more difficult for Jere to keep his end of the bargain. He put up a valiant effort, clutching at the restraints and the sheets and arching and squirming as much as possible, but after what seemed like an awfully long time, he felt his resolve slipping and he started thrusting the tiniest bit.

Wren pulled back immediately, but Jere noticed that the look on his face was more of an expression of pride than of irritation.

"So needy," Wren chided. "Well, I did warn you, didn't I?"

Jere nodded, unable to say words.

Wren straddled him, too quick for Jere to follow with his eyes, and Jere found himself looking up at his lover, intimidated.

"Answer," Wren coaxed, his fingers cupping Jere's chin and rapidly growing hot.

"Y-yes?" Jere managed, the combination of fear and arousal making him stutter.

"Close your eyes." Wren's voice was smooth and calm, but when Jere hesitated, he felt the hand on his face growing warmer. He closed them, gasping when the uncomfortable heat was immediately withdrawn, along with the weight of Wren's body. Jere felt Wren slip out of bed.

"Good," Wren sounded satisfied. "Keep them closed."

They had used a blindfold in the past, but Jere enjoyed the challenge of keeping his eyes closed. There was no force necessary; Wren demanded it, and Jere complied.

The room was silent for a few minutes, much longer than it would ever have taken Wren to do anything, given his speed gift. Jere started to shift, feeling nervous. "You're still in here, right?"

Jere was greeted with more silence. His first instinct was to open his eyes and look, but the thought of disobeying made him squeeze them more tightly together. It felt like hours had passed since the last time Wren touched him, but it could only have been minutes.

A hot, unyielding grip surrounded Jere's cock, and Jere jerked before he could stop himself.

"You don't learn, do you?" Wren asked, his voice unusually low and seductive.

Jere whimpered, then whimpered again when he felt the temperature of Wren's hand starting to increase. He held still then, very still, almost afraid to breathe as he wondered just how much he could handle, how much Wren would want him to handle.

He didn't have to wait for very long before he felt a sharp bite on the inside of his thigh. He moaned, careful not to move, but he cried out as he felt Wren making a slow trail with his teeth, bringing his mouth closer and closer to Jere's cock, which was growing hotter by the second. It wasn't unbearable, not yet, but Jere couldn't help but wonder how much more he could take, how far Wren would push him. Wren had been practicing, but did he really have adequate control of his gift?

"Wren—"

By the time Jere opened his eyes, Wren had already placed his hand over them. "No," Wren whispered firmly. "I'll tell you when you can open your eyes again."

Jere allowed himself to be pushed back, trembling in fear. He didn't protest, and he forced himself to relax as Wren placed a matching line of bites across his other leg. As he calmed, he adjusted to the heat on his cock, allowing himself to feel the pleasure of it along with Wren's slow caresses. Finally, Wren returned his mouth to Jere's cock, taking it in his mouth and swallowing him deep. Jere forgot about everything else but the familiar warmth surrounding his cock and the order to keep his eyes closed.

Jere couldn't help but thrust up into Wren's mouth again, and he yelped as he felt a sharp pressure on the head of his cock, as Wren caught him purposely with his teeth. A moment later, Jere whimpered as he felt the heat rising again. Wren wasn't using his hands, this time, he still had his lips wrapped around Jere's cock. As he took Jere further into his mouth, the heat increased, and Jere pulled at the cuffs in a desperate attempt to stay still. He knew that Wren could heat up any part of his body that he wanted to, in theory, but as far as he knew, Wren had focused the majority of his practice on his hands. He shuddered, uncertain whether pain or pleasure was responsible. Either way, he didn't care. He wanted more contact, more touch, more of Wren's heat.

"I take it I've gotten you warmed up?" Wren asked, hot breath blowing over Jere's cock with each word.

"Yes," Jere managed. Saying the word made him realize that

he had been begging senselessly for a while. His throat was dry. "Please. I need you."

Wren gave him no time to think or adjust before working his fingers in, fast and demanding, as Jere struggled in the restraints, unable to keep up with the onslaught of sensations reaching his body. Wren's mouth was hot on his cock, his fingers felt nearly as hot inside of Jere's body, and Jere was suddenly aware of how defenseless he was. His life was in Wren's hands, but he had never felt safer. He relaxed, feeling his body open to Wren and sensing Wren's satisfaction though the mind connection.

Wren removed his fingers and stretched up along Jere's body, rubbing against him. Jere savored the warmth of his lover and the pressure of Wren's cock hard against his ass. He arched his back, trying to get closer, and Wren started kissing his neck, holding him in place by his hair and by pinning him down with the rest of his body.

"Please, fuck me?" Jere begged. "I want you so bad."

"Soon enough," Wren promised, continuing to grind against Jere, kissing and biting his neck until Jere was reduced to nothing more than helpless whimpers. It seemed so long since they had just been fucking and enjoying each other, not worrying about slaves or work or social problems. Jere felt like they were the only two people in the world, and he never wanted it to end.

Wren entered him in one long, fast thrust that had Jere gasping and clutching at the cuffs, begging and pleading incoherently for more and less and faster and slower and everything all at the same time. Wren kissed him and fucked him hard, fast, and hot, pounding into him with his cock and his tongue and touching him all over with his hands. It seemed like everywhere Wren touched burned, hotter and hotter, and Jere couldn't decide whether to dread the touches or look forward to them. He begged, pleaded, not quite sure what he was begging for, and he finally felt Wren's hands settle, one on his throat, the other on his cock. Jere couldn't help but try to squirm away from the imminent threat.

"You think I'll choke you?" Wren asked, tightening his grip the tiniest bit on Jere's throat.

"Please..." Jere whimpered, unsure of what he was even begging for. A part of him loved the tight grip Wren had on his throat just as much as he loved the burning hand on his cock.

"I want you to come," Wren hissed. "I want you to come, now, with my hand around your throat, and your cock burning for me."

Jere couldn't help but feel even more aroused. He struggled to work himself harder on Wren's cock, pulling his own cock in and out of Wren's tight grip, and he came unexpectedly and forcefully. Wren held on for a few minutes longer, pounding into Jere and making his body shudder with the almost painful pleasure and aftereffects of his orgasm. Finally, Wren cried out in pleasure, and Jere felt him come as well. Jere was exhausted and more content than he had been in days.

"Open your eyes," Wren ordered, making Jere realize that he still had them closed. The first thing that Jere saw was Wren's smile.

"Your mouth," Jere managed, staring at Wren in disbelief. "So hot."

"I thought you might like that." Wren sounded quite satisfied. "I've been practicing, but I wanted it to be a surprise. I figured you'd stop me if you didn't like it."

Jere took a few deep breaths, calming himself as Wren unfastened the cuffs and cleaned them up, wiping the sweat from Jere's body as well as his own.

"I don't think I ever want you to stop," Jere mumbled, suddenly drained and eager to do nothing more than collapse into Wren's arms. "That was amazing," Jere added after a few minutes. It had been a while since they had fucked with no concerns and enjoyed it *that* much. "It's been a while since we've really been on the same page."

"If we fuck that much better when we're on the same page, then we should never *not* be on the same page again," Wren teased, pulling Jere closer. "We're better when we're working together."

"We're better at everything when we're working together," Jere agreed. "We're partners in this thing, you know."

Wren smiled a little. "Is that what all that 'we' and 'our' business was about, earlier?"

Jere nodded. "It has been for a long time. At least, I've wanted it to be. I know, it's kind of defeating the purpose to say that I wanted it to be, without asking you, but... well, we've discussed it, and I'm shit without you. Maybe I wasn't in Sonova, and maybe I won't always be, but right now, I need you, and I want you by my side, partners, forever."

Wren stared at him for a moment, his face a little happy and a little hopeful. "Forever, like...."

"Like, that time Isis asked if we were married and I told her she was being ridiculous but actually I guess that's kind of how I feel about you." Jere let the words come out uncensored, hoping they just made sense. "I mean, I know we're not, not really, and I know it's not even possible, and I don't know if or how it changes things, but really, anything like that would just be some sort of stupid recognition from the state and I hate this state anyway and don't want them knowing anything about my life, but I do want you knowing that I love you and that's not changing and I want you in my life forever."

"Is this the part where I say 'I do' and then we kiss and live happily ever after?" Wren teased.

"This is the part where you say whatever you really want and then we kiss and then we probably still argue sometimes and everything's not perfect but we work at it and we do it together."

"You'd make a terrible children's story writer," Wren commented, pulling him close. "But yes, I do want whatever the hell this is, and I love the thought of us being partners on everything. I'm in it with you."

They kissed, sealing their unofficial and untraditional agreement. Jere knew it didn't change anything, and yet, it changed everything.

We do our best to proof all our work, but if you spot a text error we missed, please let us know via our website Contact Form at http://forbiddenfiction.com/contact

Author's Notes

Isis was the first character that I created for this entire series. I envisioned a very damaged girl who would struggle to heal in the very strange situation of being owned by a doctor who bought her with the noblest intentions. This doctor developed into Jere, and Wren his cynical assistant.

Even conceiving a plot with these three was difficult until I filled in the back story on Wren and Jere, and thus, Inherent Gifts was created. I was delighted to return to the very first idea almost a year later, picking up easily where I left off. Seeing these three characters finally come to life and interact with one another was an experience many months in the making, and I plan to spend more time telling the stories from this world.

Currently, I am working on the third book in the series, where the characters are in established relationships, but struggle with changes in the society around them. They seem to have grown so much, and the challenges have grown accordingly. Boundaries and expectations are tested for everyone, making it an exciting addition to the series.

About the Author

Alicia Cameron has been making up stories since before she can remember. After discovering erotica during a high school banned books project, she never really turned back. She lives in Denver, Colorado with a tiny dog and rabbit who conspire regularly to distract her from doing anything productive. By day she works in the mental health field and is passionate about youth rights and welfare. In her spare time, she enjoys traveling, glitter, and punk rock concerts.

About the Publisher

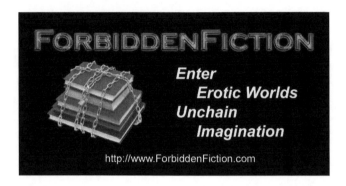

ForbiddenFiction.com is a publisher devoted to writing that breaks the boundaries of original erotic fiction. Our stories combine intense sexuality with quality writing. Stories at Forbidden Fiction.com not only arouse readers through sensations, but also engage them emotionally and mentally through storytelling as well-crafted as the sex is hot.

ForbiddenFiction.com is also designed to be a social reading environment. You'll have fun even if just reading the latest post each day, yet you will have the chance for so much more. Readers and authors can be part of ongoing discussions of specific works and individual authors as well as more general topics.

Sign up for a FREE Membership today at ForbiddenFiction. com